THE PLACE OF QUARANTINE

Vadim Babenko

Ergo Sum Publishing

w w w . e r g o s u m p u b l i s h i n g . c o m

Published by Ergo Sum Publishing, 2019

Translated from Russian by Simon Geoghegan and Vadim Babenko
Russian text copyright © Vadim Babenko 2018
English text copyright © Vadim Babenko 2019

E-book ISBN 978-99957-42-31-7
Paperback ISBN 978-99957-42-32-4
Hardcover ISBN 978-99957-42-33-1

This novel is a work of fiction. Names and characters are the product of the author's imagination and any resemblance to actual persons, living or dead, is entirely coincidental.

Cover design: damonza.com
Editor: Bill Siever

www.ergosumpublishing.com

PREFACE AND ACKNOWLEDGMENTS

This book is a work of fiction. The research efforts of its main protagonist cannot be considered scientifically legitimate – however, I have aimed to keep them as close as possible to genuine theories developed by serious scientists. I have also tried to avoid anything fundamentally impossible from a modern scientific point of view.

I'd like to express my sincere gratitude to all those who have helped me in my work. I would especially like to mention Giuseppe Vitiello, whose articles, advice and consultations have played a significant role in the formation of the book's most important concepts. The main one – the application of quantum field theory to the modeling of human memory and intelligence – in many respects echoes the works of Vitiello, including his publications in co-authorship with Walter Freeman and others.

Many thanks are due to Andrei Parnachev for our conversation about superstrings and branes.

And finally, a special thanks to Alexander Bobkov, who agreed to read through most of the manuscript and made a number of valuable comments.

For self is the lord of self, self is the refuge of self

– Gautama Buddha

The notion of an immortal mind is no more fantastic than the very fact of its existence

– Theo

AWAKENING

CHAPTER 1

FIRST, A SOUND is born – as if a copper string is trembling nearby. A tender echo responds at the farthest point of my consciousness, near its borderline. Then comes the notion that out there, beyond this border, is where my cradle once stood. Someone has willed me to abandon it; there is no return.

The sound becomes louder, more distinct, sharper. It contains a myriad of harmonics, each living its own life. Their chorus is unbearable; it grows, it drives me crazy – and suddenly breaks off at full crescendo. Silence reigns, and held within it a memory of the cradle, its final, barely perceptible trace. Its elusive image, the shadow of a strange, very alien yearning. As if someone has exclaimed, "What a pity!" – and then it's gone, the trace lost amid a multitude of others. The sound of the copper string returns but now it is not so loud and is quite bearable. Contours and lines emerge out of the gray haze like an image on photographic paper. Little by little, they meld into a single whole to form a meaningful picture.

I see my hands resting on my knees, a flight of stairs, a handrail and walls. Beneath me there are more steps; I sit, hunched over, staring at the floor. My mind is empty; all I know is that this is the first time I have been here – on these steps, on this staircase. I sense that I am capable of remembering who I am, but I don't have the strength. I am happy just sitting like this, doing nothing, not even changing my position. Staring at the concrete stairs and not thinking about anything.

Time passes and suddenly I am aware that I have been idle for too long. Something is urging me from within; "Theo," I murmur out loud, and I know: this is my name. The sound remains; in search of its source, I look around me. Then I glance up and it becomes clear – there is no taut copper string. It's all much more trivial: a dingy fluorescent tube hums and crackles over my head. It'll burn out soon, I note mechanically, and I shudder – somewhere below a door slams.

Immediately, I start to feel extraneous sounds pressing in from all sides. It seems I can hear footsteps, laughter, irritated voices, a child's wailing. I can hear car horns, screaming sirens, the noises of the city. Roaring waves and howling whirlwinds, the rustle of grass, leaves, paper…

I am anxious; my recent serenity evaporates. The door slams over and over again; I get up and lean over the bannister. There is nothing to see – down below there is only darkness and a flight of stairs disappearing into nowhere. "*Mierda*," I whisper, starting back; my head is beginning to spin. It's already clear I can't stay here – and cannot afford to lose any more time. I give myself the once-over and see a gray coat, brown pants and a pair of blunt-toed boots. My outfit doesn't impress me, but I have no choice in the matter. I raise my collar, zip my coat right up to my chin and take a step up the staircase.

Everything goes quiet again, as if on command; all that can be heard is the squeak of the soles of my boots. I climb several floors, each indistinguishable from the last. Every landing has a single bare door with no number or nameplate; there isn't the slightest murmur coming from behind any of them, only deathly silence. I don't dare knock, and, moreover, I have no desire to see anyone. I am devoid of any desires whatsoever, but I do have a purpose, although for now it's unclear even to myself. Landing after landing, I keep climbing. There is a musty smell in the air; the light-gray walls are smooth, with no cracks or graffiti. "There is no life in this building," I whisper to myself – and then, suddenly, I see the door on the next floor slightly ajar.

At the door stands a woman of about thirty in a blue cotton dress and summer shoes. She has lovely legs and an open, welcoming smile. I freeze in a daze: her presence is unexpected, hardly possible. I have almost become convinced that I'm all alone in this house and in this whole strange world. The woman is entirely real, however. "Welcome," she says, opening the door a bit wider. Then she introduces herself, "I'm Elsa." I just look at her, bewildered. Her voice echoes in the emptiness of the stairwell and seems to resonate within me, like the buzzing fluorescent light down below.

Then I realize it's foolish to just stand there and enter in through the door, squeezing past Elsa on my way. She exudes warmth and a fresh fragrance, resonant of juniper and vanilla. For a brief second, it occurs to me the scent of her sex is probably as sweet as an exotic fruit – and I pass through into the living room and look around. Elsa closes the door, throws the chain and follows behind me.

"This is the living room," she says. "There's not much furniture but we don't need any more – at least to my taste."

Indeed, there is only a table, some chairs and a large sofa, which looks uncomfortable. There isn't a single lamp, but soft neutral light streams in from the walls and ceiling. In the far corner is a kitchen with a chrome sink and an electric stove. To the right – a window; I go up to it and look outside. There is a mountainous landscape with pine trees and snow. Something vaguely familiar that pricks my memory.

"Don't believe what you see," Elsa says with a snicker. "It's only an image; there are a lot of different ones. And please, do introduce yourself!"

I turn around – she is standing there with the same welcoming smile. "Sometimes they call me Theo," I murmur cautiously, intrigued by the sound of my own voice. It sounds familiar; "Yes, Theo," I repeat and try to grin in reply.

"I'm *very* pleased!" says Elsa, moving closer. "I've been so lonely on my own..."

I notice that when she speaks, her lips morph into an indistinct, blurry O. For some reason this doesn't surprise me.

"I've already been here three days without a roommate," she adds. "It's a bit long, don't you think?"

I simply shrug and look out the window again. A squirrel jumps in the branches of the nearest pine tree, soft snow sparkling in the sun. I don't think I could imagine anything more real.

"Elsa," I ask, glancing at the squirrel, "please, explain to me what's happening. Where am I, what am I and who are you? I can't remember a thing – was I ill? Have we been abducted and taken prisoner?"

Elsa stands next to me, running her finger along the windowpane. I note that she has finely manicured hands.

"You're not going to like my answer," she says, pausing slightly. "And it's not likely to help – but I frankly don't know how to say all this. I myself thought they were making fun of me…"

She falls silent, then turns toward me, "Well, for example… Now your head is empty, but perhaps you remember what a guest house is?"

"A house for guests. A house… We are guests…" I repeat after her. "And so what?"

Elsa frowns. "Or, maybe, you remember what a hospital or sanatorium is? Or, perhaps, a colony for plague victims, quarantine…"

As she says all this, she stretches her fingers – first on one hand and then the other.

"Hospital… So that means it's an illness, right?" I try to look into her eyes. "Or some sort of accident?" Then a shudder runs right through me. "A colony… What is this? An epidemic? Some sort of terrible virus?"

"Oh, fuck…" Elsa says and looks me in the face. Then she throws up her hands, "No, you'd better look at this!" She goes to the kitchen cupboard, opens the door and holds out a laminated printout.

"This was lying on the table when I arrived here three days ago," she says angrily. "Can you imagine what it was like for me? You remember what the word 'death' means, don't you?"

Yes, for some reason I do remember this word. It evokes a sense of choking, the clang of iron, bad blood. Something that erases all meaning, like a damp sponge on a blackboard. A place where the sound of the copper string is lost and fades.

"The farthest point" rushes into my mind. "A cradle beyond the border…"

"Tantibus, the eternal nightmare," I mutter, but Elsa shakes her head.

The sign is spelled out in capital letters and no punctuation:

WELCOME
YOU HAVE EXPERIENCED CORPOREAL DEATH FOR
THE FIRST TIME

"Nonsense!" I think to myself irritably and read the next lines out loud.

THE DEATH OF THE BODY IS NOT AS SIGNIFICANT
AS YOU MIGHT THINK

And then:

THERE IS NOTHING TO FEAR
YOU ARE IN QUARANTINE

"There is nothing to fear," Elsa repeats with a nervous laugh. "Over the last three days I've gotten used to the idea. Admittedly, I wasn't that afraid in my old life either."

We fall silent for a minute and look at each other. Then Elsa takes a step forward and stands next to me. I can sense her breathing, her warmth.

"You died *back there*," she says quietly. "It is better to accept it; there's no hidden agenda. I know this all sounds crazy but..."

To me, it doesn't sound like anything. A complete absurdity, the dissonance of harmonics in the unbearably sharp copper sound. And – a premonition waiting nearby.

"In quarantine..." I murmur and move away from the window and Elsa. I sit down on the sofa and rub my temple with the palm of my hand while trying in vain to understand the meaning of the words. Then I say, "Nice joke," and attempt to crack a smile. But the smile won't form; my jaw is clamped tight.

Elsa waves her hand in annoyance. "I knew it! I knew I wouldn't be able to explain it to you. This is no joke – *out there* you no longer exist. It's all over – *finita*, forever, amen. You'll remember soon enough, trust me. And then all your doubts will vanish away."

I can feel myself getting cold; I'm shivering. Thousands of thoughts swarm in my head but my memory is empty. No, it's not quite empty, not quite. Something is stirring within it, some small fragment, a trifle. Something is creeping up on me – gradually, slowly. And suddenly it rolls over me – a nightmare of premonition, an inescapable horror. Choking and chilling me like a huge wave…

I squeeze my eyes shut, maybe I even scream, drowning in an ocean of fear. An image flares up behind my retinas like a magnesium flash: a man on a motorbike in a black jacket with a rider sitting behind him, his face concealed by his helmet. And the dull sheen of steel – a pistol in an outstretched hand… I remember: next there will be a gunshot and instant, terrifying pain. I can sense with every nerve that this really did happen to me. Then something else emerges – a house in an olive grove and a woman in tears; with her is a balding man with a twisted mouth. A wild jungle and a large river. The streets of an old city that I somehow know to be Bern. And then everything fades; not even a hint remains. I am sitting on the couch, my face clasped in my hands, in a strange world that no one can imagine.

Then, little by little, my overwrought mind calms down. Somehow gathering the courage, I pry my eyelids apart. Elsa is standing next to me, looking at me considerately and shaking her head.

"I was exactly the same," she says. "Also here in the living room, but sitting at the table, not on the couch. My first memory was of a helicopter flying over the sea, and a sudden explosion. Or rather, just the beginning of the explosion, a ball of flame, engulfing me from the right… Yes, it's not easy to get used to at first. But now do you see that all this – the quarantine – is true?"

"Almost," I answer curtly. The thought flashes into my head: I should probably do something. Maybe I should jump up, make a break for it, down the stairs and out onto the street? To disprove and expose this deception, if it exists, to simply check it out for myself, without Elsa. Without any laminated printouts or fake landscapes… But no, I don't have the strength to act or even to contemplate doing so.

Elsa sits next to me, stroking my hand. I can barely feel her touch, but something passes between us all the same, a certain hint of intimacy. For a quarter of an hour we stare at the wall opposite us. Then she says, "Okay.

I think you'll soon get used to it, like I did. You are a man after all; it feels foolish to feel sorry for you. And now…"

Fixing her hair, she gets up and with a gesture invites me to follow her, "Let's go!"

Obediently, I get up, and we go toward one of the two closed doors. "Here," says Elsa, "this is your bedroom. I don't want to leave you, but they warned me to avoid lengthy contact on the first day. So, off you go, stranger… who goes by the name of Theo. Get your head together and I'll see you tomorrow."

My head is spinning; flecks of light dance before my eyes. I really want to be left on my own. I nod, open the door and close it firmly behind me.

The bedroom has the same neutral light emanating from the walls and ceiling. To my surprise, it has no bed – only a soft armchair with a coffee table standing in front of it. On the opposite wall is a large screen. My room is more like a small cinema for private viewings than a bedroom.

I go up to the window; it looks out onto a small glade in the middle of a forest. A deer stands next to the trees, sniffing the air keenly. It doesn't interest me – I recall that it's only an image. A deceptive image – how many more like it are there?

"How many…" I mutter and suddenly feel an acute yearning for Elsa, from whom I have only been parted for a minute. My loneliness is as immeasurable and overwhelming as my recent fear. As if I've been left all alone, face to face with the boundless cosmos, the scale of which cannot be encompassed by human thought. I don't want to remember, and thinking frightens me; my only wish is to have someone's presence near – and I am barely able to suppress the urge to return to the living room or maybe even knock on my roommate's door. Something prompts me not to do this. Having taken a turn around the room, I sit down in the armchair and am just about to close my eyes when the screen flickers to life; a human face appears on it.

I see a high forehead with a small depression in the middle, sharp cheekbones, a tapering chin and sunken, sphinxlike eyes, slightly elevated at the corners. His lips are compressed into a thin line, and his unblinking gaze is directed straight at me. I am certain I have never known this person – no matter how hopeless my memory is.

"I am your friend," he says crisply and clearly. "Your helper. Or perhaps your mentor or your counselor, your therapist. My title is not important; just take it as read that I am your Nestor."

He is straitlaced and markedly formal. His lips do not move in sync with his words, but this doesn't bother me much. Anyway, it's better than just an indistinct O-shaped mouth.

"You are not obliged to reciprocate my efforts or even my friendship," he continues, "but you need to know you don't have many allies – in fact, not more than two. Every *quarantiner* has his or her own Nestor – and, of course, a roommate in the apartment. The others are unlikely to be inclined to socialize with you."

"Theo, my name is Theo," I say, leaning forward. "I'm happy to meet you – and I have lots and lots of questions!"

Somehow, it almost becomes clear: all this, the entire situation, is anything but a prank. Neither a pointless trick nor a joke that has yet to be explained to me. My yearning and loneliness recede; I feel a surge of energy and a feverish desire to get to the bottom of everything at once.

The man on the screen shakes his head. Nevertheless, I continue, "Tell me, is this really death? Because I remember being shot… But what about *after* death – what is this place? And the main thing: *How* did I get here?"

Nestor wrinkles his mouth and raises his palm. "No, no, wait," I say, not wanting to stop. "Can you tell me if anything is real here? Is there at least something tangible, solid and anchored, or is all this just an illusion, worse than a dream? Elsa smells of juniper, but I can't feel the touch of her hands. The window has an image projected onto it, but what is beyond the window?"

"Here we go again!" Nestor chuckles. "At first, everyone is concerned with the same things – looking out the window or hugging their roommate… The words differ, of course, but the thrust of the questions don't."

He glances down for a second – perhaps to look through his papers – and then adds, "Tomorrow you will read our Brochure for new arrivals – as a first step, so to speak. It's interesting you mentioned your dreams right away; they have a big role to play here. You will soon come to understand:

each dream is like a swim in the open sea far from dry land. A journey – through fragments of memories, semibroken pathways and connections."

"Soon…" I repeat after him and fall silent. The questions that have been bursting to come out suddenly seem superfluous, pointless. A new thought pierces me like the point of a blade.

"Tell me, Nestor…" I begin, then clear my throat and ask cautiously, "Tell me, Nestor, am I immortal?" My voice lets me down; the last word comes out as falsetto.

Nestor raises his eyes toward me. "Are you afraid of immortality?" he enquires curiously. "Or are you already afraid of death again – having barely succeeded in living through it, if you'll forgive the paradox?"

"But who…" I begin again and fall silent, not knowing how to carry on. My eyes become heavy, my ears start to ring – a long, drawn-out note like the thrum of a copper string.

"In fact," Nestor says suddenly, "it seems thoroughly unfair to me that you are so lost and confused – although, to be honest, who can one blame for injustice. But we do know that the notion of rebirth with one's memory and 'sense of self' remaining intact should not be an alien concept to you, Theo. You are not a typical case – no ordinary 'newcomer' with a file just one page long."

He looks down at his papers again, then raises his eyes and exclaims, "Just take the quantum field that you predicted! Or the new type of quasi-particle. Or, say, metaspace, which tells us more about you than the entire contents of your file!"

"I can hardly remember a thing," I murmur as if trying to justify myself. Suddenly and swiftly, I am again completely drained of strength. My thoughts become confused; I feel overwhelmed by drowsiness. With each passing second, it sucks me down deeper and deeper, like a thick, sticky whirlpool.

Nestor waves his hand, "Yes, yes. Your memory will return – that's what you have been put here for, just like everyone else. This is not a problem; you have no problems at all now. They have been left in the past – but you will have to remember how they started, what caused them and what they became afterward. You will have to recall the sheets of paper covered with symbols, your equations and your theories, and the *dance of the conscions…* It will all come back to you – but later; that's enough for today. You have completely exhausted yourself. You need to sleep – for now, without any dreams or visions!"

And with that, the screen switches off and the back of the armchair reclines backward. My eyelids close of their own accord, flashes of color dance in the darkness and words spin in my head whose meaning is not clear to me: "firecrackers, gunpowder, pirates…" Suddenly, symbols flash before my eyes – a fragment of a formula chalked on a blackboard, an integral sign, the Greek letters pi and theta. They are important; they cannot be wiped out easily – neither with a damp sponge nor by any thought of one's own demise.

There is one other thing that I need to know right away. "Listen, Nestor…" I say with the last of my strength, without opening my eyes. And immediately fall into a deep sleep.

CHAPTER 2

THE NEXT MORNING, emerging from oblivion, I look around me and take stock. The room has not changed – it still has the same neutral lighting, the screen opposite and the window with its fake landscape. My body is not feeling the effects of my night spent in a semisitting position in an armchair; my head is clear, and my mind seems strong enough. I remember yesterday – the stairwells, the door to the apartment and Elsa's smile. Then – a motorcycle with two riders, a gun aimed at my chest. New memories also flicker past, one after the other like lightning flashes. Some people, loud laughter – and suddenly, piercingly: anxiety, fear. But not fear for myself.

I screw up my eyes and see a fragile Asian-looking girl with a slight squint and a streak of bright-red hair. Her face moves very close; I rub my eyes with my fists, driving away the tears. "Tina…" I whisper, and I want to scream but somehow restrain myself. I gather my strength and try to think clearly: Tina – I remember we were together, even if only for a little while. I remember I had to save her – but from whom? What kind of danger was she in?… Steam from the pavement, hot, humid air, smoke from braziers and the exhaust of the cars – the smells of a big city seem to tickle my nostrils, but I cannot connect them with anything. I remember only that something was left unfinished – and suddenly a motorbike rider wearing a matte-black helmet fades in again. This is the very last moment before the shot: the realization of the disaster, the acute, instantaneous yearning for Tina, desperation at my own helplessness and… Here the memory fails, the chain is broken. In my head – only the remnants of my voice, "Ti…na."

I suddenly understand: death is more than an eternal nightmare. More than a damp sponge, erasing all meanings, or the silence of a copper string. Bad blood is not at its core; at its core is the loss of those who are dear to you. Parting – forever? Parting from Tina – and who else?

"Forever…" I say out loud.

For some reason, my voice sounds false, falsehood insinuating its way into the very word itself. I look around me – I am surrounded by falsehood; my thoughts have nothing to cling to. "Where am I?" I ask myself, losing my temper: enough fooling around. It's time to admit I am evidently the subject of some experiment. What did they give me – a drug, a hallucinogen? It's a cruel joke – but what's its purpose? And when am I going to be able to wake up?

Then I hear a cough and reluctantly open my eyes – forcing them apart. The screen on the wall has come alive; Nestor is on it, staring directly at me. "Hope you slept well," he says. "Your day is going to be quite eventful."

I peer silently into his face. Like yesterday, there is something about him that tells me things aren't that simple. All my doubts recede; I'm almost ready to believe that everything is for real. That they're not playing with me – I have indeed died, but now I am alive again, no matter how wild it sounds…

I would very much like to clear everything up at once, but again, I can't find the right questions. The silence drags on; I'm painfully lacking for words.

"What is the 'dance of the conscions'?" I ask finally, but all I get in reply is a condescending grin.

"*That* you will tell me yourself," Nestor says. "And fairly soon, I hope."

I just throw up my hands in dismay. "Although," he continues, "you mustn't get ahead of yourself. We have everything you need here for your convenience – providing your expectations of convenience are not unrealistically high. And, most importantly, don't forget: you have a roommate.

A female roommate, if I'm not mistaken; the creation and separation of the two sexes is one of nature's most ingenious moves!"

"Yes, that may be," I agree, "but all the same…"

Nestor shrugs his shoulders, looks down, leafs through something and suddenly says, "The session is over."

"Already?" I ask, surprised, and exclaim, "Hold on, hold on! It's not my roommate I need right now. You are my helper and I need help: please explain at least something to me, even if briefly… You are my counselor and I need counseling; there's too much going on that I don't understand!"

"Counsel is provided according to the schedule," Nestor grins again, and I sense there is no arguing with him. "*According to the schedule*," he repeats with emphasis, "and the schedule states that right now you should be socializing with your roommate. She's probably waiting – so show a bit more consideration." And with that, he terminates the conversation without so much as a goodbye.

I continue to look at the blank screen for a minute or two; then I get up and go to the window. Behind it is the same lawn, but now without the deer. With its disappearance, the entire scene looks somehow too static, as if the animation has been turned off.

Opposite the window are sliding doors. This is the entrance to the bathroom, where everything is shiny and clean. I look at the ceramic toilet bowl and shrug in bewilderment. Then I go up to the washstand and turn on the tap – I see that water really does flow from it. I put my hands under the cold stream and splash my face with pleasure for a long time, not worrying about soaking my clothes.

Straightening up, I regard myself in the mirror – my features are familiar to me, although only vaguely. After washing up, I feel my skin tingling slightly, but that soon passes. I touch my forehead and cheeks with my fingers – my sense of touch feels slightly delayed, as if it's being transmitted via digital protocols. I do not need a towel; there is no trace of the water on me. The floor is also dry – now that *is* convenient, just as Nestor promised.

"Well," I say out loud. "There's nothing else for it. Socialization with my roommate it is then."

I leave the bathroom, open the door to the living room and immediately see Elsa sitting on the couch.

"Well, about time!" she exclaims. "I was going to knock on your door myself. I've been waiting and waiting – and all you can do is sleep. It's really not much fun being the first to move in!"

Today she is wearing a pants suit, high-heeled shoes and a white blouse. She looks like an advertising executive or a successful insurance agent. I regard myself and frown – yesterday's clothes look rather forlorn and shabby.

"Good morning," I greet her. "You're so beautiful – I'm really impressed. How did you sleep? Do you have your own Nestor?"

"Of course I do," Elsa replies. "Everyone has a Nestor. He's such a sweetie, isn't he?"

She gets up and offers me her hand, "I'm sorry if I sounded reproachful. I'm not angry with you at all. We should avoid quarrels; they're the last thing we need!"

I think I understand her very well. "Now let me tell you about the apartment," continues Elsa, "but first let's play…"

She goes to the kitchen shelves and beckons me over. On the shelves are a lot of utensils – enough for a small family. "A small demonstration," she says, taking a soup plate and suddenly, without turning around, hurling it at me. My body reacts: one leg bends slightly at the knee, my head feints away from the impact, my shoulders twist and my hands are thrown slightly in front of me. I instinctively take up a fighting stance as the plate whistles past, hits the wall and silently dissolves into it, leaving no trace whatsoever.

"Did you see that?" Elsa shakes her head. "And look at you, ready to spring into action. Relax, we're not fighting. I'm just showing you how things are here. And here's another trick – look…"

I grin, relax my muscles and lower my guard while she approaches me, swaying her hips. She comes up close, very close, and then suddenly takes another step, passing right through me. I don't feel a thing, just a whiff of juniper, and Elsa smiles as if nothing has happened.

"Believe me, I did that very tactfully," she says. "Out on the street, some people are so *rude* when they walk through you, the fuckers. Someone did it to me on my very first day, the bitch… Sorry for my language – in fact, I rarely swear. I'm a well-brought-up girl from a decent family."

"Do you really smell of juniper?" I ask.

"A fake," she replies with a wave of her hand. "As you see, we are more like phantoms than people with real bodies. You, for instance, have no smell at all. It's a pity – in my first life everyone remarked on how nice I smelled."

The careless ease with which my roommate talks about her "first life" grates on me. It seems suspicious… What if she is also a part of this conspiracy, one of those who are against me? I feel my earlier doubts returning but put on a brave face, trying to keep them hidden. Maybe Elsa is just being too lighthearted – and, besides, she's been here three days already; she's had some time to get used to it.

Then we find ourselves in the kitchen again; Elsa smiles mysteriously and sends a pile of plates flying onto the floor – with the same effect. "Don't worry, I'm not a drama queen," she reassures me. "But it's not only drama queens who smash the crockery every now and then. Oh, while we're here, have a look in the refrigerator. Do you like fried eggs? I'll be fixing you your breakfasts. The ham and eggs here smell like the real thing. And even seem to taste of something!"

We go into my bedroom and head straight to the bathroom. "A fake," says Elsa, running her hand around. "There's little point in washing, and you certainly don't need the toilet bowl. Although I admit, I do love the showers here – you know, the sound of the water and the warmth. It's so relaxing – a haven of peace. And my bathroom is the color of a translucent wave. The color of a calm, tranquil sea. By the way, are you surprised that the first thing I check in a man's bedroom is the shower? Ha-ha – only joking. I'm a *very* good girl!"

Leaving the bathroom, Elsa looks around my room and notes with satisfaction, "It's just like mine. Here's the dressing corner," she leads me to a large full-length mirror. Next to it is a fitted wardrobe. I open the door – it is packed with clothes. Elsa giggles, "I haven't once succeeded in getting fully naked, can you imagine?" Then she points to the coffee table, "Here's the console. You can change anything – the wallpaper, the view, the lighting…"

I tap the glass surface. It turns on; it's touch sensitive. I run my fingers over the buttons – everything works: the curtains move, the walls change colors. There is an indistinct, barely discernible pattern on them – I go up to it and peer at the strokes and swirls.

"Like milk dissolving into coffee," says Elsa behind me. "Or the traces of the wind on the sand."

"A fractal[1]..." I mutter, but the word has no meaning to me. "Or maybe the stone garden in Tiahuanaco."

I am reminded of something, but only dimly. Yet I know: it was quite important! I whisper and listen to its echo: "The comprehension of one's own mind – links of an endless chain of questions. A strange attractor[2] – a line in multidimensional space – a self-sufficient, self-organizing entity. The fading of consciousness – a broken fractal line. The links become shorter, shorter, but it is nevertheless infinite..."

"What, what?" Elsa asks. "Are you all right?"

"Yes, more or less," I say pensively. "It's just that before, it seems, I thought a lot about that – the patterns in a coffee with milk. Never mind; let's go and have a look at your aquamarine bathroom."

We inspect her bedroom, which is no different from mine, and then return to the living room and sit down on the sofa. "Now," says Elsa, "get that stone garden out of your head and concentrate as best you can. This is the instruction manual for life here: they call it 'the Brochure.' To be honest, I've already shown you the most entertaining things, but my Nestor said it needs to be read. And yours did too, probably."

In her hands she holds the Brochure, as she called it, a booklet with a black-and-white cover. "Quarantine" is printed in bold in the middle of it. "You must read it all," Elsa tells me. "You'd be better off doing it here, with me. If you have any questions, I'll try to explain."

Clearly, she doesn't want to be alone – just like me.

I open the booklet. On the first page, in the top-right corner, where an

---

1   A self-similar geometrical figure, each part of which has the same properties as the whole.

2   A pattern in a phase space toward which a nonlinear dynamical system tends to evolve.

introductory quote would normally be placed, the word "*QUARANTINE*" appears again, and a little bit lower, "*Be grateful!*" The text proper begins on the next page. Point number one states, "*Everyone should remain in Quarantine until they are fully ready to leave.*" And, just below, point two, "*Once you have left, there can be no returning to Quarantine. No exceptions.*"

"So far it all seems pretty clear to me," I mutter. "But of course I'm happy to sit here with you. Oh, look, we can take walks outside. Ah, yes, you mentioned some incident on the street…"

Elsa glances over my shoulder. I read on, "*To exit the building you must use the private elevator, located inside the apartment next to the front door. Opening the front door is not recommended.*"

"*You should only go for walks during the daytime. Walking in the dark is not recommended.*"

And further:

"*Swimming in the sea without a bathing suit is not permitted. No exceptions.*"

"So, there's a sea here?" I ask Elsa.

"Oh, yes," she replies, "very much so. And it seems very, very real to me. You can see it from the bedroom – here in the living room, there are always just images beyond the window."

"Let's look at it now," I suggest. We go into Elsa's bedroom. She confidently presses the buttons of her console and nods toward the window, "There you have it…"

Beyond the window is a fabulous ultramarine seascape stretching right out to the horizon, a bright sun and white launches and yachts. Below us is a seafront with a balustrade, full of people. Almost everyone is walking in twos – leisurely and slowly; they're clearly not in a hurry. We are high up, and I cannot distinguish their faces. A set of concrete stairs leads from the seafront to the rocks near the water. I see several bathers, all dressed in bright yellow. Some are simply lying on the rocks, apparently sunbathing.

"Idyllic," I grin. "Is it like this every day?"

"Well, no," Elsa makes a denying gesture. "This is the first time I've seen the sun. They seem to be quite capricious about switching on the weather."

"'According to the schedule…'" I murmur quietly, but the words don't register with Elsa. Perhaps her Nestor uses different terms.

"Yesterday there was a strong wind," she says. "Wind, storm clouds, everything was very dark and gloomy. And the waves – no one dared climb into the water, although it's probably safe here. I mean with our so-called bodies…"

She is standing right next to me. Obeying a sudden impulse, I try to put my arm around her waist, but my hand hangs in the air – Elsa avoids it, takes a step away and toward the center of the room. "Ice maiden!" I think with irritation. For some reason, there seems to be a catch about this as well, some unnecessary conceit.

Soon after, we return to the living room and sit down on the couch a little apart from each other. "I didn't like going out alone," Elsa confides. "Everyone – just everyone! – looks you right in your face; it's so annoying. I complained to Nestor, but he told me it's only natural. Everyone's got the same thing on their mind, he said. They're looking to meet somebody they knew back *there* – that's all they're concerned about. And for me, it's not such a big deal. Back *there*, I wasn't close to anyone."

"Close? To anyone?" I repeat and suddenly recall Tina again. Recall the name, a bright-red streak of hair and a sense of anxiety, sucking at me from inside. My roommate notices something, moves away a little and looks at me askance. I remain silent, having nothing to say – and nothing even to think about. The flashback burns and torments me, but no threads reach out from it. My memory is helpless – how long is this going to continue?

I pick up the Brochure again. The next pages contain nothing but an endless disclaimer, informing that the administration is not responsible for anything, from the state of the infrastructure to the *quarantiners'* mental health. I skim over the paragraphs of this dry bureaucratic text and have almost decided to skip a few pages when Elsa suddenly jumps up, "Oh! We're almost late – you'd better skip to the end and read clause seven point one. Or maybe it's seven point three…"

I read aloud, *"Everyone should have two sessions every day with your friend, your mentor, your Nestor at twelve and five precisely, according to the large wall clock."*

Elsa points to the opposite wall. A round clock is hanging there whose hands have already converged on the twelve-hour mark. "We must hurry," she says, getting up. "Bye-bye."

"See you later," I mumble in reply and head toward my bedroom.

CHAPTER 3

"YOU ARE FIFTEEN seconds late," Nestor says, an acid smile on his face. "This is not acceptable. I would ask you to bear this in mind."

I try to justify myself, "I have a good reason – I was attempting to make sense of your Brochure. Not very successfully, to be honest."

"Well," Nestor scoffs, "that means you'll have to value my friendship even more!"

Today, he is wearing glasses, which make him look older. For some reason, that seems rather amusing.

"It is not acceptable to be late!" my counselor repeats and then adds, looking down, "However, Theo, you have never excelled when it comes to discipline."

"It's probably in my file," I nod sagely.

"Exactly," he stresses. "Just bear in mind there's no escaping your file. Although that's hardly going to upset you."

"Interesting," I narrow my eyes, "and where did my file come from? Did you follow me back *there?* Do you have agents, observers, spies?"

Nestor snorts sarcastically, "What a conspiracy theorist you are! Someone back *there* may well have been following you – perhaps some of the women you cheated on or the creditors you deceived – but it has nothing to do with what goes on *here.* None whatsoever – you'll be told about this in more detail soon – and the file was compiled during your birth here using special methods that would take too long to explain. There are, you know, algorithms that link together disparate fragments of memories, whirling about in the subconscious from the very first moment of life. We know how to deal with the subconscious and the fragments of it too, but, fragments or no fragments, it's the whole, the entire thing that is most interesting to us – everything that has been accumulated in your earthly brain. It is inaccessible to us and, for the time being, to you too. The memory restores itself gradually – in fact, this is the main reason you are here. You will need to work on it – fortunately, you know how to work hard, Theo. And you have an assistant – in me. And your roommate. And your dreams."

He raises his finger significantly, intending to add something, but I interrupt him, "Just a minute! Please, Nestor, could you check my file again and read to me all the fragments, as you put it, about Tina, a girl who looks a bit like a teenager. She is twenty-three, she has a slight squint and a red tress of hair. I promise I will work hard – but I need a prompt, at least a hint!"

Nestor shrugs his shoulders, "I've already told you, everything must be done according to the schedule." Then he glances up at me and unexpectedly agrees, "Well, all right. As an exception, just this once. In your file…" He looks down, leafs through something and declares, "There is nothing in your file about a girl called Tina with a red tress in her hair. At least not in the part that I have access to: not a thing!"

"Do you mean to say, there are other parts?" I ask, leaning forward. "They need to be found, a request sent – how is that done here?"

"It can't be done at all," says Nestor in a bored voice. "I have already told you everything I can. You need to work on your memory – and, right now, please get yourself comfortable; you have a lot to take in. You look better today; it's time to systematize your picture of the world. To orient you, so to speak, in time and space. As they say here, to *define a place* – a place for everything. And so, you were born…"

I make an angry gesture but understand there is no point in arguing with him.

"You were born on a three-dimensional brane,[3] when it was in the

---

3   Multidimensional physical object located in a higher-dimensional

middle of its cycle," Nestor's voice is impassive, level. "In your time, it was generally referred to as the 'Universe,' and this represented outer space in all its entirety. Or at least, this was the commonly held view – you, Theo, and certain others tested it out for yourselves. Fortunately, your critics proved to be deeply wrong..."

Nestor pauses and says, "Yes. We are discussing cosmological issues but, at the same time, considering you personally. To a surprising degree, the milestones of your career correspond to the chronology of your brane. But first – a little about the world as a whole, as we understand it *here!*"

"*Here* is..." I butt in.

Nestor stops me by raising the palm of his hand, "Just listen, listen," and continues in his monotone voice, "in actual fact, there can be an infinite number of branes, but it is unlikely we will be able to verify this. Our knowledge is limited to two: the first, on which you were born, and the second on which you and I are now situated. The space itself, in which localized branes are floating, has apparently always existed – or at least for a very long time. Branes are born and die independently of each other, passing through cycles – let's tentatively call them expansions and compressions. During each cycle there is a period of time known as the 'window for life': on your brane it was composed of – or to this day continues to be composed of – several billion of your planetary years. We know of only one place where intelligent life has developed to a significant level – your planet on which your mind, Theo, and the minds of many of those with whom you will meet in the new world were formed."

"And what about yours?" I raise my eyebrows inquiringly.

"We're not going to talk about me today," Nestor replies dryly. "Now listen and don't interrupt!

"A couple of words about space itself – it, by the way, has been given different names," he continues. "Just basic 'space,' or 'metaspace,' as you used to sometimes call it, or even 'metabrane' – meaning that it's possibly embedded into some more global structure. The latter seems an unjustified complication to me, but the term has caught on, and we may as well use it too. At least two fundamental fields – gravity and the field of the

---

space. Branes are analogous to the strings of string theory.

conscions – are global: their particles can travel from one individual brane to another. It is the existence of these forces, gravitational primarily, that is responsible for the unexplained cosmological phenomena noted in your time. And I stress: there are grounds to surmise that it is specifically the metabrane, and the metabrane alone, that emits the conscions predicted by you. This is important – very, very important!

"Very important," Nestor repeats, moving his lips strangely. "But let us go further: unfortunately, we don't have any control over the global fields. We can't send information to other branes; we cannot create messages to our former lives – or our next ones if they exist. We don't know whether your descendants are trying to contact us or not. It appears to be fundamentally prohibited: the metaspace is a strict censor of the trajectories along which the interbrane particles can move. There is only a limited set of possible directions of movement and there is global time – you cannot argue with it, and you can't turn it back. It's impossible to estimate the size of the whole of space, and we have only fragmentary ideas about its geometry – although we have managed to achieve something there. The main thing we do know is its variability: at any scale, the curvature of the global space changes constantly and with considerable amplitude. This, naturally, is reflected somehow onto the local universes, on their structure and properties – and onto their intelligent life: if it exists, of course. We can say that all of us, indirectly or directly, depend on the geometric quirks of the metabrane, but we will discuss the details of this dependence later. For now, we need only note that it borders directly on any of the points of all the local worlds. From the inside, your universe seemed like a large sphere or perhaps something torus shaped, but, from a global point of view, it is more like a long thread packed into a tangled ball or another complex but compact structure. Local branes seem to float in space, like balls of yarn in an ocean: throw a ball into the water, and every facet of it will become wet. They themselves might appear very distant from each other, looking from the inside, but still might be extremely close – imagine a tangled ball made up of a multitude of different-colored threads. You can move along one of the threads for a billion years not knowing there are others nearby – although, to be fair, there is no way to jump from one to another nonetheless... All in all, you need to remember: in the models of the world, different forms and structures are possible, but the metabrane is always nearby, and this, as you will later understand, is our greatest blessing!"

"Can I ask something?" I raise my hand like a schoolkid.

"Why?" says Nestor in surprise. "You're not going to ask anything meaningful for the moment." And he continues, "Now, each localized brane has its own physics with its values of universal constants, but some global laws remain true always and everywhere. Also, each brane has its own causality and independent time flow – that's why, for example, here in the second life, individuals coexist whose earthly lifespan belonged to different centuries. However, no great temporal divergences have been observed – no one knows why. We cannot say when – on 'our' times-cale – 'your' brane existed and images of individual human consciousness known as 'B Objects' were created. We also don't know whether your brane and your civilization still exist. At least for now, none of the new arrivals have informed us of any threatening catastrophe or the like. It's worth noting, by the way, that only human memories can help us to know anything about the first, terrestrial life. Naturally, no material enti-ties of one brane can be accessed from any other – information can only be exchanged via B Objects. Fortunately, for many, memory is recovered almost completely, which applies to scientists as well – you can imagine how passionately they have been revising every single concept since arriv-ing in this new world. You too, Theo, will have a contribution to make, and I must say, there are people who have been waiting impatiently for you here. Everyone believes you are the pioneer who connected con-sciousness with energy-matter and determined its place in the structure of space. Every physicist who lived *there* after you, but arrived *here* earlier, knows your work and that famous article of yours – and moreover, you vanished right after its appearance: intriguing, isn't it? But even if we leave all these intrigues aside, the theory of the conscions, as we see it here, contains a number of blank spaces. You, Theo, have to help fill them in – now, once you have joined our ranks, so to speak. Fill them in – and take it further; there is no end of the work to be done. Of course, it is no easy matter restoring such a complex theory from a large number of people's memories without its original source. The information has been collected painfully, bit by bit, and then, as luck would have it: you arrived in person. Sorry, I got carried away – of course, no one here wished for your death…"

He says all this without a pause, like a much-repeated official text – as if reading me my Miranda rights, "You have the right to remain silent…" Conscions… the word imprints itself in my brain. I know, many things were linked to it. More than Tina? It's quite possible. What was the formula that came into my head just before I fell asleep? Hamiltonian?[4] An action integral?…

"Let's go back to your particular brane – and take your particular life as a point of reference," Nestor continues, looking a little sideways. "Fourteen billion earth years before your appearance on it, your brane began to expand. This is important in itself, but we also note one more peculiarity that cannot be avoided, speaking specifically about you. It was the first and most vivid occurrence of a phenomenon that you have dedicated your whole life to. I'm even a little envious: you will soon remember everything, and much of it is beautiful, harmonious, stunning. It is – here's a clue for you – symmetrical, up to a certain point, of course. But you, Theo, are not one of those people who just admire beauty. You need to dissect it, to understand what underpins it. And in that, we have to acknowledge, you made quite a step forward!"

His voice finally betrays a flicker of emotion. Nestor transfers his gaze toward me, adjusts his glasses and nods encouragingly. His appearance changes imperceptibly; nearly all his official formality has slipped. He now looks at me as an accomplice, a partner in crime. He even seems to squint slyly and says, "Imagine a pencil standing vertically on its point – does this remind you of anything? Imagine a sphere in the center of the convex bottom of a bottle – does this image jog your memory? When it comes to symmetry, there's only one thing you were interested in – the moment of its destruction. The end point, the instant of breakdown, the step toward imperfection. The pencil only needs to deviate by a micron and it will never be able to return to verticality – no, it will fall with a loud clatter, frightening your fellow library users. You might even be asked to leave

---

4   In quantum theories, a Hamiltonian is an operator corresponding to the total energy of the system.

the room – you have modeled a cataclysm, a catastrophe! The moment at which symmetry is destroyed is the transition from the improbable to the probable, from the exceptional to the commonplace, from incarceration to freedom. And there is always a price to be paid for this – the release of energy!

"Yes," he continues, after a pause, "a huge surge, incredible power. It's the power of geometry – it is more implacable than any other force. Back then, fourteen billion years ago, your infant cosmos was symmetrical to the uttermost limit. It existed in the form of an incredibly complex figure, intertwined in a multitude of dimensions. To create this tangled ball required all the energy of the previous brane, which had disappeared, collapsing into itself. At maximum compression, space took on an ideal shape, turning into a tiny grain of unimaginable density and temperature. This was the limit of perfection – and its life, like the life of any ideal, was utterly short. The tension of all the tangles was so great that with the first quantum of a flaw, the tiniest fluctuation, like the flicker of doubt or a reproving glance, the irreversible happened. The pencil deviated and nothing could hold it back. The fabric of space burst at the seams with a deafening crash. Part of it rolled up again – into a narrow tube – and it remained like that forever, while another began to expand at an absolutely insane speed – along its length, width and depth. Your brane was distinguished by a huge and random stroke of luck – it turned out to be three-dimensional."

"Chance… Protein structures… Life…" I murmur quietly. Something stirs in my memory, certain equations, diagrams.

"Exactly!" Nestor exclaims, smirking – he is happy for me. Like a kindergarten teacher for her infant pupil first composing the word "Mom" from plastic letters. "It was pure chance," he continues, "and for some, including you, Theo, three-dimensionality also became a guiding light, a shining path in the darkness, drawing you ever onward toward distant horizons. You will soon remember your childhood, your school and the lessons in the physics lab you attended with such diligence. You were a typical teenager, with a fondness for masturbation, who would listen spellbound to his teacher – a sullen man with greasy hair and a humped back. Women would give him a wide berth, and he was probably also prone to pleasuring himself, but it was not this that connected the two of you. He planted a spark in you, speaking with a fervent passion about the three dimensions of your universe as a necessary condition for the existence of life. You imagined from his stories and naive formulas on the school blackboard how in a four-dimensional cosmos, everything would fall on top of each other – planets onto stars, electrons onto atoms – while, in contrast, in a two-dimensional one, everything would inevitably fly off in all directions, without ever stopping. Only in three dimensions could life be possible – and, like your physics teacher, you were struck by the fortuitousness of nature's choice. His words about 'the hand of the Creator' remained lodged in your heart forever. Then, when you got older, you began to look for the places where fortuitousness might be hiding and realized that traces of chance were always concealed in the events described as "symmetry breaking" – the disappearance of some of the universe's symmetries. And that's how you proceeded: first, there were quarks,[5] then bosons[6] – the bearers of the fundamental forces, then later – the quantum fields in the brain, the condensation of your specific quasiparticles, and finally – the conscions, their vortices and the 'recording' of our memory on the metabrane. Which is why, both in Quarantine and outside it, you are a bit of a *celebrity*. But we are talking too much about you; let's get back to the chronological order of events…"

Nestor looks down again – at my file no doubt. Then he raises his eyes and continues, "So. Fourteen billion years ago, your brane, having become three-dimensional, swelled into a huge bubble, on which seas of the smallest building blocks of matter were boiling, emerging and immediately destroying each other. At that time, once again, imperfection made itself felt: all the births and annihilations didn't add up, like cards in the hands of a card sharp. Some of the quarks remained intact; they happened to outnumber the antiquarks – one part in every billion. Not much, it would seem, but this was enough – and this asymmetry determined your

---

5   An elementary subatomic particle – a fundamental constituent of matter.

6   Particles with integer spin following Bose–Einstein statistics. Examples of bosons include fundamental particles such as photons (quanta of light).

fate, Theo. Not only did it allow for the creation of everything material, but it also enthralled you as a researcher. It was the predominance of matter over antimatter that became your first obsession!"

In the upper-right corner of the screen, a figure appears consisting of three different colored circles connected by wavy lines. Below the figure is a table filled with numbers.

"A unitary mixing matrix," I mutter.

"Yes, yes," Nestor nods at me, "It's something one never forgets," and then he produces a very strange sound. I don't realize it at first, but this is the sound of him laughing.

"I'm joking," he says. "But you were in no mood for jokes. You'd really sunk your teeth into the properties of the earliest matter that emerged in the first few moments after the beginning of the universe. Try to remember: quarks, which had only a fleeting existence, formed protons, surprisingly stable units – no longer just toy bricks, but real building blocks, the most reliable construction material. Other hadrons[7] were also created along with their mirrorlike antipodes; they all boiled together in a sizzling hot cauldron, colliding with and destroying each other and emitting new particles, more and more of them. The gigantic particle zoo was populated by its inhabitants. Everything was born of nothing – which is an exquisite, incredible notion, but there is something else we must not forget. In that hot, turbulent time, another perfection was destroyed. The forces of nature separated from each other – and that diversified your career, Theo! At first, gravity fell away; then, almost immediately, the force glueing together the atomic nuclei began to obey its own special laws – although there were no nuclei yet. And then, once matter had already become abundant, the final separation of influences occurred. All known electromagnetism detached itself from weak interactions – and this was the event of all events. In addition to the separation of fundamental forces, it led to a phase transition: matter gained mass. And you, Theo, earned a bit of a reputation, and we have to admit not the finest either!"

Nestor's eyes narrow, "Yes, yes, don't look at me so innocently." Then,

---

7   Subatomic particles that are composed of quarks and interact by the "strong" force. Examples of hadrons include protons and neutrons.

once again, I hear him produce a strange sound – his version of laughter. Having calmed down, he becomes serious and says, "Concentrate, this is important" – and again looks somewhere to the side. The figure with the circles disappears from the screen, and a diagram consisting of spirals and arrows emerges.

"This was a beautiful hypothesis," says Nestor, nodding to himself. "A viscous field, in which the scattering particles are slowed down, and its agents, the Higgs bosons,[8] the evasive carriers of new properties. A great many people rushed to study the mysterious boson, which lives for such a short time that it can't be seen directly. As with any hunt, the main thrill lay in capturing it – the finest minds struggled, searching for ways to detect the traces of its collapse in detectors the size of a multistory building. As a talented specialist, you were invited to a laboratory with access to the latest collider – a dream come true for any theoretical physicist at that time. Your team was considered one of the favorites in the race, and your colleagues spared no effort. Only you, Theo, threw in your hand – quickly stating that you weren't interested and wanted to leave. You preferred – surprise, surprise – the freedom of alternative models and your own fields and particles. Your colleagues considered you a traitor – what else could they have thought, engaged in an unforgiving scientific race as they were? In the middle of a contest for professorships, grants and, at the end of the day, Nobel prizes."

Nestor falls silent and fixes me with a look. I feel uncomfortable under his gaze. "However, I understand what repelled you," he continues. "Perhaps, the populist press was to blame – for sensationalizing the hunt to such an obscene degree. They indulged the masses and reduced everything down to the shameful label of 'God's particle' – probably, for you, that was the last straw. As far as I can judge, you surmised that God could have as many favorite particles as he wanted. You were not interested in his toys; you were looking for a gesture, a trace of an intervention made by a higher will in the 'magic tricks' of the universe. Perhaps the three-dimensionality and the quarks that had managed to survive annihilation

---

8   Elementary particle predicted by Peter Higgs and responsible for the mass of other elementary particles.

had not yet left your head. You remembered them for a long time, Theo – you are probably the sort of person who never forgets a grudge!"

"Is that stated in my file too?" I say curiously.

"No," Nestor admits, "but don't think all I can do is read what has been written down by others. I may not have discovered new fields like you, but I am capable of putting two and two together and drawing certain conclusions too. Of course, you aren't obliged to agree with me..."

He snorts, feigning indifference, but I can see he feels offended. Here is a character – with no small ego – but quarreling with him will get me nowhere. "Forget it," I say in a conciliatory manner, "That's not what I was implying. And, moreover, I don't remember anything about the new fields."

"You will," Nestor declares. "You will remember – the fields and how you were torn to pieces over some of them. For the time being, I will only note that despite your obstinacy, you gained a lot from that 'separation story.' I mean the actual separation of the fundamental forces – you worked on its secrets very hard. Was it not this that later helped you describe the activation of true consciousness? The immature brain as an unstable vacuum – I think the analogy is fairly transparent. And in general, it was very useful for you to look at the spontaneous symmetry breaking from various different angles..."

A new figure appears on the screen – it resembles a sombrero – with two equations next to it. I take them in with a single glance and a presentiment of recognition, recalling the words, one by one.

Nestor, meanwhile, waxes lyrical – on the harmony of proportion and form, on the symmetry of properties and of the laws of physics. He is most eloquent, but I barely hear a word he says. I look at the screen and tormentedly, intensely try to remember.

My thoughts marshal themselves into formations and lines; they begin to obey me. "Goldstone's potential!" I exclaim. In my excitement, my mouth goes dry. I cough and continue, "The simplest scalar approximation..." – but here Nestor makes a sign, and the figure disappears.

"Okay, okay," he waves his hand. "Let's not concentrate on your past misfortunes..."

"Just a minute, put it back up!" I almost cry. "I need it, I've finally remembered…"

"The session is over," says Nestor with a shrug. "We'll be seeing each other in a few hours."

And with that, the screen goes blank. Here in Quarantine, they're obviously not into long farewells.

Chapter 4

I AM HALF sitting, half lying in my armchair, looking at the wall opposite and thinking over what I've heard. Nestor's bluntness rankles; I swear at him under my breath, quite colorfully – realizing nevertheless that I can do nothing to change his manner. Recollections emerge and fade; my memory is readying itself for a huge leap. Fragments of formulas flash through my head – teasing, dissolving before I can catch their meaning. A long Lagrangian[9] emerges with a complex sum in square brackets, followed by an equation, which makes me uneasy. On the right-hand side is the already familiar integral; there is clearly something wrong with its upper limit… It's difficult to keep everything in my mind – I need to write it down, to reflect!

Breathing out sharply, I get up, again amazed at the obedience of my unreal body, and carry out a thorough examination of the bedroom. I go up to one wall, then another, tapping and probing; I kneel down, I run my fingers along the surface of the floor and look into the corners. Then I crumple the thick curtains in my hand, its fibers tickling my skin. The material is strange but quite real and doesn't appear to be fake. The room is not completely sterile – I find specks of dust, fragments of a pencil and some other detritus. It has all the hallmarks of a place that has been abandoned by its previous occupant. One could make it cozy again, get

---

9   A function describing the evolution of a dynamical system.

accustomed to it, domesticate its walls and its contents… I examine my hand, tapping the windowsill with my palm and then try to pinch myself, to scratch my skin with my fingernail. Yes, I feel pain, but I can't decide whether it's real or not. It seems my nerve impulses are being generated sparingly, just enough to register the sensation but not to convey it in its entirety.

Regardless, I continue my search. Nothing new is revealed – no secret doors or cubbyholes behind the mirror, no false compartments in the back of the chair. Then I open the wardrobe, push the clothes to one side, inspecting each shelf, and here I get lucky. In the lower-left corner, I discover a compartment full of diverse items, among which are two notepads and a set of pens. This is an important find – I have a strange feeling that I've almost wished them into existence, but I decide not to think about this yet. Slamming the wardrobe, I sit down at the table and try to record at least something of the fragments flickering in my head. I have a little success – just a few symbols and a summation sigma. The subintegral function has completely gone, and the Greek theta sign – I now know it stands for some angle – leans sideways on its own. "*Mierda*, bloody Nestor," I mutter. No one can hear me. After sitting for another ten minutes, I draw a female silhouette and write underneath it, "Tina." Then I scribble right next to it, "Elsa," and drum my fingers on the table…

The inset touchpad suddenly comes alive; squares and arrows appear. It's a plan of the room with a large menu above it. I jab at random – the curtains on the window draw to a close, and twilight sets in. "Hmm," I say thoughtfully and have a more serious crack at working out the buttons.

The control panel is quite confusing; some of the commands remain unclear. Nevertheless, I get the hang of most – I learn how to change the view outside the window, the color and translucence of the curtains, the room temperature and humidity. I discover the music console and spend a long time going through the tracks and styles. Then I experiment with the patterns on the wallpaper, which all remind me of the same thing – hazy milk spirals in a coffee cup. It's evidently a hint; I think about it, then try to draw something distantly familiar – swirls of hoarfrost or a perfectly formed snowflake – but to no avail. In irritation, I turn the walls a smooth light-orange color, switch off the music and get up – suddenly feeling an urge to see Elsa.

My roommate is sitting on the sofa in the living room – embroidering something on a piece of light-colored fabric. She has clearly also found something in her wardrobe that takes her fancy.

"Hello, hermit! What were you two discussing for so long?" Elsa exclaims, pretending to be angry, but I know she is glad to see me. She looks good in a mustard-colored skirt and a gray sweater, an amber necklace around her neck and a bracelet of the same kind on her wrist.

I walk over and sit down next to her. Elsa immediately pulls back a little – ice maiden! She smiles at me – cordially, politely, but somehow detachedly – and says, "This is going to be our tablecloth. I like things to have a personal touch." She puts her embroidery down on the couch between us and looks at me inquiringly, "Well, how are you? Coping okay? How's your memory?"

I admit that I have nothing to boast about.

Elsa tries to reassure me, "Don't worry. It'll come – I was the same; at first I couldn't remember anything except for that helicopter and the granite cliffs below it. And then in an instant: the explosion, the ball of flame… It's good it happened so fast – I didn't even have time to be scared. And twenty-four hours later, I couldn't stop remembering – both in my dreams and sitting right here. The resort where I was staying, my neighbors from the same building… They organized this helicopter ride over the mountains and dragged me along with them, assholes… And then everything else came rushing back: my childhood, my youth. I would go up to the window and see images – not the projected ones but things that had happened in my past. Nestor helped too, of course – he is such a kind, attentive man. You know, a man of his word!"

I give her a sidelong glance, feeling annoyed – surely it can't be jealousy? I turn away, angry at myself, and ask with a studied indifference, "Have you asked him to explain what Quarantine is? For some reason, my counselor-friend isn't inclined to expand on the subject."

"Yes, he mentioned something," Elsa shrugs. "Something about an anabiosis, an illusion… A mass illusion – sounds credible. It's fairly easy to believe."

"Easy..." I say, pondering. "And what about the structure of the world? Individual universes, each with its own physics? The metabrane that is always nearby."

Elsa grimaces, "What, what? No, nothing like that. My Nestor is too tactful; he wouldn't try to confuse me. And he cares about me – he chooses my dreams for me. I write everything in a diary – do you keep a diary? You should start; it's a good habit!"

"Another counselor..." I think to myself and try to make a joke about it, "I tried drawing a fractal instead. It didn't go well though."

Elsa waves her hand, "Don't get smart; I don't know what that word means. Have you noticed by the way that we're speaking the same language? But we can't read the phrases on each other's lips..."

Another thought enters my head. I go to my room, pick up the notebook and pencil, go back to the living room and gesture Elsa over to the table.

"Here, look," I draw a ball of yarn. "Imagine that it consists of a multitude of threads. Now visualize it floating in the ocean, every facet of it surrounded by water..."

I somewhat excitedly retell her everything Nestor has told me about the structure of space, but Elsa doesn't appear touched in the slightest. She patiently listens, suppressing a yawn, then, without uttering a word, returns to the sofa, to her embroidery. Even if she is not real, there's still something imperfect about her. An unevenness in the way she distances herself.

"Well, all right then," I say and begin to examine the room. For a quarter of an hour, I investigate every corner and feel all the surfaces, like I did in my bedroom. This elicits some interest from Elsa – she watches me for a while and then says with a laugh, "Sherlock! Yes, I also found traces of dust but, on the whole, they do the cleaning quite well here. No worse than I would have done myself."

"Cleaning?" I ask, surprised.

"Yeah," Elsa replies and explains patiently, "There's got to be a maid, right? She must come in when we're asleep or go out for a walk – like a magic fairy."

I'm a little irritated; she seems to be teasing me. "A fairy..." I mutter angrily. "What nonsense!" Then I go up to the couch and sit on the floor in front of her. Elsa continues to sew without looking at me.

"Listen!" I say. "Can you give me a serious answer? What do *you* think about all this – the other life, Quarantine? What have you managed to work out these last three days – I'm sure you've been thinking about it nonstop."

Elsa snorts, "There's no need to be rude." Then she puts her embroidery aside, rests her hands on her knees and says, glancing down at me, "Not quite. I have thought about it, but only a little – because I've been trying my best not to think. To, you know, not lose my mind – you should try sitting here all on your own!"

I don't say anything, just look away. Elsa continues, "When I woke up and went to the apartment, I sat on the sofa for almost half a day with an empty head waiting for something to happen. As if I'd woken up after a very deep sleep and for a while couldn't find a way back to reality. Then, little by little, I began to ask myself questions and provide answers to them. "Where am I? – I don't know. Am I ill? Apparently not. Was I asleep? Apparently yes, but I don't remember where... Only after I'd convinced myself I was capable of thinking straight, I got up, had a look around, found that laminated printout and remembered about the helicopter. And then I spoke to Nestor – he calmed me down."

"Do you believe in all this?" I ask, sharply sensing the irrelevance of the question.

"Do I have a choice?" Elsa sniffs. "Of course, I felt uncertain to start off – suspecting someone had drugged me and was playing games with me. Or that I was in a coma, and everything around me was a hallucination. But Nestor somehow convinced me..."

"By the way," she lowers her voice. "Initially, I thought I was being observed the whole time – by secret cameras, like in a reality show. I tried to be reserved and withdrawn and not betray any emotions – but then I got bored. Now I don't think about it at all."

"'To die would be an awfully big adventure,'" I murmur. "I'm sure I've read that somewhere."

"Yes, yes," Elsa nods. "I've also read it. And so I decided: since it's already happened, all I can do is just see how things turn out. If not in the second life itself – which I still assumed might be a joke – then at least in this specific place, in Quarantine. After all, some events take place here as well: there are the conversations with Nestor, changes in the weather – and I was also waiting for my roommate to arrive. It'll be interesting, I thought; who will he turn out to be? Poor thing – he's got such a shock waiting for him…"

She picks up the tablecloth again, spreads it on her knees and examines the embroidery critically. Stitched onto it is the word "Good," with the final letter slightly higher than the others.

"It's not straight," Elsa acknowledges, "but that makes it even funnier. Let it remain like that – in a kind of semicircle."

I get up and walk around the living room. Her lightheartedness still rankles me slightly – or maybe I'm just a little envious?

"It's remarkable," I say, stopping next to the window. "You immediately take everything as a given and endow it with rational meaning. Do you have any doubts, ever?"

"Oh, yes," Elsa looks mockingly. "Torturing yourself with doubts is so typical of you men! Be thankful that I'm not some crazy neurotic. I could be acting quite differently – I can just imagine how my mother would have been in my place! She would have given everyone in Quarantine a hard time – telling them how to behave and what they need to do. Nestor's nerves would be in shreds by now…"

She gets up and beckons me over, "Let's try it out."

We go up to the table. Elsa spreads the tablecloth, then straightens it and nods contentedly, "It's just right. What do you think – it's not too small, is it?"

"Just right," I assure her and ask, "Did you have a husband back there before the helicopter crash?"

Elsa shakes her head, "No. At least, I don't remember a husband. As I said, I didn't have anyone close to me – blood relatives don't count. It's a good thing I died young: when you get older, only those close to you can still really love you. They could have never appeared in my life, but a time when it'd be impossible to love me would have been inevitable. It would have been a very sad life!"

Leaning over, she scrutinizes her embroidery. I ask her what the entire inscription is going to be. Elsa giggles, "I'll tell you if you want. I remembered it this morning – it's a funny story…"

She straightens the tablecloth again and continues, "I was only a child when I heard for the first time that I might go to heaven… By the way, my Nestor mentioned today that this, in a sense, is true. Or at least a rough approximation of it, he said – okay, I know myself that that isn't completely so. But the main thing has been proven: after the helicopter crash and the explosion, I'm sitting here and talking to you, and I even understand who I am."

"It seems your Nestor is a lot nicer than mine," I grin, but Elsa interrupts me, "Look. Later on, the other words will go here and here…"

I examine the tablecloth and even trace it with my fingers. Then I turn toward the window – there are cliffs behind it. Huge outcrops of rock with sharp edges. Perhaps, they are similar to the ones below Elsa's helicopter when her first life came to an untimely end. My memory is still bad – I can't produce a single coherent recollection. If, of course, you don't count the Lagrangian, which is perfectly self-sufficient in its own right.

"It happened in my early teens," says Elsa, sitting down again on the couch. "I was feckless and pretty stupid and didn't know who and what to believe. And then my older sister came back for the holidays from her college and brought me a T-shirt that said: *Good girls go to heaven, bad girls go to LA*. It changed my life completely!

"Yes, it really did!" she exclaims, spreading the embroidery on her knees. "It sounds strange, but it's true. What I mean is, I suddenly understood that I had a chance – of really getting there. The chance, when offered, is always very important. I even said as much to Nancy – that's my sister's name – but she just laughed and said I was an idiot. Actually, she laughed at me all the way through my childhood – because she was taller and prettier, and all the guys would just ogle at her legs."

"Your legs are very beautiful, Elsa," I tell her quite sincerely. "They were the first thing I seriously took notice of in *this new* life."

"Ah, come on," she says, embarrassed a bit, but I can see she is secretly pleased. "Well, as a matter of fact, you aren't so bad yourself; you have nice shoulders and a strong forehead, and cheekbones… None of my men were like you – that is, none of the ones I can remember. I didn't have many men, to tell the truth – mostly because of that T-shirt.

"The thing is," Elsa continues, threading her needle, "I wanted to go to heaven *very much*. I like to take care of everything in advance – and here suddenly I saw a direct path! For some reason, I believed that slogan more than all the pastors and bibles put together. I always did what my sister used to tell me, and maybe this is the whole point – although she herself had no hope of redemption. She slept around, smoked grass and even broke the law – can you imagine it? She used to drive a car with a fake driver's license, buy booze and hang out in bars while still underage…"

Elsa grins, shakes her head and says, "As for me, I became a really good girl. I was always taught if you want to get something you need to work hard; gifts need to be earned. And this case was so crystal clear – naturally, I began to try my best! I tried almost my whole life – with some exceptions, of course. But exceptions only prove the rule… Could you turn up the light please? It's beginning to get dark, I think."

I run my fingers along the panel in the center of the dining table – it's the same as the one in my bedroom. The room is filled with soft light pouring from the ceiling. I change the shade slightly, return to the sofa and sit down next to Elsa again. As usual, she shies away from me, although it hadn't even occurred to me to touch her. Today, she does not smell of juniper. Her scent is an expensive perfume – something very adult and slightly bitter.

"Being a good girl is quite difficult," Elsa admits, without looking up. "But it's doable – and I made a success of it I guess. At least, I pretty quickly became a social outcast. I stayed away from guys, and I didn't smoke – neither grass nor even ordinary cigarettes; my idea of goodness was quite conservative. I tried never to lie and often went to church – I still remember a few of the prayers. Though, of course, I dreamed – like every girl – of becoming a cheerleader, wearing short skirts and looking stunning, so that boys, and even older men, might chase after me. But the dreams were easy to cope with."

She thinks about something, smiles at her thoughts and turns to me, "Just imagine, despite all this, I still lost my virginity very early. I just wanted to give it a try – and I liked it, but after that, I didn't sleep with a man for years. I set my sights very high and did not let anyone inside, either literally or figuratively. It didn't make sense spending time getting to know someone, worrying and suffering, when I was quite capable of doing everything myself... I only had my first real boyfriend when I was twenty-three. And he didn't last long, only a few months – and he managed to annoy me no end. When we split up, I got drunk on whiskey for the first time – even good girls have to have a break every now and then!"

I laugh and so does Elsa. "And thus," she continues, "it went on. Eventually, I found myself with no real friends; they were all bored of me. As for my admirers, one by one, they turned out to be complete bastards – I began to think I would never get married. Although I realized I needed a family to be happy, maybe even children – or, if that was too much, then at least a steady partner by my side. I knew what sort of man I wanted; I even made a list of the mandatory traits he would require. Yet I succumbed to weakness and started to date a man who didn't have them all. He was only missing a couple, but that proved to be enough: soon he had run off with a waitress from a nightclub. However, it was all for the best – after that, I burned my list and became a lot more sociable. I began to change my lovers regularly – some were even quite good."

"And what about your sister?" I ask, looking at her fingers. They are agile, graceful, and have a life of their own. "By the way, do you ever want sex here?" I add out of the blue.

"Sex isn't on my mind," Elsa responds nonchalantly. "There are lots of other things to reflect on here. And I fell out with my sister – forever. I snitched on a friend of hers who was carrying cocaine to the police. I assumed this was what any good girl would do. Nancy never forgave me – also, it was just at that time I went off to England to continue my studies. And the very first thing I saw at Heathrow airport was a T-shirt with the slogan: *Good girls go to heaven, bad girls go to London*! This threw me – and I suddenly began to have doubts about the whole notion. After that, I was no longer able to believe my sister."

She leans back into the couch and looks at the wall clock. It reads half past four – I'm surprised how quickly the time passes here.

"Soon it will be time to see Nestor," my roommate says, "and then a dream of his or my choosing..."

We don't talk about anything else after that. Elsa carries on with her fine stitching, head down and smiling at something, and I just sit there, furtively glancing at her profile. I sit and wonder for the umpteenth time – who she really is, what role she is meant to play. And how much can I really trust her?

CHAPTER 5

NESTOR GREETS ME with a curt nod. He is cheerful and businesslike; he emanates enthusiasm and confidence. He is wearing a cream-colored shirt and a thin tie and looks like a TV show host.

"So," he says, "where were we this morning…" But I interrupt him with a decisive gesture. My counselor falls silent in surprise.

"Just a minute," I ask, "first I would like to clarify something, otherwise my brain will simply refuse to function. Like, for example, why am I in Quarantine? Sick people are usually sent to quarantine – does that mean we've contracted something? And also, there's my roommate – neither death nor her new life seem to interest her. She just sits on her own, embroidering away… She simply doesn't care! I don't understand who she is – a woman, a phantom, or an illusion like the plates dissolving into the kitchen wall? A dream from my reasoning mind or the product of my drug-induced ravings? I need to know; I can't keep stumbling about in the dark like this!"

Nestor looks displeased, "I wasn't expecting this of you. We are trying to discuss serious matters, and here you are stamping your feet and insisting that we distract ourselves with these silly trifles!" He shakes his head and sighs, "All right, I'll explain. Are you sick? In a certain sense, yes. You suffer from an acutely unstable way of perceiving yourself, the world and your place in it – can that be considered healthy? The question isn't whether it is contagious or not – society just doesn't want to live with people who are utterly bewildered, whose criteria and guidelines are blurred. People who lack understanding – and therefore acceptance – who add to confusion and disorder... We need to ensure your perception returns to normal, and you have to work to make that happen. You must recall, correlate and apprehend – what the role of everything is. The role and the *place* – of you, me, Quarantine and of our lives."

"Interesting," I mutter. "An acutely unstable sense of perception... And is my 'cure' guaranteed?"

"Guaranteed? Pretty much so," Nestor grins. "In one form or another, so to speak. Sometimes radical 'treatment' is required that involves subjecting the memory to certain corrections. All sorts of things happen – for example, there are maniacs and murderers who enjoy the process... But this doesn't apply to you; there are no red flags to that effect in your file. Of course, I shouldn't be telling you this, but you are such an important person..."

He pauses, examines me for a few seconds and sums things up, "So there we have it. As for your roommate, well, that's up to you. Find a way to check her out – maybe she's more real than you yourself are? I would say embroidery looks a lot more innocent in this regard than pointless doodles of symbols..." And he grins again, nodding at my open notepad.

I frown, offended – and don't know what to say. So I just mutter quietly, "Check her out... What, take a peek under her skirt?"

"Well, that is unlikely to help you," Nestor sneers and becomes serious again. "All right, I hope we've cleared up the housekeeping issues," he declares. "Now, are you ready to listen? Then let's carry on – there's still a fair amount of time we haven't covered yet. How far did we get last time – about a second? The first second of fourteen billion years. Yes, a second may encompass a lot – almost the entire subject matter of your career..."

He lowers his eyes, flips through several pages and continues, "Let me remind you: it all began with an explosion of an ideal cosmos. There was nothing in it but space curved to an incredible extent and equal to itself in any projection, from any angle. Flawless symmetry is a dangerous thing – like flawless chastity: it's not clear what it conceals, what hidden passions...

"Then later, there were the quarks, the separation of forces, the Higgs field and the attainment of mass. Protons, neutrons, the release of neutrinos, rushing out on their eternal wanderings... Don't worry if the whole picture is a little confused in your head. It will soon pass: in fact, you understood all the physics much better than I do. Patience, patience – but for now let's continue further: from the creation of your brane to the person who you are."

"You're very eloquent this session, Nestor," I remark.

"Nonsense," he says dismissively. "Don't try to make fun of me; I'm invulnerable to your mockery. Although, of course, we counselors have bad days as well..."

He becomes thoughtful for a moment but quickly collects himself, "Let's not get distracted. I suggest we skip a few eons. Let's bypass those troubled times when armadas of particles of different types repeatedly extinguished each other. First some, then others, became dominant – baryons and mesons, then electrons, muons, photons... Then atomic nuclei began to form – it took nature a little more than a quarter of an hour to create them. And soon after, everything became frozen in the transition phase. The nuclei of future atoms and their satellites, the electrons, collided and scattered in thermal madness. The universe trembled like a gigantic gloomy cloud, developing nowhere, for the next half million years – years, not seconds! – until everything cooled down to acceptable temperatures. And then a miracle happened: light was born!

"Of course, there was no miracle at all, really," he adds a little peevishly. "Each 'miracle' has its own rationale, its own source of deception – every priest knows this well. Back then, at the time of the birth of light, photons simply broke free. They were released from their dungeon: electrons began to stick to the nuclei, forming the first neutral atoms – hydrogen and helium. And the universe suddenly became transparent! The fog cleared, everything became visible – although, to be honest, there wasn't much to look at just yet.

"And here's another thing I must mention at this point," Nestor nods thoughtfully. "Coincidences that were utterly miraculous in their own way. I mean, for example, finely tuned mass ratios: the masses of a proton, a neutron and an electron turned out to be extraordinarily precise. As a result, neutral atoms could exist for a long time without disintegrating or decaying. Yet, fortunately, they were not eternal; they were stable but not quite: warm them up properly, squeeze them together – and a transformation occurs. Atoms were capable of recombination in fusion reactions that created the vast diversity of chemical elements. After all, who would want to consist solely of hydrogen? That would be too insubstantial. But now if you please we had oxygen, carbon, iron… Enough material to build as many little galactic nests as you want!

"A mass ratio such as this is truly striking, and you, Theo, could not help but be amazed when you perceived its significance and strangeness," Nestor says, poking his index finger at me. "However, your amazement wasn't so great on this occasion – I think you were already tired of being surprised by that time. It was not the specific cases that interested you, but their generalization – the conclusion, the essence. The uniting substance, if not the uniting persona – someone whose hand you imagined was pulling the strings. Whose sensitive fingers were feeling the pulse of events and making adjustments, if something was not right. Of course, later, when you predicted the conscions and B Objects, your amazement, I think, completely fizzled out. Your piety vanished; you became used to the idea that there is neither 'a persona' nor a 'hand' – am I right?"

I make a gesture in an attempt to interrupt him, pencil in hand and open notepad in front of me. "Wait, I need to write something down," I say quickly and scribble a few words, but Nestor pays no attention.

"We'll find out later if I'm right or not," he continues unperturbed. "Meanwhile, beautiful, impressive, gigantic events were taking place on your brane. Star cradles formed and giant molecular clouds emerged, condensed and twisted into spirals. They collided and interfered with each other, causing local cataclysms. Gravitation, slowly but surely, segregated the condensations and irregularities – the embryos of stars. They spun and waltzed faster and faster in this majestic cosmic ball, becoming increasingly compressed and heating to immense temperatures. And suddenly, here and there, were explosions of the brightest light: the hydrogen atoms were too cramped. Thermonuclear fusion began – a star was born!

"Write that down," Nestor nods. "Write that down; I'll wait: those intense flashes were magnificent; there were billions of them! And now cross it out, because: it's not the aesthetics of that time that we're interested in. The important point is: it was specifically in the stars, in these natural furnaces, where the atoms were created from which planets are composed – and everything that exists on them, including you, Theo, and everyone like you. For that, you should be grateful to the first stars; after all, you are also one of their descendants. But their majestic dance didn't excite you much – your attention was directed to the causes; analyzing the consequences was a waste of time, in your opinion. That's why I only mention them briefly – although there were a lot of mysteries hiding in that period. In your time, it seemed the answers were close – the main things were apparently clear. Just a few calculations needed to be adjusted slightly, some artificial constants had to be introduced – well, you physicists are used to this. And basically, the sequence of events was described correctly: yes, the galaxy of the Milky Way was formed in the stellar supercluster of Virgo, in which one of the three hundred billion stars burned out, blazing up brightly at the end and provoking a modest cosmic drama in its vicinity. Thus, your planetary system emerged: the Sun was ignited; planets, asteroids and moons were formed from the debris of the old star – a motley crowd of celestial bodies doomed to coexistence. It was a chaotic mess then, like a cosmic communal apartment, filled with scandals and fights. The bodies collided, broke into pieces and exchanged satellites and orbits. They took a long time to get used to each other until only the most worthy survivors were left. Gradually, everything calmed down; the giant Jupiter took care of its neighbors, driving away large asteroids with its powerful gravitational field, and peace was established in the solar system. The planets fell into a stable formation and their moons took their rightful places. None of them now bothered each other or interfered with their neighbors' orbits. And, again, due to the coincidence of many factors, one of the planets – your earth, Theo – turned out to be suitable for the existence of protein bodies, as one of the philosophers put it!"

Nestor pauses and looks sideways. In the corner of the screen appears a picture: a blue sphere with the outlines of the continents. I remember having seen it many times – and I even know what it is. Probably, I'm meant to be showing emotion now – at least, Nestor looks at me in anticipation – but I feel none. The sphere seems infinitely distant and, by and large, not terribly interesting.

"Well, yes," I nod politely. "I see. Heavenly bodies, protein bodies and so on... By the way, I assume your brane is three-dimensional as well? And on it, in your life, I mean in *my* new life – there is at least something resembling a body?"

Nestor grimaces, "Don't rush. For now, I can only answer you briefly, in your terms: there is *something*. And you are strangely indifferent to the image I showed you – in your place, many others have broken down in tears."

"I'm not the sentimental type," I say with a grin. "It's probably down in my file."

"Perhaps," Nestor purses his lips. He seems to have been offended by the fact that his rotating blue sphere has not impressed me. "Well," he continues, "let's go on. So, carbon, water, proteins..."

The sphere on the screen dissolves. In its place, a chemical formula appears. An amino group attached to a radical, as far as I can recall.

"Life was capable of evolving and did evolve, although it took a lot of time," Nestor proclaims without looking at me. "Over thousands and thousands of millennia, the unremitting search, combinations and recombinations, experiments with large molecules capable of replication... For about four billion years, nature tinkered with the constituent ingredients of life, poking them in all directions and trying every possible option. Even in their wildest dreams, the medieval alchemists who searched for the philosopher's stone could not have guessed the number of trials, errors and efforts wasted in the labyrinth of evolution. For the first nine hundred and ninety-nine thousandths of its existence, your planet was not even visible beyond your brane – it was indiscernible and of no interest to anyone. Only in the last one-thousandth part – two million years ago – did the *Homo* genus separate itself from the family of the hominids, the large anthropoid apes. Then, in the last tenth of this period, just two hundred thousand years before your death – the blink of an eye, by cosmic standards – a new species was created, *Homo Sapiens*. A structure had evolved on the planet capable of interacting with the field of the conscions – the human brain – and then, only in the last tenth part of this tenth part, the first activation of true consciousness finally began to occur. The first B Objects began to appear in metaspace – where it borders your universe.

Their number grew bigger and bigger – evolution wasn't standing still. At the same time, little by little, humanity was succeeding in understanding the world in which it lived. There were important milestones – Pythagoras and Euclid; later Newton, Maxwell, then Einstein. Immediately after him came the quantum field theories that gave rise to the Standard Model; and later – string theory, M-theory, superstrings and branes. Humanity was readying itself for a decisive breakthrough, for a realization of its transcosmic role – and the necessary words began to emerge. Words are a very important step; they lead to ideas, and finally, you, Theo, came up with your work, which was mocked initially, with your hypothesis about invisible particles scurrying between worlds. This was another of the most important breakthroughs and, of course, the most intriguing with regards to each individual destiny. Your results have proved that the human mind is not simply a means of adapting to the reality in which people are born and are doomed to exist. No, everyone's mind, memory and interior world have gained a self-sufficiency greater than all earthly realities, which are short-lived and hopelessly provincial. Thanks to you, Theo, humanity has *proudly* proclaimed itself – more proudly than it could have ever imagined. Before you, there were people who thought a lot about this – I'll name just a few: Bohr, Pauli, Jung, James… But unlike you, they all fell short of the end goal – some lacked the math, others the freedom of imagination, and yet more perhaps, the disappointment with and resentment against society – to suffer unfair accusations and even subconsciously welcome them!"

Nestor pauses and looks into my eyes for a few seconds. Then he pronounces with a noticeable pathos, "At this point, I want to make an official statement. I would like to inform you, Theodorus: we here greatly value what you have done. Your merits will be noted – I guess you will be given some kind of award. Here, as a rule, justice triumphs post factum: those who in the first life were ahead of their time are held in honor here – great honor."

"Well, but…" I interrupt him, noting that this is the first time he's called me by my full name. "Wait, my theory – you are talking about it, but I don't remember…"

"You will remember!" Nestor replies, unexpectedly harshly. He repeats, "You will remember," and looks down. "Your estimated memory coefficient is very high: almost one. You should be able to recall everything, almost everything. And what you don't recall you are capable of dredging up in order to fill the gaps – you just need to try hard; it's your duty after all."

"That's funny – to whom do I owe a duty?" I mutter. "And why? Besides, you're talking in riddles, Nestor. Can I read about the conscions somewhere? About their dance – can you give me something, a research article, a scientific journal? And, most importantly, what exactly is a B Object?"

Nestor twists his narrow tie around his finger, looks me up and down in silence as if assessing a slightly disappointing exhibit. Then, just as harshly he says, "I can only repeat: I hope that soon you will be telling me about this yourself!"

"You're saying it in such a hectoring way..." I reply, forcing a grin. "Can you explain what the point of this pressure is?"

"Pressure?" Nestor raises his eyebrows. "You have no idea what pressure is. Coming to terms with a second life completely changes your mentality. Here, in our world, no one believes in naive fairy tales. Demagogues, inventors of gods, don't find it easy here – their recipes for immortality are merely an object of mockery. All resources have been invested into gaining knowledge of the world – and big investments entail big pressure; is that clear?

"As for duties," he carries on in a calmer vein, "everybody has them. Including me: it's my duty, for example, to decide right now how you and I are going to move things forward. I have to choose your first dream for you – one that will help restore your memory. A kind of potion directly from Morpheus, so to say. And..."

My counselor makes a dramatic pause and glances down, probably at my inexhaustible file. Then he looks up at me again and declares, "I have made a decision. We will start at the end and move back toward the beginning. Let's agree that the main part of the story – your story, the 'story of Theo' – culminated with your acquaintance with a certain Russian millionaire – if your file is to be trusted. And we have to trust it because with regards to you, Theo, it's all we have to go on!"

And with that, he disappears – as usual, without so much as a good-bye. I remain alone – a loneliness that is now desirable, a blessing. I need some respite – to be on my own, without counselors or helpers, without brochures, even without Elsa the ice maiden. As Nestor promised, it's been a very *busy* day. I want it to end at last.

Within a minute, my eyelids get heavy and my armchair reclines. Words and thoughts become confused in my head; my helpless memory fills with rustlings and murmurs.

Soon I fall asleep, and I begin to dream about a tycoon by the name of Ivan Brevich. And my next dream – on the next day – will also be about him. And the next one too – and the next one, and the next one after that.

BREVICH

CHAPTER 6

THREE FRIENDS – "Vanyok," "Sanyok" and "Valyok" – grew up together on the noisy streets of the Zamoskvorechye district of Moscow. They played the same games, studied at the local school and were inseparable throughout their childhood. Then their paths parted: having flunked his exams after an unhappy love affair, Valentin Sakhnov – Valyok – ended up in the army, in a special-forces unit, and for many years fell out of touch with his Moscow "contacts." Vanyok – Ivan Brevich – and Sanyok – Alexander Danilov – got into the same university, but Danilov was a poor student and, at the end of the Andropov era, was expelled for illicitly trading with foreign tourists. He managed to avoid military service with the help of a doctor relative and drifted into the antique trade, although he didn't exactly excel at it. Being disciplined and dogged, Brevich graduated with an engineering diploma but, with the Soviet Union on the verge of collapse, never put it to use. A new era of private business and easy money had arrived, and the friends threw themselves into "nouveau Russian" commerce.

For several years they were tossed on the fickle waters of these turbulent times. Together and individually, they made and lost small fortunes, learned how to deal with police and mobsters, tried their hands at all sorts of activities, until finally, by the end of the nineties, each had succeeded in his own way. Brevich established connections in the mayor's office and started dealing in land in and around Moscow, while Danilov developed a sudden interest in air-conditioners after a chance deal involving them. He bought into someone else's business, "wrested" it from an incompetent partner, then found a good supplier in Europe, and things began to develop rapidly. The machines fascinated him; he loved them with all his heart. The principle of their workings remained a mystery to him, but the results they produced – arctic cold, emerging from apparently nowhere – never ceased to delight him. He liked to stand in front of the cooling units, putting his hands in the icy blasts of air. They seemed evidence to him of the greatest triumph of the mind, and his whole business acquired a very special meaning. Danilov straightened his shoulders, stiffened his resolve and began to feel he had really made it in life.

Not everything went so smoothly for Ivan Brevich. The land contracts brought the money in, but the process was extremely distasteful. The daily grind of smooth-talking the jackals and hyenas who pressed in from all sides crushed his soul and left him with a foul taste in his mouth. What's more, in the hierarchy of players he was well down the pecking order, having to content himself with the crumbs granted to him by those with the real levers of power. This was dispiriting – Brevich was a leader by nature and could only be satisfied by being top of the pile. This servile role did not suit him at all; he would grind his teeth at night as he recalled the day's mad rush from one office to another and was desperately jealous of Sanyok, whom he barely saw these days due to a lack of time and their different business interests.

Everything changed in the summer of '98 – when fate performed another of its somersaults. In June, Ivan, utterly burned out, told himself enough was enough. Something had to change, and he decided to move to the US, to the West Coast, closer to Silicon Valley and Hollywood. He sold everything he had, including a three-room apartment on Taganka, and converted the proceeds into US dollars. The resulting capital was transferred to a Latvian bank, and Brevich had just applied for an American visa when Russia defaulted on its debts. The country's currency collapsed, Ivan's fortune increased fourfold in ruble terms, and, slightly stunned, he decided to delay his departure and see what prospects might now open up.

It turned out there was a lot to look at, and one prospect emerged right away. Two days after the "Black Monday" collapse, Brevich received a call from a very depressed Sanyok asking for an urgent meeting. Over dinner at the Peking Restaurant, he explained that he had been planning a rapid business expansion and had taken out a few loans. Now he had nothing to pay them back with: the raging ruble cash streams had been reduced to barely a dribble. What's more, Danilov had also borrowed some of the money from people with dubious reputations. Now, he was preparing for the loss of his business, his good health and even perhaps his life.

Brevich understood: this was the moment he had been waiting for. Giving sentimentality no quarter, he acted decisively and brutally. With the help of his contacts in the mayor's office, he frightened Danilov even more, leaving him with no desire to negotiate, and then bought his air-conditioning business together with its debts for a laughably small price. He let Sanyok remain in the company as executive director with a good salary but also all the hard work, and almost no shares.

Overnight, Danilov found himself transformed from a proud owner into a hired hand. He was shocked to the depths of his soul – especially at the ruthlessness with which his childhood friend had deprived him of the business he had grown almost from scratch. At first, he tried to pretend they were running the company on an equal footing, but he quickly realized his naivety and became wrapped up in himself. What made his depression even deeper was Ivan's lack of deference toward air-conditioners in general. Brevich, with his technical background, even tried to explain to Danilov what a phase transition and a Freon circle were – which Sanyok regarded as yet another example of life's bitter injustice. As for the business itself, it progressed and grew faster than ever. Successfully marshalling and unleashing Ivan's administrative resources, they swallowed up their main competitor and its developed network of clients. Vanyok Brevich was now the biggest player in the entire air-conditioner market and over the next ten years became an extremely wealthy man.

But then, in 2012, his destiny took a new twist. Ivan had just turned forty-six; he was influential, respected and rich. His life had acquired an enviable stability, and this was suddenly beginning to bother him. Something important seemed to be passing him by; Brevich began to suffer from a persistent sense of irritation and fatigue. And, after a particularly tough February full of bureaucratic hurdles and never-ending quarrels with his wife, he decided to take a break from everything and everyone.

At that moment, an opportune invitation arrived from a supplier and partner from Essen. Ivan had been working with the cheerful and ruddy-cheeked Lothar for over a year, and they were on very friendly terms – often doing the rounds of German saunas and Moscow's nightclubs. On this occasion, however, the supplier suggested moving their meeting from cold wintertime Europe to distant Bangkok, and Ivan agreed with enthusiasm.

Bangkok stunned him and somehow bewitched and lit up his soul. The city's traffic jams, disorder and heat left Ivan unperturbed. He even liked the thick, viscous air, which caused Lothar's nose to wrinkle. Subconsciously, without registering it, Ivan sensed an inexhaustible variety, unpredictability and the potential of the unknown waiting around every corner. And, from the very first day, he felt his virility revive – in contrast to the feeling of repletion he had long become accustomed to, believing that women could not interest him much anymore. Thai girls awoke something long dormant within him – and this was another big plus point in the city's favor.

His first week in Bangkok was devoted to vice. After fleeting visits to the Royal Palace, the National Museum and the two main temples, Ivan let his partner take the initiative, and they plunged into a rampant spiral of depravity and drunkenness. Lothar was a connoisseur and applied his German thoroughness to the planning of their activities. They methodically tried everything – from the go-go bars of Sukhumvit and Patpong and soap massages in large "aquarium" salons to chic karaoke and gentlemen's clubs. The days flew by in a blur of young girls' faces and bodies, with their endless "Hello, handsome," "What's your name?" and "Where are you from?" – as well as shameless "I love yous" in the hope of a generous tip…

During the breaks between the pleasures of the flesh, Lothar shared his thoughts on Thailand. At one time he had lived in Bangkok for about three years, and he'd been coming back every year since. Yet his views were largely negative, boiling down to one overriding complaint: Bangkok was a city of the fake. Lothar was convinced everyone here was out to rip you off. From pirate discs to simulated love, they were constantly trying to foist fakes on you. The whole of Thailand with its countless smiles was just a false, hypocritical facade concealing a typical third-world country where life was based on greed, envy and a strict caste system, untrammeled by any kind of humanism. Despite this, people would flock to Thailand in droves, and Lothar was no exception, a vivid example confirming the rule. Because elements of fakeness can be plausible – and here Lothar counted them off on his fingers: an illusion of friendliness, the ability to enjoy life, even the same smiles masking the unsightly side of human nature – they created a completely unique atmosphere. And of course – he spread his hands – of course, there are the women, how could we forget them…

Whenever the subject touched on Thai women, Lothar would always become gloomy and pitch more heavily into the brandy. His tone would turn moralistic: yes, he said, they are bubbly, friendly, easy and a pleasure to be with. The main thing is not to fantasize too much and never get into a relationship with them – neither with the bar "fairies" nor with the ordinary "good girls." Everything will end in disaster; it's impossible to live with a Thai – and once again, he enumerated his arguments on his fingers: they are irresponsible, unreliable and narrow-minded, and their opinions are infantile, not to mention their total reluctance to develop themselves. And besides, Lothar added, they will always find a way to outwit you. Behind their smiles and solicitude, they have very cold, pragmatic minds. And they are constantly dishonest – they learn the art of lying at an early age and perfect it throughout their lives. For a reason or for no reason, they pile one lie on top of another and never admit to being deceitful – even if you catch them red-handed. They will only burst into tears or fly into a rage while figuring out how they might deceive you more successfully next time!

Brevich believed Lothar – because he had no reason not to. He himself noticed falsehoods everywhere, but at the same time, he felt a constant lingering doubt that his judgments might have been hasty. Even the smiles of the girls from the bars seemed to make him ashamed: it wasn't all so simple. The unsettled, primitive exterior concealed an inner side that one could not immediately fathom… By the end of a week's debauchery, Ivan had suddenly begun to feel he was wasting his time. And he decided to stay for another ten days, without Lothar, who had flown back to Essen.

Brevich moved from touristy Sukhumvit to a quiet five-star hotel in Chitlom and promptly found himself in another world. All day, he just wandered aimlessly through the back streets until dusk, without seeing another foreigner. The sun was beating down, sweat streamed off him in runnels and an unfamiliar life flowed around him without a hint of fakeness. Neither the humidity and dust nor the narrow streets with their lack of sidewalks and smelly scooters bothered Brevich. He eagerly took in his surroundings and in the evening noted with surprise that this had been the best day of his trip.

Next to the hotel stood the modest office of an excursion agency. Brevich went there the next morning – just out of curiosity as he was passing by. A girl was sitting at a desk – she looked up at him, and he realized there could not possibly be anyone as beautiful as her in the whole of Thailand.

"Welcome," she smiled. "My name is Nok. If you've come for an excursion, I'm here to help."

"Yes, an excursion," Ivan nodded. "Or maybe several excursions…"

For some reason, he was feeling nervous, a sensation he hadn't experienced for a long time. He couldn't take his eyes off her and ended up looking to the side and then down at the floor, embarrassed.

"Okay," Nok continued to smile. "What dates are you free?"

"I can do today. And then perhaps another three excursions. No, let's make it five," Ivan muttered. He simply could not bear the thought of her disappearing from his life, and the remaining days – utterly dull and empty – dragging on without her.

Fortunately for him, the agency's business was fairly slow. Ivan breathed a sigh of relief and immediately purchased all her available free time before his departure.

That same day, they went to Muang Boran and spent several hours there. The time flew by – somehow they instantly relaxed into each other's company. Now that he was guaranteed Nok's time, Ivan settled back and lightened up. She, in turn, became less apprehensive about him. Initially, he had seemed too big, alien and threatening, but his first somewhat lost and boyish grin convinced her he meant no harm.

Muang Boran – a theme park reconstruction of the whole of Thailand

– deeply impressed Ivan. Nok showed him the northern province of Phetchabun, where she had grown up. Next to a pond stood a house on stilts – a nearly exact copy of her childhood home. They looked inside and walked through the rooms while she talked about her parents – prosperous corn and rice farmers. Her father was extremely conservative – not allowing her to befriend any of the local boys. "Boys are a distraction," he would say, "and you must get a scholarship to the university!" In the evenings and on the weekends, he would sit by the phone and answer every call made to the house… Nok spoke about this with a certain bitterness but immediately added that she loved her family more than anything in the world. She wasn't upset at her parents – they'd had to develop their parenting skills on her, their eldest child…

Ivan asked question after question and gradually – in the park and over a late lunch – learned her life story. Nok was twenty-eight years old and had spent the last twelve of them in Bangkok. Before that, she had never traveled outside her village, where she had lived like any other country girl: cleaning the house, looking after the buffalo and helping out on the farm. She spent a lot of time with the other village children – they invented games, explored the forest and, during the rainy season when the river broke its banks, they would jump from the trees straight into the yellow water and have swimming races… It was a happy period, but then the time came for her to grow up and Nok was sent to live with her maiden aunt in the capital, where she spent her final school years. Her aunt had been strict, and life in the big city had been suffocating compared to the freedom of the village. There were no wide-open spaces, no forests and no buffalo; cars and people hustled and bustled everywhere.

Nok only became accustomed to the city after she got into college with a scholarship, to her father's immeasurable pride. He arranged a celebration for the entire village and even gave Nok permission to move from her aunt's house to the dormitory. She liked to study and, besides, she discovered she had a gift for languages. This allowed her to visit Australia on an exchange program and find a job in a good hotel. In five years there, she worked her way up into a management position but suddenly felt a longing for independence and opened her own excursion agency. Business wasn't steady but Nok wasn't discouraged – she still had her own apartment, an old Honda and lots of plans…

What Nok didn't tell Ivan about was her personal life, which had not been a very successful one. The problems began with her move to Bangkok – she'd felt like a provincial, with little in common with the local children. Her facial features betrayed the fact that she was not from the capital – and she was also taller than most Thai girls. Her light skin made things easier, but she was still uncertain about her appearance, which was compounded by her inexperience with the opposite sex, thanks to her father's heavy-handed vigilance. Nok had been tormented with self-doubt right up until the end of school, and her confidence only picked up with her success in English. By the age of twenty, she'd had a Thai boyfriend: a student, like her. In accordance with tradition and the expectations of her family and girlfriends, she considered it only natural to marry him, have children and live with him for the rest of her life, but this was not to be. Two years into the relationship, the mother of the "groom" declared there would be no wedding because Nok was from the north, and everyone knew that northern girls were lazy.

This was considered a disaster by everyone, and especially her girlfriends. During this difficult time, Nok did a lot of thinking that would change her take on life. She decided she was no longer interested, first, in other people's opinions and, second, in Thai boys her age or even Thai men in general, with their overbearing, overprotective mothers.

Later, she took two foreign lovers, one quickly after the other. Things were simpler with them – she didn't have to pretend to be less intelligent than she actually was, constantly repeating, "Oh, I'm so stupid!" or "Oh, I'm so silly!" to please a partner's male ego. Therefore, after spending only a couple of weeks with her first *farang*, Nok began to think he might be the "man of her dreams." This notion wasn't mutual, however: there were too many attractive girls around and his attention began to wander. A month later he broke up with her – once again, Nok took some time to get over the experience, but in the end, she did.

Later, she met another European; they dated for about a year but then he suddenly left Thailand and stopped answering her letters. Nok wasn't even surprised, taking it as a matter of course. She now understood clearly: it was all down to karma. She was destined to be unlucky in love, and besides, there were so few suitable men in the world that it was highly unlikely she would ever meet the right one. The only thing to do was remain calm and not take any amorous misfortunes to heart.

Of course it was easier said than done, but Nok managed to convince her friends of the sincerity of her new "doctrine." People began to pigeon-hole her alongside Western women – progressive and independent, knowing what she wanted from men, and building her relationships with them on the basis of cold reason. Nok told herself and others that she had erected a wall around her heart, and only she would decide when to open a door in it and by how much. This sounded convincing enough – many believed and even envied her. The only problem was the rather lackluster way she implemented this progressive concept in practice: she hadn't had a boyfriend for over a year now.

Nevertheless, Nok tried to remain optimistic. She was constantly underlining the advantages of her situation – for example, the wall encircling her heart allowed her to be relaxed and laidback when she socialized with men, which helped her business. And that's how it was with Ivan – all the more so because as a woman she intuitively sensed the strength of his personality. Strong people put her at ease – they weren't constantly looking to assert themselves. With them, you didn't have to pretend, which is what Nok valued above all else...

They returned to Bangkok late in the evening, and Ivan, slightly hesitantly, invited her for a coffee. "Of course I'll come," Nok joked, "how could I refuse? After all, your time isn't up yet!" For some reason, Ivan felt flustered and clumsily tried to explain himself, which, in turn, embarrassed Nok. They ascended to the bar on the roof of his hotel, with a fabulous view of the city. It was already getting dark, and the lighting was on. The setting was suitably romantic, but Ivan didn't know how to take things further. As a result, he simply accompanied Nok back to her car and went to dinner alone, irritated at his own awkwardness.

The next day, they went to Ayutthaya, the ancient capital of Siam, which had been razed by the Burmese. Nok came in a different outfit and had done something with her hair that made her look unfamiliar. Ivan didn't immediately recognize her and was met with an ironic joke as if they had been old friends – she was already relaxed and used to him. On the way, acting as his guide, she regaled him with a barrage of historical facts, but Ivan was only halfheartedly listening, turning toward her to get a better view of her from the side. Nok's profile was much more interesting to him – it seemed to hint at her own fascinating history that weaved a solid, seemingly impenetrable shell around her. This impenetrability greatly annoyed Brevich; he ruminated over it almost the entire journey.

At the parking lot, Nok bought a fresh coconut and stuck two straws into it. "I'm a coconut milk addict," she confessed to Ivan, inviting him to share it with her. Then, with the coconut in their hands, they entered the gates of the old city and wandered for a long time among the stones and ruins, the statues of the Buddha and the dilapidated temples.

As they approached the moat that surrounded the fortress wall, Nok said, "The Burmese laid siege to Ayutthaya for six months, but it didn't fall until someone betrayed a secret entrance through the city's sluices."

"Yes, yes," Ivan nodded absentmindedly, wondering to himself who would help him find the hidden way into Nok's soul. Sadly, it wasn't available on any map. He, naturally, suspected she might also like him but had no idea what was really going on in her head.

Then they returned to the hotel's rooftop bar. Again, for some reason, he failed to invite her to dinner, merely escorting her back to her car, but on the way, Nok brushed against his hand several times, and, as they said farewell, she pretended to stumble and held onto his shoulder for a brief moment.

"Wow," she said, "you are electrified; it seems sparks are flying between us!"

Her words and the sensation of her smooth skin excited Ivan to fever pitch. He set off to roam the streets, took a wrong turn and spent a whole hour wandering around in the dark, tormented by the humidity. Once back at the hotel, he hurriedly changed, went back to the bar, sat down at the same table and took a long time over his gin and tonic while pondering the day's events.

The events seemed strange, weird, unfamiliar. He was a grown man and had always known what he wanted, whether it could be achieved and how to make it happen, but now he wasn't so sure. He was immensely attracted to Nok – despite all Lothar's warnings and his own past life, including his experience as a Russian businessman who had been through a lot. He firmly believed: if something looks too good to be true, then it certainly is. Then it must be a trick played by this city of fakes – but what this trick might be and where it might be concealed, Brevich didn't understand and didn't want to guess. He desired only one thing – to see this girl who was more charming than any other he had ever known as soon as possible. To once again feel the incredible pleasure of being with her, watching her and talking to her. Unlike other women, she was so natural in everything she did! At the same time, she was intelligent and, yes, she was sexy – in a special, exotic way. It was just a pity he couldn't work out how to take things to the next level…

Ivan's thoughts raced about in his head, colliding and interfering with each other. Yet no one looking at him would have said he was a man tormented with doubts. He sat there leaning back in his chair, staring into the distance with a blissful smile on his face. Above the skyscrapers, the stars filled the sky, on this hot Bangkok night.

CHAPTER 7

THE NEXT MORNING, Nok drove Ivan to the west bank of the Chao Phraya River. After making the obligatory tourist visit to the Temple of the Dawn, they joined the narrow highway, turned south and spent half a day in the suburb of Tonburi, where life didn't appear to have changed over the past hundred years. Brevich hungrily took in everything around him – the old houses almost swallowed up by lush thickets of vegetation, a small floating market for those "in the know," an orchid farm on the side of a *khlong* canal, locals traversing the labyrinth of confined, palm frond–canopied streets on their bicycles... Yet another side of Thailand was revealed to him. Occasionally, Brevich even began to experience a special feeling toward the country and its people – but wasn't able to grasp it. His mind was completely occupied with thoughts of Nok.

On this third day, she had changed yet again – as if casting off a veil, now allowing Ivan to see deeper inside. Still, not much was revealed to him; he just noted that, despite her modern city clothes, her smile, gestures and the features of her face were in harmony with those of her surroundings, including their neglect and poverty. On the way back, looking out of the car window at the interlacing bushes and lianas, the floating carpets of flowers on the small ponds and backwaters, Brevich reflected on Thailand's hothouse climate: everything here grows so rapidly, abundantly and wantonly. As do Thai women, who also flourish in the humid moist heat, like the bright fantastical flowers of their forests. A great many things may be born and survive in the hothouse air – perhaps this explained their tolerance to life in all its various forms and manifestations? Their ability to love life, whatever it may be, their inherent compassion for all living things – no matter how unusual and unfamiliar. And, just like flowers, they would open up to others gradually, not immediately...

Later, they had lunch at a restaurant by the river. They sat there for a long time; Nok recounted the story of her first love and the canceled wedding, and he surprised himself by telling her about his wife and how they had long ago lost interest in each other. Then Nok drove Ivan back to the hotel and, as usual, he invited her up for coffee. They set off toward the elevator, their hands brushing next to each other. On the way, she took out a flyer from her bag. Ivan leaned over to see better, inhaled the scent of her hair and suddenly felt so close to her that the next step happened by itself.

Half jokingly, he told her that the rooftop bar wasn't the only nice place in the hotel. There was his room, for example – and, by the way, he had some real vodka from Russia, which he was sure she had never tried. Nok laughed – no, she didn't drink strong spirits. Ivan laughed too – well, then, he could reveal his other little secret: he had stashed away a couple of coconuts. "Wow," Nok replied – also half jokingly, with a sly smile – "if that's the case, then how could I refuse..."

The entire exchange was relaxed and cheerful, without a hint of awkwardness or shyness. Ivan wasn't sure if she had taken him seriously and would agree to go to his room or not. Yet once in the elevator, he pressed the button for his floor, and Nok made no objection. Leaving the cabin, they went down the corridor, still brushing hands. Once inside the room, he immediately embraced her. She did not resist.

Afterward, they both felt acutely hungry, went to the Chinese restaurant next door and ate and laughed heartily. Ivan constantly caught himself thinking that he hadn't felt this good for years. In the sexual afterglow, Nok was more beautiful than ever, and he was proud of this stunning girl sitting next to him. He was pleased with himself as well – he felt young again and a powerful burst of energy coursed through his veins. It was as if his life was just beginning, and he felt capable of so much...

They spent the rest of the week in Bangkok, never leaving the city. In the mornings, they would meet at about eleven; Nok would suggest a tour and drive Ivan to a new place, where yet another side of the city would be revealed. Two or three hours later it would already be unbearably hot, and they would look for a good foot-massage salon and then lunch in a café – here again, it was Nok who would take the initiative. She was very attentive to Ivan's needs and especially what he ate – she constantly asked him if everything was to his liking, whether it was too spicy, whether he wanted another beer. She was fervently interested in his opinion about Thai cuisine and regularly alternated between Eastern and Western places, although she herself didn't like *farang* food, leaving most of it untouched.

After lunch, they would go to his room and spend the afternoon there until supper. Nok always brought a change of evening clothes in her car – dinner was Ivan's domain, which meant expensive restaurants and bars with live music. Then they would go back to his room again, and early in the morning Nok would return to her apartment, never staying for breakfast. For some reason, she felt this would preserve her "good girl" image.

The moment the door closed behind Nok, Ivan would begin to miss her, and by the time they were due to meet again, he would be in a serious state of anguish. With her arrival, however, life would get back to normal – she was a great healer of distress. A new series of kaleidoscopic events would commence – the city, Nok, food, then Nok again, her voice, her words, her body… The scenery, images, sounds, smells collided and interspersed, mirroring the turmoil going on in his head. Things would only calm down and come to a stop at night. Nok would fall asleep instantly and not wake up until morning, while Brevich lay awake for hours. He gazed at her face – tirelessly marveling at the flawless harmony of her features – and tried to understand for himself the nature and meaning of their "affair."

Of course, the affair was extraordinary and wonderful. And – still as incomprehensible as it had been on the first day they'd met. Nok had occupied a big place in his heart, but he could not define its boundaries, let alone give it a name. Similarly, he could only guess what she thought about him and their relationship. Every day he learned many new things about her but nevertheless felt she remained a closed book to him.

Ivan knew that Russia was full of women who were generous with their love. He recalled them – Muscovites and Petersburgers, thickset beauties from Novgorod and Samara, dark-eyed Cossacks from the Don, fair-haired girls from the deserted Moscow suburbs desperate for tenderness... Many had been good and pleased him in their own way – leaving nothing in reserve, sharing themselves and receiving in turn. Brevich had long been convinced that nothing could surprise him, but Nok had succeeded in becoming something unexpected, new. She didn't do anything special in bed; she was just totally sincere. Her scent with its aroma of cloves kept him in permanent anticipation of intimacy. Somehow she knew how to excite him with the slightest casual touch. With her, it was as if he had returned to his youth, a time of fevered desires. He had become indefatigable again, constantly ready, capable of everything – but of course, it wasn't only about this.

Ivan tried to formulate what it was exactly – and gave up at each attempt. He simply felt he was in a place of extraordinary mental comfort, which Nok could create without the slightest effort. At the same time, she was by no means submissive or obedient; she had her own opinions on everything and it never occurred to her to keep them to herself. On one occasion, she declared, "You make the decisions and I will follow them and you – but if I do not agree with something, I'll tell you about it immediately." And that is exactly what she did, surprising him with a combination of feminine pliability and unshakable firmness, which would manifest itself in everyday trifles. The firmness, he knew, had nothing to do with a desire to insist on her own way. Nok only wanted to protect him from things he would probably not like – so that when he was with her, he would not experience any adverse emotions. This was unfamiliar – the care that his previous women had shown for him had never been so complete. And for some reason he sensed that her solicitude for her man would not dissipate soon; it would be long lasting...

Here, on the question of longevity, Ivan rebuked himself furiously. However much he wanted to believe otherwise, he had no doubt their romance would end with his departure. Their environments were too different, their countries too far apart – he understood, it was very difficult to argue against this. Nothing could survive such long distances, and their cultural differences would soon become a problem... Even thinking about it was painful. As a diversion, he scolded himself, trying to imagine everything from a different point of view, to remove his rose-tinted spectacles. He deliberately recalled Lothar's diatribe: without exception all Thai women are masters of deception. Lothar had lived here for years, he'd had time to figure things out. Nok almost certainly had some kind of agenda, a selfish motive…

Ivan turned to look at her face, her black hair scattered on the pillow. Right away it became crystal clear: Lothar's views were irrelevant to them. Lies, self-interest… What utter nonsense! Nok only ever gave, without demanding a thing from him in return. She even tried to pay her way in restaurants and bars – Brevich had never seen this before. If she had a hidden plan, it was hard to imagine how sophisticated and cunning it would have to be.

He sighed, tossed and turned, sometimes getting up to drink a glass of water. Returning to bed, he would change tactics, telling himself it was ridiculous to imagine such a girl could seriously become infatuated with an ugly, taciturn, middle-aged man like himself. It was she who was wearing the rose-tinted spectacles – she had invented a fairy tale for herself without any plan whatsoever. Thai women like to imagine all sorts of things; they live in a fantasy world filled with ghosts, spirits and dreams. Soon the veil would fall from her eyes, and she would see him for what he was: much older than her, battered by life and not at all positive. Between them were the language barrier and a large number of other issues, which would require a lot of work. No doubt Nok would wake up to that; hence he needed to simply enjoy the moment. All the more so since she, happily, never bothered him with questions – either about the future or their feelings for each other.

This really was the case, although she did once ask Ivan, as if in jest, "Do you think you could love me?" Brevich was so taken aback he started coughing, and Nok immediately set about easing the situation – by trying on clothes in front of the mirror, making funny faces and taking selfies. The topic was never raised again – including the last day before his departure, which arrived suddenly and inevitably.

It was Saturday; in the morning, Nok took him to a Buddhist temple. Having given the monks food offerings, they spent two hours at a meditation ceremony. The process entranced Brevich with its steady, unhurried rhythm. Thais – young and old alike – came in, took off their shoes, sat on a wooden platform and closed their eyes. Cameras stood on three sides – concentrated, serene faces floated across large screens. Brevich observed this incredibly slow-moving action, practically inaction, as if it were a fast-paced thriller. Its stubborn, unstoppable development seemed to comprise the quintessence of all realities, which began to open up to him – ever so slightly – and even the Thai incantation amplified through the loudspeaker acquired meaning. It was probably talking about a different life, the life that Brevich wanted to transform his own into.

He asked Nok what the words were about. She said they were the words of the Buddha. About the soul and what's reflected in it. About the end and the continuity of everything. About the way the things you do return back to you sooner or later – with the inevitability of predestination.

"I thought so," Ivan nodded. It seemed to him that all this really had been there in his thoughts.

"'The ocean tastes of salt, but its dharma has the taste of freedom,'" Nok translated.

"I thought so," he muttered, remembering her scent of cloves and her salty-sweet taste.

"'Let those who can hear respond with faith,'" Nok translated.

"Yes," Ivan said. "I thought so."

Suddenly he felt a powerful urge for faith – not in any deity, but in what was going on around him. A belief that this was not a fantasy that will disappear tomorrow, but something unshakable and real. He desperately wanted the course of his and Nok's "story" to enter the same slow, meditative rhythm – or even stop altogether.

But no, stopping was impossible. The ceremony ended, an elderly monk came out onto the dais and began to talk with those assembled, and Ivan and Nok went back to the car. She drove back to her apartment, and Brevich, suddenly feeling overwhelmingly weary, returned to the hotel and slept a heavy, leaden sleep right through until dusk.

In the evening, they met at a mall famous for its movie theater – Ivan had said he'd like to watch a new American blockbuster. But in fact, he wanted to buy Nok a farewell gift, considering it his duty. His plan was simple – to take her to some expensive boutiques, where she could choose whatever took her fancy. The ploy had always worked in Russia, but Nok flatly refused his offer. Avoiding his eyes, she joked, "You don't have to worry about leaving me something to remember you by. I'm hardly likely to forget you as it is."

Brevich just nodded, took her by the hand and led her up to the second floor, to the jewelry stores, knowing she wouldn't protest openly in public. Ignoring her round pleading eyes, he went into the first available shop, where a flock of mewling salesgirls descended, their tenacious, predatory gazes fixed on him. Ivan frowned and snorted, but in a moment an elderly Chinese manager appeared who at once assessed the situation. With a single gesture of his little finger, he waved the girls away and, sensing Nok's discomfort, sat her down at a small table, where a cup of coffee instantaneously appeared. Then, for the next five minutes, he conducted a quiet conversation with Brevich, and by the end of it, Ivan had bought a bracelet worth several thousand dollars. He put it on Nok's thin wrist himself, and they left the store accompanied by envious glances.

After the movie, there was dinner on the roof of one of the city's skyscrapers. At Brevich's request, they were given a corner table next to the safety rail – like the bow of a ship rising above the city on the crest of a powerful wave. Night had already fallen, with Bangkok stretching beneath them like a chart of the stars. Nearby a neon light gleamed; everything around seemed fanciful and ethereal.

Nok asked to have her photograph taken against the backdrop of the night city – she walked up to the fence and turned round to him with a serious, unsmiling face. The wind caught her hair, sweeping it up; she raised her hands to catch it and the bracelet slid from her wrist to the middle of her forearm, its diamonds sparkling and flashing. Her thin dress clung to her body and her entire being seemed poised for flight, almost breaking loose from the floor to be borne away – upward, onward... It lasted for only a few seconds, but Brevich experienced and absorbed each gesture and moment – forever searing them into his memory. He even thought he heard some indistinct words – possibly the words of the Buddha. Finally, the course of nature slowed down; everything froze, stopped. And – there and then rushed off again.

Life continued on, and time flowed inexorably – in the clatter of crockery and the music from the bar, in the obsequious smiles of waiters and the rapid replenishment of drinks and dishes. It was still the same Saturday – and it was coming to an end. Despite the romantic atmosphere, the dinner flagged somewhat and the conversation failed to flow. Nok behaved strangely, making silly comments, ordering cocktails and setting them aside, reproaching Ivan, jokingly, for being old and overweight and for not speaking Thai. Brevich tried to make witty lighthearted replies, but they did not come out right – and for some reason, she failed to understand his English.

That night they both slept little – just lying in each other's arms, after short, perfunctory lovemaking. In the morning, Nok took him to the airport. Registration was quick; afterward, they stood for a few minutes at the VIP turnstile, lightly touching each other like a couple of teenagers. Summoning all her strength, Nok pronounced the customary phrases – wishing him a comfortable flight and expressing the hope she would see him again. Ivan remained gloomily silent. She added with a smile, "There are many clichés on this subject; you don't even have to make them up. Just read them on the internet and console yourself with the one that's most apt. Such as, 'Everyone has their own life to lead.' Or 'Everyone needs to move on...'"

Brevich moved to embrace her for the last time, but she suddenly recoiled, looked into his face and exclaimed almost with hatred, "Don't you dare forget me!" And a second later was holding him tight in her arms, clinging to him, pressing her whole body against his. He whispered something to her, knowing in his heart that "to forget" was exactly what he intended to do. It was the right and reasonable thing for both of them, and the sooner it happened, the better.

In the departure lounge, Ivan switched off his phone and threw away his Thai SIM card. On the way to the plane, he talked angrily to himself, remembering like mantras his suspicions and nocturnal ponderings. But his words wouldn't flow, and by the time he had reached his seat they had ceased to mean anything. He suddenly understood with the utmost clarity that there was nothing to ponder about. Nok simply loved him with all her big Asian heart – every minute, every moment. At the same instant, he realized how insanely bitter it would feel never to see her again. He knew only one method to fight the pain of this awareness – alcoholic oblivion. And so, Ivan Brevich spent the entire flight seriously drunk.

CHAPTER 8

NOK HAD A terrible three weeks after Ivan's departure. The dust settled, and it became clear: her world had changed forever. At its core was a void – she had never previously imagined there could be such a huge empty space. What's more, she had learned something about the walls that surround human hearts – if you're happy with someone, they get thinner and thinner with each passing hour. Her own "wall" had crumbled without a trace after their first night together. Now it made no sense to hide this fact from herself.

She had no one to complain to, no one to confide in. Her girlfriends would never have understood it – there was no way a "good" Thai girl could possibly have gone to bed with a married *farang* on their third date. If, however, at a stretch, one were to throw modern progressive notions into the mix, explaining everything in terms of gender equality and a simple desire to have the same fun as men, then it wasn't clear why her heart was troubling her so much. The "progressive" Nok should have been in control of the situation and not lost her head by falling in love – even and in spite of her hateful loneliness…

One evening she was watching a Thai television drama featuring a heroine who had discovered she could travel into a different time through an old mirror on her wall. There, quite predictably, she fell in love. A drama ensued, threatening a doubling of her being, a sea of troubles and a mountain of woes. In the end, she had to choose between reality and the looking-glass; the heroine ended up smashing the insidious mirror, thus closing her way to the other world forever… Wiping away her tears, Nok went into her bathroom and for a long time stared at the mirror above the washbasin. It wasn't going to transport her to distant Russia or the recent past, when Ivan had been with her and held her in his arms. Yet she was sure: a different world did exist – and her own parallel future was waiting nearby. She, too, would have to make a choice – with or without a mirror – and there would have to be some sort of sign.

It didn't take long for the sign to manifest itself. Soon after, Nok suddenly felt ill while climbing the stairs to a skytrain station. Her eyes clouded, and she sank down onto the platform, losing consciousness for a few seconds. An elderly woman standing beside her helped her to get up, led her to a bench and asked what had happened. Nok replied, "A darkness came over me." And indeed, while she had fainted, all sorts of horrors had loomed up at her – undefined, terrifying shadows she didn't want to recall.

The next day, she discovered she was pregnant. "Which part of the country are you from?" the doctor asked and made a joke about the fecundity of Nok's home province of Phetchabun. Nok smiled back at him, happily, almost serenely. In some strange way, the news reassured her; she realized: here was the indication from fate she had been waiting for.

Her thoughts and feelings became clearer, her picture of the world falling into place decisively. She easily found answers to the questions that had been bothering her – it had seemed there were a lot, but in reality only two were important. An abortion was out of the question – for a Buddhist it would have been the most terrible sin, causing irreparable damage to her karma. That meant, Nok told herself, she would be having a baby. And simultaneously she acknowledged: Ivan, the child's father, was the only man she wanted to live with. It wasn't just a question of her feelings – they had not vanished, but now something else was added to them. Nok's mind returned to basics; the challenge she now faced was to create a decent life for her child. The answer to this challenge was obvious: Brevich. He was the solution to her problems, filling all the empty gaps perfectly.

To assure herself of her decision, Nok did what any Thai women would have done – she went to see a fortune-teller. The latter was a young woman with large and powerful features who immediately stated, "You're pregnant, aren't you?" Nok nodded silently. The fortune-teller laid out her cards, studied them for a long time, shuffled them around the table and then declared with a sigh, "Your chances of being with the man you love or remaining alone are approximately equal. You're not going to like this, but, believe me, fifty-fifty isn't such bad odds. I can see your man – he is big, tall and much older than you... A *farang*, of course."

Nok muttered timidly, "He has a wife."

"So what?" The fortune-teller shrugged. "His wife, obviously, is no longer of interest to him. Since she has allowed this to happen, she must be a worthless woman – he will leave her and never remember her again. He has simply had no reason to think about it, but now – now there is you and what you are carrying in your womb!"

That very night, Nok leapt into action. She had kept Brevich's business card, but this turned out to be of little use. Two of her emails were returned – having failed to make their way through Ivan's company's spam filter, which was a mystery to Nok. The next day, she rang his office, but this also led nowhere. Ivan's foreign contacts were limited to Germany, and, knowing German well, his secretary hardly spoke any English. She failed to understand Nok's accent and did not delve into the situation further, instead simply choosing to hang up. Nok called again – with the same result. Then, after a short period of reflection, she took the most improbable decision: to fly to Moscow, find Ivan there and talk to him face to face.

If Nok had discussed this with others, they would have undoubtedly dissuaded her, and the trip would never have happened. Journeying so far on her own, and especially to cold and unfriendly Russia, would have been unthinkable to any of her friends. But there was no one to advise her; her girlfriends remained in the dark. She hadn't said a word to her parents either – the news of her pregnancy would have been a great blow to them, an indelible and shameful stain. Of course, her father would have immediately searched for some local groom or other and paid him for his silence to save the family's honor. This was the last thing Nok wanted, so she made up a story about going on vacation to Singapore, took all her savings from the bank and set off into the unknown.

Nok landed at Sheremetyevo airport late at night at the end of a windy, damp March. Her cheap hotel room was terrible and barely fit for habitation. All morning she felt sick, could eat nothing and didn't even know where or what people ate in this strange country. It was cold outside; sleet and snow were falling. Nok asked the elderly concierge to call her a taxi, barely managing to explain herself to him. The taxi driver circled the back streets for an hour before finally bringing her to the required address and asking for a completely absurd fare. Nok was unable to argue; then, having paid him off, she went into the building and showed Brevich's business card to a gloomy guard with a crumpled face. There was some confusion, and she was told he was not in but would be back later. She sat on the couch next to the reception desk – frightened, tired and feeling completely out of place in this impersonal office foyer.

Things hadn't been easy for Ivan either after his return from Bangkok – the same emptiness oppressed him from all sides and showed little sign of abating. Nevertheless, he did not entertain any doubts about the finality of their breakup. Brevich was adamant there was no way the relationship could survive them living in different parts of the world.

He returned to his usual Russian life, plunged into his work and drank heavily. A couple of times, he tried to let off steam with expensive prostitutes, but this only left him with a feeling of disgust and an even greater yearning. Then he took a sudden and unexpected step – he left his wife and initiated divorce proceedings. All her attempts to get an explanation were unsuccessful – Ivan avoided any contact.

In the days' bustle and commotion, he almost succeeded in erasing Nok from his head, but during the drunken evenings, the memories returned irrepressibly. He surrendered – to them and to his thoughts – wandered gloomily through the rooms of his rented apartment, went to the window and looked at the Moscow night sky that was so different from Bangkok's. For half an hour, for an hour, he just stood there, frozen, then poured himself another whiskey and sat down at his computer. He searched through forums and blogs on the web, looked for stories similar to his own, hoping for healing and to sober up. Desperately, he wanted to be sure he had done the right thing by breaking up with Nok forever and not building castles in the air. But, as if in spite, what he found was quite the opposite: other people's castles seemed to be standing firm. Thai girlfriends were not ideal, notable neither for their sophistication, intellectual refinement nor any special kind of mystery – qualities more likely to be found in Russians. But at the same time, they possessed a very powerful source of feminine integrity – something that everyone seeks but almost none find. A quality not easy to describe and explain, not immediately noticeable, but once perceived, unmistakable – and, according to the accounts on the web, Thai women had it in abundance. And, Brevich now understood, there was much of it in Nok too – as there was much of Nok in each moment they had spent together. No, she did not push herself forward or intrude and she was not talkative; she simply offered her entire being to him – intending it only for him, thus forming a strong sense of belonging between them. It was a kind of generosity he had never encountered before – and for her it was as natural as breathing… Brevich recalled his past, his two former wives, one fiancée and a dozen long-term mistresses. They had all liked to stress how they had given him their all! At the time, it had seemed to him they really had offered him a lot; now those words only elicited a sarcastic sneer.

He also read about the other side of Thai women, about their vengeful cunning, their fury in an argument, the infantile superficiality of their views and their inability to plan ahead. All this, for some reason, did not negate their surprising appeal, which was deeper and broader than everyday life, money, domestic squabbles and every commonplace sentimental dream. There was some invisible, inexplicable humanity in relationships with them, capable of providing protection from disappointments and spiritual wounds, like a guardian angel. It was probably an illusion but an alluring one nonetheless. Others had tried to describe it awkwardly, and Brevich had attempted to analyze it himself – but to no avail. These were subtle matters that evaded verbalization. All that remained was bitterness and a sense that he had refused to see something immeasurably important through to the end…

Ivan cursed, frowned and drank even more. Then he began to look for stories of a different kind, as if searching for a remedy. With a wry grin, he read the revelations of sex tourists, types like Lothar – about their amorous "triumphs" bought with money, about the deceptions and artifice, infidelity and cunning lies of the semiliterate bar "fairies." It was sobering; little by little Brevich seemed to get back onto the road to recovery. Sometimes he even thought about whether he should get himself an Asian-looking "sugar baby" – for example, a Tartar or a Buryat – to accelerate the healing process. It was at this very moment that Nok appeared in Moscow.

Brevich arrived at the office within an hour and a half – almost running into the building without looking around. Nodding to the guards, he headed for the elevators, but the receptionist called to him, pointed to the sofa and said uncertainly, "Over there…" Ivan froze to the spot, then walked slowly up to Nok, who stood up to meet him. "Why are you here?" he asked. Nok replied, "I'm going to have your baby." They looked at each other silently for a few seconds, then Ivan canceled all his meetings, put her in the car and took her home.

Removing her shoes in the corridor, Nok leaned against the wall and whispered, "My energy is spent." He gently helped her undress, carried her to the bedroom and laid her on his bed. She immediately fell asleep; Brevich sat for a while next to the bed, leaving her on only a few occasions to fix himself a drink. But the alcohol had no effect on him; now, with Nok by his side, he felt completely sober. And he was soberly aware that these were the best minutes of his forty-six-year-old life.

In recent years, Ivan had really wanted a son – an heir, to carry on the family line. He had often talked about it with his wife; they had even tried to have a child, but nothing had come of it. Brevich suspected she had been secretly taking precautions – her comfortable, carefree life was far too dear to her, and children did not fit into her idea of happiness. Be that as it may, it mattered little now – when he heard Nok's unexpected news, Ivan felt as if everything in his head had fallen into place. The circle had reached its logical conclusion; his thoughts had acquired harmony. He saw himself at the beginning of a path leading to the creation of something genuine. Something incredibly important – and no obstacle would get in his way.

Over the next three weeks, they barely spent a moment apart. Then they got married – because of the pregnancy, the doctors advised Nok not to fly to Thailand, and the wedding was held in Russia. Brevich exhibited his strengths to their full degree – nothing could stop him. A dozen petty officials suddenly found themselves a lot richer, but every single bureaucratic issue connected with the marriage was resolved in the blink of an eye. Just as quickly – and very brutally – he concluded his divorce with his wife, giving her what he thought she deserved: an apartment in the center of Moscow and some money. She became indignant and started to talk about a full-fledged division of his capital and business, but Brevich pressured her, threatening to leave her with nothing, and she signed the papers. As a result, one beautiful April morning, Ivan and Nok found themselves standing in front of the registrar at a local registry office.

The only people present at the wedding were their families – Brevich's father and mother, Nok's parents and her younger sister Pim. Ivan got to know his new relatives on Skype – it was not easy and happened in several stages. First, Nok talked to her mother who, having sighed and wept a little, quickly realized that what had happened to her daughter was not a fantasy, but an irreversible fact needing to be accepted for what it was. They set about discussing the main question: how to break the news to Nok's father that his pride and joy was pregnant, stuck at the edge of the world and planning to marry a foreigner whom neither they nor their neighbors had ever met. The discussion went on for two days and a detailed plan was hatched, but even this was insufficient to avoid her father's wrath. He shouted and cursed, flatly refusing to admit the obvious; he blamed both mother and daughter for their folly, claiming that *farangs* were not to be trusted, Nok had been duped, Ivan would soon abandon her and the whole family would lose face. Nok, however, remained unperturbed, knowing that her mother, Brevich and the future child were all on her side – and in the end, common sense did prevail. Her father's anger softened to forgiveness and he agreed to talk with Ivan, which took place in the presence of Nok and her sister.

To everyone's surprise, they got along quite well, and then Brevich arranged for their trip to Moscow, providing a luxurious program. He paid all their expenses and on the very first day not only ceremoniously presented the head of the family with a generous *sin-sot* – "ransom" for the bride – but also organized a fun-filled tourist schedule with their personal Thai-speaking guide. This greatly impressed the family, and Nok's parents came to the cautious agreement that their daughter had been unexpectedly and unusually lucky. Her father, however, added that they still needed to be on their guard with Ivan. You need to have your finger on the pulse and be ready for anything, he insisted. Out of habit, Nok's mother agreed with him, not seeing any reason to argue. Although, in fact, she really liked the big silent man with the grim face that instantly transformed the moment he looked at her daughter.

After the wedding, which was held quietly at home, Brevich promised that in a year he and Nok would come to Thailand for a considerable period. He even agreed to another wedding ceremony – a Buddhist one this time. That finally inclined her father to fully accept Ivan – especially when he imagined how envious the whole village would be when they set eyes on his new son-in-law. So, on that positive note, Nok's family set off for home, and the newlyweds were left to start their life together, full of minor cares and pleasant trifles.

Brevich rarely went to the office; his entire attitude toward his business cooled. He knew this created consternation, and his colleagues were gossiping that the boss had gone off the rails, but he didn't give a damn. Soon he realized that – for the first time in his life – he was deeply in love. He felt fully in possession of what he loved – and he was well accustomed to taking responsibility for what he possessed. When Nok cautiously hinted that her family might be hoping for some material "support," Brevich only shrugged. For him, who always paid for everyone and everything, it seemed only natural. In addition, the size of the expected assistance was laughable by his standards, and the very fact that he could offer it won him great respect in the eyes of his wife. For her, this was the finest of his masculine qualities, and in return, she was happy to express all the best sides of herself. Sometimes he would joke to himself that business-wise their marriage had been a very good "deal." Maybe that was why he had fallen madly in love, like a teenager, at his age?…

Still, all joking aside, he was perfectly capable of looking at what was happening seriously. Of seeing and acknowledging that fortune had really smiled on him this time. It was undoubtedly a level of happiness he had never experienced before. Other people's opinions, rumors and gossip did not bother him in the slightest; his and Nok's cultural differences no longer frightened him – especially when he reminded himself of the pretentious nonsense he had experienced from girls who shared his culture and spoke the same language. And he knew: Nok would genuinely love their child. This was much more important than anything else.

Time passed swiftly, tempestuously and richly. Brevich was overflowing with positive energy; he thought he could move mountains. Most of this energy was directed at organizing their everyday life. The very best that Moscow could offer, from doctors to beauty salons, was identified, verified and placed at Nok's disposal. Ivan searched and found food she was used to and a pile of films with Thai subtitles – even some classic Soviet comedies, which they heartily laughed at together. He showed her the city, took her to its museums and performances at the Bolshoi, which delighted her immensely. Before going to sleep, they would have long talks – about which country it would be better to live in or who their son would resemble – they already knew Nok was expecting a baby boy. Looking after her was an extraordinary pleasure; Brevich felt that every minute of his existence was filled to the limit with meaning. He was living in an idyll in real life; he was aware of it and not even surprised. For some reason, it seemed perfectly natural and could not be otherwise.

And then the idyll turned into tragedy.

CHAPTER 9

IVAN BREVICH'S NEW life wasn't just the subject of idle rumors and gossip. In at least one person, it provoked intense hatred. That person was Inna Vitzon, his ex-wife.

Inna had been brought up in a very straitlaced, very "Moscow" Jewish family. The diploma she had received from what people called Inyaz, a prestigious university in Soviet times, gave her cause to believe that by marrying Brevich she had raised his social status. Her family was of the same opinion, despite the fact their well-being depended entirely on Ivan. Brevich was not particularly bothered about this: he didn't take his relatives seriously. But for Inna, everything was serious and always had a strictly defined place. Nothing in her life could be deemed insignificant – because her own significance was beyond measure.

Now – seriously and definitively – Inna hated her ex-husband. There was so much hatred that she could not keep it bottled up – it had to be released in some form of revenge. Strangely, this made Inna resemble Thai women, who, she believed, embodied in the person of Nok, had caused this catastrophe in her life. What she now felt about Brevich had much in common with the famous saying of all wronged Thai wives: "Death is not enough!"

It wasn't his adultery that constituted the essence of the catastrophe – Inna could easily close her eyes to that. Their lack of interest in each other was mutual, and both had had more than one liaison on the side. The crux of the matter lay elsewhere: Inna had been shaken to the very core by the way Brevich had ended their marriage. And this was something she was not going to forgive.

Over their years together, her own complaints had accumulated too. There was a lot of irritation on her part, mainly because she had been unable to experience the true taste of success, despite having all its attributes. She held Brevich accountable for this – since there was no one else to blame. To make matters worse, he completely failed to see any grounds for her disgruntlement – his unceremonious response was that Inna needed to get off her backside and do something with her life. That really offended her; she believed – and often intimated so to her friends – that her husband didn't understand and didn't want to understand.

This was why, when Ivan for no apparent reason announced his intention to divorce her upon his return from Bangkok, Inna, despite at first being taken aback, quickly pulled herself together. She sensed that a project worthy of her had finally materialized – a long-term *enterprise* that could be undertaken with great enthusiasm. The aim of it was to suck Brevich dry. To exhaust him with the most grueling legal proceedings, to sue, sue and sue again... Inna's eyes sparkled with renewed vigor; she was filled with energy as if the years had dropped off her. Soon, with the help of two lawyers, an action plan was developed full of stratagems and cunning, but then Nok flew into Moscow and everything came to naught. Brevich was completely unbending, explaining both to Inna and her lawyers that with his connections she could end up homeless and penniless. He sounded convincing; she had to accept his terms, but her anger knew no bounds. Inna persuaded herself that Brevich had caused her irreparable damage. It wasn't a question of the money – she was still getting a reasonable amount. The thing was that in a single stroke he had suddenly stripped her of the purpose in life she'd just found. And for this, she told herself, Brevich would have to pay.

After several sleepless nights, she hatched an intricate scheme. The main role in it was to be played by the Danilovs – Sanyok, who had his own accounts to settle with Brevich, and his wife Tatiana, whom Inna had known since her youth. Back then, they had been close friends, but later their friendship had given way to jealousy and envy. This was now going to prove useful.

The first step had seemed the most difficult but had been achieved with ease. After a "chance" meeting with Sanyok next to his office, Inna had invited him for a coffee, and within a few days they were lovers. Using attention and flattery, she deftly ignited his passion and then just as suddenly announced they were splitting up.

"I've realized we're better off parting ways," she shrugged at his bewildered consternation. "You're clearly a loser, and soon you'll be out of work altogether. My ex is going to fire you; he can't forgive or forget that the business was once yours, that you were the real trailblazer. And it also irritates him that you really love those stupid machines of yours – which he doesn't. Your wife told him they turn you on more than she does… By the way, you do know she's slept with him for almost the whole of last year – just to spite me? He told me all about it; we used to be open about these things… Tanya was constantly complaining to him you're no good in bed. But that's not fair: you're a good lover, you have such a thick, powerful cock…"

Danilov was crushed, furious and frightened. He believed every single word – in his wife's infidelity, that he was about to lose his job, and in Inna's sudden, insightful contempt, to which he was prone, having long ago lost any respect for himself. That evening, he created such a disgraceful scene at home that Tatiana packed her things and left to live with her mother. A couple of days later, he tried to make it up to her but only ended up losing his temper again and, in an attempt to hurt her even more, mentioned his brief interlude with Inna. After this bombshell, it soon became clear his wife wasn't ever going to return. Danilov repented and asked for forgiveness, but she only laughed in his face and went away with her mother to a Turkish resort, leaving him all alone in rainy Moscow.

In a word, Inna had achieved a lot in a mere three weeks. This gave her the confidence and conviction she was in the right. Soon, she called Sanyok again, said she was lonely and even wept into the phone, begging him to come and see her. They drank a lot – and, after the alcohol, clumsy sex and drunken, tearful complaints against life, the idea of revenge seemed to emerge of its own accord. Brevich was the source of all their current and impending misfortunes. He was the cause of what they had lost, were losing and were set to lose – and that meant: he should have to feel the devastating nature of loss himself. Something precious should be wrenched from him, Inna declared angrily – to show him he was as weak and vulnerable as everyone else…

Thus, an "avenging duo" was formed, and their means of revenge was worked out that very same night. Nok would have to be taken away from Ivan – even if only for a little while, but in all seriousness, without fooling around, so that he would experience the pain to the fullest. And so that he would be made to pay – with his powerless despair and money – for the return of his "plaything." With serious money, which he owed both of them!

Waking up in the morning and remembering everything, Danilov sat down on the bed, clasped his head in his hands and emitted a long, protracted groan. He realized he was about to do something savage and terrible – and somehow knew he couldn't turn back. Even the fear, which caused his hands to tremble, couldn't persuade him otherwise. What's more, he already had just the man for this sort of job: Valyok, his and Ivan's childhood friend, Valentin Sakhnov.

Valentin had returned to Moscow a long time before. At one stage he had made a good career for himself in the special forces, quickly rising to the rank of captain, but then he and his entire command had been dishonorably discharged from the army for an ugly incident in Chechnya. This shocked him to the depths of his soul – despite some disciplinary problems, Valyok had served honestly. He saw himself as a loyal officer, a patriot, and even considered the army his cherished calling, telling himself his way in life was that of the warrior. Therefore, he saw his dismissal as the betrayal of a basic notion of justice, and for a long time his mind refused to acknowledge what had happened.

For a couple of weeks, while his papers were being formalized, he wandered around in a daze, blind to everything around him. People shied away from him, taking him for a dangerous, unpredictable head case. Eventually, his stupor passed; only anger and resentment remained. Sakhnov was served his papers and went home to Moscow, but at one of the longer stops on the way he left the train briefly to buy some beer and ended up missing it after a run-in with a policeman. Without thinking twice, he made friends with the driver of a freight train and arrived in the capital sitting at the back of the driver's cabin, bawling out army marching songs and contemplating the fields, woods and villages passing by. Somewhere on that journey, he underwent a complete catharsis, and his picture of the world was fundamentally rearranged. He realized that, however things turned out, he would always remain a warrior – and his war from now on would be fought for himself, against everyone and everything.

The first thing Valentin did in Moscow was ask Brevich to make him his head of security. Ivan pretended to be friendly, patted Valyok on the back and treated him to a cognac but did not give him a job, fearing that the Chechen scandal would come to light and harm his business. Sakhnov took the rejection as another serious blow. It was a breach of the "fraternal comradeship" that he considered sacred after his years in the army. Yet he was not surprised; it was already clear: the dirty tricks fate was playing on him were all links in the same chain. His life had changed course, and he would have to accept it for what it was.

He went to work for a private security firm and after a while brought in a few former army friends. Soon, they quarreled with the management, resigned and set up their own "outfit." They would take on anything; their moral compass had long since stopped working. Money was their only criterion, and on the whole business went well. Rich clients paid generously – although the depravity they encountered in the course of their work crossed all boundaries. This only convinced Valentin all the more that his life was moving in the wrong direction, but there was no turning it around.

Sometimes, he would talk about this with Sanyok Danilov – they would call each other regularly and about once a month get thoroughly drunk together. With regret, Sakhnov noted that Sanyok had changed for the worse too. Friendship was a distant memory; the only thing uniting them now was their discontent with their lives. As for Brevich, Valentin never saw him again, but he hadn't forgotten and wasn't going to forgive the snub. He believed sooner or later he would get a chance to get even.

And now the chance had fallen into his lap – when Danilov told Valyok about the plan to abduct Nok, he agreed almost immediately. Everything had fitted into place perfectly: Brevich needed to be taught a lesson – and this lesson would be a good one. People like Brevich should be punished, money-wise – and the amount promised to be lucrative!

The roles were split logically: Danilov was charged with financing the operation, and Sakhnov and his team with executing it. The cost of the hit, as Valentin quoted, seemed exorbitant to Sanyok at first, but after a little reflection he acceded, hoping for a generous ransom from Brevich. They agreed to share it equally, although Sakhnov had his own plans on that score. For him, this was another argument in favor of action – if he succeeded in hitting the jackpot, it would allow him to get out of business, change his circumstances and even go abroad for good. Who knew, maybe somewhere sunny, next to the sea, he'd work out where to take his topsy-turvy life later…

Valentin enlisted his most reliable people for the job. After observing Nok for a week, it was decided to kidnap her outside a secluded salon on Veskovsky Pereulok. Nok visited it once every two days and always walked home on foot – Brevich's apartment was in the next block. She was only accompanied by a single bodyguard – the special-forces guys took a good look at him and decided he wouldn't present too many problems. The operation began smoothly, but, as it turned out, the plan hadn't covered every eventuality.

The man guarding Nok was from the tough neighborhood of Lyubertsy and had an identical surname and nickname – the Horse. His level of training wasn't comparable to that of the former commandos, but he was an extremely strong and experienced street fighter. When two strangers in masks suddenly appeared out of nowhere, he instinctively feinted slightly to one side. As a result, the devastating short blow aimed at his temple didn't fully connect, and, as he fell down, he managed to roll over, grab his gun and randomly open fire in his semiconscious state.

Almost all the bullets went astray, except for one – it hit Nok and inflicted a fatal wound. In the last few seconds of her life, several images flashed before her eyes. She saw her father and mother in the doorway of the house on wooden stilts. Then – the yellow river and her favorite buffalo. Then – the face of her unborn child, looking a bit like an alien. Then – nothing more.

Within an hour of the botched kidnapping, the perpetrators had disappeared from the city, and Valentin called Danilov saying they needed to talk urgently. They agreed to meet in a quiet section of the park where they had once played cops and robbers. Alexander arrived first; Sakhnov saw him from his hiding place behind the trees. Sanyok stood and smoked, nervously shifting from foot to foot – although he had no idea what had happened or what was awaiting him.

Stretching out his hand, Valentin calmly said, "Hi!" Then with a single, barely perceptible movement he knocked Danilov off his feet and, kneeling over him, slit his throat – carefully avoiding any blood, as he had been taught in Chechnya. For a few brief moments, he stood motionless, contemplating the dead body of his childhood friend. It was clear: fate had led him to exactly this juncture, having elected the most misguided path possible. Then he carefully wiped the knife, threw it into the bushes and walked away.

CHAPTER 10

THE NEWS OF Nok's death plunged Ivan into a kind of stupor. He felt almost nothing and was oblivious to the world around him. His receptors were not working – his brain no longer processed their signals. As if it no longer cared.

Nevertheless, functioning on autopilot, he was able to deal with the most pressing matters as efficiently as ever. First of all, Ivan called Pim, who spoke a little English. Choosing the simplest words, he told her the tragic news and asked her to help him talk to her parents, having prepared them beforehand.

Pim agreed; they all met on Skype the next day. Ivan was confronted with two people who had visibly aged, crushed by their grief. He spoke slowly, enunciating each word, "Nok is no longer with us. And neither is our son. All I can do is to bring her body over for the funeral and find those who are responsible. And I will do this."

Nok's father got up and left without saying a word. Her mother covered her face with her hands and burst into tears. It was clear there was nothing more to say. Pim signed to Ivan to hang up.

Two days later Brevich was sitting on a plane along with Nok's embalmed body. This was his second trip to Thailand, a journey of sorrow. He spent the entire nine hours of the flight barely moving, staring unseeingly in front of him. As soon as the steward pronounced the word "Bangkok" over the PA, the anesthetic stupor began to fade, giving way to despair and pain. It rolled, crashed and retreated like the waves of the dull gray ocean.

Brevich understood: the ocean knew no bounds. Everything connected to Nok had been and would continue to be limitless. What he sensed now was only a premonition of something terrible waiting ahead. He knew it would come and was ready to accept it, but for now he still had a straw to cling to, an illusion of invulnerability. In a sense, he and Nok were still together. She was almost there next to him, on the same airplane.

And he desperately held onto this, clenching his jaw, hunched in his soft armchair. He could picture her face with his mind's eye – a face alive and full of joy, the way he had been used to seeing her. The shadows of his thoughts were bound to the image with a steel chain. Their writhing remnants encircled it, seemingly emitting sounds – bitter, howling moans. Then their rumbling echo dispersed – as they were ripped away from the circle, floundered in swamps, sunk in quicksand without forming themselves into anything of substance...

He brought Nok's body from the Bangkok airport to her parents' house in a specially ordered limousine and settled nearby in the only hotel in the area. That evening, the first of the farewell ceremonies took place, and the whole village gathered. Ivan did not take part; he just watched, standing to one side. Any rite, whatever it meant, seemed false to him now, superfluous.

Nok's body lay on the table, covered with a veil. Only her head and right hand were bare. People came up to her in turn to pour a little sweet, floral-scented water on her hand. As the mourners all went back to their places, an elderly monk intoned a singsong prayer. It all lasted a long time; Ivan was silent and frowning as if sensing that Nok was moving away from him with each new ablution.

Then the same monk tied bracelets twisted out of white thread around her wrists and ankles. The table with the body was decorated with garlands of flowers. Their sweet aroma made Brevich's head spin. He went out and walked back to the hotel, feeling with acute clarity that time was flowing through his fingers like water – and soon Nok would leave his life forever...

In accordance with Buddhist tradition, the final leave-taking lasted five days. Ivan would arrive around noon and sit next to Nok until dusk. At about six, once the heat had abated a little, the monks would appear at the house and the prayer ceremony begin. After that, everyone would disperse, and Ivan with them. The only person with whom he exchanged any words during the day was Pim. Nok's mother spent all her time in tears, dealing with domestic chores, and the father just wandered around the house, his face frozen, enveloped in a black cloud, not speaking to anyone and not seeming to notice Ivan at all.

At the hotel, Brevich would eat something hastily, without tasting it. Then he would take a bottle of Thai rum to his room and stretch out on his bed. He was absorbed by the night, by its hot, sticky darkness. A quiet reigned, accentuated by the cicadas and the barely audible swish of the fan blades over his head. Ivan was transported to another reality, plunged into a trance. Again, as on the plane, Nok appeared in his mind's eye, laughing, full of life. Her face was bewitching; he meditated on it like a crystal ball.

For the first four nights, his visions were very specific. Brevich recalled and resurrected all the days they had spent together. From their first meeting to their first intimacy, from their separation to their marriage and then week after week of happy life in Moscow... The look she gave him at the Bangkok airport. The meeting in his office in front of the astonished security guard. Morning breakfasts in their sun-drenched kitchen. Visits to the doctor and long examinations of the ultrasound pictures... All this appeared before him in strict chronological order. The images were vivid, like in a waking dream or under the influence of a powerful hallucinogen. It seemed that he could hear Nok's voice, could recognize her scent.

Then, without warning, his mind was immersed in a muddy fog. All the pictures disappeared; he was seized by a total, blind frenzy. Ivan clenched his fists as if sensing his fingers on the throats of his enemies, the perpetrators of his grief. He tore their flesh and destroyed their souls, inventing the most appalling punishments. His heart raced; his breathing became irregular. He understood that his rage, expanding to the very limits of the universe, was killing, strangling him – and he took a long swig from the bottle, attempting to curb the madness of his rage. He couldn't allow himself to die until due revenge had been taken.

Just before sunrise, he finally fell into a doze but soon emerged from it, greedily gulping in the air. He had dreamed one and the same thing, albeit in different guises: Nok was in trouble and he could do nothing to save her. It was unnatural, unbearable – for him, accustomed as he was to being capable of resolving anything… Brevich, who had not experienced fear in a long time, really began to be terrified of this dream. And he could not rid himself of it.

As he was going up to his room on the fifth and final evening, Ivan suddenly froze on the spot. He was pierced by the sudden realization that tomorrow Nok would disappear permanently, forever. Brevich ran down the steps and set off at a fast walk back to the village, weaving in the dark. He was driven by the thought that he must do something, postpone it, prevent it…

The street on which Nok's house stood was illuminated by two dim lights. Approaching, Ivan noticed a silhouette on the porch. It was her father; he was standing and looking out into the distance, all alone against the whole world. There was so much hopelessness in his posture that Brevich immediately understood: nothing could be changed. He retreated into the shadows and for about half an hour watched a man who was a stranger to him yet evidently suffering as he was. Then he went back to his cramped room, to the swish of the fan and his bottle of Sangsom.

That night, his recollections became blurred for some reason; Nok's face faded. Details of reality gave way to abstraction – a series of chaotic images from his life proceeded before his eyes. He seemed to be watching his past from a distance, from an alien space, moving arbitrarily from point to point, from one moment to another. In black-white-gray flecks and trembling sine waves, he recognized the years spent building up his business, success and wealth, the sequence of women, mistresses, wives. Everything gleamed weakly, barely distinguishable from the background. And then an incredible surge of amplitudes and colors beyond all conceivable scale. A furious dance of analog signals, renewed youth, an excitement with life and… a return to grayness but this time without the harmonics: a void. The future did not exist; in its place was a gaping abyss. Somehow, existence was only possible here in the room of a cheap hotel with a fan under its ceiling, dispelling the murky darkness…

The next day, Nok's body was burned in the crematorium. The

ceremony with fireworks and firecrackers, donations to the monks and a bountiful feast, lasted a long time, from morning till dark. It was a Buddhist celebration of death, a festival of liberation from the earthly hardship, a step toward reincarnation. But for Ivan and for Nok's parents, it merely held a grief before which any religion was powerless.

Brevich sat the whole evening hunched over an untouched plate, staring at the floor. He did not touch a drop of alcohol, remaining completely sober and immersed in himself. Toward night, when the friends and neighbors had finally left, he stepped outside and sat down on the steps, holding his head in his hands. Maybe for the first time in his life, he felt utterly lost, not knowing what to do, where to go, how to save himself.

Then Pim came up and sat down beside him. She wanted to help him somehow. "You know," she said, "there's a room in the house... Nok spent her childhood in it and slept there whenever she came to visit us. Would you like to see it?" Ivan nodded silently.

Pim talked to her mother, who had no objections. Brevich was taken to Nok's room and left on his own. At first, he sat at her desk – clean, without a single spot – then began to pace from corner to corner, noiselessly, like a caged animal. His state of mind worsened. Despair and pain circled him, spinning like demons somewhere nearby. Brevich could feel their breath, their irresistible might.

Suddenly a floorboard creaked underfoot. This distracted him; he stopped in his tracks and then, stepping cautiously, went up to the shelf on the wall. There was a stack of notebooks; Brevich began to leaf through them absentmindedly, one by one. In the semidarkness, in the light of a dim lamp, he was looking at Nok's handwriting – initially a child's hand, diligent-neat, then becoming stronger and more adult. He ran his finger along the lines, trying to understand the meaning of the Thai letters clinging to each other, forming an intricate filigree...

In one of the notebooks, Ivan found pages with short poems translated into English – probably an exercise. He began to read them absentmindedly, hardly registering their contents – and then froze suddenly, stumbling upon four lines, underlined in red. His legs collapsed beneath him; he sat down at the desk. Staring fiercely at the lined page, he repeated the words to himself, moving his lips, whispering them aloud.

You will lose me in the cold night, under a blanket of hostile dark-ness, but we will meet under another Sun, if you look for me hard enough, he reread again and again. Sparks flashed before his eyes; his thoughts seemed to have gone berserk. The dams had burst, overwhelmed by this final drop; the flood gushed forth. And swept everything away.

In those few seconds, Ivan understood: his mind was irrevocably changing. Either it was becoming free, breaking all its bonds, or dragging itself down into the worst possible dungeon – that was immaterial; they were one and the same. To hell with names, to hell with demons; only this newly found essence could lead to panacea and salvation…

He now saw everything clearly, without impediment. Nok had not left him; it was all an illusion, a trick played by the hostile world. The small, limited world – their shared cosmos stretched far beyond it. Nok had known it, sensed it before they had met. She had given him a sign in advance, prepared a supremely clear message. Saying everything without omissions, without reservation!

Ivan sat over the open notebook for several hours. In the middle of the night, Pim brought him some water with lemon and a bowl of rice. He turned to her, and she took a step back, seeing the fire burning in his eyes.

"There is a spirit of sorrow in him; he is fighting with it," she told her mother, but that was a long way from the truth. Ivan no longer had time to mourn. He was a man of action; he knew how to achieve his goals. And now he had the most important goal in life.

Step by step, a plan of action was building itself in his head. Brevich was aware of the complexity of the task, but he had no doubt a solution would be found. Sensing that he wasn't ready to guess at it yet, he didn't try to give any meaning to the notion of "another Sun." He simply knew that this place existed.

THEO

CHAPTER 11

"I WAS BORN on an island by the sea, but it was nothing like the sea here. There were cliffs and seafronts and beaches – but not at all like the ones here. There were idle vacationers, stalls and cafés all along the promenade and indifferent, ruddy-brown hills with villas scattered over them like lumps of sugar.

"My arrival into this world was celebrated triumphantly and opulently. That morning, my relatives unceremoniously broke into the ward where my mother lay, having barely recovered from giving birth. They picked me up in their arms, pinching my cheeks with their dirty hands, poking and dandling me until I was screaming hysterically. They wanted to make sure I was one of them, a member of their tribe – I did not yet have the strength to genuinely disappoint them. My first days at home were just the same, with a series of feasts, which knocked my parents off their feet in a frenzy of hospitality, to share their joy with our huge family, although there was not yet much cause for celebration. Like all newborns, I was nothing more than a conglomeration of biomass, an assemblage of macromolecules, and no one back then could predict with certainty whether I would develop into anything more. Nobody knew, but my family believed in me – as all families believe in their babies all over the world. And I lived up to their expectations: when I was six, the main event of my lives took place, no matter how many of them I've ended up living. No one noticed and appreciated its true merit, and I myself only understood it much later – and at the time only felt it as a slight shock…"

I recount this to Elsa as we are walking along the seafront under the burning sun. This is the third week of my stay in Quarantine. During that time, much has changed and much has become familiar. You can get accustomed to any place – especially when there are no alternatives.

The environment doesn't seem hostile to me anymore; I no longer flinch at every extraneous sound and don't see a trap in every word or sign. My subconscious is working hard, and this effort is yielding fruit: little by little, I adapt to the fact that I have been reborn and some kind of life awaits me after Quarantine. I reflect on that and pose questions – to myself, and to Nestor – although for the time being almost all of them remain unanswered.

My relationship with Elsa has also become different. It happened abruptly, right after an accident that gave us a serious fright. It was its incongruity that startled us – as if the well-oiled mechanism of this place had suddenly failed. As if some external threat had intervened in the serene, smooth-running course of things.

It all happened on one of our first outings together when a seven-story building we were walking past suddenly began to topple over. It collapsed downward – as if a powerful explosive charge had blown away its foundations. There was a roar; huge lumps of concrete flew down from above and rolled from our left directly at us and beyond – toward the balustrade and the sea, and other terrified passers-by. We were enveloped in a cloud of dust that filled our nostrils; I heard screams from all sides. Elsa also seemed to be screaming…

Before I had time to think, I grabbed her hand and dragged her forward, expecting to be hit at any moment, realizing there could be no escape or salvation for either of us. But we escaped – half suffocated, half blind from the dust. Coughing and catching my breath, I looked around: a dirty cloud behind me was rising up to the sky. Then it began to dissipate and soon disappeared without a trace: there was no sign of any debris or suffering victims on the promenade. Everything looked exactly as it had before, except for an empty gap in the row of buildings like a missing tooth.

Credit to my roommate, who recovered quickly. Soon, albeit somewhat neurotically, we were making jokes about the incident and each other. "Now, you are a real hero," said Elsa with a shake of the head and recounted a story about one of her boyfriends, who had been mugged with her in the center of New York.

"Do you know what *that* hero did?" she chuckled. "He ran away like a startled deer, leaving me on my own. Just shouted at me to catch up with him – and then claimed later he had acted like a man. That he was showing initiative, leading the way... At that moment, I decided I wasn't going to live with him anymore – and that was one of the wisest decisions of my life!"

After the incident with the building, her remoteness evaporated completely, as if a switch had been flicked inside her. We even began to make physical contact: occasionally Elsa would take my hand in hers, touch me on the shoulder or even brush against me with her thigh. It didn't get any further than that, though – the ethereal nature of our bodies hadn't changed. Nevertheless, I found out a lot more about her first life – in great detail, she talked about her parents' estate with its horses and polo grounds, about her student days in Arlington and her first job in the local mayor's office... She would recall these past episodes in large chunks and immediately share them with me. I listened to her, slightly envious – my own recovery wasn't going that well. I have had some progress, however – a few things have returned, and besides, I've learned to cherry-pick my dreams to gradually fill in the blanks. By myself, without Nestor – although, of course, in the early days he provided a lot of assistance.

He has also made mistakes, though: the dreams he chose for me about the Russian millionaire Brevich were no help. My mind was unable to follow a logical chain toward the past, as Nestor had expected, and this clearly bothered him. "No more 'starting at the end and moving toward the beginning,'" he announced. "We will focus on your childhood and on mathematics – we need to move sequentially, with no detours!" So that's how we are now progressing – with varying success.

Occasionally, I still think about Brevich, but in vain. A few random details emerge for a moment: a hot night in a hot city, a large gloomy bar, drunken faces. Then my memory blurs into a wall – a hot wall. Neither

Tina nor the slightest trace of my theory and mysterious particles float to the surface. Nestor's hints about the field of the conscions are like an excruciating itch – at times it becomes so unbearable I have to shut my eyes and cover my ears with my hands. Then I pester him again with questions, but he just brushes me aside with vague allusions. Some of which I am now sharing with Elsa.

The seafront is gradually filling up with people. Today we went out early, among the first to do so. I continue my story, "For no reason, I started shivering and broke into a cold sweat. Then my head began to spin and my temperature rose. My mother put me to bed with a moist towel on my forehead. Everyone thought I'd become sick – with flu or something worse – but they were worrying in vain. There was nothing wrong with my health. What had happened to me was what the majority of my contemporaries experienced sooner or later. What you and everyone else here in Quarantine went through as well. I attained consciousness – true consciousness. I detached myself as a form of living matter from all other species, genera and families – in the broadest sense, far beyond the bounds of recognized taxonomies. To borrow a popular term, I became a *human being*!

"No, it was not the angels who helped me, nor benevolent holy spirits or any of the gods invented by humankind. My consciousness was awakened, brought to life by a very real field of particles. I don't know the details, but my Nestor insists that the flow of the conscions, propagating through space, has interacted and resonated with my brain – and fallen into a trap. I have integrated as an individual into the structure of the universe!"

I'm feeling inspired; it seems to me I am propounding matters of great significance. Matters important to both of us – and not only in a global, cosmic sense. There is a much more specific implication: this morning it was finally explained to me why Elsa and I are sharing the same apartment and what is expected of us in this regard.

We are a localized team, so to speak, a small crew united by a common goal. I was informed about this by a rather grumpy Nestor today. He was silent for a while, pursed his lips, then finally said, "Well, I suppose it's time to get down to the main issue. So far, you've just been relaxing here, like in some health resort. Mostly sleeping and dreaming..."

He was being unfair; my dreams were taking up as much time as was stipulated by the Brochure. When I was awake, I tried to work, tormenting myself with negligible progress – and, I should add, without much support from my mentor-counselor-therapist. Nevertheless, it seemed to me we had become used to each other, found a common language – and over the last few days Nestor had been quite nice. But today he has changed abruptly.

Yet, arguing with him is useless. "Well, to the main issue, then," I shrug. "I thought it was the theory of the conscions, but if you now think otherwise..."

Nestor grins, "And what can you tell me about the theory of the conscions?"

"Not much," I admit. "Only what I've heard from you: imprints of consciousness, vortexes of some sort, images of memory on the meta-brane – and that I supposedly discovered it all..."

Nestor interrupts me with an impatient gesture. "Children's fairy tales," he says. "Who are they going to convince? Myths and legends – who is going to believe you and believe in you, me perhaps? I don't think so; I'm not that gullible. I need a theory, a proven theory – then I will agree you've reached one of your goals. Then I will be able to check a box on the task list I have in front of me."

"I'll let you know – as soon as it's ready," I answer dryly. "I'm trying my best to make progress."

Nestor purses his lips again – evidently underwhelmed by my efforts. Then, after a pause, he repeats, "Now, to the main issue!" – and leans forward, so that his face fills the entire screen.

"I suspect..." he says insinuatingly. "I suspect you, Theo, still don't sufficiently appreciate the significance of a phenomenon staring you in the face – every day, just as my task list does at me. I suspect you accept it as a given and categorize this given as a chance occurrence, thereby nullifying the importance of a fact that you should have thought about a long time ago. With your analytical mind... I'm surprised, surprised!"

He leans back and regards me like a schoolboy who has flunked his spelling test again. "You mean…" I begin, but Nestor does not let me finish.

"Exactly!" he exclaims. "Yes, precisely that. How naive it is of you to think you and your roommate have ended up here in the same apartment by coincidence, without any underlying reason! Extremely naive; indeed it smacks of willful blindness. But you're not blind, Theo – not by a long stretch…"

I demand an explanation. Nestor explains. Tersely and not very clearly.

"You have to work together," he says, staring at me intensely. "To reveal the causal connections – at least, one of them. Your memories must intersect at some point in space and time, and this point needs to be found – you cannot just wait for it to appear on its own. That's the *main* issue – and you both need to make more of an effort to resolve it. You need to apply yourselves, to search diligently for a path, to try, try and try again. And remember, Theo: honesty, uncompromising honesty – that's what will lead you out of this impasse!"

And on that note, we part. Now, on the seafront, I am making an honest effort to "search for a path" – or, at least, so it seems to me. Elsa, however, is not overly impressed. She waves her hand, interrupting me. She is clearly annoyed, "Are you incapable of remembering anything *normal* – like where you lived? Like what sorts of women you had – why you've been telling me nothing about your women? Or how you spent your childhood? Maybe you were a bad boy – and now you're ashamed? Maybe you used to tear the wings off butterflies and torture cats?"

I can only shrug. In my opinion, I'm talking about the most normal thing in the world. But I'm not angry with Elsa; it's not easy for her either. It would appear her Nestor has not been very kind to her this morning.

Elsa came into the living room after me and immediately said, "I'm sorry, but do you mind if we skip the fried eggs today? I'm not in a good mood – most probably I'll get them all wrong."

She was wearing a modest knee-length dress, flat shoes and no jewelry. Her hair was tied back in a low knot. She looked like a corporate lawyer or a PA to some big-shot executive.

"Okay," I responded in a deliberately cheerful tone and sat down at the table, opening my notebook. Elsa, instead of settling down on the couch with her needlework, went to the window and pressed her forehead against the windowpane. It was clear she was out of sorts.

"Everyone is always demanding something of me," she said dully. "And when they stop demanding, it turns out I'm the one to blame."

"What happened?" I asked but got no answer. She stood for several minutes, angrily examining the landscape beyond the glass, then paced around the room, stopped at the kitchen sink and began to wash the plates, which were already perfectly clean.

"It's very calming – have you ever tried it?" she said turning to me. "I always used to do this when I'd quarreled with someone – or worse."

"No, I haven't, but I'll take your word for it," I reply and suggest going for a walk.

So, here we are walking along next to the sea, hand in hand like a happy couple. The small waves disintegrate into slithers of light; it's painful to look at them. But we aren't looking over there – like everyone else, we are peering at the people we meet, searching their features in the hope of recognizing a familiar face. A false hope, a naive expectation. We are surrounded by strangers – most of them are middle-aged, no older than fifty. I have already learned from Nestor that this has nothing to do with their age when they died. The external appearance of the people in Quarantine is formed artificially from scraps of visual memory, regenerated during their second birth. And also from their files – which, in my view, are not particularly useful.

After a pause, Elsa says in a conciliatory tone, "All right, I was only joking. I don't really think you used to torture cats. I'm just irritated – we've wasted so much time! Although I don't know if that's good or bad."

"Whatever the case," I reassure her, "it is not your fault."

Elsa shakes her head. I'm already well acquainted with her overdeveloped sense of responsibility. "Yes, probably," she says, "but still: it's not at all clear where to begin. As far as I understand it, I need to be fully open with you, not concealing anything. Like with a doctor or a shrink – and not keep any secrets as I would with a boyfriend or a husband. I've already told you a lot, although not everything of course – but I didn't know!"

We arrive at a café with a terrace. As usual, all the tables are occupied. The *quarantiners*, ensconced in wicker chairs, closely examine the passers-by. In their tall glasses, variously colored drinks: all sweet, cool and fizzy.

"Ah," says Elsa. "I so miss alcohol!" I agree, understanding her well.

A singer with a guitar sits on the sidewalk leaning against the railings, tanned to a nut brown, with long hair and sunken eyes. We stop at the balustrade a couple of paces away from him to listen. Several other people stand next to us; a middle-aged man smiles at me, and I nod back amiably.

"*Oh, what are we drunken bums gonna do now?*" he sings in a hoarse baritone. "*How can we live now that Elsa has gone? Our bar bereft of her big breasts and thighs…*"

"Did you hear that?" I say with a grin. "He's written a song in your honor."

"So you think my thighs are big, do you?" Elsa says, offended.

"Joke!" I rush to reassure her. "You know your legs are your strong suit."

"That's what everyone used to say!" she declares. "Until they met my sister, of course. And did you notice how *honest* I'm being with you?"

A young woman passes by, alone, without a companion. She walks, smiling to herself, not paying attention to anyone around her. Some look her up and down and follow her with their gaze. I also watch her go.

"A newcomer," says Elsa. "A new arrival who has just moved in and is living all alone. I was exactly the same – I used to go down to the sea and wander around aimlessly… It seems so long ago – like an eternity. And my Nestor seemed so sweet back then!"

Obviously, her morning session with her Nestor has been a bit of a drama. I even feel a little schadenfreude. Although, most likely it's just jealousy.

"You know," Elsa looks up at me, "somehow after this morning's session, I don't want to leave Quarantine at all. I sensed so much indifference toward me… Do you think they'll kick us out as soon as we find this connection between us? This invisible link – I didn't really get what it's all about."

I hasten to calm her, "No, the Brochure stipulates otherwise. Although it doesn't contain a word about any invisible link."

The singer starts a new song, "*How can I love you with all my heart when I know there'll be another life? And I don't know whether I'll meet the one I loved so much in my past one..."*

"How true!" Elsa exclaims. "Don't you think? It's a good thing I didn't love anyone in my previous life. Let's go."

We wander farther along the promenade, squinting in the sun. "'How can I love you with all my heart...'" purrs Elsa, nestling into my shoulder. I smell a faint trace of the perfume she's wearing today – something subtle, exciting, bitter.

"Generally," she says, "to fall in love, you have to choose someone accessible, who is in close proximity. Maybe there just weren't the right people around me. And here – the only accessible man is you. It would be so easy to choose you! It's a pity I can't allow myself to do that – everything here is so artificial, unreal. I don't feel like getting deeply emotional; it would be better if we just remained friends. Ha-ha, imagine you are, you know, *a nice guy*, the sort that girls always just want to be 'good friends with.' Although, with our bodies here, that doesn't make much difference. And in return, I promise I won't pester you with questions about your feelings – like, whether you love me or not and, if so, how you'll prove it... Do you like this deal?"

"Suits me," I nod and smile at her with a slightly insincere grin.

"Today I talked to Nestor about it – about accessibility and so on," Elsa continues. "But he just kept returning to the same thing – that you and I being together was no accident. I even thought: maybe he just wants to find out what's going on between us? In general, he's become a real bore, the sort of man you know you'll never sleep with – from the first moment you set eyes on him!"

She laughs ambiguously and falls silent. We walk on for another couple of hundred meters and, without saying a word, turn back.

"Well, what about you?" Elsa turns back to me. "Have you remembered anything about your Asian girl with the red streak in her hair? Tell me about her – I'll understand. And I'll tell you something else about Nancy or Dave in turn. Or, do you still want to talk about those particles and fields of yours? I'll try *very* hard to listen, honest!"

CHAPTER 12

THAT EVENING I tell Nestor, "My roommate hasn't been herself all day. Her counselor has started behaving differently – what is this, some sort of Nestors' plot? Or a conspiracy, more like?"

Nestor mutters, "Conspiracies, conspiracies… Anyway, you should try to adjust to her. You should appreciate her, think what this is all about. Adapt as you go along, maybe even set an example – although, of course, expecting that of you is a vain hope. You are extremely focused on yourself – like all creators of theories."

He is calm and benign – there isn't a trace of this morning's irritation. We exchange a few more pleasantries, then Nestor says mysteriously, "Symmetry… I would suggest you focus on symmetry. At least on the word itself, if not on the overall concept. This is my advice to you – perhaps the best I've given this week!"

On that note, our conversation ends; I soon fall asleep and have a dream I have chosen for myself. There are no concepts or clever words in it; I am whisked away to an island with black sand, to the childhood of my first life, to the instant when I first became aware of my "individual self" and, instantaneously, its brief and finite nature. Yet again, I see my confusion, my fear – the fear of death that will someday come for me – I remember how it used to torture me at night. I remember how I bit my pillow, lying in a sweat, unable to move until some noise outside would bring me back to reality, forcing me to wake up. Then I fell asleep, and in the morning, in the bright light of day, I recalled this fear in a detached way, like a bout of illness that has been left in the past. I remembered it and – in a mature, truly adult way – reflected on the instability and incredible transience of everything. And I concluded: mortality can only be justified by some great achievement – and fantasized vigorously what this achievement might be, what awaited me, what would be my mission.

I did not share these thoughts with anyone – neither my mother nor her relatives, whom I spent most of my days with. My home life was not a happy one. It was at that time my stepfather appeared in my life, a puffy, balding man with moist breath and an oily gaze. We took an immediate disliking to each other. I avoided him as much as I could, and for about a year we managed to coexist without incident, but then my mother had to go away for a couple of days and, having gotten drunk he decided to reach out to me – in the crudest sense of the term.

It happened in the evening, in the kitchen, where I was warming up my dinner – a *stifado* stew and braised beans. My stepfather came up from behind and put his hand under my clothes, but I managed to twist away and throw the contents of the pan in his face. He stepped back with a yell, then recovered a little and was about to rush at me, but I had already grabbed a knife, a trusty heavy-duty santoku, and he thought it best to leave me alone. I spent the night with the knife in my hand and told my mother everything when she asked the reason for my stepfather's burns, but she didn't believe me and started screaming, accusing me of malicious lies. I didn't blame her – seeing the terrible helplessness in her eyes. After that, I was twice taken to a psychiatrist but not in earnest and, in my opinion, without any definite purpose. And then through my stepfather's uncle's connections, I was brought to Athens, to the office of a very attentive functionary. He had a number of conversations with me, and before I knew it I found myself in a very different country, full of wind and rain and devoid of sun...

I spent my entire adolescence there, in a boarding school on the shores of a leaden sea. Then I got into a good, reputable university, but those years fly past incoherently in my dream, and once again toward morning it's dominated by the same balding man, his scream and his lascivious, twisted mouth. I do not want to look at him; I already know where this evil memory is leading – and try to push it off, drive it away. It retreats but I wake up understanding that its time will come.

In the morning, Elsa greets me warmly. "I've made it up with him," she says first thing. "He's become nicer, changed his tone. Nevertheless, I've forgotten nothing – it's now clear: if we were on earth, nothing would have worked out between us. He just doesn't satisfy my list of traits."

I look at her in some bewilderment.

"Nestor," she explains and pulls a face, "You are so slow sometimes! Maybe you also wouldn't have passed muster for my list... Come on then, tell me what you dreamed about."

I share my dream without concealing anything – omitting only a few details. "That's interesting," Elsa says politely. "Interesting but completely foreign to me. By the way, for breakfast I made you a mushroom omelette. I'm afraid it's slightly burned – I'm sorry. I'm not very good at omelettes – I used to try to surprise Dave and then another man but could never manage to get them right. Once Dave even shouted at me – in San Jose, on the first day of our vacation..."

She talks about her short break with her boyfriend. It's all as alien to me as my Greek island is to her. Then we go to my bedroom to see what the weather has in store for us today. Outside, there are clouds, wind and the same gray, inhospitable sea I caught a glimpse of in my recent dream. We decide to give our walk a miss and settle ourselves down as usual: I at the table with my pencil and paper, she on the couch with her needlework.

I draw a sloping pebble beach with gulls hovering overhead. Then, skipping to another country and another time, I sketch two spired towers – this is the town hall opposite the university building. The towers are the same, indistinguishable – "Symmetrical," I say aloud, causing Elsa to glance up at me. I continue, "They are translationally similar. The symmetry of translation... The energy-momentum tensor remains conserved..."

This inkling of recognition is so strong that I know it is no deception. I scribble something meaningless and indiscriminate under the towers and suddenly, of its own accord, my hand produces a familiar equation. I've seen it before and it makes sense – I understand its meaning well. I've been tinkering with its variations for a long time – since my youth. Since my first romantic jousts at the mysteries and conundrums of the universe.

I freeze, and yes: the veil falls from my eyes, scraps of formulas line up in a logical chain. This is a breakthrough, perhaps the most important since my arrival at Quarantine. Sensing my physics finally returning to me, I take a new sheet of paper and scribble and scribble…

Nestor was right: the notion of symmetry has occupied me since childhood. He was also right about my physics teacher, a heavy-drinking descendant of impoverished Russian aristocrats – I remember his stooped figure and trembling hands. He was kind and deeply in love with his science; he would tell me stories about my own ancestors, about Euclid and Plato, who took great pride in symmetry, as they took great pride in beauty, and he would add with a grin, "In general, modern science has not moved on from them that much; it's just gone a bit deeper into the details." He would bring me books – I understood almost nothing of their contents, but occasionally I would experience insights, glimpses. Certain symbols and words would suddenly become meaningful, and I was suffused with a premonition of immeasurable depths of meaning – I knew that sooner or later they would submit to me. Then there was boarding school, where the physics that had been hiding behind a looking-glass, like an amorphous figure, began to turn into something with firm contours and later – to disintegrate into parts that were closely connected. The equations no longer seemed like cryptograms with a hidden code – it was the richest of languages, perfectly intelligible to the initiated. Then it was time to go to Bern, to the university – and there everything that had seemed like a piece of unread prose suddenly turned into poetry consisting of the most complex forms, the true manifestation of the harmony of the world. I finally felt the power of proper, pure mathematics, fused to my chosen science like a Siamese twin. The presaged depths of meaning started to emerge – reaching them required the greatest effort, but the most precious rewards waited there. At least, that's what I wanted to believe.

As Nestor had correctly noted, my path to the secrets of nature had started out from the very first moments of the universe. Specifically, from the asymmetry of baryons[10] – the predominance of matter over antimatter,

---

10   A family of elementary particles. Baryons include protons and neutrons, for example.

which resulted in the emergence of the "material," out of which all heavenly bodies, including our planet and everything on it, were made. At the university, I finally learned how this was formulated in modern physics – at a lecture on baryogenesis, which was delivered by Professor Kertner. We listened to him with bated breath – the story he recounted was a gripping one. It turned out baryon asymmetry was still unexplained, and Kertner revealed intriguing details to us: he hypothesized on the nonconservation of the baryon charge and exclaimed, "But why is the proton so stable then?" He cited examples of parity violation and immediately demonstrated why this does not suffice to explain the superiority of matter over the antipode. He placed particular emphasis on quarks – wrote out the main equation of chromodynamics on the blackboard, circling a part of it with his piece of chalk and in his excitement almost shouted, "Here it is, the possibility of a violation of balance that could explain everything! Here it is, the chance, but nature rejected this chance! We know this, if for no other reason than because the neutron, as its name suggests, really is neutral, despite everyone's efforts to prove it has at least the slightest dipole moment.[11] We call this the *strong* CP problem – at least, we had sufficient sense to acknowledge the strength of our incomprehension… I'm joking here, of course: it's only 'strong' because it refers to the strong interactions inside the nuclei. But the play of words is amusing – sometimes words reveal more than we initially plan…"

During the lecture, I became tremendously agitated. I felt the professor was addressing me personally, looking directly into my eyes. It was as if together we were lifting the curtain, looking into the innermost secrets of the world – and I realized I could no longer remain on the sidelines. I needed to give a sign, a signal – that I would also shoulder the responsibility for all this. Burning with bashfulness, I caught up with the professor at the door of the lecture theater and asked where and how I could learn more about the asymmetry of baryons. He gave me a sideways glance, nonchalantly directed me to a postdoc by the name of Gunter Stadelmann and promptly forgot about my existence.

---

11   One of the physical quantities characterizing the electrical properties of the system.

Gunter did not have any time for me and was incapable of explaining anything anyway. He could only write out formulas on paper and poke his finger at them, accompanying this gesture with inarticulate scraps of phrases.

I said to him, "I want to understand why there ended up being more quarks than antiquarks."

Gunter grinned, "Well, you won't understand it right away."

"I know, I know," I waved my hand. "What I meant was: a baryon charge – yes, okay, but what about the combined parity...? Let's accept, the problem really is 'strong,' but there should have been attempts to somehow explain, to understand!"

Then I fell silent and blushed painfully, but Gunter looked at me with some interest. His grin grew wider; "However, yes! Parity, quark..." he nodded. "There were attempts. What do you know about it?"

I confessed I knew almost nothing. Gunter thought for a while, rummaged in the cupboard and threw three heavy volumes onto the table in front of me. On top of them, he added several academic journals and said, "Read these. And here, have a look at the Lagrangian, for example..." He scribbled down the already familiar equation on a piece of paper; I sighed and thanked him hurriedly. My eyes were burning and my entire being was singing.

Needless to say, I gave myself up to work with all the fervor of youth. And was immediately possessed by a great dream – to succeed in doing what no one else had done, to find the first causes of the apparent first causality, to explain why the proton is stable and the neutron is neutral, why nature behaves precisely in this way. I was working hard, ploughing through integrals and tensors, complex functions and covariant derivatives – and learning to see through the walls, through the leaden shells of ignorance, the basalt strata of incomprehension. The goings-on in the very interior of matter, inside the atomic nuclei and their fragments, resonated in my soul like the most harmonious music. I was astonished at the way concise mathematical constructs described the incredible intricacy of reality – much of which didn't look real at all. Quarks, their generations and the mass difference, their complex color space... Gluons,[12] carriers of

---

12   Elementary particles responsible for the interaction between quarks in quantum chromodynamics.

the strong force, also differing in color... Freedom in close proximity and captivity at a distance, the inability to break out of the mysterious confinement... I read about quantum chromodynamics as if it were a gripping detective thriller, I raved about it to everyone, including my friends and the girls I met. This repelled the friends and especially the girls – which didn't upset me in the slightest.

Above all, I was fascinated by the most fundamental part of the theory – the concept of gauge fields. Its power was striking: a mere handful of hypotheses about the invariance of certain properties gave rise to equations that described the entire dynamics of the microworld. Fields and forces were needed only to compensate for imperfection, to return symmetry to its proper pedestal. It was the triumph of mathematics in its most prominent form, and I spent many hours wrestling with calibration transformations, Feynman diagrams and action integrals, Green's functions and Gell-Mann matrices. I tried to get a feel for the finest minutiae, the significance of each variable, each parameter, sign, index – and finally, after months of furious labor, mastered at least a part of this extremely difficult mathematical apparatus. I mastered it – and ran on ahead, immediately rushing to test it in practice.

My all-consuming dream and ambition pushed at my back; I couldn't wait to make big strides toward it. Far from knowing everything required either from the books lent to me by Gunter or from the relevant scientific articles, I nevertheless understood where the roots of the "strong" CP problem lay. Its source was a special anomaly, a nonlinear term in the Lagrangian function, describing the dynamics of quarks. The anomaly explicitly violated the combined parity and this, as Professor Kertner had told us, seemed natural: here it was, a trick of nature that had led to the emergence of matter. But practice showed: this was not so. For the entire theory to hold true, the nonlinear part would have to become negligibly small. This could only be achieved by zeroing out its multiplier, a certain angular parameter, denoted by the Greek letter theta. The CP problem was reformulated as follows: Why is the theta angle incredibly close to zero?

"Revealing!" I thought, remembering my childhood, the ruins on the hill and the inscriptions in the ancient language. Even back then I had imagined hidden meanings in the Greek alphabet – and now it had been reduced to a single letter for me. The theta angle had its own secret; it could not be just a simple constant, chosen at random by the universe. Its smallness should be a consequence, not a cause – a consequence of unknown processes invisible to anyone. The apparent simplicity would have to be a collision of complexities – an elaborate mechanism competing with an even more elaborate one, a struggle not for life but death, mutual death in battle... And I, putting aside any further study of my books, began to ponder over the mystery of theta.

At first, nothing worked out; my calculations showed only one thing: mathematics allows for an infinite number of possible worlds with various nonlinear multipliers. Why had nature chosen zero or a vanishingly small value? Equations provided no answer; then I began to search for the connection between variations in the theta angle and the other properties of the whole system, all the interplay between gluons and quarks – and soon noticed that theta's different values do not just simply emerge but only do so along with "phase rotations" of the quark fields. All these rotations were permitted, they were equal, if only... And then it dawned on me: they were only equivalent if the quark field didn't interact with something that might compensate for the rotation, causing the quarks to get stuck and gain mass. It was like Higgs's famous example – and I fearlessly expanded the Lagrangian with a new term, transformed it into the canonical form, compared its structure to the structure of the nonlinear anomaly and saw that they essentially coincided. Moreover, after calculating the real functionals, I found exactly what I expected: the most probable, the most stable state of the system – its energy minimum – is obtained precisely when the rotations of the new field together with the quark field fully compensate the anomalous vortices. My new angle of theta derived from the old one – from *any* old one! – as a result of the compensating interaction, must be strictly equal to zero in our real, not an imaginary, world. Well, how about that for a solution!

A new interaction and a new field meant the emergence of a new particle. I saw it in my Lagrangian – there it was, in square brackets, concealed in a standard mathematical transformation... Squiggles on a piece of paper had been converted into reality, living for a micro-moment and obscured from everyone. From everyone except me; this particle had evidently failed to hide itself from me. Well, it needed to be named... I thought about it a little and chose the most natural name. I called my particle the "Theodorus boson," or the "theonon" for short.

I gave it its name and repeated it aloud to myself, over and over again, in every way possible. I repeated it – and I swelled with pride. I'm only twenty, and, see, I've already solved one of the greatest problems of physics. Recognition awaits me – yes, for sure – and maybe even a Nobel prize – right away! And then – what will be next? It was scary to imagine the prospects opening up before me...

Neglecting my studies completely, I tidied up the sketches of my theory of the theonons as best I could and, burning with impatience, showed it to Gunter. He glanced at it briefly and said with a laugh, "Ah, the queen's approach..." I shook my head, puzzled. He rummaged around in his cupboard, slipped me a few photocopies, and then, on the move, pointed out a series of errors and incorrect assumptions that blew my "theory" out of the water. I wanted the ground to swallow me up, my pride turned to ignominious shame, but Gunter was impressed all the same. He looked more closely at my formulas and muttered, "This is elegant, yes. And here: that's a bold transformation – and a correct one, it seems. You've been very deft with the pseudoscalar field..."

The articles he gave me described Peccei-Quinn theory. They introduced the concept of axions, hypothetical particles designed to solve the strong CP problem in much the same way as I had chosen. The axions had not yet been found, but no one could deny their existence either. I saw this as an encouraging example: a lot of wriggle room was permitted in modern physics – for all its seemingly unassailable harmony. Its buildings contained secret doors, disguised windows, passageways and loopholes, allowing one to penetrate into a hidden world full of mysteries and to find there – what? Something that had hitherto been unknown before me.

This was my first attempt at creation, at thinking outside the box – and overall it was a positive experience; I had been blessed with beginner's luck. I was crestfallen, but I was happy – especially as the next day Gunter Stadelmann invited me to work with him. He spoke with Professor Kertner, and I was officially added to the staff of the scientific group at the department of theoretical physics.

Gunter was working on the problem of color confinement – trying to understand why quarks do not "wander around on their own," but are always combined in twos and threes in accordance with certain color schemes. Nobody knew why. No one had so far succeeded in explaining the phenomenon mathematically or "deriving" the confinement from the known fundamental laws. There were a few hypotheses, and Gunter was investigating one of them – the screening of color charge. The plan was that I would be doing the same when I was ready, and I began to prepare myself – in earnest! Having just soared to the heavens, I was brought back down to earth again, but the heat of the stars had not melted the wax in my wings. I was full of desires and energy.

Moreover, as Nestor had noted, I had moved one step further regarding the evolution of the world: from immeasurably high energies and quark-gluon plasma[13] to the slightly cooler "hadron phase" of the universe, when constituent particles, including all known protons and neutrons, were formed from quarks. The hadron universe was structurally richer than the quark-gluon one, and the equations describing it were much more complicated. Now there could be no neglecting a single nonlinearity or feedback. The approximations that worked well in the extreme case of free quarks failed at low energies, leading to singularities,[14] which, one way or another, needed to be eliminated. This was achieved using elaborate procedures – the most complex mathematics, which I had not yet mastered. To be up to the job, I needed to improve my theorist's skillset to the highest level in the shortest possible time – and I succeeded, although it was not easy. I did it – and began to see the light, casting off my blinders, as if I had climbed up a hill in the middle of a boundless forest and could make out a part of the landscape. I started to understand what I was doing and why, how it related to the general structure of the world. It was the happiest of sensations – I became free and all-powerful. I myself

---

13   Quark-gluon plasma is a state of strongly interacting matter in which quarks and gluons form a continuous medium and can propagate in it as quasi-free particles.

14   The point at which a mathematical function strives toward infinity or has certain other behavioral irregularities.

could formulate scientific tasks and assess their complexity, significance and place in the big picture. For the first time since childhood, I felt like a kid left on his own in a toy store.

And I really was left on my own. Seeing how tirelessly and fearlessly I grasped at everything, Gunter was at first taken aback but then resigned himself to my restlessness and even began to encourage it. Sometimes he very tactfully warned me about hidden dead ends or, more often, suggested shortcuts, but on the whole, he agreed with my somewhat chaotic free-ranging search. Also, it became clear that I was very good at solving equations – almost better than he was himself. I was helped by an unmistakable sense of what works and what doesn't that usually only comes with experience, but which I developed almost immediately on my own. Therefore, I would get results quickly and efficiently without wasting time. Even Professor Kertner became interested in me a year later and began to invite me to his private seminars.

I was oscillating between very different models of quark interaction. I tried computer simulation and analogies with quantum liquids and even superstring theory. I saw how the familiar equations of chromodynamics miraculously appeared in other formal systems that seemed to be very different. This promised some new perspectives, connecting physics to other sciences that I knew little about. I felt it was too early for me to approach these distant realms. So, having toured diverse regions and spheres, I returned to where I had started – to the Lagrangians and gauge fields, to the magical power of abstract mathematics that gives birth to the physics of the world. I had made a circle, one of many, and returned to my starting point – but already as a different man.

Symmetry, like a guiding star, drew me toward it again, but now the noisy raptures of childhood gave way to a silent piety, an understanding of its supreme role. From the images and forms – in my teen years – to the symmetry of properties – in boarding school – to the preservation of parity and the reversal of time... At the time, I believed I was approaching the summit, when in fact I was still tramping away in the foothills, not daring to raise my eyes from my feet. The real ascent only began at the university, when I learned about the invariability of the laws of nature in different metrics and reference frames. And then came the time when

I was able to properly appreciate the turning point in the physics of the twentieth century, a revolution in consciousness, a change of perspective. Like in the fairy tales, symmetry was turned into a handsome prince – from being merely a consequence, an interesting property, it became the origin, the essence. If previously it had been noticed by observing nature, now symmetry itself predicted how all real, observed nature would behave. Assumptions about its new forms became the primary source of physical theories!

Realizing this fundamental difference, I no longer felt a childish, but a mature, adult delight in the true beauty that determines everything. I realized: what interested me most was its rationale – how and why it arises, how it then manifests itself. The life of beauty was a struggle – a struggle against imperfection. To preserve it, every point of space required "compensation," "calibration" – and out of this requirement came all the physics of the modern world, all the fields and the particles carrying them, all that is visible and tangible around us… I decided this was precisely what I wanted to focus on. And that was exactly what I told Gunter Stadelmann.

By that time, Gunter had made quite a lot of progress himself. His manipulations with quark colors were original and very promising. Naturally, he assumed I would also concentrate on his developments. Nevertheless, he did not oppose me.

Our conversation took place on a cold autumn day. "Well, yes, yes," Stadelmann chuckled, twirling his fountain pen in his fingers, and asked with a grin, "You have your sights on something global, don't you?" I just shrugged. He nodded, as if he understood, and suddenly suggested, "Shall we get some fresh air? Grab an umbrella…"

Through the miserable, drizzly rain, Gunter took me to the Albert Einstein Museum. It was deserted; we spent about an hour wandering around the small apartment in which Einstein had created his first theories. I examined the copies of his letters to scientific journals that had not taken him seriously. I imagined how, rejected by official science, he would write out his formulas on the kitchen table while his wife rocked their child in the adjoining room, behind a shaky screen. It was here that he experienced to the fullest that very revolution, that pivotal moment – but without anyone prompting him: he was the first. The first who dared to think differently. He had started with symmetry and obtained from it new laws on the dynamics of the universe. It was the turning point. In a sense, the point of no return.

Then we went to a bar and, for the first time, got drunk together. I excitedly and verbosely tried to prove to Gunter what Albert Einstein's secret had been – and Gunter tried to prove the same to me. He – Einstein! – had been told that he had not been fit to pursue serious physics – yet he was unable not to think about it or, more to the point, was incapable of not *feeling* what was overflowing his soul. The notion that he perceived with his whole being – a symmetry, a similarity, the covariance of space-time – set him on his course and did not allow him to waver from it. The cornerstone change of the paradigm before Einstein was beyond the power of the human mind – or maybe simply before him, no one had been *feeling* with such passion? Passion protected him from the horror of looking into the bottomless depths. It allowed him to embrace the unembraceable while at the same time keeping the whole picture in mind. Thoughts lined up in a closed loop; an idea flashed – and was caught in this loop. And he, Albert Einstein, tamed the idea, formulated it, expressed it aloud...

It was me who used the word "passion," and Gunter agreed with it. We became comrades-in-arms on that day; it marked the moment of our solidarity. Of course, the symmetries and similarities in our science were not the ones that Einstein was thinking about. We were dealing not with global space-time but with the invariability of equations under shifts and rotations, interchanges between "left" and "right" particles and so forth. This invariability was hidden deep in mathematics; it could not be directly observed, and, despite being in step with the experiments, our theories were not completely accurate. We worked with approximations in different energy scales, and the most interesting thing was concealed from us: when changing from scale to scale, from magnitude to magnitude, not only the form of the equations but also their internal properties changed. The world, "cooling down," moving from high energies to low, became less symmetrical – spontaneously, by itself, without outside interference. Matter acquired new shapes; new structures arose in it – this was progress, movement forward, but nature had to pay for this, renouncing part of the perfection.

It was the spontaneous violation of symmetry that became the focus of my interest. I wanted to get inside, to find out how it happened and at what expense. What was this mechanism of transition in which matter becomes different?... Thus, I concentrated on the jump from free quarks to "color slavery," from plasma to hadrons, when fermion[15] loops start to appear in the equations and it is no longer possible to disregard the non-linearities of the gluon fields. Loops meant bound states – mesons, protons and neutrons. They described the world we are familiar with, coinciding amazingly with reality. It was wonderful, but there was also a strangeness: the symmetry of the initial high-energy formulas was lost – and as a result, we had half as many composite particles as we might have had, and some of them were inexplicably massive. The inexplicable to me was like a red rag to a bull – I scowled at it and charged headlong into the fight.

My goal was again utterly ambitious – Gunter turned out to be right. Just as I had two years earlier, I wanted to create my own theory, to find the first principle, to look into the deepest of abysses. I wanted to understand, right down to the smallest detail, how mysterious metamorphosis takes place, who participates in it, changing the world when crossing the boundary beyond which quarks can no longer live alone. There were many options, and I chose the most difficult of them. Again, as in the struggle with the theta angle, I began to introduce into the equations new degrees of freedom, fields and particles unknown to anyone. They lived immeasurably briefly, leaving no trace behind in the most sensitive detectors but fulfilling their kamikaze missions, permanently changing the properties of the matter that we see and from which we are made. They had perished but had bequeathed a result, and I set myself the task of restoring justice, of unveiling them, of at least giving them names, if not the rewards they deserved...

Similar approaches had been tried before me. They belonged to the "technicolor" theories, using the unobservable, "technical" fermions, which were making the vacuum nonempty, forcing the real quarks to slow down within it. I worked tirelessly, introducing newer and newer

---

15   Fermions are particles with a half-integral spin value, obeying Fermi-Dirac statistics.

terms into equations, varying the degrees of freedom and gauge fields. Multitudes of new particles arose in my formulas – they were exotic, living only for a very brief moment, but in that instant they succeeded in breaking the symmetrical initial state of the whole system of gluons and quarks, making some heavier and destroying others, giving impetus to stability before disappearing from the scene...

I fumbled about with "technicolor" until my graduation from the university. My efforts didn't lead to a full theory, but some results were worthwhile. I was noticed and criticized to keep me in order, and I began to feel I had rightfully joined the theoreticians' community – a peculiar caste, living in its own peculiar world. And of course, I now considered myself an expert in that very passage through a special point – in the spontaneous violation of the symmetry of the processes of the microcosm hidden from our eyes. Later this concept played a crucial role, and at that time I was only secretly proud – of myself and with myself, not quite understanding why. From that pride, I came up with new words – not without reason: the spontaneous "violation" was not a violation at all upon careful examination. Similarities in the equations did not disappear forever but had been carefully hidden, as if concealed up a magician's sleeve. The higher symmetry of the laws of nature was here, but we were only allowed to touch a single version of the implementation of these laws. This far-from-novel idea would give me no peace for some reason. I savored it from all sides, enjoying it as if I had been the first to come up with it. And I gave my own name to the process of spontaneous violation: I called it the "cunning trick" – like coding it with a cipher, a secret message to myself. A message that could be read and unraveled when needed.

Meanwhile, the time came to defend my master's thesis, which I did brilliantly. Gunter was pleased with me – and soon we discussed our future. He received an invitation to Heidelberg, to one of the world's leading laboratories, and Professor Kertner promised to arrange for me to go there as well. It was not easy, but he used his connections and kept his word.

Overall, it seemed that a bright, cloudless future was waiting for me.

CHAPTER 13

HERE IN QUARANTINE we have been enjoying clear, cloudless weather for the third day in a row. Nevertheless, Elsa and I don't go down to the sea but sit at home. We were recently caught unawares by a new glitch in the reality here – a hurricane, knocking over the trash cans and tearing the roofs off the stalls. It flew in suddenly and almost knocked us off our feet; we took refuge behind the balustrade and waited for the strongest squalls to pass, clutching frantically at the railings. Others who could, did likewise – the seafront was emptied in an instant, garbage hurtling along the shore, the wind howling and whistling nastily. The sound was full of hopelessness, despair – and Elsa wandered around with a gloomy face all evening.

"I don't understand," she told me. "Are they provoking us or, rather, are we provoking them, and they're just reacting as best they can? Or is it one and the same thing?"

I just shrugged – I'm not as sensitive to the instability of the environment as my roommate. In her first life, Elsa also perceived the slightest hint of instability as a personal affront. I am well aware of this, along with many other things – I have already learned a lot about her. Over the past week, she has recounted to me in great detail her adolescence, her fairly insipid youth and the years she spent growing up, which were not marked by a great deal of variety either. We laughed together at her short-lived passion for collecting – when she was fascinated with oddly shaped items.

She could spend hours looking at some strange stone, imagining where it had come from and the places it had been, and then suddenly turn against it and throw it away. Then she became captivated by chemistry – mainly because of her love for smells, through which she seemed to perceive the world. Soon enough this passed as well, Elsa got into college, studied English philology, read a lot of books and even attempted to do some writing herself. Some of her articles were published by a local newspaper, and her desk drawer was filled with scraps of verse – mostly about solitude and the world's imperfections. Sometimes she wanted to misbehave but her obsession with being a "good girl" did not allow her to go far. She tried to find excitement in something moderately extreme – surfing, rafting, skiing and even parachute jumping – but nothing took her fancy. After every adrenaline trip, she would settle back into her favorite armchair with a sense of relief and a cup of hot chocolate and wonder what her acquaintances saw in all this nonsense…

Not so long ago she suddenly asked, "Could you draw me that picture of yours with the tangles of yarn? The ones that were floating in the ocean – which you and your Nestor were philosophizing about."

I obediently drew the image and tried to explain something, but she stopped me and gazed at the drawing for a long time without saying a word. Her strained, frozen expression even frightened me a little, but then Elsa brightened up and became her old self again.

"I can't understand why you're so obsessed with this," she said. "What's the use of your intertwined worlds if you still can't travel beyond your own thread? I don't see worlds here at all but something else – and I now realize why this yarn annoys me so much. I've always imagined my life differently – easier, as if charted with straight lines. Each segment – a defined stage without any deviations. One attempt after another to live the same way as other people – and to derive satisfaction, if not pleasure, out of it!"

I joked in reply, "So that means going in straight lines, sliding over the surface, never penetrating the depths? Moving from marker to marker, from beacon to beacon – do you not think this is a case study of you?"

My words made Elsa angry and she sulked all evening and all the next morning. She was unfriendly at breakfast, playing the role of waitress and asking sarcastically, "Seeing as you're so smart, what would you like to order, maybe some fancy delicacy or other? Today we have very good stewed penguins!" Then she began to whisper something barely audibly, and when I asked her to repeat herself she chuckled, "Are you a bit deaf? Then read my lips!" And she muttered something indistinctly while I looked in confusion at the blurred spot where her lips should have been.

But then the hurricane happened, forcing her to forget the perceived insult. Now we are on good terms again; our apartment is a safe refuge and there's no dragging her away from it despite the sunny weather. We sit at the table, I work on my equations, and Elsa, after borrowing a piece of paper, writes some words, short sentences, and then crosses them out one by one.

"It's pointless!" she announces suddenly. "It's not working out. I wanted to surprise you, but for some reason, my memory won't let me do this." Then she explains, "I was trying to remember my poem – the only one that ended up being half-decent. In fact, it was so half-decent that I got frightened, crumpled it up and threw it away. And I never wrote poetry again!

"It was about the good girls," she adds after a pause. "And, in general – about how I see the world and everything on it. Although it was only eight lines long – can you imagine? At the time, I realized writing was not for me. I can't stand digging deep down inside myself."

Elsa gets up, opens the fridge, takes a bottle of ice-cold cola and offers it to me, "Do you want one?" Without taking my eyes off my notes, I shake my head. She goes up to the window with the bottle in her hands and raps her fingers against the glass, "Hey, hey!"

I look up. "It's another squirrel," says Elsa. "They seem to have multiplied recently. Reproduced virtually as a result of illusory coitus..."

I look at her, at her silhouette, gracefully inserted into the rectangle of the window and suddenly ask, "What do you think would have changed in your life, if you'd known for sure there would be another one?"

Elsa shrugs, "Nothing. Except, perhaps, I might not have been in such a hurry to throw away that poem of mine. I would have paid a lot more attention to it. But all in all... I always thought I'd enjoy myself while I was young. Later – put up with getting old; then grow really old, begin to get ill and hate my body. Finally, I'd die, and life as such would be over. And then, I'd probably go to heaven – this was what I believed with all my heart. Now, I've been promised something like a new beginning, with all the hassles that go with it, and, once again, I have to trust – not Nancy, but Nestor and the Brochure. And so, will it continue? Will I have cause to hate myself time and time over?"

I know she is poking fun at my question, and I grin, "Just think that you'll always be young."

Elsa snorts, "What am I, a complete fool?"

Then she picks up her needlework and sits down on the couch. She sews with a fine stitch, inclining her head slightly. I contemplate to myself: What would have changed in my first life had I known that the end was not the end? On the whole, not very much – only, perhaps, I would have had a reason to try even harder. To be more motivated – knowing that what you have achieved will not be lost so soon, that there is a chance at another future around the corner. One chance, then another… That's no small thing. A step or two closer to immortality.

Yet I had tried as hard as I could as it was – I doubt I could have done more. In much the same way as I couldn't have straightened my path in life, avoiding diversions and false steps. When the future seems clear it is always deceptive – I learned that from my youth. And experienced it fully after my university studies before moving to Heidelberg.

Yes, my future seemed enviable, but confusion reigned in my head – and the problem was not in the formulas, not in integrals and matrices. What troubled me was the everyday life that existed around me, beyond mathematics, outside the university walls. My feet weren't planted firmly enough on the ground; I seemed to be dangling in a void. There were plenty of footholds – society offered them in abundance. But its offers were increasingly irritating me – and most of all I was frustrated with the city of Bern, the sated self-satisfaction that it embodied.

After a certain time, its essence – despite Einstein and the university – began to corrode my mind. I looked around and saw a deformed space like a reflection in a distorted mirror. A bourgeois perspective of the world irrevocably collapsed into a cone. The indestructible walls of the shopping arcades and the boutique windows that stretched into the infinitesimal distance were actually being condensed from infinity into a small neighborhood, which was becoming increasingly claustrophobic. Its borders shielded against passion and madness, from every chance accident imaginable. The world narrowed rapidly, like a power series; it converged to zero. I began to be afraid of falling into a vortex, into the area of its convergence, to become infected by the world, as if it were a serious, incurable disease.

Like all students, I was poor, and my contact with bourgeois life was infrequent. But it did sometimes occur; one such occasion took place a month after my thesis defense – and it changed my life. Gunter and his wife had invited me to dinner to celebrate my newly acquired status. I was grateful to them, but as soon as I entered the restaurant, I realized my resentment had reached the boiling point and would not be easy to control.

Gunter was not aware of any of this. He was proud of himself, proud of me, pleased with everything. As for me, I was sitting on tenterhooks. The finest foie gras melted in my mouth but tasted of nothing. I drank exclusive red wine from Pauillac province, and it seemed my glass was filled with sour, blood-colored water. I saw: the state of symmetry, when all paths are open and all possibilities are equal, was at the very point of disappearing. I was at the edge of the funnel leading to the bottom of the parabola, into the energy abyss. It was the surroundings that pushed me there – gently, but resolutely, uncompromisingly...

Gunter's wife must have sensed something – and she looked at me furtively, as if assessing me, trying to fit a label. Her glances hinted at what would soon be controlling me: all the other looks, words and conventions that form the basis of this world. They – like pseudo-Goldstone bosons,[16]

---

16   Goldstone bosons are particles that, in quantum field theory, appear during spontaneous symmetry breaking.

like magnons[17] in a ferromagnet or phonons[18] in a crystal – create a viscous field of collective opinion, fetter everyone with chains, preventing them from escaping from their eternal local vacuum.

I, in turn, assessed her too. I knew she was a good wife: she was smart, beautiful and supported Gunter in every respect – because he never attempted to step beyond the borders. But I saw her protective shell – the invisible "bourgeois bitch shield." It fit her to a T, hugging her figure, emphasizing her finest charms. She and all the women nearby were wearing it – for protection against those who did not want to play by the rules of their sated, self-regarding lives. Against those who didn't agree – as a matter of course – to become their property, to be tamed…

In the middle of the meal, Gunter proposed a toast to our future success. "No one shall be our equal!" he exclaimed. "Let the whole planet acknowledge that quarks have unconditionally submitted to us – we will look into their souls and capture their hidden essence. We may even be dubbed the Lords of the Quarks – Mr. Gunter 'Quark' Stadelmann and Mr. Theo 'Quark' Stamatis!"

For some reason, this touched a nerve with me. The very word "quark" suddenly became unpleasant. I frowned and told them a story about an actor who had never made it in Hollywood but had, nonetheless, won fame and fortune. It was a Pampers ad that had made him his money and catapulted him into the big time. The whole world loved him; he was even given the nickname – "Mr. Pampers…"

"In my opinion," I said, "we are no different. And Pampers for some reason remind me of quarks!"

Gunter laughed politely – thinking I'd had one too many. His wife, however, was not so easily fooled. A distant threat dawned on her; she narrowed her eyes and said in a velvety voice, "Theo, Theo, you need to get married – do you have a fiancée? I know a few very nice girls who would suit you."

---

17   A quasiparticle corresponding to a quantum of spin waves in magnetically ordered systems (for example, in permanent magnets).

18   A quasiparticle corresponding to the quantum of vibrational motion of the atoms of a crystal.

I thought to myself: here – I am being pushed into the same lot as Gunter. He doesn't seem to mind – but how would I find it? To penetrate under the invisible shield, one has to ask submissively. One has to lower his eyes and acknowledge his role. The role of a beggar – this self-satisfied world can never allow a man to exhibit his strength. Only one thing is ordained for him: to provide a comfortable way of life – for those wearing the protective shells who hold him in their possession. A woman of bourgeois society knows she is always right. Her principles are unshakable – because the comfort of her world is so complete. Her set of rules and opinions are localized in an energy pit, from which they cannot be shifted by any external force. The pit is as deep as her comfort level is high – they are, like the sine and cosine, functions of the same variable. What was this variable? I couldn't say. I only knew that I didn't want to depend on it, ever.

The impression made by that dinner did not dissipate the next day; I felt it had settled onto my soul for the long haul. I tried to get used to it, to live with it – and then took it away with me on a short vacation. The purpose of the trip was twofold: I really needed a rest and also considered it my duty to see my mother – for the first time in years. Thus, at the beginning of July, I hired a car and drove through half of Europe to Greece, the country where I had been born and which I now barely remembered.

For about a week I wandered aimlessly around Athens. I took in the litter-strewn streets, the dusty squares full of Albanian pickpockets; I climbed up to the Acropolis along with the tourist crowds. I dispassionately registered the cries of the traders in the fish market, the procession of fans from the Olympiacos stadium, a short violent fight next to a bar... The city was boiling with life; I imagined my desk, my notebook with my formulas – and a chill I had never experienced before ran down my spine. It seemed that something important, the real essence of life, would pass me by – was already passing me by! And I didn't know how to catch its shadow...

The meeting with my family was scheduled for Saturday. My mother and stepfather came to Athens – the idea of going to the island and socializing with a noisy crowd of doting relatives was unbearable for me. I had brought Swiss chocolate and cheese and tried my utmost to be nice, but the meeting was still a failure. We did not know what to talk about, and besides, I noted how weary my mother had become, how her eyes had faded and her shoulders stooped. This, of course, did not improve the mood; I was sorry for her, but I could not help her and said goodbye at the first occasion. She went to a department store – to buy gifts for her relatives – but my stepfather latched onto me, saying he wanted to buy me a drink and have a talk "man to man."

This was the last thing I wanted, but I couldn't find the courage to turn him down. We drank *tsipouro* in a bar nearby, ordered another one, then another. My stepfather looked at me ingratiatingly; he confessed he wanted to make it up to me, to leave our "little misunderstanding" behind us, to return us to a semblance of a family. I understood what he really wished – to insinuate himself into what he believed was my "success," into my career, about which he didn't have a clue. He thought I was definitely on the way up, and he was trying to create a foothold – to somehow use it later to his own advantage...

After another round, anger and contempt finally began to well up inside me – toward him, toward his loser's nature and his cheap hypocrisy. I told him we would have a reconciliation, but he must truly confess so that the whole world would hear. So that God would hear – I knew he was outwardly pious, like most Greeks. I don't know what came over me, I had no plan, but my words rang out firmly – and, to my surprise, my stepfather accepted the challenge. His eyes flashing greedily, he gave a crooked grin and muttered, "I agree." And asked me, finishing the remains of his brandy, "Where? And how?"

Without a second thought, I said, "On Wolf Mountain. At the summit – there's a church where, according to rumors, sins are forgiven."

We paid, and I took him to Lykabettos – up a winding path with steps. My stepfather staggered; he was drunk; large drops of sweat flowed down his face. I watched him with detached curiosity, wondering if I wanted his heart to fail right there and then. We reached the top without incident, however. My stepfather, panting and pouring with sweat, went into the church, knelt down and, gazing heavenward, began to whisper something. This lasted for a few minutes, then he heaved himself up, went outside and said, "God forgave me; I feel it!"

There was triumph in his voice; he evidently imagined he had deceived and outwitted me. Suddenly, my rage grew to unimaginable proportions.

"No," I shook my head. "No, this is not enough. In addition to God, you must be heard by people, the whole city!"

"Well, what are you proposing?" he asked, knowing I was running out of arguments.

"Address them from here," I nodded to the observation deck near the church. My stepfather stood silently as if failing to understand. "Address them!" I repeated insistently; it was as if I was being pressed by someone else's will.

He shrugged, grinned and went to the railing. "From here?" he said impudently. It was clear to him that I was not going to outplay him, that I was driving myself into a trap.

"No, it's too low," I said. "Too little effort; it's unworthy of this moment. Climb a bit higher – as high as you can."

He nodded, gave me the thumbs-up and climbed onto the concrete base of the railings. They barely reached up to his knees. I already knew exactly what was about to happen, what would probably now come to pass. I understood, but there was nothing I could do – to restrain either myself or this alien will.

My stepfather turned toward the city stretching out beneath him. A gust of wind blew; he swayed slightly but then straightened himself, raising his hand upward – like a great orator, a Pericles or a Gorgias. I thought: here, it was a hint – but only a hint, no more. The external will did not intend to take things too far. I confess, I even felt something like regret – and then my stepfather cried out asking for forgiveness in front of a group of astonished tourists. His exclamation attracted the attention of the souvenir seller who was sitting with his hawker's tray right there next to the church. He turned around, saw my stepfather standing on the fence and, waving his hand, shouted at the top of his voice, "What are you doing? Get down right away!"

My stepfather glanced at him with the same self-confident smirk – when suddenly another gust caused him to lose his balance. He made an awkward movement, his knees seemed to give way and he disappeared, hurtling downward with a scream that seemed to contain more surprise than horror. Everyone rushed to the railing. My stepfather lay far below, on the rocks. A dark stain was spreading out from his head.

Then the police arrived; the long, tedious interrogation lasted until evening. By the time I left the police station, it was already dark. I wandered around the city, not seeing anyone around me, and then, close to midnight, found myself in a small bar in Plaka. I ordered a drink, noticed a young woman with straight black hair nearby and struck up an idle conversation with her. For some reason, she didn't push me away, and a quarter of an hour later I realized she lacked the "bourgeois bitch shield," which I already couldn't imagine the entire opposite sex without. Her name was Camilla; she was from Mexico. Her two-week tour of Europe was coming to an end in Athens.

I told her, "This afternoon my hatred killed a man."

"I just don't know how I am going to live with that," I added.

And I said some other things as well, but all this made no impression on Camilla. She did listen to me attentively, however, and told me in return about her family business. I did not understand everything; her English was peppered with Spanish, which I barely knew at the time. It did become clear to me, though: in her world, death was treated without piety.

She liked me; we spent the night together – at first I was depressed and restrained, but afterward somehow I forgot everything and cleaved to her flesh, dissolving in it again and again. Then I dozed briefly – in the darkness of forgetfulness, without dreams. Then, next morning, I saw her next to me – and was amazed at a sense of closeness that I had never known before with anyone.

We went down to breakfast together. Camilla chatted about this and that, and I looked at her unceasingly. When we were getting up, something clicked in my brain; my world had altered, and I with it. As if someone had changed the backdrop in a theater – I suddenly saw myself in a different reality and Camilla next to me in it. My former life was forgotten in an instant.

That same evening, we flew together to Mexico City. On the plane, I wrote a long letter to Gunter Stadelmann – as if attempting to explain but in fact trying to convince myself of something. I almost believed at that moment that science was not my true path. There was too much left out beyond the brackets of our formulas; the calculations were precise but took far too long – I did not have enough time for them. They would not lead me to the root, to the core, to what destiny had really planned for me. Witnessing the death of my stepfather was a sign: physics could not relieve me of my fears. Maybe this meant it was time to stare them in the face?...

Gunter was not impressed with my letter – he never forgave me for deserting him. As for me, I joined my girlfriend's family business. They lived in a large hacienda on the outskirts of the capital. Officially, they described their activities as "import-export," but in fact, it was the usual smuggling – the illegal flow of goods into and out of the country. I told her father: I want to be in Mexico, to be with Camilla. I'm willing to do almost anything, but I refuse to shoot people. We agreed to this, and I was taken on to their staff.

I spent four years in Mexico. There I became a man, conquering my weaknesses or, at least, a large number of them. I often had to travel to the border, "to resolve issues" with suppliers. I learned not to be afraid of heat and swamps, poisonous spiders and snakes. With Camilla, I learned not to fear women – and to respect, to appreciate them. Did I learn not to fear death? Probably not. But I got to know what it was like to be close to it.

I would have lived there for longer, but suddenly the equations of quantum chromodynamics began to appear in my dreams – almost every night. Then they started to come to me during the day as well – my tranquility was gone completely. It became clear: Mexico City was only an episode, which was coming to an end. Physics was authoritatively calling me back, and I could not lie to myself any longer. It really was my path – no matter where it was to lead me or whether I had a mission or not. I understood this and decided to return to Europe.

Before leaving, I wept bitterly, burying my face in Camilla's knees – although for a long time now I had not been inclined to dramatic gestures. She smelled of copal incense and sweet sweat; she smelled of home. She could not leave with me; her place was here with her family. To part with her seemed inconceivable, impossible. I knew I was losing my guardian angel, and I felt the onset of a loneliness like none I had ever dealt with. But Camilla let me go calmly. She said, "I expected that sooner or later you would be drawn back. And now I see it's time for you to go!" And she looked directly at me with her shining black eyes. And struck a chord that I would later never forget.

On my return, I wrote to both Stadelmann and Professor Kertner. Gunter did not answer me, but the professor responded and helped. Through his good graces, I got into Hamburg, to a respected university with a good physics department – and, as a result, moved on to the next stage in the evolution of the universe: from strong interactions to the separation of electroweak ones. The group, which agreed to take me despite my years of absence from science, was getting ready to process the results coming out of the upgraded Tevatron collider – humanity's first serious attempt to catch the elusive Higgs boson. Like many other laboratories around the world, we worked our way through a huge variety of particle interactions, their births and decays, their transformations into one another – hoping to reveal the detectable trace of the mysterious boson that theoreticians needed so badly. It would be proof that one of the main pillars of their castle was not imaginary but real.

It's hard to convey the enthusiasm with which I got down to work. Even the tritest cliché wouldn't have been an exaggeration: I just put my nose to the grindstone and gave it my all. I worked fiercely; nothing distracted me – neither entertainment nor socializing beyond the confines of science. Camilla was with me – albeit unseen – for quite a while. Even when her image began to fade, she still helped me immensely. She was my inspiration, then – a shadow of an inspiration, and later – only a memory of an inspiration that had once been. But even a memory is better than nothing.

Three years later, I received my doctorate, having done work on refining the mass of the Higgs boson and its derivatives. By that time, after all the delays, the collider finally went into operation, and our group joined one of the collaborations analyzing its data. It was the most tedious but necessary work: day after day, week after week, we calculated and recalculated, checked and rechecked the probabilities of the events and reactions that might be caused by the presence of the Higgs boson. Almost the entire brainpower of the world's particle theorists was focused on capturing it, on minutely studying an imaginary map of the area where it might be – in order to drive it into an ambush, in some hollow or clearing by a river. And once there, immobilize it and force it out into the open, to be presented to the world...

The routine boredom did not bother us – everyone understood the significance of the project. At first, I, along with others, worked with genuine excitement, but soon I began to have my doubts. Something was wrong – the hype the populist media had created around the boson began to grate. The fervent determination to catch it right away, by whatever means possible, was irritating.

"Now, there's no way anyone could admit the boson might not exist at all. It would probably be easier to invent it," I joked at lunch one day, but no one smiled. The stakes were huge; the expressions on my colleagues' faces made it quite clear: this subject was no joking matter. And then in the evenings, almost secretly, I began to assess to what extent the rebels might be right – those who suggested that the Higgs boson, most probably, did not exist in nature.

My calculations convinced me: the rebels were in with a chance. Everything that our sensors might detect could be explained in a different way, without the presence of the notorious boson. Its place could well be substituted by certain kinds of composite fields...

I showed my rough estimates to Professor Kertner. To my surprise, he did not try to dispel my doubts but, on the contrary, strengthened them by sharing his own. "Yes," he said, "let them discover something that behaves the way a scalar Higgs particle would behave. Let them publicly say that the mechanism for the separation of weak and electromagnetic forces is thoroughly understood, that victory is ours. But do you not think, Theo, that when the universe is cooling down, too many different symmetries are broken independently of each other? Chiral, conformal, electroweak – and each has its own mechanisms and particles. It's not economical – and, at least for me, there is a certain concern that crops up. There even arises the question: What if all the forces were separated for one and the same reason? Imagine an army of additional fermions that began to interact with everything in a row right after the era of the quark-gluon plasma. At low energies, they cannot be seen singly, but their bound states – yes, why not? Maybe the Higgs boson, even if it is caught, is only a special case, one of?..."

I remained quiet, knowing where this conversation might take me. I kept silent and sensed a decision growing within me – which nobody was going to like. Especially Professor Kertner, who had twice taken it upon himself to support my career!

"By the way," the professor continued, "have you read the latest articles on the theory of 'technicolor'? I suspect you will be overcome by nostalgia. The world has moved forward – now we know how to change the energy scale smoothly. There are no more meaningless leaps – read the latest papers. This may be a key to unraveling the mystery!"

I beseeched him, "Professor, stop tormenting me – are you doing this on purpose? I know, I can't let you down again!"

"Forget it," Kertner said with a frown. "Life is short. And the productive part of a scientist's life is even shorter. You'll have about fifteen years before you will no longer be able to create anything new. You should not be worrying about other people's feelings."

I could see he was speaking earnestly about something he rarely expressed out loud. I heard in his words regret for his own fate in life, which seemed to be so successful. I immediately remembered the university, Gunter, the feast of ideas from endless conversations, all the intellectual freedom of those years. And I cleared my throat and said in a voice I could barely control, "Professor, I want my own theory and nothing else. I'm stuck in a swamp – and cannot believe I have no mission, so to speak. Sorry for sounding so melodramatic, but my goal, whatever it may be, cannot be reached by taking tiny steps. I have to make a bold leap…"

My words sounded incredibly foolish. "I'm sorry," I added, but Kertner merely shrugged. The next day I went to the head of the group and announced my departure. Having once again committed an act of scientific treachery – from an outsider's point of view.

I quickly managed to get a new job – at the same university but in the neighboring wing – and found myself in a completely different world. Compared with the collaboration and the grinding toil of the scientific rat race, it was a haven of peace and quiet. I was forced to teach but accepted this as an unavoidable evil, the price to be paid for my freedom. I had a lot of time left for research, and I hitched myself to my formulas like a faithful old workhorse to its harness. Fatigue did not exist for me; I did not allow myself to notice it. I just clenched my jaw and ploughed my way through the maze of the most complex transformations – onward, ever onward.

Chapter 14

"GOOD MORNING," SAYS Nestor. "I have an idea. Why don't you show your roommate a couple of equations?"

"Why?" I ask. "What will they do for her? She'll just get bored, immediately and irrevocably."

"Give it a go," Nestor continues. "Nothing ventured, nothing gained. And she, in turn, might teach you how to embroider..."

He laughs his strange laugh. Only then do I understand he is joking.

"It's always nice," I say sourly, "to start the day with a good, funny joke."

"That's true," Nestor nods and purses his lips. "But seriously, you never know what might prove useful. If I were you, I wouldn't be so quick to knock my jokes. After all, as far as I can see, you still haven't made much progress."

"We are trying," I mutter. "You can put that in my file if you want!"

I'm upset because, in my opinion, we really are making progress. Elsa and I spend ages patiently listening to each other's memories. We have even plotted charts on paper; we mark the points and shade the squares; we are looking for a chance moment – a chance intersection in our first life, even if it was only for a brief instant. In a word, we are not standing still, and Nestor knows this full well. He knows, but almost every day he nevertheless reproaches me for being idle.

"And how is your physics going?" he asks.

"It's progressing," I reply curtly. "I'm minimizing the set of technical fermions."

"A jolly time," Nestor nods and adds, "Although, of course, not the brightest in your life. Yet you are still a long, long way off…"

"Listen," I say with irritation, "really, I…"

Nestor stops me, raising the palm of his hand. "Don't be angry," he says in a conciliatory tone. "I'm not berating you. My remarks aren't meant to be a criticism but rather a stimulus. Think hard about the word – 'stimulus'; it might help you jog your memory. And don't get so upset: no one is hurrying you; no one is reproaching you for not returning our hospitality, so to speak."

"Yeah, right?" I raise my eyebrow ironically. "Well, it feels like I *am* being reproached – specifically by you, Nestor. And by the way, talking about hospitality: Could you finally let me in on a little secret? How is everything set up, what are the principles of physics at work here? Or, to be more precise, the Quarantine Principle?"

Nestor frowns, "It's a long story. And there's no point – this 'secret' would only make sense to an expert, and you have no relevant expertise. Just accept that here, in Quarantine, you are present as an entity, some sort of essence of yourself. Everything that is visual is merely an illusion, as it is everywhere, always."

"I may not be an expert, but I still want to know!" I insist. "It's important to me; I need the details. Tell me something at least; I'll pick it up easily – I'm good when it comes to science."

"Everyone thinks so at first…" Nestor grumbles.

I sense that the session is about to end, and I hurriedly add, "Hold on, hold on! Don't go yet; tell me how the entities are structured, what is their meaning? For example, Elsa seems to emanate a vibe, a certain female heat – is that an essence? Or is that also distortion, fake? If so, then I have to admit, it's been done very well. Sometimes I dream that in one of my lifetimes I will succeed in dragging her to a hotel room, plying her with whiskey and screwing her brains out!"

Nestor looks at me and says nothing. I continue heatedly, "Well, if you can't tell me about the fundamentals, then talk to me about your world, about the second life. How it works – are there physical bodies? At least I want to know, will I still have my beloved, manly prick?"

"This is the fifth time you've asked this," Nestor replies seriously. "And my response is always the same: there is *something*."

With that, our conversation comes to an end. I go to the living room, greet Elsa and give her one of my sheets of paper, covered with the quantum field theory equations.

"Here," I grin. "My Nestor suggested you take a peek at this."

Elsa obediently looks at it, then puts the piece of paper on the table. "Gibberish!" she exclaims angrily. "It seems your Nestor is a bit crazy. He doesn't seem to understand at all what may be of interest to an ordinary girl."

"Maybe he doesn't," I say, going over to the window. "As for me, I understand perfectly – one of my girlfriends explained it to me very well…"

Outside the window is a forest, an impassable thicket. I start to tell Elsa about Hamburg. She interrupts me – "Stop! I'll bring our spreadsheet!" – and runs to her bedroom. "It's not really a spreadsheet, it's just a diagram," I mutter to her departing back.

Yet I must give her credit: this is her idea – to put the coordinates of our memories down on paper. She looks after them jealously and takes the chart with her to her room at night. "I want them near at hand," she explained to me. "It's always useful to have something nearby in case they accuse you of being lazy. I think my Nestor now sees I'm not really into him anymore. And when a man loses hope, he can become very exacting!

"Dates!" Elsa commands as soon as she returns to the living room. "Dates and places…"

Then I relate to her: how I used to walk to the university along the muddy streets of the Turkish quarter – savoring the smells from the coffee shops, hurrying to be in time for my first lecture, after which precious hours of freedom awaited. How I used to work on my formulas till late and then cycled along the empty sidewalks – and the city seemed to become more tolerable to me. I would return – soaked and happy – and sit down again at my desk, despite the grumbling of my girlfriend, Gertrude. I lived with her for about a year after I had finally decided I'd forgotten Camilla forever. I hadn't really, but I felt I needed the stability and order that Gerti had provided in abundance until one day she collected her things and disappeared from my life.

It happened suddenly, although it had probably been brewing for a while. One evening, on my return home, I began to talk to her about the fermionic vacuum before I'd even closed the front door. I had been thinking it over on the way home and was unable to keep my thoughts to myself.

"Yes," said Gertrude, "it's all very interesting, but you know, I've finally realized I want to live with a normal person."

"Well, then you probably need to find a normal person," I replied jokingly, but somehow the joke fell flat. She gave me a long look and nodded, "Right. I'll just have to find someone else then." And she left me forever, although for a while I couldn't believe she was serious. I just couldn't accept it – I phoned her, wrote to her, tried to get her to meet up and talk...

"I've got it!" Elsa declares. "You're all the same – you, your Nestor... Let's go for a walk; the sun is out again."

She carefully folds up our spreadsheet-diagram, which has several new points on it, and says angrily, "*They* are annoyed we're not making much progress. But what do they expect from us – we're not fully fit. After all, we are in Quarantine!" And then she grins, "It's so strange: at the word 'quarantine' you imagine being locked behind doors, isolated, almost like prison – but in fact, this is the closest you can get to freedom. You can do – almost – anything you want, and you – almost – don't owe anything to anyone. You show you're making an effort, fulfilling your little debt – and that's all; you can go and do what you like. If, of course, you don't get blown away by the wind or crushed by a collapsing building..."

We go out onto the seafront, which is as crowded as ever. Elsa takes me by the arm – with pride and what seems to me a proprietorial satisfaction. We wander aimlessly, not talking, only glancing at the people we meet, catching each other's eyes and hastily looking away. Like playing a familiar game that never gets boring.

I'm still hurt slightly by the memory of Gertrude, who'd rejected me so unceremoniously. "You know," I say to Elsa, "when I was at the university, when I first started studying science, I always hankered after sex. After two or three hours with my equations, I'd be overcome by an unbearable desire."

Elsa looks at me slyly. I continue, embroidering my story somewhat, "In the evenings at student bars, after a few drinks, I'd tell the girls about gluons and quarks, looking deeply into their eyes and sending them the thought signal: 'I want you! I want to do this and that to you!' It acted like an explosive mixture. They sensed my thoughts – and went with me to my place. They themselves dragged me to bed; they demanded, 'More, more...' I couldn't express how grateful I was to them. I called them princesses while they were with me. And then they returned to their humdrum lives, turning back into secretaries, hairdressers, salesgirls..."

"Well," Elsa replied, "I'm glad you got so lucky. And now I understand – you showed me your scribbles this morning not just to impress me and to pretend to look smart. You did it because you're a pervert, some special kind of pervert. You should continue like this – I might get interested. I have to confess, I'm a bit of a pervert myself – I've always wanted a man to not only give me oral pleasure but do exactly *this* and *this* – she whispers in my ear what she has in mind. "Can you imagine such a thing?"

"Very much so," I grin. "I think most girls want the same. And those who don't at first usually develop an inclination for it later."

"Is that so?" Elsa pouts her lips. "Are you calling me average and ordinary again? All right then, so be it, but I love myself just the way I am!"

"In a certain way, I love you too – just the way you are," I say in a conciliatory tone, speaking the truth. "And believe me, I am sure the way *you* like it is unique – it does have some special flavor of perversity..."

The singer with the guitar has no audience today. He sits silently, hunched over and looking sullenly at his feet. Nevertheless, we stop – it has become a tradition for us. The singer nods to Elsa, totally ignoring me. Then he strikes a chord and starts, "*Oh, infamy! Oh, the boundless vanity of pride! I tried to break free of every net. And end up here – what a laugh...*"

I freeze as if in shock; something pierces me like a needle. Turning toward the sea, frowning, I try to hold onto a thought that is slipping away. And the singer sings:

"*I will sweetly self-destruct, drink bourbon by the quart, to deaden my longing for Elsa. I'll smoke several packs a day – let my lungs burn and decay. Let my liver die – anyway, I have so many lives to come. Don't let*

Elsa return – my longing is dearer to me than she is while there are packs of smokes and endless gallons of whiskey..."

"Infamy!" I repeat and then say to Elsa, "I'm sorry, I need to go home."

"We've only just come out," she sighs in frustration but nevertheless obediently follows me.

I look at the nearest clock – there is still time before the next session with Nestor.

Elsa mutters, "You're lucky of course I'm a bit submissive in a sense..."

I repeat, "I'm sorry," and glance with the utmost tenderness at her profile.

Back at home, I rush over to the table and start scribbling – the sheet of paper is rapidly covered with formulas. I recall *how* it was – and when, where and what. Why I left Hamburg, bidding farewell to science – seemingly forever. How I got disillusioned with the whole world and even conceived a hatred – not so much for the world, but for myself.

My theory, explaining in detail how the division of the fundamental forces occurred, was ready in a year and a half. Many things fitted into place: the quarks' flavors,[19] their masses, the unusual decay of the kaons[20] and other oddities that had seemed inexplicable – before me, I repeated to myself, inexplicable before me. Now, the explanation had been found – without the elusive Higgs boson and almost without any fine-tuning. Clearly, I was impatient to bring it to the public's attention, and I did – a bit too hastily. I rushed and shamefully overlooked a singularity in one of the functions, which reduced everything to nothing, requiring a revision of most of my approach...

The mistake was picked up almost immediately – and was then savored by the scientific community for several weeks. My former Hamburg colleagues were especially zealous in their criticism – they still had not forgiven me for my "betrayal" for the sake of my vainglorious goal, which had led me to commit such a blunder. Others were also caustic in their

---

19   A flavor is the common name for a series of quantum numbers characterizing a type of quark. Many of their features do not yet have an explanation.

20   Elementary particles of the hadron family.

remarks – my article really was ambitious in the extreme, laying claiming to far too much all at once. I even suggested that all physics, as we now know it, has become what it is under the influence of certain external fields, originating in invisible dimensions, in global metaspace. My equations allowed for such a hypothesis – and of course, this attracted attention and elicited an additional stream of ridicule. Then everything died down, the story became an amusing but forgotten incident, and I was left in smoldering ruins, a void, of no interest to anyone.

Probably, certain fragments of that work would have made sense. If someone had brought a team of a few eager postdocs together, they would have put it into proper shape within a year, and its true value would have become clear. But, of course, no one was going to waste their time on this. My theory was declared dead, dumped into a shallow grave and sent to oblivion. And the fault was all my own – in my rush to prove that mine was the correct path, I took too big a step. My legs had parted ways and now I was sitting in a dirty puddle. Perhaps because I had been too eager to be first, to get ahead of others.

My downfall was devastating, monstrous – and I could neither cope nor find a justification for it. I had no one to complain or to apologize to: Gertrude had left, Gunter didn't want to know me, and Professor Kertner had been working in the States for six months; I had lost contact with him. We did not correspond and, truth be told, it was too embarrassing to discuss with him what had happened. After suffering alone for a week or two, I decided to give up science.

The decision was easy – it was plain to see. I no longer wanted to think about great missions and grandiloquent goals. I desired only one thing: to be of use to the world. My skills, my trained mind should not be wasted – and, having prepared a detailed resume, I sent it to headhunting firms all over Europe. The first to respond was an agency from Switzerland, which offered a choice of three potential employers. One was in Bern – to me it seemed to be a sign. I wrote back that I was ready to come in for an interview.

Thus, the next big change in my life took place – I had come around full circle and ended up at one of its starting points. I soon realized I had done the right thing: now my work was quickly, almost immediately, rewarded with appreciation. My results were put to use right away; they were trusted, they were highly valued – and, in turn, I tried as best I could.

Our middle-size company was engaged in the microbiology of the brain – with an emphasis on the methods of its control. We had a "client," about which the management spoke with significant expressions on their faces. It was believed its name should be kept secret, although the aims of our operations were obvious. Obvious and not completely harmless – which did not bother me in the slightest.

I was paid good money for my math, and my skills were in great demand. My colleagues – biophysicists, neurophysiologists and psychologists – had only the most basic mathematical tools at their disposal. And the need for them was enormous: we had been accumulating a huge amount of data. On the condition of anonymity, difficult patients – schizophrenics and epileptics with electrodes implanted in their brains – were brought to us from clinics throughout the country. They were valuable specimens; with their help we could measure what was going on inside the brain, in the neocortex, responsible for the higher nervous functions. With the other subjects who were mostly healthy, it was only possible to work on the surface of the cranium, but the amount of information was increasing rapidly anyway, and there were problems processing it. Our researchers were drowning in it, hopelessly lost in the dark. It was my job to significantly improve the situation.

They gave me two programmers to help and were prepared to be patient, but they didn't have to wait long. Within three months, meaningful patterns – periodic curves, clusters of stable form, contours of distributions with pronounced maximums – began appearing on the graphs and diagrams. I removed the statistical noise, normalized the scales and put the data types in order, abstracted them, representing everything in a single way – with wave packets, averaging the activity of neurons at any distances and for any timeframe. Thus, we acquired a universal language describing what happens in the brain. Then I reorganized the information space, redefining it in other coordinates. The Hilbert transforms were very helpful – they allowed me to reduce the number of variables and select the main ones, reflecting the true dynamics of the whole system. My programmers also applied themselves diligently – and the terabytes of figures, which my colleagues had lost all hope of sorting out, were reduced to gigabytes, quite manageable and visualized in an appropriate way. Both previously accumulated and newly arrived data were now quickly transformed into images that were comprehensible to the eye. The scientific team took heart and rushed to rethink their hypotheses, and I acquired a reputation as the local genius who could solve problems regardless of their complexity and nature.

These first months I worked extremely hard, only taking breaks to sleep. But gradually, my methods were put into action and the need for my participation was reduced. Powerful computers digested the massive volumes of numbers, the printers diligently excreted graphs, and my colleagues were quite happy. From time to time, someone would ask me to recalculate something with different algorithms or with better accuracy, but this wasn't difficult and didn't take much time. I even began to get bored – but after a chance conversation with Tony, my boredom evaporated entirely.

Tony's group was researching memory. They studied the brain's reactions to external stimuli – pictures, words, melodies, both new and already familiar. The task was to find out exactly how memories are kept. To understand the storage mechanism and then learn to reach into people's heads with an invisible hand and take control of the process.

Things going on in the memory were now being described using the same universal language – the wave packets calculated by my programs. At first, the biologists got excited – it seemed their eyes had been opened. The parameters of the electromagnetic waves really did change from stimulus to stimulus. The brain reacted differently not only, say, to smells and photographs, but also to different smells and different photographs, while identical stimuli, in contrast, led to similar reactions, to similar charts and images on the screen...

The correlation was obvious, yes, but other problems immediately emerged. Brain reactions were similar but not completely alike. The correspondence between the stimuli and the patterns of the amplitudes and phases in the wave packets was not definite, and besides, the dynamics of these patterns puzzled everyone. It was impossible to explain why very different parts of the brain suddenly began to work in unison: the waves coming from them changed their amplitudes together and became synchronized – their phases seemed to "cling" to each other. This was contrary to the traditional view of the direct responsibility of certain neurons for certain fragments of memory. Memories were "blurred" almost throughout the entire neocortex – at least, that is what the experiment was asserting. And, what was even more inexplicable, the synchronization was established instantly – significantly faster than the neurons could "reach out" to each other.

Tony's group reacted in a way that was typical in corporate science: they closed their eyes to the inexplicable and tried to eke out a practical result from what they thought was more or less clear. In their heads was one and the same model: a fragment of memory is a group of neurons and their connections, a static imprint of the experience that can be identified and influenced. They put the inability to identify these groups down to inaccurate data – and rushed from one technique to another, endlessly changing the ways of recalculating. Therefore, I worked with them more often than with others.

One evening, Tony came to see me – tired, his eyes sad – and informed me of another setback. I began to ask questions purely out of sympathy, and we ended up talking until evening. It was then that I first heard about the problem of the spatial diffusion of memory and the instantaneous coordination of actions in different regions of the brain tissue when we try to memorize or recall something.

I asked, "Why not?" Tony explained, "Because it's just not physically possible." He drew me a detailed anatomic diagram of how an external stimulus – for example, a picture – is transformed into a signal that arrives in a certain place in the brain, to a local neuron group. Then, how the cells of this group fire messages to one another through synaptic connections[21] – and the more often the same picture appears before a person's eyes, the stronger these ties are, and the memory of it is more reliable. I nodded; everything made sense. "But," Tony said bitterly, "unfortunately, look here and here…"

---

21   A synapse is the place of contact between the nerve cells through which nerve impulses are transmitted.

We studied the printouts together – yes, there was no doubt: the behavior of the electromagnetic waves calculated during memorization-recall did not in any way confirm his model. Instead, *large* communities of neurons from *different* areas of the brain – not small localized groups – were working in concert. And it was not at all clear who was commanding them, who was giving the go-ahead and then monitoring the amazing synchrony of actions.

I asked, "What have other people found? Maybe it's only a matter of the accuracy of your measurements, and your instantaneous correlation is a decoy, a phantom?" Tony was offended, "We're not complete simpletons!" Then admitted, "At least, no more than anyone else." And he explained that this consistency had already been observed for decades, but no one had come up with a worthy explanation. Neurons "communicate" through electrochemistry – these processes have been studied well. It is known for certain that chemical reactions are way too slow, and the fields from ion currents are way too weak, to manifest themselves so quickly and at such distances. Therefore, everyone simply accepts as a reality that another means of "communication" exists, but no one has had time to find out what kind that might be.

"In any event, *I* don't have the time," Tony added irritably. "It'll have to be left to those who are engaged in *real science*! The pure scientists who like to boast that their hands have not been sullied by money and their souls by mammon. They have time on their side; they're not constantly being prodded in the back, but I – I need to solve the tasks set me by the management. For example, how to influence memory using an external high-frequency field. How to implant an electrode in a specific place and remove unnecessary recollections. How…" He moaned a bit more and then left. Perhaps he felt better afterward.

Once on my own, I postponed all business for the day and sat pondering. I pondered at home as well, until late evening, and then long into the night, lying awake, unable to sleep. I did not come up with anything intelligible, yet I realized the problem was of great interest to me, something I had not experienced for a long time. My gut feeling told me it contained a huge layer of the unknown. And what's more, I had time! By morning I had decided how I was going to proceed.

First of all, I had to figure out how the brain and memory work from the point of view of advanced science. I buried myself in articles and books and soon became convinced the phenomena Tony had told me about really did exist. Everything was as he said: nonlocal, instantaneously established correlation had long been observed in experiments. All these years, people had tried to ignore this – because no explanation could be found. The scientific mainstream, supported by all recognized experts, was still searching for "memory imprints" – the same ones that Tony's team was looking for. "Imprints" were understood to be small neuron groups responsible for specific memories. Money had been allocated for it and the media talked about it, conveying the concept of imprints to the curious wider public. Thus, everyone was moving in the same direction – without even trying to raise their heads, change their perspective or take a different viewpoint.

At the same time, the specifics of the interaction between neighboring neurons had been meticulously analyzed. Scientists had investigated to the finest detail how dendrites and axons[22] are arranged, how synapses work, how the connections between the brain cells are established and strengthened, creating the aforesaid imprints. It was all very fine but, from my point of view, did not bring us any nearer to understanding memory. Local groups of neurons – both inside and outside the imprints – certainly played some role, but only an intermediate one. Their function could not be the central one – not least because the imprints themselves were not all that stable. The brain tissue showed amazing plasticity, evolving and living a complex life – the brain was constantly reacting to the outside world, adjusting to it. Streams of stimuli, signals from receptors, led to the reorganization of neural connections, and it was impossible to predict in advance exactly where and how they would change – or, perhaps, disappear altogether. No neuron group – including "memory imprints" – could survive for even a month in a static, unchanged form. But our memories are tenacious – many of them remain for decades…

Thus, the following picture evolved. Experiments had shown that memory is nonlocal. From our own experience, we knew that memory

---

22   The structural elements of neural cells.

is stable. Neuron-synaptic models explained neither the nonlocality of memory-recall nor the stability of the memory. And although research-ers, with incredible stubbornness, continued to look for answers within the framework of the classical imprint doctrine, it was clear that this path led to a dead end.

In particular, I became aware of two things. First, when studying how memory works, one must consider neither individual neurons nor their local groups but the brain as a whole. Nothing can be explained by moving through the synapses from neuron to neuron; the neurons do not engage in the recall process one by one, interacting just with their neigh-bors; they all work at once, each cooperating with each other regardless of their location. And second, the mechanism of the nonlocal interaction of neurons was the key to unraveling the mystery. The spatial correlation Tony observed, which instantly arises during memorization or recall, is not a secondary effect that can be dismissed but the very essence of the phenomenon. This mechanism is triggered by an external stimulus – a smell, a word, a face in a crowd – but then acts by itself, providing some dynamic that is unknown to us. A fragment of memory is not an element of structure. It is not an imprint involving a particular group of neurons; it is some kind of dynamic process.

I began to read the articles again – looking now for alternatives to the generally accepted approaches. For about a month, I had rifled through everything that had been published recently – in an attempt to find allies who would understand the problem the same way I did. There were almost none; for the vast majority, memory was associated not with dynamics but with static, structural elements. Some had tried to interpret the plasticity, the reorganization of synaptic connections, as a dynamic mechanism of memorization – but this, in my opinion, was naive and did not explain anything.

I almost despaired, nearly resigning myself to the fact that the mys-tery of memory is unresolvable – and then a work published as long as thirty years ago caught my eye. I glanced at the annotation and was aston-ished. And felt something vital had slotted into place.

A long, long time ago, the author had taken a step that I had lacked the spirit to take. He had seen what I saw: the same long-range correlations throughout the brain, the same stability of memories, the independence of memory from the fate of individual cells. He, like me, and contrary to the prevailing views, had realized that we need to step away from electrochemistry and locality – to accept that neurons and synapses are not enough. Yes, they play a part in memorization but only by acting together with something else... All this was familiar – the same thoughts tormented me as well – but the author had gone a step further and had made a breakthrough. Assuming there is *something* different, he disengaged himself from specifics. He began to seek an explanation in pure mathematics – firmly believing that a consistent mathematical theory always corresponds to some kind of physical one that, perhaps, we are not yet aware of. He looked at the problem from above, with an unbiased eye, asking the question: What *in principle* could be the explanation for the properties of memory regardless of the known components of the brain? And he saw what it might be and was not afraid to proclaim it out loud.

I cursed myself roundly for having wasted so much time in vain. Now, in hindsight, it seemed I had always sensed what it was all like but had not dared to admit it. It had just been too strange to think about quantum fields and the condensate of bosons in warm, wet matter. The word "quantum" should be forbidden, forgotten: the human brain was a macro-, not a micro-, world. Neurons and biomolecules were too large and distant from each other to be considered quantum objects... But what if we assume some other hypothetical "agents" exist in the brain and live in accordance with quantum laws? They needed to be extremely small; there might be an almost infinite number of them – and here the physics I knew so well could come to the rescue. More than once it had manifested itself where there seemed to be no place for it – throwing a bridge between the micro and macro, explaining how the micro-level order becomes macroscopic, observable with the naked eye and stable for centuries. Just take crystals for example – no one would consider a diamond to be something imaginary and unsteady...

I finally sensed where the key to the mystery lay. The order that comes out of disorder, the asymmetry that comes out of symmetry... I said in a low voice, and then repeated out loud, "This is it, the 'cunning trick'; it has raised its head and is peeping out from under the covers." I myself had been uncovering it many times – even if in another medium and at other energy scales. I could not break free from my science, no matter how I tried!

I hurriedly looked through the article – some of its notions seemed naive in the context of modern science, but the main idea had been stated clearly. I knew exactly what now was required of me. The author was long dead, but I was alive, and I was capable of doing much. I sat down at the table, wrote out on a piece of paper the Hamiltonian of a quantum system consisting of many interacting particles and immediately sensed a feeling of utmost harmony enveloping me. Once again, I was back where I belonged and doing what I do best.

CHAPTER 15

MY COLLEAGUE, IN his article published long ago, had only outlined the basic principles. Memory, he wrote, is formed by *two* related mechanisms, not just one based solely on neural cells. Neurons enter into the game first: responding to external stimuli, they begin to "fire" electrical impulses. But their role is auxiliary – through their activity, they only help other participants living in the microworld. Neural signals trigger not the classical but *quantum* dynamics of the hypothetical micro-objects that fill the entire space of the brain. Disordered initially, they transform into a state of stable order and maintain this order, like atoms in crystals, exchanging quasiparticles – collective excitations, the waves of some sort of field. These quasiparticle-waves create an oscillatory background that affects the neurons and in turn regulates and coordinates their work. This dynamic interplay between neurons and micro-objects is a fragment of the memory, and the collective oscillations are some kind of code that, once it emerges, is stably stored in the brain. It condenses in the lowest energy state, the so-called ground state, and can then be reactivated by a familiar stimulus – forcing the brain to enter into the same dynamics, "recalling" what was remembered earlier.

Thus, the brain – or, more precisely, the part of it responsible for memory – was considered as a single whole, where all components simultaneously interact with each other. This fundamentally differed from the traditional models based on the individual elements of the whole "seeing and hearing" only their nearest neighbors. The two main things – the nonlocality and stability of memory – were now explained in a natural way: first, the oscillations of quantum micro-objects were distributed throughout the entire brain, so that each point instantly received information from the other points regardless of the distance between them; and second, these oscillations require almost no energy in their ground state. They do not die out like classical macrowaves; they are capable of living in the brain for a very long time: in ideal conditions, forever...

The author did not attempt to identify these micro-objects; he just postulated that they existed. And he demonstrated with precise mathematics how their presence could cause the observed memory properties. I repeated his calculations – everything was right. Out of disorder – suddenly, spontaneously – order arose, reducing the dynamic symmetry of the system and leading to the emergence of quasiparticles, bosons of a certain type that preserved this order, kept it in place. If those oscillations-bosons really modulated the way neurons work, then all the oddities on Tony's diagrams would have been logically explained. And the neurons played their role too: they gave a push, they initiated the spontaneous symmetry breaking, thus launching the mechanism for the formation of order. Probably, I thought, among these neuron activators there are very important ones, sitting at key points – could they be the "imprints of memory" that mainstream science was so preoccupied with? Yes, you can damage memory by killing individual neurons – but the memory is still not stored in them; they are just a means, a trigger...

Within a week or two I was assured of the potential power of the combined neuron-quantum paradigm. I was assured – and right then hit a wall, got stuck by the fundamental question: But what exactly are these "quantum micro-objects"? I was not going to accept anything mystical; they had to be perfectly natural, habitually material... At first, I didn't have a clue and even began to fear the puzzle would remain unresolved. But pretty soon I found a solution – or, to be more precise, it had been found before me.

It turned out the thirty-year-old theory had undergone some development. Several people had picked it up during a surge of interest a while back, and one came up with a very simple idea: the mysterious "micro-objects" were nothing other than water molecules, which as everyone knows make up ninety percent of the brain. After reading about this, I was amazed at how obvious his guess had been – and wondered why it hadn't occurred to me. In hindsight, it was all so clear: of course, water molecules are small enough and possess a dipole moment, which has rotational symmetry. This rotational symmetry gets broken – crudely speaking, the dipole vectors become aligned in one direction. An order emerges and the released energy is transformed into joint vibrations, which eventually pass to their ground state and remain there – always ready to be excited again. It's so natural to assume this if you simply write down the levels of organization of living matter: cells – macromolecules – water!

Surprisingly, this was the last significant breakthrough in the "quantum" model of the brain. Soon, related articles stopped appearing: no one wanted to spend time either in criticism of this theory or in its progress. The interest of the scientific world dissipated, having barely been piqued – due, I'd guess, to the overall complexity of the model as well as the impossibility of its practical verification. Without an experimental proof, the chances of the benefits – generous grants and publications in prestigious journals – decrease rapidly to naught. Fortunately, I needed neither publications nor grants. I sensed the approach's potential and could afford to spend time on it. As much time as it would take.

And I proceeded further: I had to move from the *ideal*, infinite and cold "brain space" isolated from information noise to a *real* case – to a finite brain that lives in a certain thermal regime and is bombarded by signals from a multitude of receptors. Water dipoles appeared before my eyes as if they were alive. And indeed they were – first, they oscillated, vibrated all the time; and second, they supported memory, thought, the essence of our lives. It might seem their orderliness was fleeting, unstable. They had many enemies – thermal effects, quantum fluctuations, the constant discordance of signaling neurons. But some things worked in their favor too – for example, the unique property of quantum field theory, so-called negative entropy: quantum order was energetically more favorable than disorder! The breakout of symmetry "released" part of the energy, like setting a ball in motion down a hill; this reinforced the stability of the ordered patterns – and, so, strengthened the memory, prevented it from dissipating, dissolving. And it gave additional strength to me; I felt that the microcosm was on my side!

Of course, in a limited, not infinite space, the life of the quantum condensate, which coded memory, became finite, and the Goldstone bosons acquired the prefix "quasi" – they gained mass and used up energy, albeit only a little. And the areas of coherence, of the synchronous operation of remote neurons, also became different, ranging from extensive to very small ones, from large parts of the brain to only a few hundred cells. Much, though not all, depended on the subject of the memorization – on how much the brain allowed itself to "concentrate" and linger on something. How long the neurons have been signaling about that something – say, a pungent smell or a beautiful face – into the water matrix, into the space of the dipoles, expanding the limits of their influences. The "reminders," repeated stimuli, were important too – they supported coherence and widened its boundaries... All this, taken together, brought the theory closer to reality: the brain modeled on paper began to live, to change its states, constantly moving from symmetrical to asymmetrical phases, not freezing in one infinite, perpetual order, as in eternal ice or a hard crystal. Some fragments of memory vanished in a few moments, forgotten, erased by fluctuations; others were remembered for a long time and recalled easily, always ready "at hand." Everything looked as if it were in my own head – maybe not exactly but quite similar!

Then I went on to study the connection between dipole waves and neurons, to establish the link between the quantum micro and the classical macro. It was necessary to at least demonstrate the possibility of the interaction, to reveal its probable mechanism. The search for "intermediaries" between neurons and water dipoles took a while – I had to read a lot of scientific books and articles to get to the tiniest details of the structure of the neural cells. Finally, I understood: the answer was hidden in microscopic threadlike protein structures – countless intertwined filaments creating their own intricate networks, distinct from the network of neurons, both inside and outside the brain cells. Excitations of the electromagnetic field propagated along them, giving a push to the ordering of the water molecules, and this order was "felt" by other filaments, in other cells as far away as you like. Thus, neurons, without knowing it themselves, sent each other instantaneous signals at great distances, coordinating their work. The coherence of water dipoles determined the correlation of the work of the neurons, which was established very quickly and was preserved for a long time!

Dutifully, I paid a lot of attention to the temperature effects – they represented a great danger. Quantum condensate in a warm, living environment – it sounded suspicious, even a bit wild. Everything turned out all right, however. The concentration of bosons, collective oscillations, was sufficient to withstand thermal energy, to erect a barrier between the symmetrical and asymmetric. They did not allow memory to be erased, to return the brain to a state of forgetfulness, an empty sheet. Moreover, a significant part of the water matrix was penetrated and permeated with the same protein filaments. Their elements possessed their own dipole moments and, involuntarily, helped to fight attempts at reestablishing disorder – as if "sensing" that a coherent state is the most advantageous one and protecting it, providing a screen, a defense…

In about six months it became more or less clear to me: the idea proposed thirty years ago did not contradict the observed facts nor the biophysics we now know and accept. My calculations indirectly confirmed: it is quite possible that our brain functions precisely in this way and our memories are not static "imprints" but resonances of dipole waves interacting with neurons throughout the neocortex. It is in these waves, in the excitations of the dipole matrix, with a lifespan of a couple of seconds to dozens of years, that everything we remember is encoded.

I tried to talk about this with Tony once or twice, but with little success; he showed almost no interest. I think he did not understand much – quantum field theory was too alien to him. But at the same time his sad, yearning look pushed me onward. I felt responsible: for the quantum model of the brain, which, having been someone else's, had now become my own; for the efforts of Tony, his group, for everyone else, daring to try to get close to the most important of mysteries – how we remember and think. There was no high-flown ambition behind this; I only knew I had to give it my all and keep advancing. And there were plenty of advances to be made – so far, despite my model's strong points, I could not solve its main problem: why new fragments of memory, while "entering" the brain, do not make the old ones disappear forever.

The system of water dipoles coding the memory had one undeniable property: its states could not pass into each other. Once the dipole matrix had fallen into an energy minimum and been placed into some kind of order, it could not be "reordered" in any other way. The system needed to jump "upward," to again approach toward symmetry, toward disorder – and only then to slide into another local vacuum, having encoded something new. The problem was that the old code was erased during this process. Mathematics demonstrated that two different orders – two different memories – could not exist simultaneously without interfering with each other.

This appeared to draw a fat red line through my theory, but I did not allow myself to become discouraged. I knew the model was correct, I felt it with every fiber in my being – but at the same time I could see no way out of the impasse. Of course, one could consider the spatial division of ordered areas, but this assumption seemed far-fetched. It was clear to me that each memory could be encoded on as large an area as you like – it could even be the entire brain at once; otherwise, the whole point of the concept would be lost. The brain cannot be divided into many small principalities, each of which is responsible for its own allotted recollection. No, as I had already told myself many times, the solution lay not in the structure but somewhere in the dynamics. It was obvious that I hadn't fully understood the dynamics; I was missing the most important part.

Until a decent idea presented itself, I decided to bring the model closer to reality – in particular, to take into account thermal energy exchange with the environment. The brain is a very thermostatic system, its temperature being almost constant – therefore I did not expect any surprises from the thermal exchange. Nevertheless, I decided to pay some attention to this aspect.

It was not easy to introduce this into my equations – and I felt a bit unsure. Quantum field theories, as a rule, deal with isolated systems, whose total energy remains constant. They prefer not to bother with dissipation, but there had still been attempts to formalize it properly. And one of them gave me the impetus to make a breakthrough.

The approach was based on the idea of describing the environment subjectively, as it is "seen" by a quantum system immersed in it – for example, by the brain. This subjective image was represented by a similar system with the same number of components but reversed along the time axis. The system seemed to interact with its own reflection in the mirror of time – strange as this sounded, the authors showed that the energetic balance with the environment was strictly maintained in this way.

Initially, I did not give this work much attention until suddenly I began to feel something nagging at me from the inside, some elusive idea that was about to surface. It revealed itself when I was in the shower, getting warm under the hot water. "Here it is: heat exchange," I muttered to myself ironically, groping around for that slippery train of thought. Then I sighed and drew an unhappy smiley face on the steamed-up wall of the shower cubicle – and looked in the mirror, where my emoticon was reflected. For some reason, I rubbed out the downward smile and drew it back the other way up. The picture in the mirror changed accordingly. The face with its curved smiling mouth continued to look at me with displeasure – as if irritated by my stupidity. "It's still looking at me in the same way," I thought to myself. "Maintaining its balance – its, ha-ha, emotional balance… But on the wall, the face has become different!"

I jumped out of the shower, hastily dried myself and ran to the table. I began to write things down – using words rather than formulas and scratching the paper: thermal transfer means doubling the degrees of freedom. The ban on the transition of stable states into each other refers to a *duplicated* system. To the totality – to the brain plus the environment – and not just the brain alone!

Adding an exclamation mark, I looked for a while at the sentences jumping out at me. Then I got dressed and sat down to work – calmly, realizing that the decisive step had already been taken. It just needed to be described mathematically. I doubled the number of oscillation modes holding the system in an ordered state, adding "reflections" coming from outside, and – observing the energy balance – equalized the contributions of the direct and reflected quanta. This gave me a basic equation specifying the constraints on all the dynamics. The solution turned out to be easy; I singled out those parts that corresponded to the states of the brain – as one would expect, these were *different* patterns of excitations. Different states of memory, independent of each other, arising every moment and living of their own accord. The brain was creating them, adjusting to the surrounding environment, which is always different. Thus, the brain was getting enriched by experiences, as if by frames on a photographic film. And the state of the entire system – the brain plus the external world – was localized in proximity to the same energy minimum, rising slightly above it and falling into it again!

I realized: the capacity problem in my model had been resolved. Different quantum condensates – different modes of dipole waves, encoding a multitude of memories – coexist simultaneously, like a myriad of colored shades in a single beam of white light. They are waiting for their time to be activated, at the signal of certain neural groups, to become dominant for a brief moment – as a fleeting recollection or thought – or perhaps for a long time, if the corresponding stimulus is persistent enough. Then they are replaced by others – "coded" in the dipole matrix or emerging anew. The brain works tirelessly, gathering new experiences and adding them to those that have already been accumulated, and none of them interfere with each other. And the guarantee for this is the ever-changing surrounding world, which the brain senses through receptors, cerebral fluids, the capillaries and blood vessels. The brain interacts with its environment constantly, every moment while it's alive – this interaction is the substance of its existence, like the existence of any other type of living matter!

Everything fell into place; my quantum model became logically complete. It was amazing – to see through abstract formulas how memories were created and stored, how they gradually blurred and died. How they were activated, summoned into life – some more willingly than others, but for each of them, at least a little bit of work was required. It was natural – otherwise, it would be impossible to dwell on a single notion. Consciousness would simply jump from one recollection to another; the process of thought would become impossible. At the same time, the transition between energy minimums was fast and fluent: interaction with the outside world provided agility and flexibility of thinking... Flexibility of thinking... *Thinking* ...

And here, at this point, on that very word I felt like I had been doused with icy water. The delight of comprehension turned into confusion and vexation – I sensed, almost physically, that once again I was hitting a brick wall. Yes, I understood – in general – how we *remember* but still had no idea how we *think*. My model described in detail direct links between external stimuli and brain responses, but this was only suitable for very basic functions. For animal instincts and the ability to survive – but not for an intelligent human being, capable of fathoming thoughts immeasurably beyond our feral needs.

From scattered fragments of memory I needed to advance toward the connections between them, to the transitions of one to another, and then to associations, categorization, abstractions… I knew this was a huge step, one could say a leap across the abyss. Reflecting on this, I felt I was failing – and, in addition, other memory issues remained unclear. I could not understand what makes us able to distinguish subtle details with such confidence – for example, how we recognize a familiar face in the crowd, having only glanced briefly and obliquely at it from a distance. How a few carelessly sung notes allow us to recall the entire melody; how a chance phrase in a conversation reveals all the weaknesses of a companion – even if we had never heard those exact words from him…

The stimuli are never identical; they can be similar but no more than that. How does our brain nevertheless infallibly and instantaneously choose the correct memory without getting it confused with others? I was convinced that a certain general principle was behind all this, according to which the states of the brain are organized and interconnected – so that navigation between them is carried out with astonishing efficiency. And I didn't even have an inkling of this principle, this underlying fundamental law. I had no decent ideas – until… Until I met Kirill.

CHAPTER 16

I'M SITTING IN the armchair in front of the screen, glancing at my watch for the hundredth time. Something strange is happening: the evening session has been delayed – and not through any fault of my own. The screen is dark, Nestor is not there, and this is completely inexplicable.

At seven minutes past five, I begin to panic. It seems to me that my mentor will never appear. That no one will appear – with difficulty I suppress a desire to rush into Elsa's bedroom and make sure she is still here. I force myself to calm down – this is ridiculous, of course. It's just my nerves, my tortuous attempts to move on with my physics, to recall more…

"Everything's fine, fine," I mutter aloud, and at that moment the screen comes to life. Nestor seems the same as usual; he is focused, neatly dressed. I look inquiringly, but it doesn't even occur to him to apologize. I'm not offended, however; I'm too glad to see him. I even forget my determination not to ask for any assistance and instead of greeting him blurt out, "Nestor, I need help!"

"Yes, of course," he says and inclines his head to one side. Now that my theory has begun to take on features, Nestor has changed again; he has stopped nagging and has turned into an efficient manager. "What do you need – my opinion? Information? Friendly support?"

I explain, trying to sound calm, "I'm at an important stage, but I'm treading water. I know there is a key – it goes by the name of Kirill. The key is in the word – it is a *key* word, leading to a key idea that isn't coming to me. Leading to a thought about thoughts – what do you say about this?"

I am being deliberately inarticulate, and Nestor, of course, recognizes this. He looks down and says importantly, "Well. The name Kirill is in your file." Then he adds, "You're right about the key. You are approaching something – it's a serious moment. I can help you but please bear in mind that by doing this, I'm taking a risk. I'm risking giving you a false hint, confusing you. Fooling you with a thought about thoughts. And at the same time – no matter what I do, you'll achieve your goal, stumble across the focal point. A paradox? – Yes, it's a *key* paradox. Yet at the moment you won't understand its essence…"

He is evidently mimicking me with his choice of words. "Of course I won't; I'm not smart enough," I say, offended.

Nestor nods, "Perhaps, that is so! But don't worry, no one else in your place would understand either. You only have to believe: a false hint is a false idea… A false idea doesn't have the right face. A false face, a *lying* face, ha-ha-ha!"

As I fall asleep, I think with irritation – it's easy to talk in riddles, to shroud everything in fog. To make someone lose their train of thought – why do we not lose track of our thoughts all the time? Even in spite of all the hints… I reflect with the last ounce of my strength, and then I fall into the darkness. Into the dream Nestor has chosen for me, a dream about Bern – as I knew it in my maturity, not in my youth.

The city had not changed, but I had become different – and immediately realized I was no longer afraid of its sated, self-satisfied quagmire. Its essence now lay not in the gleam of the store windows, not in its bourgeois well-being, but in the fine rain, the tedious drizzle that poured down from the sky day in day out, without ceasing. Passers-by huddled under the arcades, in the twilight of the covered galleries, caught in the shopkeepers' clinging tentacles. The central part of the city seemed to be ensnared in an invisible enticing web. Rain and shopping galleries – it was a combined idea, a conspiracy against consumers' wallets.

It was crowded under the arcades but the streets themselves were empty. I was wandering alone along the wet sidewalks, the hood of my raincoat up. The city had little to offer me; it no longer had any riddles or secrets. There was neither Gunter nor Professor Kertner, and the intoxicating spirit of learning was long gone. Only a trace of Albert Einstein remained.

One time, I went into the university and was struck by its shabbiness. In the building where my old department had been located, everything screamed of lack and want. Ascending to the second floor, I peeked into the library and read the timetables for the seminars. Their subjects were impressive; researchers here were still engaged in serious matters. And the world continued to allocate to them pittances, crumbs, spending the rest on toys for the crowd... I went out into the street, to the observation deck named in honor of Einstein – and for the first time noticed it overlooked railway tracks covered with litter. In front of me were the dirty concrete and the unsightly graffiti – and beyond sneered a wealthy city with no desire to know anything about science in general, let alone a small gathering of theoretical physicists breaking into the very secrets of the universe.

On the weekends, I would sometimes go to Einstein's apartment to gaze at the two cramped rooms and the rickety dressing screen, at the baby carriage for his small child who probably cried at night. I looked at his ads offering lessons for three francs an hour, at a blunt reference letter from a professor from Zurich stating that Einstein was not an able student, that physics was too complex for him and he should try doing something else... Afterward, I always felt the need for broader horizons, a wide-open space – so I turned toward the Theaterplatz and headed out onto the bridge, to the river, where there was a lot of light, despite the cloudy sky. I'd walk in the riverside park for a while; then I would return to the enclosed web of galleries and arcades, to the traps for the deep-pocketed, to the crowds of tourists and the bourgeois insularity of their views. And there, as if to spite my surroundings, I would think again and again about the might and power of the human mind. For the umpteenth time, I would try to imagine how analogies and associations are created. How the leaps are made from specific details to generalizations, to abstractions. Why do thoughts that seem to be inspired by very different motivations converge? Why does our brain not get lost in a maze of constantly changing states but confidently finds a way to a correct conclusion?...

I knew the questions but had no answers. Understanding would not come; all hypotheses seemed fruitless. I despaired, I was angry with myself. And then – then I met Kirill.

It so happened that in the evening, after dinner, I went to the bar of one of the hotels. The place was crowded – the hotel was hosting a symposium of cardiologists. With difficulty, I found an empty table, and a few minutes later a stranger joined me. He looked slovenly and somewhat arrogant, but I didn't have the strength to turn him away.

He sat down and introduced himself, "I'm Kirill." Then he awkwardly shook his head and dropped a napkin on the floor. I told him my name in reply and out of politeness asked, "You're probably a cardiologist?"

Kirill immediately started up, "Certainly not! I'm a mathematician!" And he asked with evident sarcasm, "And you I suppose are a doctor?"

After hearing I was a theoretical physicist, he nodded indifferently and lost interest in me. I was struck by his vain posturing. "And what do you specialize in?" I asked in an equally indifferent voice, showing I couldn't be bothered about him either.

Despite this, Kirill's eyes lit up. "In a subject that's more natural than all others!" he declared hotly. "In something that keeps the whole world running. You probably know about dynamic chaos – which is, in truth, deterministic, not chaotic; it obeys an indisputable order. I'm trying to enlighten these ignoramuses on how the human heart actually works."

His tone was comical, but I saw that his posing was not without foundation. "We, in some ways, are allies," I told him. "So, how's your enlightenment going?"

"Not particularly well," Kirill admitted and had just started complaining about his colleagues when a waitress brought him a coffee. He immediately made a scene with her, claiming he had ordered something else and appearing even more unpleasant than before. He was sarcastic and rude, knowing the woman couldn't answer him back. I felt ashamed and almost decided to pay up and leave, but the dispute ended, Kirill returned to his science and his manner changed abruptly. I glanced at him and was amazed at how utterly inept he was in every respect – except for his highly trained mind.

"You, of course, will immediately start looking for a contradiction!" he exclaimed. "Determinism is predictability, reproducibility; chaos is exactly the opposite. You think I painted myself into a corner – but no, I did not! The behavior of a nonlinear system appears chaotic at first glance; it seems *random* – but that's only because we aren't attentive enough. It's just that a tiny initial difference – a micron – quickly leads to a huge divergence in what happens later. You've probably heard about the so-called butterfly effect. I'm sure you are no stranger to pop culture..."

He accusingly jabbed his finger at me, but I didn't take offence; I was listening with ever-greater interest. "So, it turns out," Kirill continued, "you launch a double pendulum a thousand times, and it produces a thousand completely different curves. You may think this is a matter of chance, and you hastily put a label on it – but you're wrong: the randomness of the pendulum is not real; it is a phantom, a ghost. What's the difference, you may ask, between two kinds of randomness, imaginary and authentic? You'll ask, and I will answer: the difference, the principal disparity, is causality. It is precisely the presence and absence of causality that distinguishes between traditional and deterministic chaos. When a system behaves erratically under the influence of unrelated events, this chaos is true, it is real. It can only be averaged out by statistics, which, you will agree, is not interesting: statistics emasculates the essentials. But, when connections between events emerge – as the literati say, *things happen for a reason* – 'chaos' becomes predetermined; it can be studied; one can look into its depths. And there, in the depths, amazing events take place – always, everywhere, in the heart, in living... Real chaos is death, but deterministic chaos is life!"

I listened to this unkempt man, I looked into his eyes, in which at that moment the cosmos was reflected, and it seemed I was hearing great music, the purest of melodies. And the reflected cosmos resounded, it lived – in accordance with some higher order. I sensed that this mode of existence is the most precise, the truest.

"But!" Kirill exclaimed. "But, looking into the depths, you cannot restrain the nature of disorder, even if the most comprehensible reasons explain it. The first to understand this was Poincaré, a Frenchman, who was objecting to another Frenchman, Laplace. You may remember that the latter asserted: if we learn all the connections between the heavenly bodies, then we'll be able to calculate at any moment their mutual positions and influences on each other... He thought he was singing a hymn to the human mind, but in fact he was only underlining its, the mind's, overconfidence and naivety. And Poincaré demonstrated this with just a few bodies – three were enough. The disorder immediately raised its head and, with a flick of its mighty tail, sent Laplace's dreams crashing to earth. Understandably, Poincaré became pessimistic – no predictions are possible in unstable systems, he declared. And I quote: 'An absolutely insignificant reason, eluding us in its minuteness, can cause a substantial effect that we cannot foresee. We have a random phenomenon before us...' – and here he was not quite right. But it was tough for him: he did not have a computer; he could not study phase portraits over and over, as we do. And yet he – a great man – proposed that a nonlinear dynamic regime, a deterministic chaos, is recognizable in its own way! He described – romantically, in the French manner – what an attractor, a portrait of chaos, an image of nonlinear dynamics, might be.

"Of course, you know what an attractor is?" Kirill looked straight into my face. "A state of equilibrium, for example – simply a point; periodic motion – a closed curve, a so-called limit cycle... Now we know: 'chaotic' systems also have attractors, their 'disorder' converging toward certain trajectories. Only these attractors are atypical – they are strange, and so they are called: *strange* attractors. Nonlinear dynamics is nonperiodic – therefore the phase trajectories do not intersect. The nonlinear regime is unstable – thus the system easily jumps from one section of the attractor to another. Here again, it is appropriate to recall the butterfly effect – and it's funny that strange attractors sometimes resemble butterfly wings, but the most amazing thing is how correctly Poincaré described them. 'Something like a lattice, a fabric, a net with infinitely tight loops; none of the curves should ever intersect themselves but should coil themselves up in a very complex way to intertwine an infinite number of times...' Think about it – sounds like poetry, right? And he saw it all with just his inner vision, without having a powerful processor or a multipixel screen!"

Scorching myself, I swallowed hot coffee, my third or fourth cup already. In my head, the parts of the puzzle were quickly falling into place. And Kirill carried on, "Deterministic chaos is a rule, not an exception! It is everywhere, it imposes itself on us, and we – we turn our heads away, pretending not to notice. We are trying to remove the noise, smooth up the fluctuations, *linearize* – oh, it's a terrible thing, linearization! Linear approaches, linear minds… Of course, it's easier like that – otherwise you would need art, not just craft. You yourself know very well that nonlinear equations in general cannot be solved…"

He decried the short-sightedness of the world, and I nodded back, sensing, almost physically, that I was finally about to understand – both memory and thought. Understand how the brain builds chains of reasoning, categorizes and generalizes, moves from subject to object, associating one with the other. I had just heard of deterministic chaos for the first time, and yet I had become immediately convinced it was the source of the order I needed. I didn't know anything about attractors, but somehow I realized it was they that act as the navigators in the brain's manifold states.

We stayed up very late. I barely asked any questions and made no notes; I just listened. The next morning, I realized that I remembered and understood everything. The concept of an attractor was obviously connected with the principle of minimal energy. I roughly estimated the properties of phase trajectories, minimizing the free energy of my system. As expected, they satisfied the conditions of deterministic chaos. The superposition of the brain's stable states was an attractor of a certain type – the same strange attractor Kirill had been talking about. An intricate figure Poincaré had described, much more complex than ordinary circles and spirals…

I immersed myself in chaos theory – wondering how I could have gone so long without it. Little by little a new picture of the dynamics of the brain was emerging – and I sensed it was accurate and true. The brain, recalling a familiar smell or word or, say, reanalyzing an idea that has already been formulated, "moves" through states that are close to those that had once been formed and "encoded" in the quantum condensate. The brain's accumulated experiences, as well as the thoughts linking them together, are mapped into a hierarchy of converging trajectories: attractors in the space of states, attractors in the space of attractors, attractors in the space of attractors within the space of attractors, and so on. It was categorization, abstraction through the hierarchy of attractors, that explained both the incredible sensitivity of the brain to external stimuli and the flexibility of human thinking, the ability to form thoughts through associations and analogies. Events that evoke memories – for example, the flash of a face in the crowd, or the slightest trace of a smell – did not lead directly to the goal. They only defined the regions of the "attractors' landscape" at different levels of abstraction. And then the brain "swirled in," as if through a funnel, into the desired area of the phase space, entered the required dynamic mode deterministically and purposefully, obeying the laws of chaos, which was not chaos but the highest order. Order, defining the laws of thinking!

The recognition path went "down" from categories to specifics, but specific memories and thoughts could also "ascend" toward abstractions – and not necessarily to those with which the thinking process had started. The smell of wine could remind one of a wine stain on a tablecloth; this, in turn, might elicit the color of the dress worn by a woman once loved; and that might lead to thoughts of love, infidelity, loyalty and betrayal, transience and the meaning of life. From information to fragments of knowledge; from words to meanings – this was the essence of cognition, the essence of the mind's power. Now I could imagine the details of this process with ease, as the most natural thing. Neurons fired signals, providing the boundary conditions, allowing the "fall" into the necessary attractors, the re-creation of familiar dynamic modes. The corresponding types of dipole waves resonated, "jumped up" to higher energy levels – and in turn affected the neurons, controlling their signals. Or, if the information was new, then no resonances would emerge; the entire system of neurons and dipoles would pass through new chains of states, new attractors would appear and their codes would be added to the quantum condensate. That's how everything we think, rethink and remember is created and summoned to life.

The question arose: What provides the "mobility" of thinking – transitions from one memory to another, from image to image, from word to word? How does our brain "reselect" attractors, moving from thought to thought? The answer came easily – I just had to take a close look at the properties of encephalograms. The coherence of neural groups would arise almost instantaneously. The unity would be created in large regions, live for a couple of hundred milliseconds, then disappear for a dozen milliseconds, then reappear, but in some other areas – these were the very same patterns Tony's group was observing. Now I understood their meaning perfectly. There were pauses in the stream of "thoughts," moments of a loss of coherence – a return to disorder, thanks to which the brain could move freely from attractor to attractor at any level of abstraction. Dynamic modes replaced each other abruptly, in rapid leaps. This opened the way for analogies and associations, generalizations or, conversely, for concentration on particulars. This also ensured a constant readiness to respond to a new stimulus, to accept a new challenge from the outside world.

Soon it also became clear to me what the purpose of the brain's plasticity was, of its relentless, scrupulous restructuring of neural connections. The aforementioned "memory imprints" were, in fact, a "map of the terrain," the result of the adaptation of brain tissue to the prevailing order of thoughts, to the types of the mind's work that currently were the most important. Speed and clarity of thinking were provided by optimal initial conditions – the "push," after which the ball rolls down the hill in the right direction. Neurons, sending signals to the system of water dipoles, provided this push – helping to choose the correct subspace of attractors and to "leap" swiftly to the most suitable among them. Synapses, neural connections, formed a "landscape of attractors," delineated boundaries, placed survey markers. Each individual brain seemed to adapt anatomically to the most frequent, intense memorization, recollections, reflections. It adapted to them but did not imprint them – contrary to the popular "neural doctrine." Synaptic connections only represented the extent to which a particular brain is adjusted to the realities, agile and able. Memory and thinking are the prerogative of a *trained* brain, not a brain "full of neural records" in contrast to an "empty" one!

This explained so much! This allowed human beings to develop themselves, to become smarter, to improve their "picture of the world." The more often each specific brain passes through a particular dynamic process, the easier it can return to this process – this *is* learning, training. The more often you think about something, the longer you remember it, the less effort you need to come back to this subject. And, after coming back to it, to move forward toward new hypotheses and ideas…

So, the concept of deterministic chaos put everything in its place. The main principle of the dynamics of the brain was now completely clear. I knew, I felt: a thought, a memory is a "strange" attractor and it cannot be otherwise. And of course, I wanted to look at the thought-attractor eye to eye. I set out to re-create it on paper or on the monitor screen – to get a phase portrait of the process underlying intelligent life.

Of course, this was a very ambitious task. A consistent whole would need to be deduced from fragmentary, incomplete specifics. I began reconstructing the phase space from data sets – combining and comparing the amplitudes and phases of the neural waves at different moments in time. And I made a bold assumption, which turned out to be correct: I proposed that the form of the attractor should be the same at all levels of the brain's functioning – when responding to stimuli like smells and sounds, when converting memories to words, and when abstracting, generalizing. That helped; similar structures started to appear in the streams of data. For a long time, I could not visualize them properly, but I finally found the solution – the coordinate structure in which the encephalograms obtained from different patients under different circumstances were projected into similar curves. Taken together they formed a picture – an attractor, localized in an enclosed space. I investigated this as far as was possible – and yes, indeed, it was "chaotic," it was "strange": the system never repeated itself; the line did not intersect but gradually filled a certain region, interwoven in the most complicated way. This was a portrait of the dynamics of the mind, the crown of evolution. I gave it a name – the "face of thought." I printed it, hung it over my desk and looked at it for a long time as if trying to reach even further, deeper. And then I got on the tram and went to Bern University.

I climbed the long stairs to the physics faculty building and went to the back entrance, leading to the Albert Einstein observation deck. I looked around, glanced down at the graffiti and railroad tracks. Then I came up to the memorial plaque, made a curt bow and said, "Thank you. You gave me the courage."

And apart from Einstein, there wasn't really anyone I could talk to. I realized this especially keenly when I wandered one day into Tony's group's seminar. They were discussing the same old problem: Why does one and the same stimulus – in this case, a smell – elicit brain reactions that are not one hundred percent similar? Why is the correspondence between the stimulus and the neuron activity only approximate, albeit statistically significant? Why does the intensity of the stimulus change almost nothing?…

The biologists were arguing fiercely and tirelessly, but I could see they were going around in circles. It was not in their power to escape from it – and I could not resist, I intervened. In a few words, I tried to convey to them what was now for me completely obvious. Somewhat inconsistently, hastily, I spoke about the water matrix and the dipole waves, the quantum condensate and memory codes, the landscape of attractors and the role of neurons, the navigators in its labyrinths. I explained that the brain's response can never be the same, and its clarity and intensity are determined not by the force of the stimulus but by the brain's internal dynamics. A few molecules of perfume can lead to the same reaction as a whole bottle poured onto the floor. A casually dropped word can cause a torrent of memories – more powerful than a persistent repetition of the same phrase. Stimulus is not a pump that supplies energy into the neurons' network. No, it is only a trigger that launches an internal mechanism…

Of course, they did not understand me; they looked at me wildly, as if I, when speaking about the most familiar things, were using words that made no sense. As if I were presenting them with entirely incomprehensible nonsense. I proposed that they at least let me clarify what I was saying in more detail. But no, they did not want clarification; they had no desire to leave their comfort zone. Then I made my apologies and left – once again feeling an immeasurable loneliness.

That evening, I decided that my theory must be published. It had to become accessible to those who, at least at some time, would be worthy of it. Those who might be able to gain from it the impulse to push onward, even if it were only to happen in thirty – or three hundred – years in the future.

CHAPTER 17

WE HAVE AN early morning; I am sitting at the table watching Elsa cook the fried eggs. A few minutes earlier I had had a minor quarrel with Nestor – over nothing in particular. It's my fault – the last two days I've been wound up and my nerves are on edge. Everyone knows the reason – Nestor, Elsa and me as well. I'm at yet another impasse and my counselor hasn't yet found a way of helping me.

What's more, he is, as usual, playing around with allusions and innuendo. "It's important. More important than you think," he said in response to my story about deterministic chaos and the "face of thought." And he added with exaggerated regret, "It's a pity you don't know why yet."

This annoyed me, of course, and then he also hinted at his role in choosing the dream about Kirill. He made it sound as if the whole theory was in some way down to him – which made me even angrier. I said something to him in reply, to which he merely nodded and then switched off the screen in silence. Now I am sitting, dissatisfied with everything, and looking gloomily at Elsa.

Fortunately, my grumpiness doesn't bother her in the slightest. She puts the frying pan on the table and says jokingly, "What else do you want? Tea, coffee? A dance? Maybe a blow job?" And adds with a snicker, "You know, not long ago, I had a very sensual dream. But I couldn't recognize the setting – I mean the place and the time. That's why I didn't tell you about it, I'm sorry. You're angry about something – not at me, I hope?"

I dig into the fried eggs, which really do taste good. "No," I say to Elsa, "I'm annoyed with myself – and, it seems, I'm still not angry enough. Tell me something, provoke me, make me really mad..." And I continue my thread of thought using highly technical terms, knowing that she doesn't like them, "Excite some dipole wave in my memory, drag it out from the bottom of the parabola. It's sleeping there in the energy minimum, encoding the recollection I'm hunting for."

Elsa is animated, "Aha, that is, you want me to tell you something nasty, and you'll then invent a story about me?"

I shake my head, "No, you'll only act as a catalyst, as an external stimulus, and afterward my brain will move along the chain of associations – somewhere in the distance, probably, away from you."

"Aww," Elsa pouts. "And there I was thinking..."

"But," I continue, "if you keep repeating the same thing to me every day, then, at some point, my neuron connections will readjust themselves. My brain will be returning to you with its thoughts over and over again, no matter what you talk about!"

"Well," says Elsa, taking my empty plate, "how could I turn down such an offer? I *can* tell you this: in my first life I was also often mad at myself. Basically, when I was being carried away in the wrong direction – and everything I did was misguided. For example, I once cheated on Dave to convince myself to break up with him..."

She talks about a chance encounter with a traveling salesman from Texas. She didn't like anything, especially the way he pestered her with his caresses, which weren't to her taste – but she tolerated it, wanting him to climax and leave her alone. For a long time, this didn't happen, and when it finally did, in response to his questions, she confessed that it hadn't been that great.

"Why didn't you say anything?" the Texan asked. "Why didn't you push me away?"

"I didn't want to bother you," Elsa answered honestly.

"You put up with that for my sake?" He was amazed and started making a long-winded apology...

"He really felt guilty," Elsa tells me; "he was very uneasy. I had no idea that Texans were so self-conscious. I became uncomfortable myself;

I suddenly felt I had complete power over him, albeit for only a minute. I could have forced him to do whatever I wanted – buy me a handbag or some shoes, for example… It was an unpleasant feeling, I realized then: having authority over a man was not for me. Too much gets dragged up from the hidden depths – I looked down there and did not want to look any more. After that, I didn't allow myself to be generous with my lovers – it's like winning with the help of an unfair trick. Unselfishness is too powerful a weapon, with too rigid a trigger!"

Elsa turns on the water and sets about washing the dishes. I reflect on her story. I like it; for all its banality, it has a hint of the absurd that appeals to me.

"Your turn," says Elsa. I tell her about my last girlfriend from Bern, a Turkish bus driver. She was insatiable; her temperament shook me time after time. I once asked her as a joke, "You probably like a man with a large 'appendage' – after all, you're the commander of a pretty big apparatus yourself?" And she laughed, "Well, no, I'm quite happy with your average-size willy…"

Elsa looks at me slyly, "Well, if you're talking about such things, I've got something else to admit. I sometimes thought I would end up empty-handed, so to speak, at the core moments, because my clitoris wasn't sensitive enough." She giggles. "But on the other hand, I didn't believe it could have been otherwise: good girls should be vaginal, not clitoral – for some reason, this notion remained stuck in my head. Perhaps, as you mentioned, those were my neuron connections, right? So, in general, I was a bit of an oddity, yes… Well, are you pleased with me? Did I help you free something from out of the bottom of your parabola?"

Then we move to the window and stay there together for a while. Elsa asks, "Could you clarify with your Nestor again that they won't force us to leave here after we do what they want? The instructions in the Brochure are all very well, but I'd still like to double-check. And I don't really trust my own Nestor anymore…"

I nod in silence. Elsa adds thoughtfully, "There's something in what you said to me once about always being young. I'm not growing old here in Quarantine, and, likewise, I don't have to live through the idiocy of youth again when you never understand what's what. I'm in my prime here – why should I have to leave it?"

I put my hand on her waist and send a tantric message of tenderness. It even seems I can feel her response, the heat of her blood. The *flow of her blood*... and then something dawns on me suddenly. I say, "Elsa, you are priceless!" And rush to find a pencil and paper.

The future publication of my theory had to be approached carefully. I knew that my quantum model deserved a long life, but I clearly saw the dangers it might face once it stepped out into the spotlight. It required protective armor against unfriendly arrows – I understood that well. First, I had to delineate the model's boundaries – its territory, its claims – without detracting from its value but also avoiding any superfluous assertions. And second, I needed experimental support – not necessarily direct and explicit, but I did have to have at least something tangential. Otherwise, the whole concept remained a hypothesis, a mathematically proven fiction.

In terms of the boundaries, everything was clear. The theory explained the underlying mechanisms of the formation of memories and thoughts but did not say much about the global, principal meaning. It answered the question "how?" without touching on the "why?" In other words, I didn't even get close to the subject of real reasoning, real consciousness – which places humankind apart, distinguishing it from all other species. Memory and the ability to think, to construct at least basic logical chains, are not the exclusive prerogative of *Homo Sapiens*. The key moment is self-awareness and self-perception, stepping into the loop: "I perceive," "I perceive that I perceive," "I perceive that I perceive that I perceive..." *Cogito me cogitare,*[23] as the great philosopher put it. The human mind for some reason turns away now and then from the external world and concentrates all its power on itself. The human mind reinterprets itself, reworks the knowledge it already possesses. It is this trait that immeasurably increases its strength, allowing it to escape beyond the boundaries, the narrow limits of reacting to the environment and to step out toward infinity, to the point where there are no limits. This is what allows humanity to stand proudly.

---

23   "I perceive that I perceive."

In the loop "I perceive," "I perceive that I perceive" and so forth, there was some sort of closed circuit, a constant feedback, a back-and-forth exchange – but consisting of what and with what? Or, sometimes I would think to myself with a chill running down my spine, consisting of whom and with whom? Nothing from my theory provided me with any clues. I decided not to torment myself with this just yet, faintheartedly leaving the issue to philosophy and not physics, and busied myself with another, vital question – a link between my theoretical calculations and at least something that could be observed in an experiment. And I soon concluded there was only one way – energy exchange. A comparison of energy flows computed from my equations with the real data accumulated by our firm.

The energy of the brain was being studied by a special laboratory. I knew its boss, Albert, who had a shaved head and looked like a thug. At the company he was known as "the man who lives in the bloodstream." It was specifically blood – bright, arterial, nourishing the cerebral vessels, and dark, venous, cleansing the brain of carbon dioxide – that served as his research environment. Using the most modern equipment, Albert's staff could accurately determine the oxygen consumption at any area in the brain at any moment in time. I often helped them with the analytics and had direct access to their data. Thus, I had irrefutable experimental evidence showing when, where and how much energy is spent in the brain tissue.

Good news immediately emerged: the form and duration of the energy cycles – both the experimental and theoretical ones – matched very well. Their amplitudes, describing the *amount* of energy consumed by the brain, also coincided perfectly at *certain* stages of the brain's work – but only certain, not all. This news was bad: my model was supported by experiments only during periods of routine brain activity. When the brain had to work hard – being confronted with something difficult that required more than the usual effort – its energy requirements increased greatly. In my model, they increased too – but to a much lesser extent. The model did not explain where the energy went.

Of course, this was an unpleasant surprise. I didn't believe the theory was wrong, but the mismatch meant it was at least incomplete. I checked the calculations again and again but was unable to find any mistakes. I soon understood, however, that those periods when the brain had been subject to a serious workout had not been reflected in the encephalograms I had used to calculate the model's parameters. Tony's laboratory had discarded stressful situations as being too extreme and confusing the general picture.

Realizing this, I went to Tony and persuaded him to repeat the measurements on several patients, offering them complex logical tasks. He didn't understand why I needed this but agreed, sensing he owed me a favor. For several days, his group was busy with my request and the resulting encephalograms confirmed: when engaged in active thinking, the "analytical power" of the brain really jumped up. The groups of neurons signaled to each other much more intensively – this was not surprising; I was expecting exactly that. I also expected that the connection between the neurons – the coherence of electromagnetic waves, their phase entanglement – would become more firmly established, reliable and stronger. But for some reason, the experiment didn't show that: the areas of correlated neurons did not change in size, and the correlation itself became different – more *diminished* than pronounced, as if slightly blurred. It was there, no doubt, but I was bothered with a sense that it was just an echo of more significant correspondences and connections. I felt I was merely looking at a screen on which shadows danced and all the important actions were going on behind it.

Signaling neurons seemed to be trying to convey a message – to someone, somewhere. Their "perseverance" increased by an order of magnitude, which obviously explained the excessive energy I had observed. As for the "fuzziness" of the correlation in the neurons' joint work, this hinted at the complication of a conveyed message: if previously the neural cells had been beating it out on a drum, now they were collectively playing a harmonious, exquisite melody. What did it mean; why did the brain need this?

I reasoned: in the terms of my model, neuron groups' "messages" represented the initial conditions for quantum processes. The complexity of the messages meant that the conditions were becoming more intricate, and the increased intensity of neuron firing made them more stable. This stability, in turn, implied that some stricter order was maintained in the system, that the system remained in a state of reduced entropy for an extended time. I could assume that the collective excitations of the water dipoles were reaching increasingly higher energy states – and so the thoughts became clearer, more precise. Most probably, this was indeed the case, but this was not enough. The calculations showed that the excess consumption of energy could not be explained in this way. In addition, I suddenly realized: the protracted orderliness of the water matrix should expand the "territory" of the neural correlation, involving more neurons in the joint work. But this did not happen either: synchronization became more stable and lasted longer, but it was localized in the same areas. Finally, I focused on this particular anomaly – at least it represented a strict fact.

I made an obvious assumption: if I do not see a "quantitative" increase in the correlation – reflecting content, knowledge – that means I'm not looking properly. It should exist in some more sophisticated form, and I need to take a more focused look. I saw only one source of sophistication – the incredible complexity of the brain structure. And I began to read articles and books, trying to understand why the brain is arranged in such an excessively complex way, what the essence of this excess is and its meaning. And most importantly – by what laws is this complexity organized?

This time, the breakthrough came of its own accord. Without any external factors – there was no publication dug up from the annals, no chance meeting with some unpleasant character, not even a puzzled smile in the shower. I just sensed and absorbed the collective opinion that had been set down in one form or another practically everywhere. For a long time, it had been expressed repeatedly and quite clearly. Many others, most likely, had had nothing to apply it to. But I definitely did.

The anatomical structure of the brain, its extremely intricate, irregular form, possessed the same property as other irregularities around us. They concealed self-similarity, independence from scale – the very things described by fractal mathematics developed in the last few decades. This fact was interesting in itself, but to me it had a special, extraordinary importance. My phase portraits of cognition, the "faces of thought" – like all strange attractors appearing in chaotic dynamics – were manifesting exactly the same properties…

One morning, I just took a blank sheet and wrote down an idea that had suddenly become obvious to me. The phase trajectories of memory and thought were converging to fractal-like figures. The brain, while developing, also evolved into a fractal-like structure. In both cases, time created order in chaos according to some sort of fractal principle. So, it was natural to propose: Perhaps this was one and the same principle?

I began to investigate the fractal-generating functions, searching for those that might be applied to both the configuration and the dynamics of the brain. Those that would reveal strict regularities in an apparent irregularity and allow for a formal comparison of their features. It soon became clear that yes, I was right, the properties of "geometric" and "dynamic" fractals were similar – or at least very close. The same types of formulas described completely different things – the geometry of the brain and the dynamics of its work. This was an important stage in the development of my theory, although at first I didn't realize its fundamental importance, only sensing a hint at it. But even a hint was enough to understand that fractals were a universal language through which I was being sent a prompt. And there was no brushing it aside.

The next step was obvious – the prompt had been formulated very clearly. I saw a hidden – fractal – order in the formation of the structure of the brain, one, and in its movement from state to state, two. This was related to the brain as a single system, as a whole. So why not get inside the whole, to the level of neurons and dipole waves – three! Neural coherence – knowledge, thought – is also nothing more than regularity arising from disorder. Maybe fractals would help me to identify the concealed part of it, for which I had been unsuccessfully hunting? Perhaps I could take a peek behind the screen on which the shadows were dancing, and confront the actors face to face?

There were several ways to explicitly introduce a fractal principle into my model. I chose the most direct one: I changed the coordinate system, representing each of the coordinate axes by the set of values of a certain fractal generator. A "certain" one, but not quite: following the logic of the emergence of my idea, continuing to assume that the same laws govern both structure and action, I linked this function to my "face of thought" through its main property – the dimension of the generated fractals. The resulting equations looked scary at first, but soon I adjusted to their complexity and, with the help of some advanced methods, managed to simplify them, to transform them into a convenient form. And then they revealed to me their hidden meaning.

Under specific boundary conditions – if the protein filaments, the means of contact between the micro and the macro, were intertwined in a certain way – the system of water dipoles would acquire a topologically nontrivial order, "packaged" into fractal structures. The "quantity" of order became large – it could be infinitely large – but in three-dimensional coordinates it remained localized in the same modest limits. The coherence propagated inward along the fractal trajectories. Thus, a small area of the brain encoded an almost unlimited amount of knowledge…

I pictured this visually: water dipoles were not just lining up in the same direction. Their vectors, like needles, formed the most complicated, highly organized figure, which flickered and trembled but remained stable for a fairly long time. I knew that this was it. The excess energy was spent precisely here – on the transition of regions of the brain into a new ordered state. Obviously, in addition to the usual coherence, an additional order was established and maintained in the brain during active work, reflecting the same dynamic regimes, the same memories and thoughts, but in a different way. And again, the question arose: Why did the brain need this?

There was no answer. I continued to work away using the most complex mathematics. It was natural to call this emergence of a new order "fractal symmetry breaking." This required, first, the nontrivial initial conditions and, second, overcoming a large energy barrier. The two corresponded perfectly to the incredible complexity of the brain and with the excessive energy consumption due to the more intensive neuron work. The symmetry broke down, and then, as always when this breaking occurs, the emerged order – my fractal order – was maintained by quasiparticles of a certain kind, the joint oscillations of dipoles – that very same flickering and trembling of the highly organized figure. The "cunning trick" – it was so familiar to me. I had mastered the methods of its analysis perfectly.

And here as well: I saw the quasiparticles in the products of matrices; I could almost grab them with my hand – but no, something prevented me, forbidding the path from the imaginary, illusory constructs to real ones. Solutions to the equations of motion for my quasiparticles were physically impossible. Their calculated speeds turned out to be greater than the speed of light.

So, fractal coherence was excessive but did take place. Quantum oscillations that preserved it could not exist but existed nonetheless. These two facts were obviously connected with each other. But how, how? Only one explanation came to my mind. Something had to slow down the quasiparticles, act as a "brake" on them. This meant they were *interacting* with something – and that was their key role. Through them – through the quanta of dipole waves maintaining the fractal order – *the human brain was interacting with some unknown field!*

I formulated this concept on an ordinary gray, rainy day. In my office, I just sat down at the desk, looked at the formulas and added another integral to the right side of the main equation. And then muttered, grinning, joyfully like a child, "Interaction, interaction… The geometry of the macroworld is translated into the microcosm… Here's your interfusion of scales, no matter how speculative it may sound!"

So, once again, the components of the most complicated puzzle had been put in place, set into their grooves and perfectly attached to each other. So many things were clarified at once, in a single stroke! The essence of my model, its quantum nature, had manifested itself in all its might. The step into the microcosm not only explained the stability of memory, the sharpness and flexibility of thought. This step opened a door in the solid wall put in place by classical physics. This new interaction… It occurs only when the water dipoles are ordered fractally. This, in turn, becomes possible when the initial conditions – neural impulses – are specifically nontrivial: and here is, we repeat, the "excessive" complexity of the brain tissue. The synchronization of the neurons that we observe in encephalograms is only the beginning of the process. The brain focuses on a certain thought, and if the concentration is strong enough, a fractal order appears in the matrix of water dipoles, reflecting this thought. Where an order arises from the symmetry breaking, there are quasiparticles, quasi-Goldstone bosons – and they, as we see, perturb a certain external field. The brain exchanges energy with this field and this means... This means it is exchanging information!

I swayed in my chair in a euphoria of insight. Color spots flashed before my eyes in which all the answers were encrypted. Exchange, feedback, consciousness, true consciousness... I strained with all my might, trying to retain the words and meanings, to link them together, to take a step beyond them. It was an enormous effort, and I seemed to be close, right next to something vitally important – but suddenly my thoughts became confused, exploding like fireworks. My head spun, and I passed out – right behind my desk. Then I woke up, covered all over in a sticky sweat, and realized I could not get up. My temples were burning with fire; I had a fever. Helplessly, I'd fallen face first onto the table and stayed there half sitting, half lying until lunch. One of my colleagues found me and called an ambulance.

The doctors said I was suffering from flu plus fatigue and nervous exhaustion. I stayed in the hospital for almost a week. On the second day, one of my bosses visited me and gently but insistently recommended that I take a vacation. He was right – I had not had a break for nearly two and a half years.

In the luxurious ward overlooking the river, I finally sensed just how much my quantum model had drained me. I could not think of it; my mind protested; it seemed I was almost going crazy. Sometimes, at night, hyperspace filled with a shimmering substance – the unknown new field – appeared before me. Strange voices sounded in my ears, repeating in different ways, "I perceive that I perceive that I perceive..." I woke with a start and lay awake until dawn, trying to think soberly – and they were gloomy thoughts. The repetition of what had passed – a "new field" had already been in my life, and more than once. There were also hints of other spaces, and behind them – past failures, defeat, ignominy. I knew that above all I did not want to be this ashamed again – either before others or myself.

After leaving the hospital, I tried to play with the model a little more. I transformed in different ways the equation with the new term on the right – randomly changing the set of quantum degrees of freedom, giving the mysterious field a chance to reveal itself, to "catch" my quasiparticles, to increase their mass, to restrain their mad dash. What I ended up with was nonsense; divergences emerged everywhere. When I tried to remove them, new, even more frightening ones appeared. I didn't know what to do. And most importantly – did not want to know.

Realizing this, I resigned myself and put in a request for a vacation – as if turning my face back to the ordinary world, to the city I had so often despised. Turning and announcing to them – I'm yours, forgive my pride, grant me your little pleasures. I wanted to go somewhere far away – and I chose Thailand, having read travel stories on the web. Soon, I was sitting in the cabin of an airliner, heading east. I looked down at the banks of clouds and thought about almost nothing. Only imagined the sea, the sun and – affectionate and graceful Thai women.

THE DANCE OF THE CONSCIONS

CHAPTER 18

"LET'S GO TO your bedroom," Elsa says. "We need to choose your clothes."

I halfheartedly try to protest, but she is adamant – she gets up off the couch and drags me along behind her.

Today is an important day: I'm about to have a serious talk with Nestor, summarizing what we have achieved so far. This is a joint decision by Elsa and me – however, we are not totally clear what our objectives are. It's just a vague sense of urgency that both of us have felt simultaneously.

In addition to this inkling, there is a formal reason: I have recalled a considerable part of the theory. It's almost logically complete now – I have remembered everything right up to my fainting fit, Bern's hospital and an airliner flying over the clouds. My memories cascaded in like a raging torrent; I barely managed to transfer them to paper. There were formulas, facts, notes and sketches – at times, all mixed up in a heap, not easy to sort out. I worked during the day, in the living room, and sometimes in my bedroom instead of sleeping – in contravention of the schedule, with permission from Nestor. Surprisingly, I didn't get tired – that's one of the advantages of a fictitious body. Some of the math hasn't come back to me yet, but I know it won't be long; I'll soon be getting the hang of it.

Elsa spent nearly all her time on her embroidery. Our tablecloth is now covered in inscriptions: in addition to "Good girls go to heaven...," we have "Virginity is curable," "Dream to dare," "Love your enemies" in large letters and a few more random words. While I was hard at work at my desk, she would sit at her regular place on the couch and look over at me with some envy, maybe even jealousy. I understood her – fully occupied by my theory, I couldn't give her enough attention. We still kept to our usual routine, however: joint breakfasts, walks along the embankment, attempts to somehow link our memories – which, to be honest, Elsa put a lot more effort into than I did. She basically became the mistress of the house – mistress of our everyday lives, of our surreal world and, in a sense, mistress over me. At least, that's how it seemed – as for me, I was incapable of thinking seriously about anything except quantum fields and fractal structures.

And then, a few days ago, I suddenly had a dream about Tina. It was bright, short and completely incoherent. There were flashes of pink taxis and sheets on an unmade bed, fragile nudity and shameless groans, a view from a window onto a jungle of skyscrapers, myself sitting in front of a pile of paper covered in formulas. I remembered a word from the dream: "Bangkok." I repeat it to myself in my head, soundlessly. I repeat the word and a smell emerges – a mixture of musty cellars and smoldering coals, hissing oil and roast meat on skewers, fish sauce, coriander and tamarind. I feel, I recall – the unbearable sun, the moist, humid air, the taste of sweet coconut milk fresh from the nut, the taste of Tina – also sweet, somewhat reminiscent of coconut, but incomparable to anything in the world…

None of these details led anywhere; no veils were revealed, no covers were pulled back. I still couldn't work out what took place, what happened in that hot, noisy city between me and a girl with the looks of a teenager. After that I tried with all my strength – to make a breakthrough, recollect, grasp – but to no avail: the theory would not advance and Tina no longer appeared to me. I only dreamed of the familiar: the clouds below the airliner and the equations with the mysterious field on the right, which I did not know how to approach. And last night I saw Brevich – not the way I knew him before, in my first dreams here, which Nestor had chosen. Now he seemed different – almost insane, driven by fate into a corner. And ready to do anything to pay fate back.

In the morning, I told Elsa about this, and a certain shadow flashed across her face. A hint of recognition or a glimpse of doubt – and she suddenly admitted she was anxious for no reason. This was all the more strange – because the dream had alarmed me as well. It was then we decided: it was time to have a frank talk with my Nestor. To lay all our cards on the table – so he would also reveal whatever he had hidden up his sleeve. If, of course, he had anything up there.

"All the Nestors are liars!" Elsa declared. "But we must do something anyway. Somehow, neither of us are feeling ourselves – isn't that right?"

Now we are standing in front of the wardrobe, and Elsa is rifling through it purposefully. For some reason, it seems to her my appearance is going to be important for the upcoming conversation. "None of these are right..." she mutters. I wait patiently. Finally, an austere dark suit and white shirt are presented to me. "Here, try this on," she says, looking at my figure skeptically.

"Would you mind turning your back?" I ask. "I don't know why but I feel a bit awkward."

Elsa snorts but obediently turns away. I put on the things she has chosen. "Oho!" she exclaims, turning toward me again. "It fits *really* well. I had no idea you were so handsome. I don't think Nestor will be able to resist you. It's a pity, of course, he's not gay – although you can never be certain... We've got an hour left – is there anything you need to prepare or write down? Or maybe you'd like to eat?"

An hour later, I am sitting in front of the screen. At exactly five o'clock my counselor appears and looks me up and down with unconcealed surprise.

"Just trying to guess," he says at last, "whether you're going to a wedding or a funeral."

This pronouncement is followed by his peculiar laugh. I wait patiently until it recedes and say, "Nestor, I want to provide you with a summary of what I've recalled so far. I am ready to share everything I've remembered – there is a lot of important stuff – and in return... I'd like... No, no, let me recount it first – without concealing a thing."

"How open of you," Nestor sniffs. "Practically a *coming-out*, one might say. Well, go on then, do tell – now I understand why you've been so secretive these last few days."

He's right – up until now we've been playing some sort of game of cat and mouse. I've been talking about my progress in hints, not getting into details. My counselor, in turn, has hardly been asking any questions, only making his usual witticisms, both to the point and off it.

"Yes," I agree, "I am being extremely open. And that's official, I repeat, *official*. I'm going to reveal to you and your experts everything I have, without reservations…"

Then, over the next forty minutes, I describe the quantum model of the brain up to the moment when my memories were interrupted. I describe it all but in a coherently concise way, accessible to a layman, with just the minimum of formulas. Having finished, I lay a few sheets out on the table, covered with equations. They contain all the accompanying math – again, in very condensed form.

Nestor listens to me with an impenetrable expression on his face. Then he looks over my papers and asks, "Is that all?"

I shake my head. "No, not all!" – and tell him, significantly less coherently, about my latest dreams, about Brevich, Tina and, most importantly, about my and Elsa's uneasy gut feeling. I make a point of particularly stressing this, even adding a little intrigue, but it has no effect on him whatsoever.

This, of course, makes me angry. "My calculations," I exclaim, "I know, they are somehow connected with all this!" And I add, "Elsa – why did that shadow pass across her face?"

Nestor remains silent. I repeat with annoyance, "Why? I need your help – again. *We* need your help – Elsa is with me on this – and we are asking you to look hard, do some digging about, fish around, cross-reference… After all, you are my counselor, and don't forget: we're talking about the theory of the mind here, nothing less. Remember, you yourself did mention the importance of my role!"

Nestor looks at me, his eyebrow raised, as if waiting to see whether I want to continue or not. Then he nods, "Yes, nothing less" – and tries to make another sarcastic comment about my suit. It isn't funny; I just grimace. He puts on his serious face and sighs, "I'm disappointed!"

"Please explain," I propose.

"Willingly," Nestor agrees. "What you have told me is not of much value to us – it certainly wasn't worth getting dressed up for. I had already guessed you were getting somewhere – judging by your equivocal hints and despite your childish game of hide and seek… But as far as the mind is concerned, I cannot agree with you, not at all. As I see it, you haven't yet gotten close to the nature of the human *mind*. And most importantly, *what is the B Object*?"

I become agitated; my cheek begins to twitch. I even seem to have broken into a sweat underneath my fine suit. Nestor continues unperturbed, "Besides, you are surprisingly persistent in your delusions. You don't listen to anybody – yet I've already said this more than once: your file doesn't contain a single word about a girl called Tina. So I have nothing to dig up, fish out or cross-reference against."

His imperiousness is solid, like thick armor. "In my opinion," I say irritably, even cantankerously, "in my opinion, you simply don't want to make even the slightest effort. It's not clear to me what you're doing here at all, except cracking lame jokes…" And I add, "By the way, what do you think your superiors will make of all this? Are they going to be pleased with you, or maybe as *disappointed* in you as you are in me?"

Nestor frowns, "Your threats are pathetic. Do you want to complain? Okay, by all means, go ahead. For example, you can write a message on the promenade sidewalk with white chalk. Oh, what a pity – you have no chalk… Well, then, why not just go down to the seashore and scream – maybe someone will hear you!"

"Ha, ha. Very funny!" I say.

Nestor continues, "But you're right about something. You're correct as far as my superiors are concerned. They are likely to be as unhappy as I am myself. Because it is indeed strange that your file doesn't contain a thing about this Tina whom you keep coming back to relentlessly, again and again. There's nothing either about Tina or the B Object – it's as if your memory is hiding them away somewhere, protecting them against strangers. In the backwoods, where there's no getting to them – even if… Even if we assume they do exist!"

"You mean to say…" I begin to raise my voice, but he interrupts me, exclaiming even louder, "Just you wait a minute! Just cool it with the resentment; otherwise I may also get offended, and I have good reason. Really, why do you only see me as some callous, self-obsessive career type? Why do you fail to notice the sincerity of my words, my genuine and unfeigned bewilderment?… You are a callous egotist yourself, Theo; you don't have the ability to put yourself in someone else's shoes, to feel, oh, their pain… An egotistical, self-centered character, but there's nothing to be done; I am duty bound to live with it. Because I have obligations," he assumes a dignified air, "yes, obligations, and now, as it happens, I need to move on to the next of them. Its time has come – I need to tell you how your theory and the *place* it occupies are seen here, in our society. By all means, let's 'cross-reference,' as you put it – allow me to provide a summary as well, even though I haven't dressed myself up as an undertaker. So…"

I wave my hand, trying in turn to interrupt him. I want to make an objection – I also have something to say about sincerity, genuineness and callousness. But Nestor does not react; he isn't even looking at me but down – probably at some of his papers.

"So," he repeats. "Of course, we have our own theories of everything. Theories of the mind and theories of the universe – recognized *officially*, so to speak. The only problem is that they are incomplete; they have blank spaces in the most prominent places – and when you showed up, there was a flash of hope that with your help we might succeed in filling some of them in. Well, that hope is still glimmering, but I have to admit: so far you have filled in almost nothing. You are wandering along the same border that we are – it's a bit strange, isn't it? This is something worth thinking about, not shaking your fists at and getting confrontational about!"

I snort indignantly but keep quiet. "Some of our knowledge," Nestor continues, "came from your world, from those who remember your article and subsequent works by others. The remainder is the result of our own studies and efforts. Both parts, it should be noted, agree with each other perfectly – and much of 'Theo's theory' has been stringently reconstructed. First, it's about quantum mechanism – including heat exchange with the environment, which provides memory capacity. And second, the concept of attractors as navigators of memories and thoughts. And we'll begin with them – with the pleasant. With the amazing and extremely important. Get yourself ready." Nestor purses his lips and speaks with great emphasis, "You are about to hear. Something. Quite amusing!"

I shrug, demonstrating my readiness, and he pronounces insinuatingly, "Attractors… In Theo's theory they are given a great deal of attention. As much as they have been in our works – and that is deserved, undoubtedly deserved. Unfortunately, here, we do not have the opportunity to experiment with what you had available to you – the brain of a *Homo Sapiens* from the terrestrial world. We cannot reconstruct the attractors you got on the basis of real data. But, even in books, in long, boring novels, a crucial role is sometimes played by pictures, and this is so here too: some of the newcomers who lived after your death perfectly remembered the illustration from your article, the very same 'face of thought' you hung over your desk. We clung to it like a straw, and the straw turned out to be strong. We restored it carefully, like a wanted man's photofit. We blew the specks of dust off it, discarded everything superfluous and made a comparison – it is clear with what: our 'human brain' here can be investigated thoroughly! And so: the kind of attractors navigating in our 'consciousness' undoubtedly resemble your 'face,' Theo – the 'face of thought,' I mean, not your sullen physiognomy. Apparently, our minds here and your earthly ones function similarly. The realities are different, but the principle is unalterable – how do you like that fact, it is *amusing*, isn't it? Well, I did promise… And now, with your calculations, we can probably verify this – here I must give due respect to the revelations you've made today. They do provide something – admittedly, I didn't show it, but believe me, my soul rejoiced!"

Nestor pauses, cocks his head to one side and looks at me for a few seconds. I, too, remain silent, mulling over what I've heard. For some reason, it doesn't surprise me in the least.

Not seeing any reaction from me, he sighs briefly and says, "Let me clarify. I also rejoiced because the whole concept, the universality of the principle, goes further. Much further – it is by no means confined to the mind alone. This is an unexpected development, astonishing to any mind – if you'll forgive the pun – capable of comprehending it. But we'll save it for later – really, we don't want to get ahead of ourselves. We must focus on the most urgent issues, and therefore: now to the main one of these. Or rather, to a fairly sad one…"

All his animation seems to have dissipated. He frowns, sighs again and then talks, tediously and at length, of the attempts to formalize the interaction of their "brain" with something external. Their problem is the same as mine: there is no doubt that an interaction exists, but they are unable to put it into a consistent theory.

"Yes, we also see an excess – an excess of energy consumed during intense thought," Nestor says with a clearly displeased expression. "Yes, we have also come to the idea of fractal ordering, which is fairly obvious. In our equations – and they, I'm sure, resemble yours – divergences of a certain type appear, quasiparticles that violate physical principles – all that is familiar to you, isn't it? We are trying, like you, to introduce some compensating field – which, thanks to your good graces, is called the field of the conscions... Overall, we have to admit: we and you, probably, have similar things in mind, pursuing the same goal – and so far, suffering the same setbacks. Our calculations do not give us what we all long to see, touch and feel, even if only on paper. We cannot get solutions in the form of stable localized vortices: those very B Objects, in which, as you put it in your article, our memory is 'recorded.' For some reason, it is precisely this part of your theory that has been impossible to reproduce."

I again make a gesture of protest. "I know, I know," dismisses Nestor. "Yes, no one is arguing: the indisputable fact that consciousness doesn't die with the brain clearly speaks in your favor – in favor of you personally, Theo, and these Objects of yours. It's just a pity there is nothing *more* to say about them for the moment – and yet so much rests precisely on them. The most important consequences, the most thrilling, incredible mysteries... And where are they, the B Objects? Alas, they are nowhere in sight – do you now understand my impatience, my disappointment? Of course, I can see some specifics in the numbers on these papers of yours – they may prove useful. But something tells me that there won't be a decisive breakthrough."

He pauses, and for a few minutes we just look at each other. Then I clear my throat and say, "Could you provide me with a description of *your* theory of the field of conscions? Even if it is incomplete, even if you and I have been stuck in the same places."

"Impossible!" Nestor declares. "It's not even up for discussion. All the experts have unanimously agreed that our theory will only throw you off the scent. It will send you on the wrong course – can we risk that? Of course not – but I will take the liberty of saying one thing related to it. Purely to encourage you, give you a gentle nudge…"

He looks away and continues after a short pause, "We, after all, have had successes too. Our equations have allowed us to obtain some specific types of solutions, different from yours – and they are extremely important. But the B Object still remains the main prize. We must understand what it is – in a strict mathematical sense. If you only knew what prospects this opens up… It's a pity we cannot talk about them now. Later – it can only be discussed later!"

"Well…" I say and spread my hands. I have nothing to add, and there's no point in making objections. I just know that very hard work awaits me and cannot be avoided. Already now, in advance, I feel weary at the thought of it.

"Yes, and by the way, I cannot help but note," Nestor suddenly comes to life again. "There is one more consequence of your 'official' summary. It's now clear: from today onward, you can only count on your own memory – neither I nor your file can help you now. This is a new turn of events; admit it. I will cease to be your adviser, let alone your mentor. I will remain only as your friend – yes, sometimes in life you can't choose your friends. Well, and I'll still be your therapist – like, you know, almost every friend is in their own special way."

Thus, our session comes to an end. That night I have another incoherent dream. It contains an elusive hint at an elusive smell. At an elusive, somewhat stringent taste.

I wake up refreshed, rerun everything I have heard from Nestor in my head and go to the living room, without deciding what I'm going to say to Elsa. Still wearing my shirt from yesterday, only with the sleeves rolled up, I try my best to radiate confidence and optimism.

Elsa, as usual, is standing by the stove preparing breakfast. Hearing me, she turns around and raises her eyebrows inquiringly.

"There is some interesting news," I say with exaggerated enthusiasm. Her face immediately takes on a somewhat bored air. Nevertheless, I continue, "We now know: in this world, the brain works in the same way as it does in ours – in what used to be ours…" And I exclaim, "It's a pretty amazing fact!" – thinking that I sound remarkably like Nestor.

Elsa nods silently and turns back to the stove. "Yes, probably," she says, stirring something in the pan. "So, overall, if I understood correctly, nothing worthwhile happened, right? But I'm sure you did everything exactly as was needed!"

I tell her briefly about yesterday's conversation, adding that I do not have a counselor as such anymore. That he is now just a "friend" – and I can't expect any help from him.

"An interesting development," Elsa mutters thoughtfully. She walks up to the cupboard, takes a plate from the shelf and abruptly turns toward me.

"Just don't forget..." she says. "Don't forget: you have me! Even if my body is fake and I don't understand much about your abstruse scribbles. By the way, I was just thinking... Could you show them to me again? I don't know why, but all of a sudden I really want to take a look."

"No problem," I shrug, go to my bedroom and bring her several sheets of paper.

Elsa puts my breakfast on the table, pours the coffee and, while I'm eating, examines the mathematical symbols, moving her lips as she does so, as if repeating something to herself. She even runs her finger along the lines like a blind person reading braille, and then she begins to ask me questions, "What's this? And this? And this one in brackets?"

I explain, at first briefly, but soon get carried away. Forgetting my food, I talk eagerly about neurons and synapses, about protein filaments connecting the micro and the macro, about symmetry breaking and water dipoles lining up in a row. Elsa, of course, understands little but sits and listens patiently. After I've finished she is thoughtful and quiet as she picks over her embroidery on the couch. I try to work, but to no avail – my thoughts are scattered, and I am unable to concentrate.

The midday session with Nestor is over quickly – we don't have much to say to each other. I return to the living room, wait for Elsa, and we go for a walk.

The weather is splendid and the seafront is full of people. There are no empty places in any of the cafés. "I'd really like a fresh grapefruit juice," says Elsa, and we stop at the kiosk. We get in line and suddenly find ourselves at the center of a conflict.

Standing in front of us is a couple whom we've met two or three times before – a young man and an older woman, both tall and aloof, with unhealthily puffy faces. They are having an argument – a rare event in Quarantine – hissing at each other and exchanging unpleasant looks. I hate to see this and really want to leave, but Elsa looks at the fruits with longing, and I decide to wait.

Soon the woman declares to her companion, "I've had enough of this, *basta!*" – evidently intending to abandon him. I'm standing in her way. "Excuse me," she says irritably, and, not waiting until I step aside, passes right *through* me, as if there's nobody there.

I don't feel anything, but it makes me angry. "Hey, lady," I say after her. "Didn't they teach you better manners at charm school?"

The woman turns around and bursts into a malicious tirade. "Who are you to pass judgment on *me*?" she shouts. "You're nothing but an uneducated redneck, a savage – how dare you talk to *me* like that?..."

Of course, I am at a loss for words, but Elsa is quick to enter the fray. Without hesitating for a moment, she grabs someone's glass and hurls its contents right into the woman's face. My assailant falls silent, leaving only Elsa's voice audible: "You bitch, keep your mouth shut! He is more educated than any of us and all the Nestors put together! There is a million times more on a single scrap of what he writes than in your entire imbecile brain. You are at the bottom of the parabola – just sit there and don't stick your nose in where it doesn't belong..."

I'm amazed – I would never have imagined Elsa capable of such vehemence. Flushed and furious, standing tall, like an Amazon protecting her tribe. Everyone around is stunned too. All eyes are on us...

However, the fracas doesn't last long. The man leads away his companion, who is still so shocked she hasn't fully come to her senses. Elsa and I leave as well and soon we are sitting on a bench not far from the street singer. She sips her grapefruit juice and squints into the sun. It seems to me that today she is especially, defiantly beautiful.

Meanwhile, the song we hear is quite strange. "*Katie has left us, her boat floats up an invisible river. Along an apparently nonexistent river, lying in dimensions inaccessible to the eye. No one can tell if I'll see Katie again, but there's hope – it's in the complexity of a Lagrangian. It's in the diagonals of the tensors of my world...*" I hear and wonder whether this is really happening or if I'm only dreaming.

"What beautiful words!" says Elsa. She snuggles up next to me; I sense her warmth. I sense her in all her entirety, even her soul. The way she belongs to me, her *lack of indifference.*

Then we leave. "*The Southeast awaits you – with slender girls whose yonis taste of coconut...*" the singer trills in our wake, but I'm not listening anymore. The new word drills into my brain. Against the background of the silvery sea I see a silhouette. I see brushstrokes carelessly made by black raven hair and bright-red lipstick...

That very evening I recall how I met Tina.

CHAPTER 19

I HAD INTENDED to spend just a few days in Bangkok and then head on to Phuket and flop for a couple of weeks on the beach. My plan was simple: to do the obligatory rounds of the temples, follow the guidebook routes and in general "get to know" Bangkok as well as any other moderately curious tourist. Almost immediately I regretted coming to the city at all. The hotel was dirty and too expensive, with very small rooms and nonexistent service. The surrounding streets were almost impassable – because of the countless food stalls and motorcycles weaving along the sidewalk. Thousands of cars poisoned the air, their drivers ignoring pedestrian crossings. Everything was alien, difficult and irritating. I decided the place was not for me; it sucked out my energy, dissipated my thoughts and sapped my strength. But on the third day, I met Tina and everything magically changed.

I saw her on a skywalk, on the way from the overground station to one of the shopping malls. The journey was a short but tough one: the humid heat enveloped me like a cloud, and my clothes were sticking to my body. To avoid going too fast, I fell into step with a girl about ten meters ahead of me walking more slowly than the other pedestrians. We moved like a single entity, without getting closer to each other; the crowd flowed around us. I observed her from the back – fragile shoulders, slender legs, a bright streak in her hair. She had an exquisite languidness, a natural grace about her and – something else. We entered the mall together, an oasis of coveted coolness. She settled at a table in a café near the entrance, and, on a whim, I sat down there as well, not far away. She did not seem to notice me or anything else around her. Her demeanor betrayed not just a reverie but a certain intense concentration. A focus, not typical of Thais, and – something else besides.

The girl spent about half an hour in the café – and in all that time I didn't take my eyes off her. At first, she wrote something in a small notebook; then she fiddled with her phone. I could not approach her and strike up a conversation; there was an aura of inaccessibility around her, an elastic shell, lines of a force that enclosed her in a dense cocoon. Then she asked for her bill, and I realized she would now disappear from my life forever. To get up and pursue her would have been stupid, so I sat and just watched her pay and leave, walking away with her graceful gait. I followed her with my eyes for as long as I could, then looked at her empty table and discovered that, yes, she had disappeared but not quite. On top of the enclosure next to her chair lay her forgotten glasses case. I took it, intending to give it to the waiter, and, after a moment of hesitation, looked inside. There was a note in Thai and English: "I often forget my things. Please contact me, if you find this." Underneath this message was her phone number.

In a quarter of an hour, we were sitting at my table together. I had called her; she had come back and agreed to have coffee with me. It was just a gesture of politeness – but I was as nervous as a schoolboy nonetheless.

She introduced herself, "My name is Tina." And she asked, "Are you here for a long time? Did you come specially to save me from losing my glasses?"

I noted her good English and responded in the same tone, "Something like that. Consider me your knight in shining armor, your Lancelot. A Lancelot whose actual name is Theo."

She, of course, had no idea who Lancelot was. Annoyed with myself, I began to spout even more nonsense. "I'd very much like to say that, yes, I'm only here because of your glasses, but I don't make a habit of deceiving beautiful girls," I spluttered, feeling more and more of an idiot. "Actually, I came here to nurse my ego. I'm not a knight but a gloomy tourist, aimlessly wandering around, surrounded by smiling Thais…"

In this verbose and not altogether amusing manner I joked for several minutes. Tina remained absolutely serious.

"But I'm not smiling," she said when I had finally stopped talking. "And you should not always believe other people's smiles. Even if you are a naive *farang* and see everything upside down… I shouldn't say this, of course – I'm Thai myself, albeit only half Thai. And I really love Thailand!"

I asked her what the other half was. Tina curtly replied that her father was a Korean businessman from Seoul. I asked how she could possibly have gone any distance without her glasses, and she, just as curtly, told me they were made of plain glass and did not have any lenses.

"Why do you have them, then?" I persevered. "Are you in disguise? Are you hiding from someone?"

She suddenly became uneasy and said quietly, "Well, maybe I am" – and turned away. Then she finished her coffee and asked, "How old are you?"

I told her my age. "Aha," she said thoughtfully and pondered something. Then she took out a mirror and made up her lips with bright, blood-red lipstick. I thought with an inexplicable sadness she was getting ready to say goodbye and leave, but Tina suddenly said, "There is one thing I'm curious about.

"It's of no consequence, but I am still interested," she continued, carefully enunciating her words. "Maybe you know: The world, the universe – what is its shape; does it have edges? Earth is clearly a sphere – but what about beyond it? Are their six flat layers, like in a cake? And above them Brahma's twenty heavens? As one monk explained it to me, ha-ha… And another thing I'd like to know: Where does time come from?"

"Wow," I grinned, not hiding my surprise. Tina's gaze bored into me. I asked, "Are you really looking for an answer?" She nodded.

"Well," I shrugged. "If we are talking about shape…"

I pontificated for quite a while – not expecting, of course, that she would understand anything. It was just nice to feel at ease, on solid ground. I told her about relic radiation and its remarkable uniformity. I explained why this allows for the idea that the curvature of the universe is constant, and, moreover, the scientific world is inclined to think it is close to zero – if, of course, we are considering an "empty" space undisturbed by gravity. Curvature imposes strict restrictions on possible shapes, and, perhaps, the most probable of them is a three-dimensional torus with a smooth surface, rather like a donut...

"Can you imagine a donut?" I asked Tina. She looked at me, all eyes. "Now, as far as time is concerned," I continued, "then out of a multitude of interpretations the thermodynamic arrow is the one most worthy of attention. There is a law: in an isolated system, entropy increases; it can't be otherwise. The increase in disorder is what distinguishes the past from the future, determining the direction of all processes. This is considered the direction of time – at least in the macrocosm we are used to. In the microworld things get complicated: for example, quantum field theory allows time to be reversed..."

At that moment, Tina made an imploring face, and I interrupted myself, "I'm sorry, all this probably sounds boring. I got carried away; it happens to me often. Would you care for more coffee?"

She shook her head. "I didn't understand much, but it was so fascinating to listen... Perhaps later you could tell me in more detail – this and maybe something else."

"Do you always ask how the universe works when you first meet people?" I inquired jokingly.

"In general, yes," she said. "I use it as a defense."

"Against whom?" I asked.

She shrugged, "I don't know, everyone." And added, "Who'd have guessed you knew so many clever words!"

We laughed, and I realized the ice between us had melted. "Are you hungry?" I asked her. Tina thought for a moment and said honestly, "Yes. Let's go to the third floor – there's a good Thai restaurant there..."

Soon we were eating – seafood salad, rice with crab meat, and chicken in something sweet and pungent. Tina ordered for both of us and then confessed, "We won't be able to eat it all, but I wanted it like this for some reason. It's not wise to come here hungry – and I did not have any breakfast and forgot about lunch."

I liked watching her eat – with a concentrated, meticulous grace. At the same time, she managed to speak volubly about herself – in response to my cautious questions. I learned that Tina was born in Korea; after her parents broke up, her mother brought her back to Thailand, to a small town in Isaan province. They spent almost three years there while the divorce dragged on. For Tina, it was a happy time – in Isaan, unlike Seoul, which she hated with all her heart, no one made fun of her looks and slightly darker skin. Then the divorce finally came through; they were given a generous settlement and moved to the suburbs of Bangkok, with good schools attended by children of middle-class folks rather than farmers. There was enough to send her to the university – where Tina graduated with a diploma in IT, after which she began to live independently, renting a tiny apartment. She had a penchant for anything related to computers, as well as a knack for cracking firewalls and passcodes. Most of her work came from small shops selling second-hand mobile phones. She didn't make much, but it was enough, and working in an office with bosses and a strict timetable would have been impossible for her anyway...

Later, we went outside onto the noisy Ploenchit Road. "It's time for me to go," Tina said and looked away.

"Can I see you tomorrow?" I asked, in a deliberately nonchalant manner, sensing my trembling voice betraying me.

Tina paused and suddenly gave me a dazzling Thai smile – the first one in the three hours we had spent together. "It's hard to imagine what might induce me to agree," she said thoughtfully. "Unless you were to promise to tell me why we can't go back in time – along this arrow of yours... Let's get in touch by text tomorrow; you have my phone number."

She left with a quick assured step – never again did I see her walking as slowly as she had that morning. She moved around the city swiftly and decisively, despite the heat. She hurtled through space, weaving past cars, buildings and pedestrians in a flourish of thick black hair and, sometimes, a flash of red lipstick.

The next day we met in the same mall, at the same café, at almost the same time. Tina, however, seemed quite different. She was withdrawn and quiet and sometimes looked around as if searching for the cause of her discomfort. I ordered her a cake with coconut; she ate it slowly, in small pieces, throwing me attentive, serious glances. Then I went to the bathroom and, returning, I saw her sitting motionless, with her eyes fixed on something utterly remote.

I joked, "You seem like you're here, but not here today." And added, "It's like you're talking with someone from some other world," and almost recoiled from her intense upturned gaze.

"I'm sorry," I shrugged, "I didn't mean anything by that."

"No, no," she said. "I just... Do you think I'm a bit of a freak?"

Her look became alert, almost frightened. I hastened to reassure her, "Not at all. I've known a lot of freaks and, no, you're not one of them."

"Good," Tina nodded. I saw she was feeling even more uncomfortable now. Then I asked, "Is there something wrong? Tell me – I'll understand; maybe I might be able to help."

She looked at me in silence; I sensed she was trying to decide something. Almost physically, I could feel her desperate shyness and – her desire to share, to relieve herself of some sort of burden.

"Well, I don't know," she said at last. "You see, this is not about the universe – I'm not used to discussing this with everyone I meet." Then, after a pause, she responded to herself, "On the other hand, you're not just anyone; you're the only person I've met who can really talk about the universe." She thought a bit more and contradicted herself angrily, "However, you are a *farang*, much older than me. It's clear you can't be trusted." And then she sighed, "But how can you not be trusted? After all, you didn't let me lose my glasses..."

She reached for her cake. Her fingers were trembling slightly. I no longer doubted that her desire to confide would prevail over her bashfulness.

"I could tell you," she said, raising her eyes again. "But you're unlikely to believe me; it sounds so stupid. Stupid and strange – stranger than all your 'donuts' and 'arrows.' And most importantly, you're unlikely to understand – even though you know so many smart things."

"It can't hurt to try," I encouraged her.

"Well, okay..." Tina drawled, folding her arms over her chest. "Just remember: I warned you." And she began to recount – incoherently at first, somewhat reluctantly choosing her words. Then she started to speak more fluently; I noticed that when she spoke, her whole body curved slightly to one side, and her hands danced in the air in a special, peculiar way. And as soon as she paused, even for a brief moment, she immediately folded her arms again, as if protecting herself – from me and everything around her.

This state of detachment and not seemingly being present was not unusual for her, Tina said. It happened to her quite often – which means she probably is a freak after all, and I'd been too presumptuous with my optimistic judgment. However, freak or no freak, she was no ordinary one because… Here, Tina was silent for a while and then blurted it out, "I really do speak to someone – constantly and involuntarily. And the most important thing is that this 'someone' comes – yes, from another world; there's no other way of putting it!"

She looked at me intently. I nodded, seriously, without the slightest hint of a smile. "There's no other way of putting it," she repeated, "and there's no need to. It doesn't have a precise name anyway, even if I were to go through every dictionary and phrasebook. I cannot even explain it clearly to myself – although, of course, I've become used to it and stopped considering it a disease, a sickness. Now I just call it a symptom – it's a step forward; a difficult one. It's a positive step – because a symptom is not necessarily related to an illness…"

Tina's "symptom" manifested itself way back in her distant childhood, soon after moving to Thailand. She began to experience odd sensations: it seemed someone invisible had stationed himself next to her and remained there, never leaving her for a single moment. He could not be touched, he was incorporeal, but his presence was undeniable. He held endless conversations with her – no, she wasn't hearing voices, but *her mind itself* was in a constant dialogue with him, in contact with him, and that's how all her thoughts were conceived. All that she could say, think, remember, arose from the presence of that "someone" nearby – or maybe "something" if one were to look from a wider perspective. Although, of course, "someone" was preferable because he already was her best friend, an intimate confidant, and she has no desire to think of him as something without a soul.

In her childhood, when it all began, she got scared and asked the Buddha to save her from this obtrusive stranger. In addition to the Buddha, she mentioned this to her mother, who became seriously alarmed and took her to a well-known local shaman. He said that Tina was being hunted by an evil spirit living in an old tree near her house and performed a tiring and distressing ritual that frightened her more than the symptom itself. After that, she decided she'd be better off not asking the Buddha for anything – and, in general, not discussing this secret "someone" with anyone.

From that moment, Tina only posed questions to and sought answers from herself. For a while, due to a lack of any other ideas, she continued to believe her "friend" was a spirit on a hunt for her, although she doubted his malignancy. Wandering around the house, she peered into the branches of the trees, looking for her "collocutor," mentally begging him to reveal himself. Then, all at once, she became disillusioned with this notion, outgrew it and immediately started to feel almost like an adult. She began to be visited by very unchildlike thoughts, and with them came various fears, some of which had remained with her ever since. Tina still did not like sleeping in the dark, always leaving the night-light on. She was afraid of heights and dogs and avoided the touch of strangers. And her main phobia was and remained the fear of death.

Over the years, she became increasingly reserved. Her peers felt her detachment, her aloofness – and were on their guard with her. She did not try to dispel their suspicions, to become one of "the gang." At school, she was teased and given nasty nicknames – because of her habit of moving her lips, as if carrying on a silent conversation. She only withdrew further into herself, and at times she would suddenly become aggressive, attacking her tormentors like an enraged cat. Once, she pushed one of her classmates who had been persistently calling her a "loony" into the school pond from a footbridge – he couldn't swim and nearly drowned. This incident made a big impression on Tina: she learned to stay away from people who might make fun of her – at any cost. Since such people made up the overwhelming majority, the price she paid was solitude. She embraced it willingly and wasn't afraid of it in the least.

She never made a single close friend. And there were no boyfriends either – despite her attractive appearance, she was not a big hit with the boys. All this bothered her very little – Tina's main preoccupation was her "symptom" and not the people around her. She had no doubt this was no accident; it was an echo of something vitally important – and she was very afraid her life would not be long enough to uncover the essence of it. For the time being, this essence remained a mystery; she did not know how to approach it. Neither religion nor the Thai myths offered anything useful. Common concepts of the mysterious and otherworldly seemed naive, simplistically primitive. As a result, she stopped going to the temples and almost forgot about the Buddha. And she treated Thai films and TV series, full of phantoms of all stripe, with condescending contempt…

"Look around," Tina lowered her voice, glancing at the tables nearby. "Everyone sitting here is convinced they share this world with a whole legion of ghosts, but to me this sounds like nonsense. I do not *share* the space; it's just that some part of me does not *fit* into this space – do you understand? Have you ever noticed how cramped together we are here? As if you're sitting in a small room with a large crowd of idiots. And in that room, there is a window, and there, beyond the window is a boundless, infinite breadth!"

It was these words that caused something to shift in my mind. I suddenly interrupted her, "Wait, wait" – and turned away, trying to apprehend this microscopic change. Tina looked at me with some alarm; I grinned to calm her, then nodded and said, "I understand you perfectly, better than you think – and, by the way… Please think hard, don't rush, this is serious: How would you describe *the place* where this 'someone' of yours is located? How would you label this place – or perhaps you might be able to just show it to me?"

"What is there to think hard about?" Tina shrugged. "It's here, around me – and around again, everywhere."

"Wait a moment; here's our world" – I drew an imaginary circle on the table. "And here you are" – I mark a point at its center – "show me where your interlocutor is? To the right, to the left, all around?"

"No," Tina shook her head, "he's here" – she made a gesture as if poking through the plane of the table with her finger. "Under the table, above the table and here, a little to one side, if you look in that direction, but the table doesn't matter; that place always remains with me. Only out there, as I said, there is none of the crowdedness we have here."

"Amazing…" I muttered, looking at her hand and rubbing my temple. "Amazing and strange, and very precise. You know, I'm working on something; I'm trying to explain how thoughts are born. Both yours and mine

– but I'm still unable to tell you in a comprehensible way. It seems I don't yet understand the most important thing myself."

The sense of a shift in my mind was still with me; I caught it. I was ready to start formulating it – in solitude, in silence.

Soon we said goodbye. "I'm leaving tomorrow," I told her. "Maybe we'll see each other again, who knows."

"Yes," she responded to my tone, "as I was saying, the world is such a crowded place…"

For some reason, I couldn't hold her gaze. "In any case," I said, looking down at the table, "I believe this 'symptom' of yours is not a fantasy or drivel. It is something very real, and you are wonderful – with or without it."

"Oh, thank you, thank you," Tina laughed, and it was a strange laugh. Then I looked at her at last and saw in her eyes, deep inside, a very adult confusion and longing. So out of harmony with her lipstick and the bright streak in her hair.

Going to the skytrain station, I muttered in different ways, "Dimensions, dimensions, there are many of them, far more than three…" I wanted to laugh, feeling an incredible burst of energy. In the car, I pressed my forehead against the glass door and looked out at the city, stretching in all directions, the skyscrapers piercing plane after plane. The train made a semicircle, turning toward the Chao Praya River; the monorail bend changed the perspective, altered the geometry – the geometry of the city, the geometry of the world. Bringing together points that had seemed dispersed, like on my fractal curves… I looked through the glass, like an emperor over my domain from the top of a hill. Gradually it became clearer what I needed to do next with the equations and the mysterious field. With the flows that establish balance – the balance of energy, the balance of consciousness…

And suddenly, I was struck by something else, like an electric spark or the overly adult gaze of a teenager. I sensed with every fiber of my body that I didn't want to, I couldn't fly away from here – from Bangkok, from Tina. I finally had real allies – maybe for the first time in my life. I could sense their lack of indifference – it was so valuable, so rare! A city full of alien realities; a girl whose life was infinitely distant from mine had suddenly become incredibly close – much closer than snooty Bern and my colleagues, not willing to open their eyes a bit wider.

Ten minutes later, on the platform of my station, I took out my phone and wrote to Tina, "I'm not going anywhere!" Immediately I received a text back with a surprised "Oh!" and after it, seven emojis in a row expressing jubilation and joy.

"Shall we meet tomorrow?" I texted and received in reply, "Yes! Yes! Yes!"

CHAPTER 20

BEFORE BANGKOK, ALL the components of my theory – neurons, the water dipole matrix and a new compensating field – had existed in the same space in our habitual three-dimensional one – without going beyond it. Of course, I had often thought of making the new field an "external" phenomenon, entering the three-dimensional world from somewhere outside, but each time I rejected this idea, hastily driving it away. I remembered too well the embarrassment caused by the ill-fated article where I'd mentioned the hyperspaces and external forces my colleagues had found so funny. To put it simply, I was just afraid – but now, having met Tina and seen how she had unhesitatingly pushed through the plane of the table with her gesture, I realized I had no right to fear. I made an effort and stopped being a coward. This was the essence of the shift in my mind – and it played a crucial role.

I went back to the hotel, to my cramped, uncomfortable room. It was a very unsuitable place, totally unlike my office or apartment in Bern, where everything had been so lovingly chosen and arranged. But I didn't have any choice, so I sat down at the narrow desk on the awkward, rib-backed chair, took a sheet of paper with the hotel logo, picked up the cheap, poor-quality hotel pen, and in these totally inconvenient conditions recorded the most important thoughts. The first of them stated: the number of dimensions of our world and the space in which my new field "lives" do not have to match. This external space could be a multi – more than three – dimensional one. The mysterious field permeates our world, as, for example, a magnetic field permeates a figure drawn on a sheet of paper placed between the poles of a magnet… Thus, discarding my past fears, I divided the two worlds. And crossed the line.

That day I sat at my equations until late at night. I twice ran out of paper and ran down to reception to ask for more. The next morning, I canceled my trip to Phuket and started to look for accommodation for the remaining days of my vacation. The thought of sand and sea only aroused bewilderment. I no longer needed rest; I was fed up with it.

Of all the areas of Bangkok I had managed to visit, I liked only the central one where Tina and I had met. I promptly took the subway to the center and, without bargaining, rented a two-room apartment on Langsuan Road. Then I brought all my things there and immediately fell in love with the place – both the street and my new home. The features of the city that surrounded me – the humid air and the strange smells, the bustling crowds on the potholed sidewalks – acquired a new status, became friendly. The short walk from my new apartment to the skytrain station convinced me every time: the city was my ally. It was ready to share with me its energy, its perpetual thirst for life.

I perceived this thirst, imbibed it, absorbed the energy into myself. And worked tirelessly, for days on end. The division of the worlds into an internal and external one complicated the theory, demanded different approaches. It seemed I was moving even further away from a result, but the complication also had its pluses: now I could toughen the criteria by excising those constructs that had no real meaning with a ruthless scalpel. The set of available options widened, but, at the same time, there were more restrictions, like levers in my hands; I just had to use them wisely. I varied the quantum variables, the degrees of freedom of my "fractal" quasiparticles – and, on the other hand, changed the dimensionality of the space from which the hypothetical field originated, its configuration, metric and curvature. The divergences in the equations disappeared and emerged again. I was wandering in a jungle of transformations, playing one anomaly off against another, trying to make them mutually destroy, nullify each other… It was a long, difficult process, and its success to a large extent depended on luck. This state of uncertainty, a random trawl in an ocean of possibilities, lasted about three weeks. And all this time Tina provided a vital foundation for my determination, an inexhaustible source of strength.

The same day, shortly after my move to Langsuan Road, we met in an outdoor restaurant nearby. It was stuffy; I was drinking ice-cold beer and telling her everything – about my work, about the mysteries of the human memory and mind, about her, Tina, and her gesture, piercing through the surface… I said to her, "I can't promise anything, but perhaps you're experiencing exactly what I'm looking for in my math. Why not concede there are people with abnormal sensitivity – who *feel* the interaction of their brain with something external. If so, then my theory could provide an explanation of your quirkiness – it would be the clue you are looking for!"

Tina didn't ask any questions; she just listened without taking her eyes off me. Only when I mentioned her "symptom" did she raise her eyebrows and mutter, grinning, "Ah, so you didn't fly here to save me from losing my glasses. You came to explain why I'm such a freak. At last – I was so afraid no one would ever come to my rescue…"

Afterward, she asked, "Can I help you in some way?"

"Yes," I said, "you can. Just be with me sometimes. I don't know why, but I need your presence."

Not surprised, she just nodded her head. "If you want, I'll come to your place in the mornings. I can bring you lunch, make you coffee. Or just pay you a visit – we are friends, after all. And friends do visit each other – sometimes quite often…"

And she began to come frequently – that is, every morning – to keep me company during the most productive hours. She would bring some street food – I'd try a little, out of courtesy, and Tina would eagerly devour the rest herself. Despite her idiosyncrasies, she, like all Thais, had a good appetite and was a strong sleeper – she talked of this with pride, as if to emphasize her relative normality. Sometimes she tried to tidy up the apartment, although it was already clean – the rent included maid service. More often, she would just sit on the sofa in a Buddha-like pose and busy herself with her phones or watch movies on her tablet with her headphones on.

Her presence helped me immensely. To know she was there, to look at her at times – it was so important and seemed so valuable! The power of her dark, almond-eyed gaze in response increased my strength tenfold. I was aware she was here with me every passing second, and it wasn't distracting – on the contrary, it deepened my concentration, sharpened my focus. I sunk my teeth into stubborn formulas, using every ounce of my courage and my resources. She believed in me – and I couldn't allow myself to linger over doubts, to assume for even a moment that my work might end up being futile.

Thus, the first two weeks passed – in the most intense, albeit unfruitful research, and in getting used to Tina's presence. She would spend most of the day with me. After that, we'd go out for a meal, and then she would leave to attend to her own affairs. In the evening, as night was closing in, we would usually chat on "Line." At first, we just exchanged jokes or trifles, but soon the tone of her messages began to change. And so did mine – I recognized it but could not help it. The platonic period of our relationship had exhausted itself. We had become tired of the pretense of hiding just how attracted we were to each other.

Suddenly, from one evening to the next, Tina began to ask one and the same thing: "Do you want to see me tomorrow?" – as if there were any doubt. And, every time in response to my surprised, laconic "Yes, of course," she would write something like: "Oh, yes, you need me for your work…"

I would remain silent. There was a tension crackling between our chat apps – as if the data-transfer protocol had special tags for it. She continued, "Well, so be it; it's good at least, you're not rejecting me outright – whatever the reason might be…" I laughed in reply, showing I was taking this as a joke. Pretending I did not understand, although I understood everything perfectly.

I knew how to be bold with women, but I felt an inexplicable timidity toward Tina. Her apparent vulnerability bothered me – and at the same time I knew she was amply protected and it'd be tough to break through her defenses. The very same lines of force that had surrounded her in the café during our first meeting were still in place, here, around her – like the invisible "someone" with whom she was engaged in an endless dialogue.

Subconsciously, I was afraid of failure, rejection. And a hint of rejection had already happened – one evening, soon after my move to Langsuan.

We were sitting somewhere, and before leaving I suddenly wanted to make physical contact – albeit without any serious intentions. I reached across the table and took her fingers in mine. Tina reacted very sharply. Wrenching her hand away, she recoiled in her chair and, as was her habit, folded her arms over her chest. I shrugged, raising an eyebrow inquiringly, and she said with feeling, with all her heart, "I can't stand lovey-dovey stuff!" There was an awkward pause; I paid the bill and we left, but within the hour we were exchanging messages again, and the next morning she came to see me as usual. This episode had not changed anything at the time, but now it was really holding me back.

Meanwhile, I sensed our mutual attraction. It tormented me, getting more and more difficult to deal with. In the evenings, after parting with Tina, I would go to the massage parlor next door, where for a surcharge the girls would be happy to offer various extras. I got up to all sorts of things with them, but it didn't help. As soon as I got home, I would start wanting Tina again. It got to the point where my desire began to interfere with my work – I could no longer concentrate on mathematics when she was sitting on the sofa behind me. It was clear: something needed to change. We had to come to definite terms – if not regarding the configuration of external spaces, then at least with the nature of our relationship.

Finally, an idea came into my head. I decided to cook dinner for Tina – knowing that the next day, on Saturday, she would be busy and would only come to see me in the evening. I found a book of Thai recipes on the web, studied it until the small hours, went to the Central Market in the morning, and then, forgetting about my formulas, immersed myself in cooking – on the whole, successfully enough. The only thing that didn't work out was the traditional Thai soup; the rest – the green curry, the rice with pineapple and especially the pad thai noodles – were rather edible. Then I called the maid in to do the cleaning, went to get some wine and waited for Tina.

She never cooked herself and was stunned. At first, she could barely cope with her shyness and sat in silence, unable to raise her eyes. I began telling her about Europe – about Gunter and his wife, about Tony with his sad vagabond eyes and macho "he who lives in the bloodstream" Albert. My account was lighthearted and funny, and Tina soon cheered up. Her stiffness dissipated; she laughed a lot and even asked for a wine – although she never usually touched alcohol. I poured her some chardonnay. She quickly drank it, got up, took a few steps around the room, came up to me and said with a smile, "You're such a big man and I'm so small, and yet you're making me dinner..." Then she added, "Perhaps there's something you want from me?" – and looked at me with her dark eyes, openly, at point-blank range, as only she knew how.

I also got up and grinned, as if responding to a joke, "If you already know what I'm thinking, then I have nothing to add." Tina took a step back, not taking her eyes off me. I could sense her expectation, even an element of impatience – and a complete unwillingness to turn back.

I advanced toward her, took her by the hand and gave her fingers a light squeeze. "Well, yes," she said, "look how the time's flown. It's probably too late to go home now" – and retreated a little farther. I followed her.

"I'll just have to spend the night at yours," she said. "Evidently, I'm going to have to repay you somehow for putting me up?" Then she took another step away and feigned a deep sigh, "What a fall from grace – to spend the night at a man's place..."

I moved toward her again, without letting go of her hand. Our eyes were locked together like the steel links of a chain.

Tina stepped back and leaned against the wall. She shrugged, "I've already told you much more intimate secrets. What's the point of concealing my body?" Then suddenly she released her hand, pulled off her T-shirt and immediately covered herself with it, muttering, "Of course, I must give you this; otherwise you might go looking for other women. And anyway, it's such a small thing..."

Her voice was trembling with tension. She turned away and confessed, "I'm afraid, but it's not what you think. I'm just terribly unsure of myself. I'm a virgin; I've never had a proper boyfriend before. You know about most of my complexes, but there's one more – I have a fear I'm not any good in bed!"

I just embraced her, ignoring her words. I had a thing or two to say about complexes myself – the entire previous year after I had broken up with my Turkish girlfriend, my love affairs hadn't amounted to much. Evidently, my theory had taken over; I couldn't free myself from it, take my mind off it. No, I wasn't thinking about my formulas during sex, but I would often lose interest – at the most inopportune moments. I'd become helpless, I'd hate myself – so now I also had reasons to feel uneasy. Yet, I tried to forget about them – surprisingly, it worked out. And we made love.

I took Tina to the bedroom, sat her on the bed, pulled off the rest of her clothes. She gave a deep sigh, leaned back and spread her legs. I buried my tongue deep inside her – she came quickly, signing to me she wanted to rest, to savor the moment. Then she pulled my head back toward her. She came again and made a gesture with her hand. It didn't express anything specific, but I understood: she wanted me to penetrate her…

Probably, it was one of the clumsiest episodes in my life – Tina's inexperience and lack of confidence were evident, and I was unable to help her much. And yet, it was one of the happiest occasions: I felt indefatigable and capable of any feat. At first, I tried to be gentle, overly cautious, but Tina suddenly screamed, "Don't mollycoddle me, be rough with me, give it to me hard!" I obeyed and took her roughly – she did not make a sound all the way through. I looked into her face but could not perceive what lay behind the new expression on it. Her eyes were closed, her lips tightly compressed. It seemed I was coupled together, not with a fragile Thai girl but with a boundless cosmos that refused to provide me with a response – perhaps because I wasn't yet worthy of it. Only at the last moment did she open her eyes, and I saw how brightly her pupils were burning.

Afterward, she sat for a long time with her legs crossed and her back straight, looking in front of her and not saying a word. I sat next to her, gazing at her in silence, not even trying to guess her thoughts. Waves seemed to be emanating from her entire body; I sensed a perplexity in her caused by something bigger than the loss of virginity. The boundless cosmos was finally sending me a signal. It was a pity I didn't know how to decipher it.

Then she recovered, stretched out her hand toward me and touched my hair as if seeing me for the first time. She asked for more wine, went to the bathroom; on her return, she lay down next to me, cuddled up close – and so we lay, it seemed, for ages. After she fell asleep, I cautiously freed myself from her embrace, poured myself a gin and sat down in an armchair nearby.

Tina's dreams were restless, unsettled; she shuddered and muttered indistinct words in Thai. I could almost physically sense that her talking with her "someone" was continuing even now – with images being created in her head, thoughts conceived, their connections formed. I remembered her in the recent moments of intimacy – her compressed lips, the amazement in her burning eyes, her demand for roughness. I wondered what it was she was looking for in this world, overcoming her fears, pushing tenderness away like a half measure. It was somehow connected with her vulnerability, with her subtlety of feeling, but I could not grasp its logic and essence. I made a huge effort, trying to comprehend at least a little bit, but I understood almost nothing. Yet a presentiment of understanding, a foretaste of a deep truth, came to me that night. For the first time, I thought about the role of consciousness and the role of the body; I separated them, imagining how we are enriched by our new experiences, and why. Are they transferred somewhere – and if so, where? Maybe experiences do not vanish in vain, do not simply die? Maybe those among us who have heightened feelings subconsciously know this and are striving to live their lives more fully, more vividly – even at the expense of damaging themselves in the process?…

I have to stress: back then I was not able to formulate all this, tie the loose fragments together. But a sense of these fragments remained within me. As well as confidence – of a fulfillment, which was waiting for me somewhere nearby. I could no longer doubt that, could not show any weakness. It had gotten closer to me, become more discernible. Because: a crucial step on the path toward it had been taken – the fulfillment of love. Even if not a word about love had been said.

CHAPTER 21

OF COURSE, OUR intimacy changed everything. Things became easier but at the same time more tangled. We each tried to cope with these complications in our own way.

Tina's next step was momentous: within a day she had moved in with me. She rang from the street-level intercom, asking for help – I ran down the stairs perplexed and saw her standing at the entrance with two large bags. For some reason, I wasn't at all surprised. To her, it also seemed natural, although at first she was somewhat embarrassed by her act. She talked as she wandered around the apartment unpacking her things, "Who would have thought it. For example, only yesterday I had no plans of living with a man whatsoever. Especially a *farang*. And a middle-aged *farang* at that. It's a good thing I don't have any girlfriends; they'd be shocked. They'd probably be saying I'm a kept sweetie!"

I also did something decisive: I extended the rent on my apartment for another four months. I did not tell Tina about it – she already considered it a matter of course that I was going to be in Bangkok for a long time. We never raised the topic; only once did she ask when I was going back to Europe. I answered honestly – that for now I didn't know – and my answer satisfied her. At least that was what I thought, and I worried myself while figuring out what to do with my vacation, which was rapidly coming to an end. After our night together, the decision came of itself – I simply realized there was no way I could leave. Having understood this, I wrote a desperate letter to Bern begging them to let me stay on as a consultant so that I could work remotely, albeit for only half my salary. They were accommodating – maybe my message managed to convey a sensation that possessed me utterly. The feeling that fate was forcing me to remain here with a powerful gesture that could not be contradicted.

Our daily routine was established right away. Tina would get up first, silently slipping out of bed; she would do some stretching and yoga exercises. Then, just as quietly, she would potter around the apartment, tidying things up, shifting them from place to place, brewing the coffee. When I woke up, she would return to the bedroom, sit by the mirror and busy herself with her appearance, applying the slightest cosmetic touches. I reclined in bed and looked at her – it was a mandatory part of our daily ritual. Often this would excite her; she would come over to me with an innocent half smile. I would drag her to me, rip off her clothes and throw myself on her fragile nudity...

Then we would have breakfast, and I'd work while Tina sat on the sofa behind me, doing her own thing. Sometimes she would do it semidressed; without turning around I could easily imagine her sharp shoulders, thin neck, brittle teenage grace. Just looking at her gave me strength and inspiration, which, I'm sure, I'd never have gotten from anyone else. Even sex with her, contrary to the laws of physiology, did not leave me drained but charged with energy.

At the same time, not everything about our intimacy went smoothly. For a while, Tina could not get used to her new state and our bedroom games. As before, she would occasionally mutter, "Lovey-dovey stuff..." – although her own tenderness could have melted anyone. And, simultaneously, she would melt herself, soaking me with her juices, which disconcerted and bewildered her...

It was impossible to predict what exactly on a particular day would bring her pleasure and what would leave her feeling indifferent or even uncomfortable. Besides, she always tried to hide her discomposure – so as not to upset me and spoil the mood. But, of course, I sensed everything – and became upset, nervous and at times would lose my erection. Then, Tina, desperate with herself, would run to the bathroom – only to come back in a few minutes and console, calm me like a wise, mature woman.

More often, however, she preferred it for me to be the mature adult. She liked being led – and this wasn't just feminine weakness, a search for a strong shoulder to lean on. By handing over the initiative, she was, for a little while, casting off a huge load – a burden of responsibility of an ambiguous kind.

Sometimes she wanted to behave like a child – fooling around, having fun, whimpering. At others, she became easily hurt, with or without a reason, and then she threw up her hands in a funny way, always repeating the same phrase: "Can you *really* treat me like this?" But then the full weight of her responsibility would fall back on her shoulders. Occasionally, during my difficult moments, she unerringly perceived my fear of failure. And she would lead me to my desk, almost by the hand, saying, "Come with me. Don't be afraid; sit down and do this. Do this well."

And I would do it – at least I'd try. Sometimes, while working, I'd suddenly feel I was desperately missing contact with her. I would make up some excuse to turn toward her, ask how she was feeling, whether the AC was too cold for her or not. Tina almost never answered, only nodded, shrugged and looked at me with a playful, understanding glance. Then she would suddenly get up, approach me, press my head to her breast and stay like that for several minutes, exchanging her energy with me. She would just stand there, not saying a word, looking into the distance, into worlds that didn't exist for others…

In my work, everything has changed as well. Our new life has strangely altered my view, my perspective. It was no better or worse; it just became different. This may have been the reason, or simply the quantity of effort had evolved into quality, but by the end of the fifth week, I stumbled across the right combination of the parameters and degrees of freedom.

This again happened in an ordinary way – everything just suddenly came together. Three multipliers turned to zero, neutralizing the most malicious divergences – and the remaining ones were eliminated by renormalization. The external space in this case could have any number of dimensions from a certain range: ten, sixteen, twenty-eight, forty-two… Each of these values assumed its own set of degrees of freedom in fractal quasiparticles "on a flat sheet of paper" – in our three-dimensional world inside a multidimensional external one. I settled on the simplest, the sixteen-dimensional case. It required only one additional quantum variable, and the equations acquired a laconic, elegant appearance. I knew: the more harmonious and compact the theory, the greater the chance it would be correct.

Thus, the mysterious field interacting with the dipole matrix was fixed, described by mathematics. As I already knew, the interaction took place when the water dipoles of the brain were arranged in a special way. Their arrangement was "packed" into a nontrivial fractal-like figure – I named this state "fractal coherence"; it emerged and was sustained thanks to the intense work of certain neural groups. They created the initial conditions, triggering the quantum effect – fractal symmetry breaking, fractal ordering – this was exactly what the "superfluous" energy was spent on when the brain was working hard, remembering and thinking. The energy was then released in a stream of quasiparticles, quasi-Goldstone bosons – they transferred it to the external field, gaining mass and slowing down. Thus, the quasiparticles, the quanta of dipole waves supporting fractal coherence, acted as agents of a previously unknown interaction – as mediators between our brain and a new field, our world and an external multidimensional space.

Now I saw this field – in the modified right-hand side of the Lagrangian I had obtained. Assuming it was the primary cause of our intelligence, I named its quanta, the particles that permeate our world and interact with the quasiparticles of the brain, "conscions" – from the word *consciousness*. And that was where my achievements ended. The formulas demonstrated mathematical consistency, affirmed the *possibility* of the new interaction, but, alas, I did not understand *exactly how* it was taking place. The equations describing the connection of the worlds lay in front of me, but I could not solve them.

A week passed, another began. I was treading water, on the verge of the most important secret, and could not move a single step forward. It was extremely frustrating to be standing on the threshold and not being permitted to look inside. Coming to a standstill was nothing special; it had happened before. It had happened often, and, like any other scientist, I was used to that. But never had I been so tormented by my incapability – too much converged together; I was sure that the result, when it finally came to me, would put everything in its place. That my theory would be completed, logically whole. That the essence of the mind and the nature of true consciousness would become clear to me. And that I would reveal to Tina the basic nature of her mysterious "symptom," unmask her inter-locutor-confidant, drag him into the light. I felt desperately impatient; all these motivations urged me on. But I wasn't getting anywhere.

As if in tune with my mental state, thunderstorms began to break over Bangkok. Every day, heavy clouds would gather by lunchtime, clinging to the tops of the skyscrapers. Soon there would be a short but furious deluge, followed by muddy streams of water cascading down the side-walks and throngs of cars frozen in traffic jams. Then we started to have problems with the electricity: it would get cut off at the most inconvenient times. Often, we would wake up in the middle of the night to a stuffy humid room and wander around the apartment like sleepwalkers in the sparse gloom of the streetlights. Then the storms went away, and the elec-tricity was fixed, but a serious conflict had arisen between Tina and me.

It had been coming to a head for quite some time; we'd been approach-ing it from different sides and had simultaneously reached the critical moment, just as we had often attained orgasm together. It all started when I told her about my success – the equations for the sixteen-dimen-sional case – although for the time being, this "success" was still illusory and eluding my grasp. I think I did it just to cheer myself up – running ahead and saying things I so much wanted to believe. Everything, how-ever, turned out differently. After listening to me, Tina shook her head, "I don't understand. I know I'm stupid, but can you draw me a picture of it, please…" – and I became confused, evasive and inarticulate. I was unable to draw something I could not see myself; it would have been the most appalling deception!

As a result, I only got angry – both at myself and Tina. The words I had let loose on the world too soon had not pulled me along with them – conversely, they had made everything worse. Seeing no way out, I began to make attempts at changing things around me – but the only thing around was Tina; the rest was not important. It started to seem to me that her presence was no longer helping but, on the contrary, hindering, leading me astray. One time and then another, I tried to work away from home, in a café next door. But only ended up achieving one thing – exacerbating her jealousy, which by that time was already making itself felt.

After that first night, Tina's mind quickly passed through several stages – clarifying our "romance" and its future. While I was occupied with global concepts – which, I thought, united her and me just as globally – Tina was thinking simply, like any woman. For several days, despite moving in with me, she was tormented with doubts – I could sense them but did not contemplate their nature. Then the doubts receded; the internal reasoning had been completed. Tina understood, formulated for herself precisely what she wanted. She decided she wanted to be with me for the rest of our lives.

Right after that, unconsciously and then quite consciously, she began to assert her rights over me. Her ownership rights – despite her youth and the disparity of our worldviews. Her position evolved rapidly, changing day by day.

It began from an inverse point of view, in a sort of emancipated way. "I'm not jealous," she told me, "and I'm not trying to tie you down. Every man should have adventures, I know. You can sleep with other women and then tell me about it…"

I was turning this into a joke; Tina was laughing. Then, in the same exalted-joking manner, she began to make fun of me. "Actually," she sighed, "you are a bit over the hill, don't you think? Just a little bit older and you'll be an ancient ruin, ha-ha-ha. What other women could there be – it's amazing you don't have a heart attack when we make love!"

At the same time, she – cautiously, as if by chance – interrogated me about every minute of the day I had spent without her. On several occasions – pretending to be playing around – she even tried to check my smartphone. I wasn't bothered – I had nothing to hide. My mind was busy with my theory and the equations that wouldn't yield. And then we had a conversation.

It happened at dinner, in a quiet Japanese restaurant. Tina started it suddenly – she had been chatting about trifles, then stopped, took a piece of sashimi from her plate but did not eat it, her chopsticks frozen in midair. She looked at me and said in a tense voice, "On the whole, I wouldn't mind if we were to be together for a long time. Maybe a very long time. Perhaps forever."

Caught unawares, I could not find an answer. The waitress came up and poured us some green tea. Tina's chopsticks trembled in the air. She laid them on the table, turned away and added, "I would like to have a child with you, but this is not obligatory. If you are afraid I'll be stressing you about children, then don't worry; it's not a big deal for me."

I caught a glimpse of something in her expression beyond her years, as I had weeks ago, during our second meeting. I now noticed it again but did the wrong thing: I did not take her seriously. Instead, I winked at Tina slyly, "I know, you're only pulling my leg. You're much younger than me, and it's too early to discuss our future, isn't it?..." Tina smiled and changed the subject. She did not raise the topic again that evening or for the next two days. Only later did I realize: it was precisely then that she had become possessed by the idea that I had a wife left behind in Europe to whom I was going to return sooner or later. She'd heard that romances with Western boyfriends often ended this way. And on the third day, there was an explosion.

I came home from the café in the evening at about seven. Tina met me without a smile or a kiss, her face in a frozen mask.

"Where have you been?" she asked.

I just shrugged, "You know perfectly well."

"Well, yes," Tina nodded, "it's all too easy – to hide behind your work, when in fact you could be doing anything you wanted. And no one would know where you were, exactly..." Then she asked, "Well, have you done much today? Have you made a lot of progress? Completed a great feat of labor? Of course, you can do much better without me!"

It was a sore spot; I flared up and was rude to her. She was rude to me back, burst into tears and locked herself in the bathroom with her phone. And from there she began sending me short messages – flashes of despair, insecurity and hurt.

"I do not want this anymore," I read. "You are old. You don't speak Thai."

"It's all unreliable. With you. Unpredictable!" I read in confusion. "I will not live in Europe. Go back on your own."

"Go back to your wife. How old is she? Fifty or sixty? Just what you need!" And after this came: "I don't want a *farang*!!" – like a scream at the top of her voice.

These condensed fragments of hastily formulated thoughts for some reason hit me straight in the heart, dispelled the illusions and destroyed the magic. I suddenly felt that behind them was a life infinitely alien to me, one unconquerable abyss after another. Everything I had closed my eyes to now reared up before me. Self-deception – there was no other way of defining our closeness. Naivety – that was the reason for my faith in the affinity of our goals, in that indistinct something binding us together with a strong thread…

After a two-minute silence, the final message came through: "Do you understand me?"

"Yes," I wrote back. "I understand."

"Okay," I wrote next. "Go away then."

And added a few hurtful, unfair words.

I was filled with disappointment and bitterness. Tina remained in the bathroom; not a sound escaped from it. I wandered aimlessly around the apartment, then changed my clothes and went out into the city, not wanting to see her or talk to her. Carrying inside my dissatisfaction with the both of us, my anguish. Nursing it like a tamed beast.

CHAPTER 22

NIGHT DESCENDED ON Bangkok. I was walking toward Sukhumvit, to the sweaty crowds and neon glare, to the countless bars and every imaginable vice ever invented by man. I stopped somewhere, ate a bowl of spicy soup, drank something and moved on. Then I had a drink somewhere else, stepped away from the central boulevard and walked and walked, veering randomly from street to street...

I traipsed around like this for hours – not knowing what I was doing or where I was going. Feverish thoughts whirled around my head – about Tina, about my theory and my fate. Everything was slipping away; I couldn't grasp hold of any encouraging feeling. Faces floated into view – old and ugly, or inviting, heavily made up – they rushed up to me and staggered away. Hands grabbed me by the sleeve, trying to sell me something, capture me, lure me, drag me away – I pulled my arm free, pushed peddlers aside, ignoring their indignant cries, and walked on, stopping only for yet another drink. Then the streets became empty; I had wandered into some desolate hole. I found myself in a very poor and dirty neighborhood next to a bridge across a rotting canal. Nearby, there were piles of garbage, a few miserable shacks and people – a fairly large group. They called me over to them; I approached, and they began to point something out to me – "Here, here!"

A man lay next to a racing bike. Quite young, white, with European features. His head was bleeding – evidently, he had tried to ride around a puddle in the middle of the road along a concrete elevation but had fallen off and hit a stone.

I instantly absorbed the whole scene with my inflamed, alcohol-addled brain. I grasped it and realized: this was a reminder, maybe even a sign. My stepfather immediately came to mind – yes, fate continued to lead me around the same themes. I remembered my childhood and myself covered with night sweat, the awakening of my fear, the fear of death – it came as suddenly as death itself comes. I remembered Tina and her fears – and, for some reason, how she had sat in the Buddha pose after our first sex, listening to something new emerging within her. I was remembering, and the same thing appeared from nowhere, kept spinning in my head: "Phase transition!"

The people around me were babbling something in Thai. I did not hear them and paid no attention. Everything seemed to have frozen; I was beyond reality, beyond events – having turned into a medium and receiving a signal. The world opened up before me, revealed itself to me – in its entirety, all at once. I perceived its interconnections, unable and not even wanting to formulate them into words, symbols, numbers. It was a sensation of extreme clarity – as if my mind had suddenly been overlaid on tracing paper with the structure of the universe and was living with it in unison. I don't know which term was more relevant here – resonance, similitude, concordance? They were all quite powerless. Words were powerless, but the feeling itself made me more than powerful, omnipotent. Everything that had happened and was happening to myself and others was becoming arranged in a series, breaking down into the most basic images, and I was capable of instantaneously grasping any or all of them.

I saw that life was a spider's web, a labyrinth full of dead ends. I could see Tina, the guiding thread, one of the many or few available to me. And my theory – it was a component, an element of the series, one of its details. I sensed that it only required a little effort on my part to find a track in its own intricate labyrinth. I made this effort; in my mind – with difficulty, with a creak – a corner was turned, and a change of the guard, a transfer onto new rails occurred. Suddenly, flicker after flicker, fragments of a new comprehension were lit up: one formula, another and yet another... An integral, which seemed to be unsolvable, broke into several independent parts… I finally saw the real meaning of some of the constructions that I had dropped for the sake of simplicity, to shorten the path. But no, the path could not be shortened. Was this what fate had been repeatedly hinting, offering clues to which I had been apparently deaf?…

Then I came to; something brought me sharply back to reality. A sound… I shook my head and heard a groan – obviously, the cyclist was alive. "An ambulance!" I shouted and looked around, but no one moved. I screamed and waved my arms, but they only looked at me silently. Then I pulled out a mobile, shoved it in someone's hand nearby and yelled in his face, "Ambulance, ambulance!" The man immediately disappeared – I realized I would never see my phone again. And at that very moment the ambulance appeared – obviously, it had already been summoned before me.

The medical team busied themselves with the cyclist, and I felt unneeded, superfluous. I desperately wanted to go home, to Langsuan, and began to ask about how to get out of there. People turned away from me, not understanding a word; I thought sadly I would have to randomly find the road back, but then an elderly woman with a flabby, drunken face and kind eyes emerged from the crowd. "Let's go," she said; "I'll show you the way."

Barely believing my ears, I asked her, "Do you speak English?"

"I worked for thirty years in the massage parlors in Patpong," the woman smiled. The smile almost made her beautiful. She seemed like a saint to me.

"My name is Som," she added. "And you're handsome…"

I followed her under the bridge, winding through the garbage heaps.

"Look, this is where I live," Som said, pointing to a hovel made out of cardboard boxes.

"Why are you here?" I asked in confusion. "You have such a wonderful soul…"

"Where else should I be?" she said in surprise. "This is my home."

Behind the bridge was a path through the bushes, and beyond the bushes – a wide highway. "You need to go there," Som pointed to the left. Suddenly we heard a shout. The man whom I had given my phone had caught up with us and shoved it back in my hand.

I wanted to give them money but discovered I didn't have a single baht. My wallet with my cards had been left at home; I had to make my way on foot; the journey took an hour and a half. I stumbled into the apartment, still not completely sober, in my sweaty clothing – and immediately saw Tina.

"Hi," she said, "I didn't leave, I just couldn't" – and she came up to me, embracing me around the neck.

I gently pushed her away and muttered, "I need a shower."

"Did you cheat on me?" Tina asked.

"No," I shook my head. "No, quite the opposite."

I went to the bathroom, but Tina followed me. She glanced sideways, standing on the threshold, and said, "So, you want to shut yourself away from me with a door? Are you disappointed? Are you going to leave me?"

I tried to smile, "It seems I couldn't part with you – even if I was disappointed a thousand times."

"Aha," Tina nodded and frowned, "but you are of course angry with me?"

"I don't know. Without you, I'm trapped in a spider's web," I confessed, revealing what I was really thinking.

"Aha," Tina repeated, growing pensive and taking a step back. I finally closed the door and began to undress. She did not go away, though, and spoke from the hall, "While you were gone, I went outside and brought back some food – sweet pork; you like it. I saw a dog without a tail. I drank tea and dropped the mug in the sink, but it did not break; only the edge chipped a bit..."

"Yes, yes," I muttered and turned on the tap. I stood under the stream and disconnected myself from everything in the blessed white noise. Then, about twenty minutes later, I left the bathroom and asked Tina to make me some coffee.

"In a minute," Tina nodded but did not go into the kitchen. She followed me around the apartment and continued to talk. "I was afraid and did not sleep," she complained. "I'm not used to sleeping on my own any more. I had to turn on the lights everywhere and leave the TV on. But even so I fell asleep just for an hour or two – and I had a bad dream..."

She spoke quickly, her words tumbling one after the other as if she were afraid that if she stopped, it would be forever. I embraced her, holding her tight. She took a deep breath and calmed down. Then she slipped out of my embrace, "Coffee... I'll be quick."

I swiftly downed the first cup and then another. My head cleared; I sat down at the table, yearning for my work as if I'd been away from it for a whole week. I leafed back through my notebook and immediately saw what I was looking for – the part of the equation I had earlier decided to omit. At the bottom of the sheet, two coupled operators, changing the behavior of the field, were frozen as if readying themselves for a great leap. For a complex transformation strangely leading to simplicity. This was a leap indeed – over the void, above the conventional, the familiar. A jump – from the interaction of fields to the compatibility of geometries. The entire system was reformulated in another way: my quasiparticles, local perturbations, produced space deformations carrying a topological charge. What had previously seemed mind-bogglingly complex, now came out naturally and simply. And I saw: these deformations twisted the field of the conscions into a vortex!

In three hours, I had derived the principal solution of the modified equations – a stable wave of soliton type. I only noticed the conscion vortex for a brief moment – but that was enough to believe in it. It was a stable wave motion localized in space around the source of disturbance – the human brain. In multidimensional reality, the brain was surrounded by conscions dancing their dance around it. A highly complex dance full of meaning – encapsulating everything we think about, everything we remember...

I named the vortex the "B Object." It was unclear where it came from – I just liked the word; it reflected the instantaneous associations flashing through my head. The associations were forgotten, but the word remained.

After that, I went to bed and slept until noon. Waking up, I saw Tina sitting nearby and looking at me. "Tina..." I muttered. "Now I know what you sense around you. You were right – it's here, here and here. It is a stable, solitary wave, a whirlpool of new particles, their dance."

She replied in all seriousness, "You are my genius!"

The next few days passed in a frenzy. I refined the theory to its final form, checked and double-checked it, scrutinized its properties. Then, convinced that everything was correct and error-free, I set about the main test – the connection with reality, the calculation of energy flows. Everything dovetailed in the best way possible; the "dark energy" of the brain – indirectly, through the oscillations of the dipole matrix – transformed into the new "steps" of the dance of the conscions. It enriched the conscion vortex of the B Object with new content – and the energy balance was strikingly rigorous. It was the most harmonious mechanism, and my formulas now described every stage of its workings!

Finally, I could say without reservation that I could see the whole picture. I could trace the entire path step by step – from the brain's response to an external stimulus up to abstract thought and self-awareness. It all started with a "seed," a trigger, some kind of image, sound, word or smell, or some other reason for exciting a particular group of neurons in the neocortex. Neurons resonated with the water matrix, activating the required dipole code, quantum oscillations of a certain frequency that had been "sleeping" until then at the lowest energy level. An interplay commenced between the micro- and macrocosm; a synchronicity in the neuron firing emerged and could be observed on the encephalograms. The brain passed through a multitude of states, perhaps previously familiar to it, circling near their attractors or jumping to others – that is, forming memories, thoughts, moving to associations linked with them, returning back, then moving away again…

The initial stimulus no longer played a role; the brain itself built chains of images, thoughts, memories – and, from time to time, became concentrated, "stuck" on certain ones. On those that were especially important at this given moment – and, as a result, the brain states forming this something became advantageous; it would pass through them again and again. Some areas of neural correlation seemed to start glowing red: a new hidden order, a special, "fractal" coherence was established within them. This coherence was caused by the ordering – again, fractal ordering – of the water dipoles, which, in turn, was supported by special types of quantum oscillations: bosons that, at first glance, could not exist according to the laws of physics. But they did exist – an external field had come to the rescue. This was my field of the conscions – interacting with it, quasiparticles-bosons decelerated, and the fractal ordering became stable!

Thus, the external field influenced the brain, but the brain influenced it in turn. A vortex arose in the flow of the conscions – it emerged and then existed, "lived" in the immediate vicinity of its source. Its dynamics were constantly changing, enriching – with the memories and thoughts on which the brain was concentrating. And then the enriched vortex, the B Object, in turn interacted with the brain slightly differently – as if providing a feedback. Consciousness focused in on itself or, if you like, "looked" in upon itself from the outside. This evidently was how insights, sudden comprehension, the formation of new concepts – all those things reflecting the real strength of the human mind – happened, as if being "prompted" externally. I no longer doubted that I had unraveled and mathematically described the mystery of the mind. And at the same time the nature of Tina's enigmatic "symptom"...

These were amazing, crazy days, the likes of which I had never known in my life. The hard work of the previous years was now crowned with success – of the greatest possible scale. To this was added the confidence that I had mastered the most important secret in the universe. And what's more, I was overwhelmed with my extraordinary intimacy with Tina.

Every evening I would describe to her in detail everything I had done during the day. She, of course, understood little, but I was sure she sensed all the most important things, transmitted them through herself. She somehow immediately believed me, believed in me, believed the truth of my discovery. And we became increasingly aware of exactly what we meant to each other.

Our link was stronger, deeper than the usual – coincidence of tastes, sexual attraction or commonly held opinions. We were connected by the greatest knowledge and we were both making a contribution toward it. We each played our own role in it – I could explain the phenomenon, and Tina could unequivocally experience, physically feel it, thereby confirming its truth, even if only for the two of us. This, as far as I could tell, made us and our partnership something inimitable, most unique. This gave huge meaning to our lives, and each of us was a source of meaning to the other. Many might not have believed it; they might have considered us charlatans and liars, losers who could not find their place in the world. But we knew what the world, and our place in it, really were.

Sensing our closeness, we did not talk about it – and never spoke about love. I diligently avoided tender words – and she even more so; it wouldn't have been her style. We just lived in our intimacy, reveled in it, not even trying to find a name for it.

The accounts I would produce in the evenings would turn us both on and always ended in sex. And our sex had also become different: within a week Tina had been transformed from an uptight virgin into an unbridled courtesan. Her shame dissipated, she now allowed anything to be done to her body. We did it in all sorts of places – on the bed and on the sofa, on the floor and in the armchair, in the kitchen next to the sink, in the bathtub under the shower... Wiry and flexible by nature, she could twist herself into the most incredible positions trying to find one that would bring a new or greater pleasure. Her subtle, barely perceptible aroma – the scent of arousal, desire, passion – seemed to permeate throughout the entire apartment. Sometimes she would say to me with a grin, "You bring out the animal side in me. When I'm with you I feel like a girl from Nana Plaza who has slept with a thousand men!"

Then, having completely exhausted each other, before falling asleep we would chat and joke: about ourselves, our lives and also – about the world's incredulity. I told her what I knew full well – about the resentment my theory would evoke, how they would look for reasons to ridicule it, to find even the smallest fault. "Then," I said with a chuckle, "we will present you as living proof; it might help. Keeping your animal side well concealed, of course..."

"Ha-ha," Tina answered me in the same tone. "I know you: you'd be dying of jealousy right away. But don't worry, we won't be showing me to anyone – because they wouldn't believe me either. You can at least do the math – and what can I do? They'll just say I'm a lunatic – we've already been over that. Or maybe they'll invent some sort of pill to cure me, so I stop sensing this Object of yours. Well, thanks but no thanks!"

And then the day came when the theory was finally completed – it was no longer a joking matter. We suddenly realized the depth of its consequences – especially the main one, the depth of which shook us to the core. And we continued to be shaken for a while, trying to cope with our bewilderment.

The essence of this realization was revealed to me on a hot, sunny morning. I saw it on paper and sat for a long time, not taking my eyes off the formulas, as if trying to find the courage to fully believe them. The crux of the matter was simple, easily comprehensible: the math demonstrated that the B Object, once created, could then exist *without the brain.* Having for any reason lost and become separated from its creator, it did not dissolve, did not scatter into nothingness. It was kind of fixated on itself, maintaining in full its vortex dynamics!

Later on, as usual, I checked everything again and again. Then I carefully copied on a separate sheet of paper the sequence of the transformations revealing how the B Object undergoes phase transitions – the first, the second one, the third one... And that night I told Tina about it – agitated and carefully selecting my terms.

She, I think, understood my emotions rather than the content of my words. Yet she caught the main thing: the B Object could not be *enriched* without a brain but is able *to live* without it, keeping what it had acquired. It can survive for a long time, maybe forever – with its conscions tirelessly dancing their dance. One that reflects everything that has been received in its time from the host-brain – the entire memory, or at least the most important fragments...

What I was saying hung in the air; it seemed strange even to me. I became nervous; trying to make it clearer, I exclaimed: "After the death of the brain, the B Object loses its connection with our world!" And I gesticulated, explaining, "Only the special quasiparticles, quanta of specific dipole waves, are able to interact with it!" And for the hundredth time I stressed the main notion, as if trying to find a fault in it: "Without fractal ordering – that is, without the active work of the brain – there are no such quasiparticles, and therefore there is no interaction. The B Object loses its energy supply and its compensating part. All its momentum becomes directed inside, toward itself, but it does not destroy it. It soon jumps into a different phase state and, not being attached to anything, moves away into space, carrying what it has accumulated. Just as a stone flies off after it's released from a sling, our memory 'recorded' onto the B Object races into the distance. In anticipation of – who knows what? Perhaps, some new fateful encounter?"

Tina lay by my side, not moving, frozen. "Your secret 'interlocutor,' plus your body, your brain – all this in its entirety is you," I told her. "Your body will disappear, but the interlocutor – that is, the B Object – will remain alive; it will then become *you*, storing within itself the experiences you have lived through.

"Your B Object, containing you within itself, will be carried away to other worlds," I went on, surprised at how stupid and pitiful my words sounded. "It will be carried away, as if on a quest – a long and endless quest.

"And maybe it will find *what* or *who* it is looking for," I fantasized, stroking her on the back. "Maybe it – that is, you – will become someone else's secret interlocutor. What would I give to know for sure…"

"If we were to know this for sure," said Tina, "then we would no longer fear death."

And after that we were silent; we just lay there, huddled together – probably thinking the same thoughts.

CHAPTER 23

TINA'S VOICE AND her words resonate in my ears. As if I'm living through that night again, sound after sound, touch after touch, and it is with some reluctance that I open my eyes – here on Quarantine, in the soft armchair of my bedroom. I open them and stare into space for a long time – remembering how in Bangkok, once the theory was finished, and the last equal sign was down in my long-suffering notebook, I went out into the city and wandered around it for hours in unrestrained euphoria. Formulas floated before my eyes, and beyond them, beyond the integrals, logarithms and matrices, I could see the whole universe and farther beyond it. I imagined stunning pictures – multidimensional worlds with exotic metrics, patterns and shapes that could not be believed in, and yet I knew they existed, me myself being an inseparable part of them. Their scale did not overwhelm me – I could see alongside them a myriad of shooting neurons, the trembling of the dipoles, the waves of an invisible field piercing the brain. I could visualize the most complex dance, the dance of the conscions, and it was no less majestic than any cosmic structure. I felt a proportionality with the entire cosmos – for myself and for every other human being.

The music thundered inside me. I walked along a crowded street and peered at the faces – of petty traders and taxi drivers and tourists crazy with the heat. I told myself not to judge them strictly; they, too, would leave their mark. Many of them had thought, felt and perhaps loved at some time or other. There are those still capable of it to this day – and everything their mind has been accumulating will be preserved and not lost. The B Objects, having left their "owners," will bring parts of their lives to other worlds. Do the other worlds need that? Maybe so; who knows – and perhaps, I thought, among these people there are those who believe they have a global role to play, even if they can't explain it in words. Everyone, probably, has moments when they feel themselves to be on familiar terms with the stars and galaxies. On the same wavelength with outer space – and then they are no longer intimidated by the immeasurable scale of time and distance. This is reflected in their faces, in their eyes – look closely at anyone doing what they know best. Perhaps, at that moment, they feel the universe itself is tirelessly caring for the integrity of their unique "I"! Is this not a reason to be proud of your superiority over mindless nature?... I felt the most acute pride in humanity. Although, of course, "pride" is not the right word. No one has yet come up with the right words for this.

I wandered around, insensible to the heat, talking to myself, grinning at my own thoughts. My delight, my emotional outburst resembled a powerful narcotic dream. Even now I am utterly unashamed when I recall it – and I remember, savor the memory, reclining in my armchair, stretching out the pleasure. Then I finally get up and go out into the living room – in the same elevated state of mind. I have several sheets of paper in my hand: a concise extract, the quintessence of my work. The sequence of the transformations deforming space, the path leading to the conscion vortices, to the stable soliton waves. To the B Objects connecting worlds – my former, terrestrial one and this strange place that I have yet to really get to know.

Elsa stands at the stove, wearing a short dress with a bow and a lace apron. She looks like a French maid from an upmarket porno. I say hello and am immediately struck by her gaze. I freeze under it, feeling pinned to the wall. Like we are midddle of a love affair and I have just been caught cheating.

"You're glowing all over," Elsa says. Her voice is calm, even, but there is an electric charge about it heralding the proximity of a storm.

"You were the same yesterday and generally every morning over the last few days," she continues. "What would be the reason for this? Let's assume: you're recalling that Asian girl of yours! Maybe you're even having erotic dreams?"

I know: a certain tension has been rising between us – I sensed it but there was nothing I could do. Thinking about Tina and reliving, as if afresh, the story of our romance and the completion of my work, the decisive steps leading to the dance of the conscions, I distanced myself from my roommate. I wasn't telling her much, keeping all the details to myself, and she wasn't pressing me with questions, although her silence obviously concealed a grievance.

"Answer me!" Elsa insists.

"You guessed right," I confess. "Something like that – plus some math. I've made progress; I didn't tell you earlier, as I was afraid of jinxing it, but now, it seems, these anxieties are already behind me…"

The echoes of the morning's euphoria linger within me; I can't believe Elsa's resentment can be serious. I'm still waiting for her to share my happiness – yet I sense how the global images in my mind are fading, and my entire accomplishment is diminishing in size.

"Yes, I remembered Tina, I resurrected my theory, the theory of the conscions," I continue, not wanting to give in. "I saw their vortices – by the way, it's thanks to them that we are here. If you want, I can tell you everything in greater depth…"

Elsa waves her hand impatiently, "Forget it. Your depths are too much for me; I won't understand them. I'm just a down-to-earth girl; I only know: your muse has finally returned to you. And I'm not fit to take her place, of course – although to be frank, muses come in all shapes and sizes… What is that in your hands – are you drawing portraits of her? Or are they your love letters?"

She doesn't attempt to hide her irritation. Not knowing how to react, I make a circle around the room, moving a chair away and putting it back again. Then I try to take a step closer to her, but Elsa pulls away and sits down at the table.

"Well," she says in an indifferent tone, "tell me if you want. We have to move forward with that spreadsheet of ours somehow" – and she purses her lips, almost like Nestor would.

I plant myself opposite and – somewhat bashfully, fitfully – I tell her the whole story. Elsa stares seriously straight at my face. When I finish – in an incoherent and confused manner, despite the triumphant conclusion – she sighs and says, "Well, on top of everything else, you were her first lover… She must have behaved stupidly and felt awkwardly shy. There's nothing more boring than virgins, is there? In any case, this Tina of yours is in no way connected with me and my past. We're treading water – as ever!"

She gets up, walks to the window and nods toward the cityscape beyond it, "It's such an annoying image! I wanted to put something better on but didn't manage to for some reason. Really, the day has started badly… By the way, don't you think it's odd that even here, with only you and me present, you need someone else to help you remember these vortices of yours? The only thing I'm good for is frying your eggs in the morning!"

For some reason my heart contracts. Elsa carries on, trying to smile, "Although fried eggs are no small matter; at least I have no rivals on that score. And you know, it seems I'm getting better and better at them – don't you think?"

I cling to her words, like a lifeline, nodding with a short strained laugh, "I have to admit, in my former life, no one ever cooked such great breakfasts for me." And I add, "As for Tina, it's complicated; there's no point in being jealous. You see, she was able to physically feel everything I described with my equations on paper. To feel and perceive the sensation – glancing at her, it was as if I myself could sense that our B Objects were next to us, nearby."

"I think," says Elsa, "the whole point is that you could physically sense *her*. It's so upsetting – having a body that can only tease!"

"I think," I reply, matching her tone, "the thing is that Tina's presence dispelled my doubts. This is the main role of a muse – not to let you have doubts!"

Elsa continues – stubbornly, as if not hearing, "It's good I restrained myself from trying to make you mine. I did it from the very first day – feeling for some reason that it wouldn't work out. And now I also understand: even if everything here were for real, even if we slept together and your head was spinning, I would still lose out to her – the one who is not just far away but is basically in some sort of other life. I would lose in every sense – I simply didn't have a chance!"

After that, we remain silent. I eat my eggs – they really are delicious – and Elsa drinks her coffee in small sips. After breakfast, I get up, put the dishes in the sink and take a blank sheet of paper.

"Look," I say and draw a human head and something vague around it.

"Oh," Elsa snorts. "It's a saint with a halo. Just don't tell me this is a drawing of yourself!"

I continue, "This is not a halo; imagine – our three-dimensional world and some wider outer space. Imagine that space above and under this sheet of paper…"

"Some men," Elsa sighs, "just don't get it the first time. You're wasting your breath; it's just not my thing. The extent of my perception is very limited."

I'm genuinely surprised, "Do you really not want to hear about it? Do you have no interest in how and where your memory is kept? It's what saves your former experience for your future lives – by the way, there could be a lot of them. They could be long – and you're not interested in their meaning?"

Elsa frowns, "What's the big deal? I've always suspected something of the sort existed – what happened once is bound to repeat itself. Things rarely end at the first attempt – which, by the way, often happens to be awkward… And as far as meaning is concerned, the why and how, I really don't care. What's important is the result – and I believe most people think the same."

"Yes," I agree, feeling nettled. "Yes, that's why it's so easy to sell the simplistic concept of God. It's much easier to understand than multidimensional spaces and quantum fields. And the *result*, in general, is the same. No wonder in my first life, theoretical physicists had such small salaries…"

Elsa doesn't smile at my joke. "If this is a reproach in disguise," she says, "then you're off the point – remember, I had my own way of getting to heaven. It may be quite simplistic, too, but at least I chose it myself. And I didn't like church, by the way; it was utterly boring there."

"Yes," I nod and look at our tablecloth. *Good girls go to heaven*… curls around under my plate.

"Yes!" she repeats after me and continues, "I just thought: Maybe you'd like me to embroider some of your equations on here? That would be another contribution – besides my fried eggs, I mean. Or, if not an entire equation, then at least a very clever word; I remember one: 'Lagrangian.' And next to it I could add your name – has anyone ever embroidered your name?"

There is a deliberate coldness in her voice, a concentration of her resentment. I merely shrug.

Then, to top it all, she refuses to go out for a walk. She just sits with her needlework on the couch, without even glancing up. I look out the window, changing the views – a first, a second, a third… Nothing good comes of it. Disappointed, I sit down at the table and fiddle about with nothing to do, drawing some random symbols instead of formulas. And then, unexpectedly even for myself, I go up to the sink and rewash the dishes on the rack that are already sparkling clean. This calms me down, and by the evening session, a part of my former euphoria has returned. After all, I say to myself, the main event of the day is my upcoming conversation with Nestor, not my quarrels with Elsa.

My former adviser and now only a "friend" appears on the screen at exactly five. "Get ready," I say to him, "it's your turn to hear 'something quite amusing.' For example, what a B Object is – in the strictest mathematical sense."

Nestor tenses visibly. "If so, then you seem to be a bit underdressed," he tries to joke. "I'd expect no less than a tuxedo…" Then he brushes his temple and mutters something else in the same vein, but his snide little jokes bounce right off me. I am full of confidence and calm – and I recount everything to him in perfect order, from A to Z: about the idea of the separation of worlds and how I came to it with the help of Tina, about the sixteen dimensions and the new quantum variable, about the field of the conscions that pervades the universe and its vortices at the source of the disturbance. I talk about waves of soliton type – the B Objects forming around the brain once it has reached a certain maturity. And then – without any dramatic pauses – I reveal the most intriguing thing: why my theory is so difficult to reproduce. I stress the need to leap to the side and take a look from another angle – in order to uncover the topological charge and deformations of the space-field. And I briefly describe the meaning of the transformation that came to me in my drunken stupor after my quarrel with Tina and another reminder of death.

"Here's the math," I say and spread out my sheets with formulas on the table. "Here they are, in front of you, the B Objects," I add, unable to resist a little pathos. "They 'record' the contents of memory during the life of the brain. Probably, not everything is recorded – I presume the memories, ideas, thoughts that our brains repeatedly return to are more likely to be preserved than others. It can also be assumed that a special chance is given to those products of thought that have been subject to a certain amount of work – when, for example, they have been reformulated several times to be verbalized in the best way. The work of a thought or on a thought is a guarantee of a kind that the thought will not be forgotten, will not be lost – either in the current life or future ones. By the way, I guess that for life itself, for the physical body, the very process of exchange with the vortex of the conscions could be unpleasant or even, in some cases, unsafe. I can imagine heart palpitations, headaches and jumps in blood pressure – sometimes of extreme magnitudes…"

Nestor snorts, "Well, this last part is just lyricism…" And he asks, "So, you're done, are you?"

"Not quite," I say, "there's something else," and I put the last three sheets of paper on the table. On them in a formal, strict format is the apotheosis of my theory, possibly its most important essence. Step by step, equation by equation – the path to this essence, to the phase transitions that the B Object is capable of undergoing without destroying itself, preserving its internal dynamics.

I say, "This is also nothing more than lyricism, perhaps, but there's no escaping it; it demands to be articulated…" And I confide in Nestor the same things I told Tina that night: how a conscion vortex, having separated from the brain that created it, continues to carry within itself the sophisticated "dance moves," keeping unchanged their most complex pattern. How it rushes with its contents somewhere far away – for a long, long time, possibly forever…

Nestor remains silent. Then I express my gratitude to him personally, underlining the assistance he has provided. I note the connection between the main provisions of my theory with the facts he has been revealing to me – albeit sparingly – from my first days in Quarantine. I mention his words about the metabrane and his hints regarding the field of the conscions, his frequent, though not completely coherent, references to the B Objects. All this, too, probably pushed me in the right direction, set the right tone. Even if it seems to me that Nestor could have been more open, we achieved the end result nonetheless; and as for his secrecy, maybe he had his own reasons for it.

Having said all this, I look at my "friend." He nods – as if to say "received and duly noted" – but still doesn't mutter a word. Well, that's his right; I put the papers in a neat pile and declare, "Allow me to sum up!" And I briefly go once again through the main milestones, the most important aspects.

"Quantum fields!" I exclaim. "They play the principal role. Quasiparticles capable of interacting with the conscions 'appear' only at the level of atoms and the smallest molecules. At the level of quanta – due to specific effects that have no place in classical physics.

"The uniqueness of the structure of the brain and its incredible complexity!" I continue. "The dense packing of a huge number of interconnected neurons. This structure is essentially nontrivial; it's based on a fractal principle, self-similarity on various scales. And the scales are converging; the boundaries between them are blurred – thus the micro and macro come into contact with each other. Our brain is a *macroscopic-quantum* system, if you'll forgive me for such a wordplay.

"And finally," I say, raising my voice even higher, "finally the main thing: the dynamic nature of memory! The fact, amazing to many, that memories are not static records but sequences of rapidly changing brain states, some specific dynamic regimes. Statics mean unavoidable death; only dynamics have a chance – of rebirth and resurrection. If the memory were stored in the form of neuron 'imprints,' it would inevitably die with the brain forever!"

At this, Nestor interrupts me, "Yeah, yeah, I understand. Why are you spelling it out to me, as if I'm a first-year student…"

He is frustrated – for no apparent reason. I shrug and fall quiet. Nestor turns away and says, not looking at me, "Well, congratulations. This is, undoubtedly, an achievement, a great accomplishment in its own way."

His behavior seems strange to me – I was expecting something different. We remain silent for a minute or so, then Nestor jerks his chin and adds, "If, of course, all this proves to be true. As we all remember, you have a history of giving in to wishful thinking!"

The expression on my face has evidently changed. "Okay, okay," he mutters, raising his hand in a conciliatory manner. "That was all in the past; turned to dust so long ago it's almost forgotten. Still, it's most likely been recorded in your personal B Object... Kidding, kidding. For some reason, I believe in this instance everything is going to be faultless. It's now up to the experts – I'll pass your calculations on to the higher authorities. And, well, I'm glad that you've been able to live through such vivid moments here. That you've experienced all this all over again – the delight of a discovery, the courageousness of an idea, the triumph of a thought..."

"Why are you being so caustic, Nestor?" I ask, surprised.

"Triumph..." he repeats, thinks for a while, then suddenly clicks his fingers in front of his nose, as if trying to drive away an apparition, and declares, "And now for something else. For the essential nitty-gritty – from your triumph to the everyday. To your search for the point at which your memories intersect with those of your charming roommate. No one can put this off, even a VIP like you. When it comes to Quarantine obligations, everyone is equal..." – and for a while, he proceeds to reprimand me like a schoolboy. At the same time, it seems to me his thoughts are wandering somewhere far away.

Just the same, I am dumbfounded by the timeliness of his scolding, its tone. My confidence evaporates along with my calmness. I let him see with my entire demeanor that I am not happy and thoroughly put out. Nestor looks at me intently as if expecting some response, but I have nothing to say, and he just nods, "Well, that's all. Or do you want me to return to the beginning and share with you all the delight of your achievement? To participate in the feast of your ideas and thoughts?"

I don't even dignify him with an answer. Nestor clears his throat and says, "Well, here's something else about delight and feasting. Have you never thought the very fact of you being *here* implies that not everything in your story back *there* went smoothly? Quarantine is no place for euphoria. And stories from the past, as a rule, don't tend to have happy endings."

With that, he disappears. I lean back in my chair and close my eyes but lie awake for a long time. For some reason, I remember my first day after my "awakening" and feel the same: a desperate loneliness, superfluousness and strangeness; Nestor, Elsa – they don't care. Their supposed indifference is nothing but an illusion that dissipates in a moment. No affinity is possible without a common goal – that has a meaning for both. A long-known truth, but it hurts nevertheless...

And I think about Tina – with bitterness, with an intense sadness. I try to imagine what happened to us after those thrilling days, how our lives developed. My night dreams are still revealing nothing about this – did we stay together for long, or were we soon parted? Did we have any children? Did Tina leave me, or, perhaps, did I leave her, disenchanted by something? What was the conclusion of our story – which, according to Nestor, had little chance of ending happily? I just hope a lot of good things took place before it came to a bad end. And that everything came to a closure of its own accord, without a disaster or tragedy, with no one to blame...

I lie and think about all this and suddenly I realize with the utmost clarity: here it is, the separation of worlds. The place of Quarantine finally presents itself as it really is – a small, congested locality, bounded from all sides. And, as if opposing it – everything that exists beyond... It was the same in my former life: the space I shared with Tina had no boundaries. And the world without each other – it was incredibly cramped. That's why she used to say: "It's so crowded here!"

I toss and turn for an hour and then another, sighing gloomily. I want to drive all thoughts out of my head – forever. There is nothing to think about anymore – it seems I have reached an understanding of everything that exists. I have learned all that is possible to learn – despair, defeat, joy at my accomplishments, true closeness...

"The dance of the consions," I say aloud, grinning ruefully at my own whisper. Then I finally sink under somewhere, into incoherent dreams. It's as if half the frames have been washed away from the film. Images and faces scurry from one void to another – and so it goes on all night.

CHAPTER 24

THE NEXT DAY, Nestor cancels the midday session and is late for the evening one by almost ten minutes. Having finally appeared, he nods dryly and just as dryly announces, "Congratulations. Apparently, your calculations are correct. The transformation that introduces a topological charge does change everything. It opens the doors, removes the veils… At least, that's what our experts are saying. They are a bit overexcited now and inclined to exaggeration."

He is serious and gloomy. I would even say he appears unshaven and has the look of a man who has spent a hard, perhaps drunken, night. There is a shadow of regret on his face over something that has failed to come to fruition. As if he's lost hope, is tired of struggling and has resigned himself.

Of course, this is only my fancy, but I can allow myself to fantasize a bit. I have completed a great feat, and now I can afford myself some slack. For example, some sort of joke – and I'm just about to make a quip about his appearance when he suddenly adds, "By the way: I will probably be transferred away from you soon. You, and the whole situation with you, have exceeded my level of competence. Although the question of my replacement has not yet been resolved. Some decisions are difficult indeed…"

This is unexpected news. I don't know how to deal with it, only I realize I no longer want to make any jokes. Nestor continues, "We will return to this later, though. And for now – now I am still working with you, and my list of tasks has not been canceled, not yet. It has even been expanded: I have to…" He looks down and quotes verbatim with a wry grin, "I have to 'bring you up to date on the same subject matter but with much broader horizons.' To put it plainly, I've been given permission to share things with you that are still within my remit and about which my competence is unquestioned. This concerns cosmology – and I should note right away: your hypothesis about the sixteen dimensions coincides with our 'picture of the world,' although its validations are significantly indirect. What's more, the other – possible – numbers of dimensions you have obtained from your equations also correspond to our most widely accepted cosmological model…"

It suddenly dawns on me, and I, not very politely, interrupt him, "Of course! I've just realized – you, Nestor… Go on, admit it – you're a cosmologist, aren't you?"

Nestor immediately takes offence, as if he's been waiting for an excuse to do so. "I don't understand what difference it makes," he mutters, puffing his lips. "Yes, I am a *former* cosmologist, and, yes, I wasn't a success, but let's just see what will happen with you in that regard. You have always been lucky, Theo – even hitting away at random, you soon ran into fruitful ideas, always getting out of dead ends. I wonder how many lives your luck will last – I mean, how much success has been apportioned to you in general."

"Are you wishing me adversity and disaster?" I ask, surprised.

"No, no, of course not," Nestor waves his hand and pulls an innocent face. "How could you think such a thing? We're almost colleagues; I would never… I just wonder how you will deal with all this. I mean your pride in yourself, your tendency to feel like you're on a pedestal…"

He looks at me point-blank, then smirks and says sarcastically, "I reckon you always dreamed you'd have a monument put up in your name in your lifetime?"

"Yes," I answer him in the same tone. "And by the way, Elsa wants to embroider my name onto our tablecloth."

"Really?" Nestor shakes his head and suddenly exclaims with genuine, sincere bitterness, "Well, there you go!"

Then he looks through something under the screen; I wait patiently.

A minute passes, then another. "Well," Nestor finally sighs, "may I continue? About cosmology – if you've satisfied your sudden interest in my career. Let's start by summarizing – reviewing the main theses of 'Theo's theory,' as they are seen in our world. I would like to ask you to confirm – if everything is right? To check I haven't gotten confused or distorted anything, inadvertently underestimating... I would advise you to make notes – you can even put down ticks; I won't be offended. I won't think you're copying me – like, you know, trying to make fun of me."

Yes, today he is being difficult. I silently take a pencil and a blank sheet of paper.

"First," says Nestor. "We believe, like you, that consciousness is nothing else but the result of an interaction with an external field. Thanks to you and out of respect for you, we are using the term you coined and are calling it the field of the conscions. Give that a tick – we have nothing to argue there. The conscions are apparently emitted by the metabrane and spread throughout the entire cosmos – you don't possess much knowledge on this yet, so here ticks are irrelevant. And finally: we are aware of just two examples of the conscions interacting with something. In both cases, it's a highly complex structure – a 'macroscopic,' as you put it, quantum system. Let's call it the 'brain,' having in mind both the one from your former world and ours here.

"Next," he continues, "the agents of interaction are a special type of particle-waves that emerge in the brain when some strict conditions are met. Be careful with your ticks now; things are going to get tricky. According to your theory, the human brain does not immediately become 'fit' for the interaction. It has to develop, reach a certain maturity; only then can a specific ordering take place in it – as a result of what you have called 'fractal symmetry breaking.' This is a quantum effect, and the quantum field theory requires the appearance of quasiparticle-bosons that support the fractal order – it is they that interact with the conscions, resulting in the formation of a vortex around the brain. You have named it the 'B Object' – yes, put a big fat tick there: we believe in it, and we call it the same. We admire it a lot – of course: in a certain sense, it is copying our personality. Its dynamic reflects the aggregate of quantum vibrations that encode our memory – and, thus, all recollections, associations, thoughts, both specific and abstract, are gradually being 'rerecorded' on it. And yet, next to this tick, you should put an equally fat question mark – there are important nuances here. You were right only to an extent, but don't get frustrated: there is a huge benefit in your error! And anyway, no one can be right about everything, without exception, all the time..."

There is a hidden arrogance in his voice. The arrogance of the cosmologist, I say to myself. And I obediently draw a question mark – so that he sees – and next to it another and a third, just out of mischief, to spite him.

Nestor snorts, "Don't overdo it. And focus: you asserted that when the conditions for the interaction disappear – for instance, if the brain dies – this is not the end for the B Object. It doesn't get destroyed, it does not turn into nothingness; on the contrary, in a certain sense it matures and grows stronger. It transfers into another phase and lives its own independent life, traveling in space until it finds, you fantasized, something suitable, a different structure, that it can 'catch onto'... Give yourself a tick – your fantasies in this instance have coincided with reality. An example of such a structure does exist – our 'brain' here. You can also add an exclamation mark – hurray! Human consciousness is reborn into a different nature. The experiences lived through are preserved in the conscion vortex; the personality does not die but regains a body and lives in this body, developing and enriching itself. Moreover, there is reason to believe that after death here, the whole story reiterates. The B Object undergoes another phase transition, once again finding something suitable for interaction – and so on. You have done some preliminary calculations showing that the Object can have many phase states – so award yourself a whole load of ticks and exclamation marks. But next to them – yes, you'll need to put another question mark, perhaps more than one. Because here, too, some of your assumptions are totally wrong!"

He nods with a patronizing grimace and adds, "By the way, I was somewhat sloppy in my wording. I was being a bit careless when I said that the B Object 'lives': the Object itself is incapable of living, although it can exist without disintegrating for an infinitely long time. Life is about development, an exchange with the external environment; life requires a body. It is the body that 'extracts' information from the outside, and the brain, as an intermediary, transmits it to the B Object. Give yourself a tick – you did mention this. And let's sum up: all this together forms a coherent concept, which, of course, is an outstanding scientific discovery confirmed in practice. I repeat: the resurrection of earthly consciousnesses in our world is not a theory but a fact. Therefore, let me congratulate you once again…" – and he claps his hands several times, apparently imitating applause. Then he says, "And now let's move from rapturous praise to a criticism – *constructive* criticism. To the question marks that are dotted all over your sheet of paper – it's not a coincidence you've put down so many. You've been feeling, I guess, that your view of things was hopelessly narrow – and, most probably, remains so!"

"Interesting…" I mutter, agitatedly tapping the table with my pencil. For some reason, Nestor's words nettle me. I recall how very recently I'd had a sense that I had mastered all the mysteries, that I knew everything of importance, and this irritates me even more. "Narrow, huh?" I repeat after him, and Nestor nods affirmatively.

"Yes, it is narrow, and don't squint at me with such anger," he threatens me with his finger. "You – and your Tina as well – have been considering the whole concept of the conscions from a very limited perspective. 'Ah, my consciousness… Ah, my memory… Ah, my fear of death…' This is the view of a pair of loners, accustomed to rescuing themselves on their own. The view of desperate, hardened misanthropes!"

I smile with some effort, trying to show I appreciate his eloquence, but Nestor is being serious. He continues, "Or you were obsessing over the fact that a human being leaves a mark in the universe, like a footprint on fresh concrete. As if your earth's humanity is something special, the pinnacle of evolution. A very parochial view, and, alas, you've not been able to overcome it. That's why it's surprised you that I wasn't overly excited when you presented me with your little secret, this transformation opening the way. You didn't even want to think that the B Object itself is only a part of the big picture. That there are people who see this picture better than you… Yes, there are those who are trying to get their minds around something more than individual destinies. Those who are not just thinking about leaving their trace on the universe but about the universe itself. No one appreciates that, of course; no one gives them due praise – well, so what? They still have the will not to turn into sociopaths and latent misanthropes – although they could… Well, okay, never mind, let's not dwell on the negative. Let's get back to the point: the point is that your Objects can have a much more global role and meaning. Don't get upset: by saying so, I'm not trying to belittle what you've done. Moreover, we can now penetrate this very meaning much deeper. But first, we need to define it properly."

Nestor assumes a dignified air, and I feel this is not a pose. His confidence is obviously growing. Something is changing imperceptibly in his face, in the position of his hands – and even his voice, it seems, sounds different.

"So, back to the question marks," he says. "Let's start with this: you assumed that the interaction of the type 'epsilon' – as we call it here – leading to the emergence of conscion vortices, is the *only* way of exchanging anything between the brain and the field of the conscions. Consequently, you reasoned, the brain must mature, ripen, before the field of the conscions will 'notice' it. Remember: the complexity of the neocortex, the special configuration of neurons, the initial conditions for fractal coherence… If these are not present, then there is no reaction from the external field, you believed – and that turned out not to be so. Our mathematicians were unable to get to these Objects of yours, but they did obtain solutions of a different type – more traditional ones, by the way. You can look at the details later, but I'll give you a rough outline: the brain – at least *our* 'brain,' which we have studied thoroughly – goes through several stages, several jumps of complexity while growing. For a long time, it does not produce a stable fractal ordering, but, so to speak, hints at it – yes, surely. Fleeting, unstable sketches of fractal order – the brain seems to be measuring itself compared to its future role. And each of these sketches generates its own quasiparticles – a brief impulse that creates perturbations in the flow of the conscions! Imagine a stone thrown into a pond – in the same way, conscion waves disperse out from the brain, and this occurs long before the brain is able to support a full-fledged Object. Furthermore, there is every reason to believe that the brains of our ancestors who lived millions of years ago were also quite capable of 'disturbing' the external field. And probably, in your terrestrial case, everything was approximately the same!"

I lean forward, fixing my gaze onto him. Nestor falls silent and makes a sympathetic face. He looks at me for a minute or two and says, "I understand this makes you unhappy. It even likely upsets you, but we have to admit: your theory only describes a particular case, one of many. Your Object is only a part, albeit the most important one from the point of view of our destinies, our egos, our personal aspirations. Well, now we have to work on a generalization, an integration of all the solutions – both for the conscion waves and their stable vortices – in one mathematical formalism. A tough job, probably a long one, but one thing is already clear. We can acknowledge that both your and our regions of space 'disturbed' the field of the conscions long before intelligent beings appeared in them. They seemed to signal to the metabrane that structures would soon be created which would be able to interact with this field, allowing conscion vortices to form or develop further. Thus, global space *learned in advance* about its special locations!"

"It learned in advance..." I repeat, rubbing my hands together and putting them to my cheeks. I ask, "Does this mean?..." – and interrupt myself, "No, it doesn't. But nevertheless, the whole picture is changing dramatically... You're wrong; I'm not upset in the least. It's just all so very new!"

"Yes, yes," Nestor gestures impatiently. "A lot is still new for you. And for me as well – one just never gets tired of being surprised by these things. Here, for example, take your second mistake: you stressed – probably to avoid any mysticism – that the meetings of B Objects with the new host brain occur randomly – if, of course, they occur at all. That each Object hurtles by itself into the pitch-dark cosmic night – as if cherishing the hope that someone needs it... It's very romantic – a poem could be written on the subject. It is a pity that its ending would be immensely sad – exactly like your reasoning about random chance. Well, you should be forgiven; you are not a cosmologist, you are not even a poet, and in general, this part of your theory was developed poorly. I'd say not developed at all, but here, in our science, we have taken it seriously. And soon it became clear: your assumptions, fortunately, are incorrect – otherwise new lives would only theoretically be possible at a probability so small it's not even worth mentioning. The conscion vortices would not have found structures suitable for interaction randomly – even at a brief glance, such a hypothesis seems strange, and if you do the calculations... So, we had to forget about the randomness and concentrate on searching for a rule – because a fact is a fact. B Objects migrate from your world to ours, and something helps them do this. What could that something be? The answer is almost obvious – nothing other than space itself. The idea is bold, even a little bit mad, but it is quite evident. We have mathematical results demonstrating its viability. And this means: the metabrane not only learns about its special locations. It also, apparently, *reacts* to this information!"

And again I look dumbfounded. Then I mumble, "Does something affect the curvature in some manner? Pseudo-gravitational inhomogeneities, energy clusters? But the effective mass must be huge for them to be at least a tiny bit noticeable..."

"Of course, you are thinking along the right lines," Nestor nods to me, condescendingly, as if I were a student. "With effective mass, however, not everything is so unambiguous, and, moreover, Einstein's equations are also a special case, valid only for your local world. Obviously, on the metabrane, the physics is different; space-time depends on various factors, and the field of the conscions is one of them. Perhaps, from the point of view of the metabrane, the creation and maturation of the conscion vortices represent some sort of advantage in terms of energy distribution. Maybe something is minimized in this way, some kind of global functional... We can only guess. I repeat: there are only hints; we are still a long way from a complete cosmological theory that would take into account the field of the conscions. But this assumption is quite plausible, isn't it?"

"Wait, wait," I ask and look perplexedly at the piece of paper in front of me. Then I take a pencil and draw something over the ticks and question marks, frantically trying to comprehend what I've just heard. Nestor calmly, patiently waits. Thus about a quarter of an hour goes by.

"Well," I wave my hand. "Let it be so... I admit, I can't grasp all this right away. I'll think about it later – and, please, can you finally give me some scientific articles, some books. And I must say: the prospect is incredibly shocking!"

Nestor spreads his hands, "I agree with you fully. It's difficult even to acknowledge the globality of it all, the unusualness of its scale... Our intelligence, our ability to think – or even the rudiments of such ability – elicit a reaction in the immeasurable cosmos. They force space, the mysterious metabrane, to change its geometry – admittedly, it's more customary to talk about these matters in the context of cosmic cataclysms, the merging of stars, the formation of black holes. And here all we have is just the birth of an intelligent mind on some insignificant specks of dust... Behold the significance of a single small human being, behold – his or her role. It does not compare with your timid mention of some sort of indistinct trace. And besides, it's such a pleasure to be aware that something is not indifferent to us. And not just something but the universe itself!"

It's difficult to tell whether he is joking or not. I'm silent, but my lips stretch into some stupid half smile.

"But let's not be too grandiloquent," Nestor continues. "We should not expend all our emotions just yet. Save your wonder; I will tell you something else soon – about the prospect, so to speak. And in the meantime..."

He touches something under the screen; then I see in his hands an oblong black object resembling a mobile phone. He looks into it, brings it to his ear, listens in silence and nods in satisfaction.

"In the meantime, we must pause briefly, and it's good – I think you need a rest too. You need something like, as they say in your world, a 'bathroom break.' Even if the bathroom here is just for show, you can still visit it out of habit. To go back to basics, ha-ha..." – and Nestor laughs his strange laugh. This time, it definitely is a joke – and he is pleased with it.

CHAPTER 25

HAVING LAUGHED HIS fill, Nestor disappears from the screen, and I really do go to the bathroom – to refresh myself. I stand there for a while over the basin, looking at my reflection in the mirror, splashing cold water on my face. I listen to my thoughts, I watch their shadows – broken formulas, exotic symbols. Half-erased images of equations, the ruins of mathematical identities. They clarify nothing – though it would be naive to expect otherwise.

"It's okay, it's okay," I say out loud. "Everything lies ahead." Then I return to the bedroom – Nestor is not there yet, but the screen is alive. An image has appeared – at first glance, it seems to be a pure abstraction, a jumble of shapes and colors. Little by little, however, I distinguish something meaningful – a myriad of multicolored threads tangled together like a ball of yarn. This is familiar – to me and even to Elsa – but this time the picture is not static; it has started moving. Looking closely, I recognize a concurrency about it, a sophisticated order. Different sections of different threads approach each other and then scatter away. From time to time, bright points of light appear on a few of them, and pale-yellow halos emerge around some of the points, like flashes of light in the fog. The points do not burn for long; they disappear, but the halos that surround them remain. They are stretched out a little, like the tails of comets, and seem to float away somewhere to other points of light on other threads, which in turn rush to meet the halos…

It is difficult to tear my gaze from the screen. I look at it spellbound and then hear Nestor's voice, measured, a little solemn, "Imagine a metabrane, and inside it a wreath of filaments, a variety of local universes. All of them are constantly changing shape – for many reasons, including the fluctuations of the metabrane's curvature. The points that light up and go out are flashes of intelligent life – that which is capable of interacting with the field of the conscions. And the halos are the collections of the vortices of this field, the B Objects… I'm sure you've already guessed from my hint: yes, the Objects do not travel in space independently of each other. They don't scurry around madly on their own or fly away in random directions. They are organized in a union, a system – this is precisely what allows our lives to 'migrate' en masse from one world to another. And, most important, as we've mentioned already: the halos and points are constantly searching for each other; they endeavor to draw closer, to intersect. In accordance with the authoritative dictates of the metabrane!"

Then Nestor himself appears on the screen. The picture moves to the upper-right corner. "Well, how do you like the visuals?" he asks. And he adds with feigned modesty, "This, I must confess, is my own work."

I see he is seeking praise and I say quite sincerely, "It's brilliant. I am impressed!"

"Oh, come on…" Nestor waves his hand dismissively and continues, "Of course, as far as the halos are concerned, we are only certain about the existence of just one of them. But, in my opinion, it's natural to assume there are many – perhaps a lot. And, possibly, from the metabrane's point of view, there is an energy advantage for them to converge toward each other. Maybe even to merge together, forming a superhalo – if you like, an abstract image of a supermind, a superbrain!…"

He's now changed again – his eyes are glowing, and his shoulders seem to have opened out, spreading beyond the edges of the screen. A totally different person sits in front of me, not at all like the petulant, thin-skinned man at the beginning of the session. This, of course, is only an illusion, but I have seen similar transformations before. Take Kirill, for instance – but, of course, he and Nestor have nothing in common. And anyway, that was another life.

"Well, okay," Nestor raises his hand as if slowing himself down. "The superbrain is only an assumption: one of a number of hypotheses that we are unlikely to test soon. Yes, one of them – and I confess: I was laughed at. Moreover, I was laughed at by my own family. You know how it is; you were mocked, too, when you hinted for the first time at the fields and forces that came from other spaces. Do you remember – during the period of your desperate struggle with the Higgs boson? Thus, it's still unclear who will have the last laugh, but let's skip this for now; let's talk about more immediate prospects. The ones I promised you – they are closely connected with the sole 'halo' we know about. We, by the way, call it the 'Cloud' – the Cloud of B Objects."

Nestor pauses and throws me an attentive, stern look. Then, as usual, he tilts his head to one side and says, even somewhat sympathetically, "Get ready. Take some more paper – you'll probably want to note down your thoughts. But don't strain yourself too much: your thoughts will be in confusion. Yes, in confusion and complete disorder – for sure."

I obediently pick up a pencil and pull a blank sheet of paper toward me. "The Cloud!" Nestor exclaims and again pauses, rubbing his face. Then he confidentially informs me, "The Cloud is mysterious; its riddles are significantly nontrivial," and looks down at his papers.

I want to hurry him up, give him a nudge; I'm almost squirming in my chair.

"And one of the riddles is entirely extraordinary," Nestor continues. "The point is: the 'union' of the Objects is not uniform. It is structured in a complex way – and, what's more, we have reason to believe… There is some certainty, supported by scientific…" He looks up at me and declares, "We are certain the Objects in the Cloud interact!"

We stare at each other, silent. Then I make a gesture, "Wait, wait, I've already considered this. I tried to check it out, at least in theory… Yes, this idea came to me, but according to my calculations, even if two brains are in close proximity, their B Objects do not interfere with each other – are you telling me I was wrong here too?"

"You were!" Nestor says firmly. "You were, and you were not. No one is claiming that by bringing your head closer to someone else's, you're going to accidentally enter that person's Object. Your brain always 'communicates' with only one single conscion vortex – but these vortices themselves, independently of the host..."

"What... Are you kidding me?" I say, knowing full well he is not.

Nestor merely shrugs. Then he continues, "I'll start from the very beginning: at some time, one of the Clouds moved close to our 'special point,' with the very world where you and I are now located. Obviously, this Cloud had been created by your intelligent life – or, at least, it had interacted with it – because here, individuals began to be born among us with a terrestrial past. Initially, they had a hard time – imagine the very first people waking up with extremely realistic memories. What were they meant to think; how and with whom could they share this experience? All sorts of things happened, but gradually, we stopped turning our backs on the facts and began to understand the essence of what was going on. The concept of rebirth – with the memory preserved and subjective features of the consciousness intact – was formulated and officially adopted. Now newcomers are given the care they need: Quarantine is, without exaggeration, the ideal way to prepare for the new reality. It's the most important step – without it, those who have been reborn would for a long time remain in a state of blindness and confusion, very similar to the one in which they'd lived their first life. We, of course, also went through many misperceptions and mistaken judgments. Our own history of comprehension was a rather peculiar one; yet everything developed much more dynamically than in your world – past collective experience did its thing. And of course, the main efforts of this comprehension were devoted to the most important factors – to the actual rebirth and the mechanisms that, despite the scale of distances and times, make it possible."

Nestor touches the bridge of his nose, as if he is straightening an imaginary pince-nez, and grins, "By the way. We already know that our local 'brain' can play a dual role in relation to conscion vortices. It is able to 'attach' to itself ones that already exist as well as create new ones in which nothing about the former life is 'recorded.' Many of those born into our reality never remember anything from the earthly one. Obviously, Objects of different degrees of maturity can coexist in the Cloud – and perhaps some people born on your earth were too 'connected' to B Objects that already existed and had been carrying a certain previous experience.

Perhaps they were tormented by memories of an inconceivable, inexplicable past, and they were not *quarantined* as they are here – I believe they were mercilessly mistreated. Your society tended to apply labels quite easily – the label of insanity, for example..."

He pauses as if waiting for me to intercede on behalf of my former world. Then he adds pointedly, "But the past is the past. We're talking about *our* rules and culture – here, earthly memories are thoroughly studied. They are like a keyhole: through it, we can look into the hidden life – the life of our consciousnesses, no matter how strange that may sound. I, of course, mean the Cloud, which is extremely difficult to approach. We cannot get inside, cannot pinpoint, examine or measure anything. Only its external features are available to us – the statistics of rebirths and memories of the previous lives, if any. And there are two main aspects to these features: chronology and grouping."

Alerted by the familiar words, I try to interrupt him – a question has occurred to me. A very important question, it seems, but Nestor only frowns at my impatient gestures. "No, not now!" He shakes his head. "Right now, you'd be better off listening. Sitting still, not intruding, not even fidgeting. Although the first part is quite boring..."

I obediently remain still. "What's not so interesting is the chronology," Nestor explains. "There's not much about it. Everything is quite logical: the new arrivals come here in approximately the same order in which they left their first life. That is why the Cloud in my image is somewhat reminiscent of a comet's tail – it probably has an elongated shape, and the earlier Objects are located closer to its head. There are exceptions: sometimes even those who have died more than a century earlier may be reborn later, but such discrepancies are rare and relatively minor – they never exceed one hundred and fifty years. Those who have left your world within an interval of fifteen or twenty years of each other arrive here in any order – either earlier, later or at the same time. The statistics we have don't show anything significant – and that's where the boring bit ends. Because there is something else that is significant indeed..." He makes a solemn face and carefully enunciates his words, "Newcomers are born in groups. Groups! How does that strike you?"

"Groups? I don't quite understand..." I mumble.

"What's there not to understand?" Nestor waves his hand impatiently. "A group is a group. To use your earthly terms, for example, in the same 'hospital' of a single 'city,' you can see the following: one day there are no newcomers; on the second there are also none; and then on the third – say, fourteen; and the day after that, none again. And so on; these sorts of patterns are the rule rather than the exception. The same is true on the scale of cities: you get hundreds of reborns in a city during one or two days, separated by almost-empty weeks. The specific numbers may vary, but the phenomenon itself is undeniable. For a while, we couldn't grasp what was behind it – those who had been born in the same group had died on earth at different times, in different places, and did not even know each other. There were no correlations – just a continuous statistical noise – but one day someone discovered a fascinating fact with absolutely incredible consequences!"

I interrupt impatiently, "In other words, some sort of correlation has been observed?"

Nestor pretends not to notice my question. He frowns slightly and continues, in a deliberately casual manner, "The fact is this. The first lives of the newcomers from the same group do intersect in some way – although at times implicitly and very briefly. The vivid episodes, experiences, sudden shocks of one always correlate with incidents from the life of another or others…"

He pauses and raises his index finger, "Think about it! Before and after the intersection, their destinies are independent: these people live and die in different countries and in different years. But their consciousnesses – encoded in the B Objects – are reborn in our world together. This rule has been thoroughly tested, and we are certain there are almost no exceptions to it. What does this mean?" Nestor stares directly into my eyes and slowly pronounces, "This means that the B Objects inside the Cloud 'recognize' each other. They 'see' each other, they 'know' a lot about each other. And they are redistributed, clustered together, *depending on their internal content*, on the experiences accumulated within them!"

I put my pencil on the table – carefully, soundlessly. Silence hangs in the room for several long minutes.

"It's funny," Nestor says at last, without the slightest hint of a smile.

"I see you've believed me right away, without even questioning what I've said. Yet many do question it – even those whose minds are far less critical than yours. Many think it's all been made up, like in a children's fairy tale. Maybe it's just *me* you believe? Am I such an authority figure for you? All right, only joking… I understand you, scientist to scientist: it's impossible to argue with statistical confirmation. Well, admit it, are you stunned? Do you want another bathroom break? It won't help: I am stunned too – to this day. Despite all the time we've had to think about it here!"

"Depending on their internal content…" I repeat after him. "In what terms can one define it, that content? How can it even be categorized? And, even at a cursory glance, this should entail a multitude of consequences…"

"Of course," Nestor nods. "The consequences are immense and staggering. The experiences of the first life affect the beginning of the second – and not just the beginning. Data from the maternity hospitals are just one example; there are others, much more sophisticated. Much less obvious – and, in general, it's not clear when and how the interaction between the B Objects occurs. Maybe it takes place not only when the Objects are released from their bodies? Maybe their attraction-repulsion manifests itself *during* life – the first, the second, the others? What if this is the hidden reason for the unexpected twists and turns of our destinies?"

He smiles weakly, "Now you may fantasize as much as you like, and no one could reproach you for lazy thinking. Any 'wisdom' bordering on dense prejudice now plays with new shades. How about this one: the adversities we face in our life are commensurate with our abilities? Or – if you wish for something with all your might, will it come true? What would an emissary of serious science say to this *now*? Here's what he'd say: Why not? Maybe what you desire hard enough really does come true, whether in this or in the next life – through the tendency of your B Object to the corresponding reclustering provoked by your thoughts? Or is it quite the opposite: What is a desire, really – maybe the Cloud desires on your behalf? Maybe the metabrane desires on your behalf – after all, the relocation of Objects in the Cloud could also be interpreted as a change in its geometry. An infinitely small change, you might say, but who knows in what ratio the multidimensional twists are reflected in the space-time of a local universe?… So yes: maybe your desires, aspirations and so forth are only *consequences* of what's happening somewhere outside – outside your body, outside your world. Moreover, maybe they are not aspirations per se but insights, some unconscious interpretations of the dynamics of the cluster to which your Object belongs? And the same can be said about our anxieties, fears…

"Or here: what about the question – the eternal question over which humanity has been constantly struggling? Is there free will, are humans masters of their lives – of all the lives that await them? The human mind – do they really control it themselves? Well, maybe they do – but not quite in ways they imagine: by themselves and not by themselves, together with others, thanks to others or in spite of… It's natural to assume that your thoughts, even if indirectly, affect your destiny. But, it turns out, it's not just yours – have you ever felt, Theo, that you are bound hand and foot by everyone else's expectations, illusions, wishes?

"How simple it is to contrive a religion on the basis of this," Nestor shakes his head. "And how difficult it is to get to the core of it – to the real, mathematical core! Stepping from the consequences to the depths, to the causes – what kinds of physics work here? How does the connection of fates function; what formulas can describe it?… Funny, almost no one can understand the 'why.' Why are the causes and depths needed if the consequences are believed anyway? Just ask a stranger: Does he think that things happen for a reason? What answer will he give you – well, if, of course, he dares to tell the truth?"

And again we look at each other in silence. I remember Elsa and her categorical "What's important is the result!" Then I cough and say, getting my unruly tongue around the words with difficulty, "But, Nestor… Does it not seem to you that explaining everything, absolutely everything, with the Objects and the Cloud is a bit speculative somehow? That it's somehow too convenient: to think up some abstract concepts and reduce the phenomena to their interaction in some ultimate outer space beyond the reach of any detector…"

"Well, yes," Nestor immediately responds. "It is, of course, speculative and simplistic, but I'd like to note one thing. The B Object has not been thought up: it exists, and someone has proved it. Who, who? Oh yes, you, Theo!"

Now it's my turn to shake my head. I'm completely at a loss for words.

"Actually," Nestor continues, "switching the question of fate to a different level of abstraction, considering it in terms of the B Objects interacting with each other, is a complete game changer. Incredible horizons are opening up; new opportunities are knocking on the door. You can try to lay a foundation under a great many things – say, under the concept of predestination, a perception of mission. Possibly somewhere inside the Object there is a concealed source of energy, a spring whose tension never lets up – now, thanks to you, we can examine it more closely. Or we can sort out in details the influence of one life on another – that includes how our previous lives affect the next... It's like taking a step toward a *mathematical model of karma* – in our world, no one laughs at the word 'karma' anymore..."

I blink, then blink again; I rub my eyes with the palms of my hands. Something strange and alarming is ringing in my head – a string? Is it just a melody, a collection of sounds? Or the shadow of a recollection, an insight, a recollection of an insight – of the deepest, most inarticulate one – the beginning of an understanding of those things that cannot be fully understood. But you can take a step toward them, to reach out with a thought. It seems I have already been doing this, already been reaching out. Someone has even prompted me – I almost remember the name, the face – a gloomy, flabby face opposite...

Nestor continues to hold forth, "No one even laughs at the word 'magic' – it's not so easy now to dismiss the inexplicable. The same applies to predictions of the future: you can look contemptuously at all the tarot cards, all the rune stones and crystal balls, you can make fun of charlatans, but who would dare to poke a specific charlatan with a finger and say – this is nonsense? It turns out that life itself is magic in some sense, or so it appears if you dig deeper. It is governed by phenomena that are incredible, unbelievable – but there is no dismissing them; they exist. Their existence is confirmed by statistics – it is impossible to dismiss statistics. Did you ever imagine that statistics and magic would be mentioned in the same context? Would be working, so to speak, as a team?"

I am listening but no longer hear him; my attention has wandered. The words "things, things... reason, reason..." throb in a staccato in my head. I can almost physically feel how my perception of the world is changing – the perception of a *grandiose* world. As Nestor and I are changing – it seems he looks at me almost with tenderness. Indeed, our entire conversation sort of hints at a certain intimacy. Matter is too subtle, imagination too brave…

Then the staccato subsides. I ask, "Nestor, why didn't you tell me about all this before? It might have saved so much time… It seems I have only now started to believe that this world – this Quarantine – is for real. Although it's difficult to explain why."

Nestor waves his hand, "Don't be *too* self-confident. You can hardly make judgments about *time* – as well as about the evolution of your beliefs. The time had to come, and it wasn't tracked by me. What to say, and when, has never depended on a whim of mine – it's not even been my calculated choice. I'm just following instructions – yes, there are others watching your personality. A whole group of experts – you understand why. And maybe soon you'll find out there are even more reasons for so much attention!"

"How soon is 'soon'?" I mumble.

"Obviously, when the *time* is right," Nestor smirks. "It's simply impossible to avoid a tautology here. I'll give you just one clue: my ticks in the task manager play an important role. Remember – the obligation, the duty of a roommate…"

"I suppose," I say thoughtfully, "the role of a roommate is somehow related to the Cloud."

"Undoubtedly," Nestor nods, "and I am even authorized to explain to you exactly how. Not in any great detail; only in the most general terms. But – this is not for today; our conversation has already dragged on enough. You'll just have to be patient until tomorrow morning…" And he disappears, not seeming to notice my gesture of protest.

CHAPTER 26

ALL NIGHT I dream the same thing – a string of characters and numbers running in an endless line. Something like a stock market tape or subtitles for the hearing impaired. Probably, my subconscious mind is trying to convey the truths to which I am still deaf. Then everything merges into a single-colored bar; soon it's swallowed by darkness, and I wake up in fright. My heart is pounding; I feel stuffy and even seem to be shivering. A black ocean almost swallowed me – it was familiar; I had floundered in it before, unable to escape. It somehow matches the feeling I experienced when Nestor mentioned karma – and then magic and something else. Later, I fall back into a slumber again. I plunge deeper and see, see… No, I can't see yet. Something interferes, envelops, blinds.

I have breakfast alone, without Elsa – she is not leaving her bedroom. I make myself a tasteless sandwich and chase it with tasteless tea. Reluctantly, I try to jot something down on paper, write out a couple of equations. Then I cross them out and go outside – alone, at an ungodly hour of the morning. I walk at a quick pace along the empty seafront and think, think, think…

The shifts in my consciousness have somehow happened too fast. My math, my Tina… Hot, humid Bangkok, my intimacy with her – and right there: the field of the conscions, the theory of the B Objects. Like swinging from an extreme to an extreme, from one layer of memories to another – but as soon as I reached the most hidden, the most important one, Nestor effortlessly tore things apart, completely changing the perspective. Now my theory is merely a special case. What I considered to be a universal achievement has been transformed into just a small step, one of many...

The next session doesn't go well. Nestor is pointedly dry and matter-of-fact, his face an impenetrable mask. We seem to be slightly sheepish with each other after the delight we experienced last time. Like the morning after a wild bacchanalian night.

He mutters monotonously, "I must remind you that you and your neighbor Elsa have been placed in the same residential block because your 'awakening' happened at the same time and place. This, apparently, means that the B Objects, the vortices of the field of the conscions, in which your minds were 'imprinted,' converged in space and time, ending up, as we say, in one group. Statistical studies show that the grouping of Objects is directly related to their contents. Not to the usual dynamical parameters but to the experiences and events of your earthly lives..."

I can't see his hands, but he seems to be clinging to the armrests of his chair as if he were in a dentist's office. His speech is formal and completely devoid of emotion. There isn't a trace of yesterday's animation.

"The grouping of the conscion vortices is itself extraordinarily important," Nestor mumbles. "This means that their 'community'– what we call the Cloud – is not static, and its evolution is not accidental. It is a dynamic system that operates according to certain laws; our goal is to understand these laws. The vortices interact, and the parameters of this interaction are the aspects of human destinies – one can say the destinies themselves demonstrate some kind of interconnection. Obviously, first of all, one needs to identify these parameter-aspects, to recognize which 'features' of earthly lives make the corresponding Objects converge, congregate together – or move away from each other, or influence each other in some other way. To do this, we must describe the destinies in some formal, logically complete language – which, of course, is a very challenging task. Choosing the right approach is difficult, but we have still made progress, and I won't conceal the fact that Quarantine is one of our most important sources of data. There are different techniques; I will not dwell on them in detail. Let me just say that one of them – which may appear oversimplistic at first glance – is exactly this: breaking the new arrivals into pairs and searching for the intersections in their memories."

"Factor clustering, concordance analysis..." I say quietly. "I read something about it – psychometrics?"

There is nothing unexpected in what he is expounding – I have already assumed all this while reflecting on yesterday's conversation. I even have my own ideas; I'd love to share them, but I restrain myself – most probably they are way too hasty.

Nestor frowns, "Psychometrics is from your past life. Our science has made considerable steps forward. Factor analysis, as you understand it, is not much help in this instance – but it is encouraging, of course, that you grasp the essence so quickly!" He grins and adds, "By the way, your neighbor was unlucky: she spent three days on her own. This doesn't usually happen, but they were busy with you for a while to ensure your file was as complete as possible. Still, some things evidently remained hidden. This Tina of yours, for example..."

I want to object but, suddenly, agree instead, "Yes, it is strange. Tina, then my theory – and what happened afterward... I'm stuck on the ellipsis, like on a puzzle. I'm mired in it, like in a quagmire!"

Nestor just nods with an expression of accentuated detachment on his face. Soon the session ends, and the screen switches off. For a quarter of an hour I sit in my armchair, thinking incoherently, then abruptly I jump up, pacing back and forth, and exclaim, "Yes, but still!..." No, Nestor's dryness does not diminish the importance of what I'd heard yesterday. Of the most unexpected, most incredible things that I'd heard... It lives on in me as if waiting for when I will take it up properly. The clustering of B Objects, the interlinking of destinies... This is a trick much bolder than those I used to deal with! Once again, I become bemused at the grandeur of the whole concept, and with this feeling I go out into the living room – hoping my roommate will be there.

And so she is. Elsa sits on the couch, in her usual place, but instead of her embroidery, she is holding a book. In recent days, she has lost interest in her sewing. I, of course, understand that neither my equations nor my name will ever appear on our tablecloth. It was just her little joke.

"Just imagine," says Elsa, seeing me, "you can order books like in the library here. I immediately asked for almost a dozen – my Nestor thought I was a bit loopy."

I note she's wearing mascara and a bright-red lipstick. She rarely uses makeup – today I fancy there's some kind of challenge in this act of hers. "Good afternoon," I mumble, chasing foolish thoughts from my head, and ask, "What are you reading?"

"A thriller," Elsa shows me the cover. "I hope the bad guys get away. Well, what's on your mind? Asian girls? Formulas? Saints with halos?"

"On my mind?" I reply, pouring some water into the coffeemaker. "There's a lot on my mind indeed. I had an important, extremely interesting talk with Nestor. And I have to admit: in about two hours he managed to recast a great deal in my head. He swept away all the boundaries; he enlarged – mercilessly enlarged – all the scopes and scales. I am still amazed – and perplexed too!"

"Wow," Elsa puts down her book. "Look at me – you haven't gotten sick, have you? So much emotion – it's something new. Usually, you're such a cold fish!"

I don't get offended, knowing she still can't forgive me for Tina. I even feel guilty of some sort of betrayal. As if I haven't fulfilled certain expectations – after all, her involvement has been for real. And even now she is not as indifferent as she tries to appear.

Elsa comes up, feels my forehead with exaggerated, comic concern. I try to hug her around the waist, but she pulls away; all I get is the scent of her perfume. We drink our coffee, and she recounts the simple plot of the book she's reading. Then we clear away the table, each washing our own cup, and go for a walk.

Today it is sunny, but the wind is strong and the sea lumpy. Elsa takes my arm, clutching it tightly; I can feel her strong fingers. And thus we wander, occasionally nodding to the other, tediously familiar couples. Hardly anyone would think that we have had a disagreement.

"It's good to walk and walk like this," says Elsa, squinting at the sun. "I'm on your arm – and, even if it's out of decency alone, you're not going to try to break free. I can be boring and quarrelsome; I can say the same things over and over – and you will still listen; this is what you have to bear as a man. This is how castles in the air are built, fantasies are created – as if someone undividedly belongs to someone else."

I breathe in the moist wind; it smells of salt and seaweed. And the subtlest sweetness, it seems to me – but the sweetness is emanating from Elsa, not the sea.

"I admit it, by the way," she says. "I'm terribly possessive by nature. Same as your little Asian – you won't contest this, I hope? That was the point of her presence, which you value so highly. A muse, not a muse, an affinity, not an affinity… A woman's interest is always based on only one thing – on a sense of ownership. At least, very soon it comes down to this – sinking to the bottom of a parabola, ha-ha-ha…"

I chuckle along with her, not even trying to argue. Elsa grips my arm even tighter.

"Your Asian girl just got lucky," she says. "Like it or not, it's difficult to compete with a living, warm body – although even this, it seems to me, may be sort of questionable too. I sometimes thought you and I would adapt; we might even like it – after all, there are lots of perverts who find satisfaction in the weirdest things. Maybe we might become an odd couple as well – some sort of perverted, bizarre couple…"

And again I try to laugh, pretending I don't notice a certain strain in her words. I turn toward her to ask about something different – wanting to change the subject – and I see that Elsa has a very sad face.

"It's funny," she says, "for some reason, my…"

There is a gust of wind that shimmers her hair. She pauses, bites her lip, then continues, "For some reason, my boyfriends never hung around. It was amusing; I even used to say to myself: no matter whether I treat a man well or badly, he's going to disappear quite soon. And now it's even funnier – despite that you're not my boyfriend and haven't vanished yet. Nothing matters: whether my skin is smooth, what I'm like in bed, if this is my first life, my second… The phenomenon takes on the property of universality, don't you find?"

It's difficult to turn this into a joke; I mumble something, but the words are awkward. A chill creeps up my back; I don't exactly know why. Nevertheless, I force myself to smile, "Well, even you're talking about the universal now."

"Why not?" Elsa shrugs. "Do you not believe in me at all?" Then she asks, "Well, who else? Talks about something global, I mean." And she adds immediately, "It's easy to guess who: it's your Nestor, of course – and that's why you were so excited this morning. You two are always pretending to be clever!"

She turns away, mutters something inaudible to one side and then suddenly asks, "Well, what was that about?"

"A lot of things," I reply. "For example, about fate. And about magic, about karma..."

"Ha!" Elsa exclaims. "What could you two have to say about karma that's new? What could *you personally* have to say that's new – if only about fate?"

"What could I?" I respond absently. "Well, maybe something..."

It's like a trigger switches on in my head: I can physically sense the ordering of my thoughts. Everything I have heard yesterday is finally beginning to take some shape – little by little, reluctantly, slowly. I feel I should help the process along somehow, verbalize my reflections, say the words out loud – to catch, to seize my emerging comprehension by its coat-tails. Only Elsa is with me – I have to tell her, and she will listen; she, too, has nowhere to escape. No matter how alien or boring it is to her.

"Fate watches over and protects you, at least for a certain time," I say. "You can't fight against it; you can't argue with it. And the basis for all this is the B Object!

"Your own aspirations expressed in familiar terms may be far from what really drives you through life. There is a reason for this – the B Object!

"The trajectory of a life path – your path – is not built by you alone. Everyone is involved – through the interaction of the B Objects!"

Having reached the word "interaction," I expect Elsa to brush everything aside, as usual, to declare it all nonsense. But she listens attentively, without interrupting. In her silence, there is no rejection – only expectation.

We go down to the sea and sit on a stone about twenty meters from the water. I become even more inspired; I level out the sand under my feet and draw pictures on it. It almost seems to me that Elsa and I are allies again – as we were a few days ago. I'm looking for the appropriate words, searching for the right meanings – and she takes part; she's with me. She's truly interested – and an invisible connection between us appears to emerge…

I tell her, "The vortices of the field of the conscions are material entities, not phantoms. They strive to group together – in the wilds of the universe, inaccessible to our gaze. This striving of theirs is governed by what is 'recorded' in them – your thoughts, your memory, everything you have ever experienced. Thus, the contents of our lives affect our subsequent destinies – they form intentions and impulses, make us change occupations and countries, connect with people and separate from them suddenly. With an ease that is inexplicable sometimes."

"With ease…" Elsa repeats after me. "With unfortunate ease – if you think about it for a while, it may be impossible to refrain from tears. But, I suppose, my Object does not contain a single sob. Maybe I should have cried sometimes, but I had no idea. It always seemed to me that the universe didn't care at all, ha-ha."

I smile back at her, then shade my eyes with my hand and look at the sea for a few minutes. Something seems to be wrong with it; the waves are small, but, for some reason, their pattern disturbs my eye. It hints at a threatening irregularity – and the white yachts, gliding along the coast, rock and buck too fiercely, as if in a storm.

Then another thought enters my head. I exclaim, forgetting about the yachts, "Yes, and by the way: maybe there is a deeper feedback! The content of the Objects determines their grouping, but the grouping can affect the content as well. The *preferable* content – meaning not just mutual attraction and repulsion, not just a drive toward continents and countries, but certain peculiarities of destiny, specific vicissitudes of life. What if a group of B Objects must, for example, minimize its internal energy? Does this not mean that some Object or other will strive to be 'filled' with a certain life experience? Is it not for this reason that an unconscious desire arises in us to experience something – time and time again? Maybe this is also the case for you – because you are destined to part with your men quickly, no matter how you would have wanted it to be otherwise…"

"The universe is a bitch!" says Elsa and takes my hand. "Well, at least you're still here.

"I understand," she adds. "Blaming someone for something is a non-starter. Many, if not all, are guilty at once!"

"Many..." I mumble. "That's just how Nestor talked about other people's desires, which bind us hand and foot. And they at the same time provide the highest degree of freedom. A mission, a true predestination – if you sense it within you, then it's also because of the whims of the Object clustering. It's also everyone else's 'guilt' – and we should thank them for it!"

The wind gets up, and it becomes chilly. Elsa turns to me and rests her chin on my shoulder.

"Imagine," she says, "this grouping of yours; it can separate forever. No matter how hard you try, you can't turn this back: you break up with someone and understand suddenly – you will not see him again, in any of your lives. This is what's really called 'never' – and it contains more terrible meanings than anyone can think of. Many words could be written about this, and they will be very miserable words!"

"Imagine," I say in the same vein, "you can fall in love with someone, and you believe this happiness is forever. You believe you have found your other half, but this is just an episode with a purpose that is not immediately clear – for example, in order for you to write a book that might not even be read. Or, sometimes, you are given a chance to learn from the same mistake: for instance, very similar women enter your life, one after another..."

Elsa is silent, as if – I would like to think – she is pondering what I've said. Then she bends down and draws a series of little human figures as if hinting at the counting rhyme...

"I like sitting here like this with you," she admits. "It's as if we're having a picnic by the sea. Very romantic – next time we need to be better prepared. If it's possible to order books, then my Nestor probably won't refuse us other things as well. I can ask for some crockery – and for a thermos, a basket. We can even bake a cake – it'll be easy to carry. By the way, I don't know why I've never baked any cookies here..."

I look at her profile, at the line of her cheekbones, her lips. Everything about her is well measured, refined, almost perfect. I want to tell her this.

"You…" I begin, but suddenly Elsa's face becomes taut, her gaze freezes. She gives a short scream, "What is this? What?…"

I turn around and see something unimaginable: the sea is swelling; a giant crest is rising out of it. A thought flashes through my head: this has been coming; we were warned – at least I was. Irregularity is never a vain threat; the intuition that not everything is quite right with your surroundings should always be taken seriously. It's a bad habit to ignore the signs!

A second later, the trough turns into a wall. In another second, the wall obscures the sky. I can clearly see it is about to crash down on us, hit and smash us – and, without a moment's hesitation, I whisk Elsa off the stone in one swift movement, trying to cover her with myself. Of course, my body is no defense, but all the same, some instinct pushes me. And, at the back of my mind, a thought pulsates: this is not the first time – we've already had a hurricane and a hail of stones…

Frame after frame click through my brain: Elsa's dark hair, the sand on my cheek. Her body beneath me, supple and elastic – I feel it almost for real. Her shoulder, squeezed by my fingers, her waist, her hips… "Click-click" – I register picture by picture, sensation after sensation. Then, at the very last moment, I look around doomed and see how the gigantic wave looming over the beach freezes on the boundary between the sea and the shore, as if stumbling up against an invisible screen. It freezes – and crawls back into the sea, producing enormous sprays of foam and a multitude of smaller waves running away from us, toward the horizon…

In a minute it's all over: the sea is still restless, but its agitation contains no threat. Everything is as it was before; only the yachts have disappeared; I don't want to think about their fate. We get up, brush off our clothes and look around. Excited voices come from somewhere; a woman is screaming. It's clear the killer wave is not a notion of our fancy: it really did happen.

"You looked pretty comical," Elsa says, straightening her hair. "On all fours, like a monkey…"

She is not overly scared, but her mood has changed. I can understand her – for some reason, the magic has dissipated along with the wave; the feeling of newly found closeness has disappeared, leaving almost no trace.

Trying to return at least a part of it, I run my hand down her back – but don't feel a thing: neither a hint of a response nor an illusion of warmth.

Elsa does not withdraw but makes no gesture in return to me either. I remove my hand, sit on the stone and regard the semitrampled little figures on the sand. Elsa sits down next to me and says, frowning, "Of course, I might find it surprising that you're not tired of saving me, although we know that these dangers are most likely not real. But no, I am not surprised; it's clear: doing this, you are thinking about that Asian girl of yours, having a guilt complex. You suspect you weren't able to save her from something, and now you don't want to be ashamed of yourself – but maybe she did not need to be saved? Maybe she didn't need you at all – I even wonder if you let your dreams go all the way, right to the end? Did you have the courage to see everything as it really was?"

"Bullshit," I say coldly. "Nothing is clear to you, and neither is it to me, and you know it, and you're just trying to hurt me!"

I say this and realize: I was searching for the right meanings, but she, not me, has hit the mark. Or somewhere close to the mark. These are her "very miserable words." For some reason, it is precisely in these words that I can see some kind of clue, a red bull's-eye in the middle of the target.

Elsa does not respond; she just silently looks into the distance. Soon we get up, climb the chipped stairs and wander along the seafront to our block.

"Actually, there's nothing romantic about a picnic by the sea," says Elsa. "You just end up with annoying sand in your shoes."

Her face is gloomy – nevertheless, she holds my hand and nestles into my shoulder. We keep step, like a small squad of a battered but undefeated army. An army retreating to the demarcation line.

"*I will settle with you by the river…*" – the words of the song reach me.

It's our singer – he is sitting in his usual place, but today there is no one around him. Perhaps the wave is to blame. His voice, as if in tune with our mood, sounds especially melancholic and hoarse. "Wait," I say to Elsa, and we stop a little distance away.

"*I will settle with you by the Chao Phraya River. In a dilapidated shack on the canal bank. Among the vines and half-rotten stilts. By the water reflecting the jungle.*"

My heart contracts. I remember Tina, our outing in a long-tail boat. A carefree tour through a maze of canals; the jokes of the boatman sitting behind us. I bought him a beer, and he became our best friend for those two hours...

"*A white bird with a black beak will roam behind the house. Our modest life will be open to all eyes – to the views of all who float past. Right by the water, we will place a Buddha, a small Buddha surrounded by candles. Everyone will see how much we love him. Everyone will see how much we love each other.*"

I stand, frozen, forgetting where I am. The song resonates deep inside me – with something sweetly sharp, incomprehensible, painful. Elsa feels it – she suddenly withdraws her hand and exclaims, "Enough! I'm going home; you can listen here on your own." Then she turns to the singer and shouts, "How much do I have to put up with this? You are always singing for him to spite me!"

He does not respond, merely plucking the strings in silence.

During the evening session, Nestor is still diffident and dry. "I will read you one paragraph," he says, flipping through something out of sight below. "It has not been written by me, so don't get critical."

And he reads – measuredly and monotonously: "...in the end, she got used to him and simply called him 'my lord.' The frequent déjà vus no longer seemed strange – she played his games, resigned to their masculine essence. All her losses were nourished by his hatred; the moans of her passion were devoted to him. She knew the flow of the Tao was tossing her, like a small splinter, together with him from one direction to another. They were hurled side by side in muddy whirlpools, and he, the 'lord,' was always slightly ahead. Her happiness lay in following his shadow; this was her special path. She often wondered on which continent, in which time he existed and only regretted that she could not love him with all her heart. For, she believed, you can love only those who are reachable, who are distinctly close."

Nestor becomes silent and rubs his nose with his finger. Then he smiles thinly with his lips, "It's an interesting passage, isn't it? Of course, this is just prose. Fiction, a tale – but still…"

He goes through his papers again, looks for something, then looks up at me. His eyes sparkle; his detachment has gone. "Still," he repeats. "Imagine, for example, a long thread with knots at different ends. Throw it on the table, make a figure out of it, join the ends together… Who knows how close or distant the points on the local branes are if you look at them from above? Those small knots of your thread on the table might be right next to each other. Who knows whose B Objects are nearby? Is this not a hint at the inexplicable unity of souls? At some special sensation of closeness to someone else, independent of your locations or social circles… Is there not a hint here of the true solidarity of thoughts or – of unrestored justice, of the thirst for revenge?"

"Or simply," I say, "at the need to be near someone with whom you are, alas, not?"

"Well, yes…" Nestor nods and immediately closes up, drawing inside himself. Now he is wearing a mask again – of impassivity and even boredom.

"The session is over," he says. "Good night."

"You're being sentimental today; you even said goodbye to me," I try to goad him, but the screen is already dead; no one can hear me.

I'm trying to get to sleep but to no avail. So I wander around the room, then go to the bathroom and stand for a long time under the hot shower, muttering, "Unity, unity…" Nestor's words do not leave my head – and it seems they've stirred something in him as well. Although, of course, with Nestor you never can tell.

Returning to the bedroom, I take one glance at the armchair and resolutely open the door to the living room. A table lamp is on; Elsa is sitting at the table and reflecting on something, her palm propping up her cheek.

I sit down next to her. "I can't sleep," she complains. "I have nothing to dream about. And don't think I've forgiven you."

She has almost the same expression on her face as Nestor – detachment, indifference. But I can still sense our deeply hidden closeness. A closeness that would be pointless and meaningless to cover up with insincerity. We are like spouses who have accumulated a lot of mutual hurt but know there's no way of getting away from each other.

Elsa seems to feel the same way. She says rather angrily, "In fact, it's you who's the possessor in our case, not me. You own me, knowing I am not going to leave Quarantine – and, therefore, your property rights are inviolable. You possess me more securely than anyone ever, more securely than your Asian girl – she could get angry, suddenly lose it, run away from you in her Asian city, in the Asian night, in her Asian world. But I can't!"

She looks up at me and continues, squinting slightly, "Of course, one could judge things more rationally: you and your Asian are no longer together – death, as they say, has already parted you. She is now who knows where, and I am here with you. Your separation is the price you paid for your possession of me, but it still hurts me that while owning me, you will be thinking about her, maybe even pining for her. For her, for your muse! I still can't get used to this. But, most probably, I will."

We keep silent. I, like her, prop my head with the palms of my hands. And I mutter, squinting at the spot of yellow light, "It's amazing – almost everything you say helps me one way or another. Maybe it's not about you at all? Maybe things I hear from you, from Nestor, have just one purpose – to lead me somewhere, provoking specific thoughts, stimulating my mind? And – as terrible as it sounds – what if it's not about Tina either? What if she – and everyone I ever once met – has been granted to me only to make my brain work?"

"The center of the world," Elsa snorts, but somewhat uncertainly, forcing herself.

I continue, "Yet on the other hand, I am dealing with the most complicated matters, but every moment I feel my dependence on the most primitive, the most simple. On the presence in my life of at least someone, albeit temporarily, momentarily… I feel dependent on a woman, on women – on those near me, whom I sometimes bring to tears, and on the one who is desperately far away. She may be in a different universe, but, I want to think, she is also yearning – or even crying without me."

"I've already told you," Elsa says coldly, "as for me, I never cry. But it doesn't mean I'm not hurt."

"Yes," I nod. "Yes, I understand."

I really do understand – knowing already what I felt today while listening to the street singer. The words didn't help me – the recognition came on its own, highlighted by the yellow spot from the lamp. It came, and I cannot dispel it; I know it will find a way back – with pain. With reminders of my anticipations, of premonitions from the past – foresights of the simplest things, well known to everyone. Like the memory of inevitability, recognition will return inevitably – you cannot escape it, even soaring through the most mind-bending theories. From equations apprehensible by only a few, you deduce what everyone is feeling – and this connects you with the ordinary, with the rest of the world. The connection may be fleeting, but it's beyond doubt nonetheless; I remember now how I looked at Tina and knew: she belonged to me, but only for a little while. I envisaged "for a little while" in its most frightening sense – and the pain from it had a sweetly terrifying flavor. And this pain was uniting me with another man – who had tasted it and become its slave...

I say goodnight to Elsa and go to my room. I choose a dream for myself – scrupulously specifying the moment from which it should begin. I do not need anyone's help; I leap off from the ellipsis of the unknown; I free myself from its tenacious hooks.

And the chain of memories unwinds: Tina and I leave our apartment in the evening, holding hands. We are going to celebrate an occasion – I have just pressed the "Enter" button, publishing my theory on the net. The party is coming – but now, falling asleep, I feel no joy. My soul is full of anxiety, and the reason for it lies in one word, in one name: Brevich. With this, I fall through – into the anticipation of pain, into the depths of sleep.

THE RESTLESS GHOST

CHAPTER 27

HAVING SPENT ALMOST the whole night in Nok's room, Ivan Brevich decided what he wanted to do with his life. With what remained of it, which he knew would not be long. Lasting just enough to find a reliable way to reunite himself with Nok after his own death.

This was not a decision born of despair – Ivan had no doubt he could endure everything, cope with it no matter what. The loss of Nok included – but living without her was pointless, ridiculous, absurd. Any alternative seemed more sensible – and now, looking from a new angle, even through a cloudy prism, he saw: an alternative was possible. He did not stop thinking about it for a minute, pushing everything else into the background. In the depths of his soul, he understood the task was enormously complex, his goal perhaps unattainable. But his mind rejected unattainability, refused to accept it.

Returning to Moscow, Ivan began reorganizing his assets. The strategy was simple: he quickly sold everything of noticeable value. Within three weeks, his company and the huge house on the River Klyazma had acquired new owners. He transferred money, a very large amount, to offshore banks and left it in cash, without investing in anything, so that all the capital would be available at any moment.

In the meantime, the investigation into Nok's death had produced results. The case was a high-profile one and was being followed closely by the press and high-ranking officials. The bodyguard, although seriously injured, had recovered and was able to testify. The abduction of the wife of a major businessman was immediately linked to the violent death of his partner. The perpetrators, despite a carefully thought-out plan of action, had been captured by a surveillance camera on a nearby building. They were identified, declared wanted and arrested somewhere down in the south of the country, near Krasnodar. Upon their delivery to Moscow, they were both given a serious going over and confessed everything they knew. And at this point the investigation stalled: Danilov was dead, and Sakhnov had disappeared without a trace. Brevich's ex-wife was summoned for questioning and released – there was no evidence against her.

Ivan followed the investigation through his main contact in the police – Colonel Sibiryakov, the head of the city department. The whole chain of events – in particular, the death of "Sanyok" and the disappearance of "Valyok" – made logical sense to him and fitted into a coherent picture. Brevich had no doubt: the crime was nothing more than an attempt by his childhood friends to avenge themselves on him. He wasn't surprised, but not about to forgive anyone either. Through Sibiryakov, he met the warden of the jail, where the perpetrators were being held, and had a private meeting with him. The latter was reluctant at first but soon heeded Ivan's arguments and agreed to take his money. It was not just that the amount was huge. The abduction of a wife, by any "criminal standards," was considered beyond the pale. The warden secretly prided himself on having retained at least a hankering for fairness, despite his job.

On the same day, both perpetrators – who had up until then been detained with other former servicemen – were placed in a punishment cell for a contrived reason and then separated and transferred to so-called black cells full of hardened criminals. Their training and toughness counted for nothing there. Soon both were badly crippled and afterward, half dead but still capable of perceiving what was happening, put through every imaginable and unimaginable humiliation and torture. Then, having lost any resemblance to human beings, they were eliminated. Ivan was presented with a detailed report, which did nothing to reduce his inner pain. Yet it spurred him into action, into implementing the main, most important thing.

Brevich did not have a specific plan; he only had an inkling: to find what he was looking for, he had to be in Bangkok. There was no logic behind it – except the memory of the outpouring of emotions during his first week together with Nok. For Ivan, however, this was a sufficient argument: the city had helped him meet the only woman he had ever loved – he would now have to rely on it to resolve a similar if not more difficult matter. He had nothing else to rely on.

A month after the funeral, Brevich was sitting in a Thai Airlines jet again. This was his third trip to Thailand, a trip of determination, a one-way journey. Ivan didn't plan to come back; he knew: his present existence would end there – having been transformed into something new and again filled with meaning. And of all possible meanings, he was interested in only one.

During the flight, Brevich was thinking about death, as he had been constantly over the last few weeks. Previously, before Nok had appeared in his life, he, like most other people, regarded death as something abstract, not related to him personally. It was a topic that never loomed fully into view – but now the question of nonexistence and its nature had arisen in its entirety. There was no dismissing it; its scale could not be diminished. He needed to find an answer – a convincing, consistent one that he himself would be able to believe in without reservation… Brevich was well aware how challenging this was. How difficult it would be to search through the vaguest matters, in the impenetrable darkness, counting only on instinct. Nevertheless, he had no doubt that a solution would arise sooner or later.

The necessary conditions were clear: it was vital that he and Nok meet again, not in the form of plants or stones but as entities with consciousness and a soul. They would have to be able to recognize each other; their memories must be kept intact. A resurrection of this sort here in the earthly world was impossible; otherwise, everyone would have known about it. That meant that existence continues somewhere beyond – this is how the idea of another space accessible from this one had gained traction in his head. Ivan sometimes even thought about it in terms of complex metrics, other dimensions, curved planes and spheres – recalling fragments of the knowledge he had picked up at college. But he could not go any further in this way – his thoughts kept slipping up on science fiction clichés, which he did not take seriously.

In his search for ideas, Brevich had been reading books all month. He dismissed the scientific literature immediately as being beyond his understanding and plunged into the psycho-spiritual and the mystically religious. The notions and canons of Jews, Hindus and Buddhists intermingled in his mind, feeding each other. He jumped from concept to concept – from Sheol to Maimonides, from the Upanishads and Sansara to the treatises of Lao Tzu, from the magical formulas of the Egyptian Book of the Dead to the grim ancient Greek myths. Sometimes it seemed he had almost found the answer; then, on the contrary, everything that had ever been conceived by humanity appeared hopelessly naive and unworthy. Sometimes – painfully, almost agonizingly – he felt that his dimmed mind couldn't cope with the contradictions, incapable of withstanding the abyss he was trying to peer into. Despair rolled over him; it was always waiting nearby, but Ivan only gritted his teeth, not letting it get the upper hand. Not allowing himself to give up and lose the hope for which he had a basis – the city where it had all begun. Bangkok had to provide him with the nudge, sending him in the right direction, leading him to clarity, to a resolution.

Exiting the terminal for the taxi stand and breathing in the thick, humid air, Brevich was even more convinced this was precisely the place he needed to be. He reserved the same penthouse in the same hotel in Chitlom where he and Nok had spent several happy days. In the suite, walking through the rooms and glancing out of the window at the panorama of buildings stretching below, Ivan felt: he had come back home. This was his fortress, his citadel, his outpost; from here he was ready to plan and conduct the final battle with the whole world. To fight the evil circumstances and forces that he wanted and had to conquer.

Brevich spent the first week after his arrival in apparent inaction. He wanted to synchronize himself with the city's rhythm, to get a feeling he was on its wavelength. He woke up around noon and sat in the restaurant for a while, picking at a late breakfast; then he would call a taxi. Without any haste, he would again drive and walk around all those places he had been to with Nok. Vigilantly peering at people, objects, at the entire surroundings, as if trying to read and unravel some encrypted code.

On the very first day, he went to Nok's old excursion bureau, which had now been turned into a gift shop. The owner, a tiny young Thai woman, started speaking to him, offering something, but then suddenly became frightened and fell silent under his gaze. Brevich turned away, put on his dark glasses, had a look at the shelves with various trinkets and left without saying goodbye. Then he drove to Muang Boran and spent an hour sitting by the entrance of the house on stilts. The next morning, he went to Tonburi, stopped by the floating market, bought an orchid in a phial and carried it around with him all day. In the ancient Ayutthaya, he wandered around for a long time in the heat, then went to the canal and looked out toward the opposite shore. Unlike the River Styx, it was impossible to cross over to uncover the concealed riddles. Neither a boat steered by some Thai Charon nor Persephone's golden branch would have been of help…

Bangkok was in no hurry to provide any clues, hiding under a different mask. Brevich knew the face behind the mask but understood that the city had no reason to reveal it – now that Nok was no longer here. Ivan was all alone in his fortress; no army was rushing to his aid. Everything and everyone around was supremely indifferent to his loss – like his acquaintances in Moscow, like Colonel Sibiryakov, like the Thai Airlines flight attendants… He was right to have come to hate the world – the world was false in all its attempts to show concern. Brevich felt this falseness in every glance, in every Thai smile and recalled Lothar's words: Bangkok was a city of the fake. It was its favorite incarnation, its most natural state – but, despite this, Ivan believed: sooner or later, something authentic would emerge. He would just need to recognize it.

Still, nothing true had emerged yet, and Brevich waited, following his established routine. In the evening, after dinner, he would go to the rooftop bar, open his notebook and try to write down some daily thoughts, seeking hidden substance in them. This would soon make him bored, and he just looked at the night panorama, spread out like a sky map. He counted the clusters of bright dots and gave them names, mentally drawing a line from one "galaxy" to another. He followed the play of the illuminations and, most of all, the signal lights on the tops of the skyscrapers, whose reflections flashed on and off in the windows as if calling to each other. Ivan saw in them allies; they were sending signs to the airplanes never going to fly here. They were signaling to the unresponsive; they strived tirelessly, despite the surrounding indifference, and he respected their efforts.

Once the bar closed, Brevich would walk to his room, lie on the bed for half an hour, then jump up, put on a pair of worn shorts and a T-shirt and head out into the night. He would take a taxi or wander off into the most impoverished, unsightly areas, walking through a web of narrow streets, strolling among the garbage dumps and ruins, the shaky houses and smelly canals. He stumbled and slipped in the dark, blundered into some rusty barbed wire or a half-rotten picket fence. Frightened by his crazed gaze, the local punks and stray dogs gave him a wide berth. Neither the dirt nor the stench bothered him. He knew he had to dive as deep as possible into the city's core. He had to get so close to the city that nothing would separate them – and perhaps then a signal would flash, a hint would be heard...

Toward morning, tired and soaked, his eyes inflamed, he would take a taxi to Soi Cowboy. The go-go bars were already closed; the priestesses of paid love had changed their outfits and had transformed back into ordinary country girls. They crowded around the street-food stalls, plastic tables and chairs, eating their late dinner, laughing and chatting with each other. Brevich bought a large bottle of Thai brandy, put it on the first table he came across, said "please" and silently drank until dawn with anyone who cared to join in. After a couple of days, the girls got used to him; no one looked at him in surprise or bothered him with questions. Some of them tried to sell him their services but soon gave up. They simply made a place and laid out food for him, which he almost never touched...

Then Ivan suddenly realized he needed to change his tactics. Some other action was required – and he already sensed what it should be. Superfluous, inept options fell away by themselves. Only one remained: Brevich was almost physically drawn to the environment where he had once touched upon the secret of the Thai soul. For two nights in a row, he dreamed the same thing – a voice from a loudspeaker, the concentrated and peaceful faces of the Thais and Nok's quiet whisper translating words that for some reason seemed familiar to him. Somewhere, in all of this, the essence of Siam was concealed, along with the essence of this city wearing its mask, pretending to be something it wasn't. Like a clown at the fair, it was adopting one guise after another, fooling the gullible with its smog and bustle, its girly bars and counterfeit junk. But Brevich was not to be deceived; he saw the entrance to the secret sluices. Concealed there was what the city and its inhabitants believed in. And Nok had believed in it as well – perhaps this was what she had been hinting at in her message? Maybe this was the starting point – from which the path he was seeking originated?

The next day, Ivan went to the nearest Buddhist temple. He managed to find a monk who was ready to talk to a *farang*, but the conversation did not work out. Besides, Brevich was irritated by the monk himself – still a young man, resembling a wily street peddler – and the tone of their discourse, which had nothing sacred about it. What's more, they understood each other badly – the language barrier was too great.

Nevertheless, using gestures and grimaces, they talked for about half an hour. The monk tried to speak about karma and the futility of human desires and then suddenly switched to the theme of the visibility of images, of the real in the unreal. "You have to think about your wife every moment, imagine her with you, keep her face before your eyes," he said. "You should see it as if in reality – like when you've smoked your fill of dope. Like when your mind starts swimming during an amazing trip…"

Brevich noted that the monk spoke about dope and trips with suspicious confidence. Then he was asked to donate a thousand baht for the temple's needs, and with that, the audience ended.

"Can you introduce me to any of the elders?" Ivan asked as they made their farewells.

"My English is the best in the monastery," the monk sneered. "The elders won't understand a word!"

It was evident he was quite pleased with himself. Ivan nodded glumly and left, utterly irritated. Once again, the indifference of the world struck the eye, enveloped him from all sides. There was no one with whom he could unite against it.

Later he visited two more temples – with much the same result. Yet he had no doubt: the starting point had been identified correctly. It just wasn't easy to get to it – and the main hurdle was the difficulties with the language. So, in the evening Brevich opened his laptop and entered

"Bangkok English Thai interpreter" into the search bar. At first, numerous companies jumped out; he gave them a miss and clicked on the first link leading to someone's personal page. There was a phone number – Ivan dialed it and heard the voice of Dara. They made an appointment to meet the next day, and this was the turning point for his whole "project."

CHAPTER 28

DARA, THE FREELANCE interpreter, had been born in eastern Thailand, in Buriram, the "city of happiness." Her mother was half Khmer, and her strong Khmer blood manifested itself clearly in Dara with her dark skin, stubborn disposition and fiery temper, which she sometimes struggled to keep in check. She was the only girl in her family and the firstborn – it was therefore considered only natural that the responsibility for providing for the household should be laid on her shoulders. Thus, at the age of sixteen, without finishing school, Dara found herself in Bangkok – where her virginity was sold to one of the bars. And before that, her mother had taken her to Cambodia, to a distant relative, a female shaman, who put an invisible tattoo onto her pubic region that would render her irresistible to men.

Dara did not hold any grudges against her family, but she realized she could only count on herself in life. On herself and on good fortune – so she diligently prayed to the goddess of happiness, Nang Kwak, every day of the six years she spent as a "bar fairy," leaving sweets in the temple and lighting at least two candles each visit. And then, at the age of twenty-two, fate cast her a winning ticket – an elderly Englishman fell in love with her and took her back to live with him in London. It was a tremendous piece of luck – Dara understood: Nang Kwak had deigned to smile down upon her. Although, she conceded, perhaps the tattoo had also played a role – so, after all, the family might have given her more than she had originally thought.

She lived with the Englishman for seven years; then he died, and Dara returned to Bangkok – with good English and some money. This allowed her to lead the independent life of a freelancer, providing services to foreign tourists and businessmen that ranged widely from interpretation to massage and, sometimes, bed. Yet Dara was discerning and did not waste herself on just anyone. She never forgot her goal: to find a new source of wealth that would be sufficient for a long time to come.

From the first words exchanged with Brevich over the phone, Dara sensed this was no ordinary occasion. And when she met him, she understood two things right away: he was rich, and something seemed to be wrong with his mind. It was a promising combination; Dara's internal sensors shuddered, pulsed and flickered into life. She immediately turned on the charm and her ability to be attuned to whatever a man might want at any given moment. And it worked, as it always did: Brevich suddenly felt that besides the silent skyscraper lights, he had found another ally in the city – someone who wasn't indifferent to his problem.

Before the meeting, Ivan hadn't planned to be too candid. He had invented a cover story, pretending he was writing a book about the afterlife and was traveling the world, collecting material for it. But Dara listened so attentively, and her gaze betrayed so much empathy, that he, imperceptibly even to himself, began to open up and little by little told her everything as it was.

They spent over three hours together in a French café at Lumpini Park. Brevich recounted the entire story about Nok: their passionate days in Bangkok, her pregnancy and their wedding, then her death and cremation. He hinted at "the other Sun" and revealed his decision to follow in her footsteps, to find her again, no matter how fantastical that might sound. He talked about his childhood buddies, Sanyok and Valyok, who had become his worst enemies, depriving his life of any meaning. About his business and former wives, about his plan, which had yet to take shape, and the words of the Buddha, which he had heard together with Nok…

Dara didn't ask questions; she sat silently, propping up her cheek with her hand. It was becoming clearer and clearer that the rarest stroke of luck was knocking on her door again. She knew *farangs*, coming to Thailand with their plans – they were all losers, cherishing the hope of avenging themselves on fate in one way or another. All of them were weak, and their thirst for revenge, their obsession with proving the unprovable, were transferred onto the only Thais willing to have any dealings with them – the girls from the bars, in whom they sought consolation for their grievances. Brevich wasn't like that – he didn't look like a loser or a weakling – but all the same, fate had caused him the most terrible grief… There was a deep contradiction concealed in this, and Dara could not quite grasp it, turn it into a clear idea. But she had a feeling: it contained an opportunity, a great chance. Everything was for real and for high stakes – Ivan wasn't going to waste time on trifles or half measures.

By the end of the conversation, Brevich was on thin ice – he had stumbled into a jungle of unclear meanings, into poorly fitting fragments he had drawn from his reading or invented himself. He began to jump from one to another – from outer spaces to the dharma of the ocean, from kabbalistic reincarnation to the parables of Ecclesiastes, asserting the dualism of "predestination" and the rejection of death. Soon he became confused and began to contradict himself – getting angry but continuing to pile complication upon complication.

Dara came to his aid – carefully choosing her words. "I understand what you're talking about," she encouraged him gently. "And you know, everything could turn out to be much simpler…"

Ivan grinned and looked away, but she caught the shadow of his gaze. She caught a glimpse – a flash of hope – and this, too, was familiar to her. Nearly every aspect of *farangs'* lives was incomprehensible to themselves and others. They were all subconsciously searching for simplifications, certain elementary truths – it was a lever that Dara had learned to manipulate to perfection. Just like her old barroom companions – and because of this, hordes of men with experience, education, families and money would fall with surprising consistency into the most naive of traps set by their barely literate Thai temptresses. The Western mind – whether sick, like Brevich's, or ordinary, healthy and rational – would turn out to be powerless in the face of primitive cunning, as if it, the mind, only needed an excuse to capitulate and surrender. Thai girls didn't try to rationalize what was happening in their lives. They just believed that the flow of events would carry them where they needed to be – and their natural lack of doubt made their words immensely persuasive. One by one, dozen by dozen, hundred by hundred, their clients would be deceived – despite the numerous warning tales that filled the net. All *farangs* badly needed simplifying formulas, and Dara understood that Brevich, too, would be unable to resist despite all his strength and wealth…

That evening, Ivan changed his routine – he didn't go to the hotel bar or wander off into the night. The silent lights sending their signals no longer attracted his attention – a new supporter had emerged, and the signs became different. Not everything about them boded well – they seemed to worry him more than lead anywhere. A light had dawned at the end of a tunnel, but he could still barely make it out. It was unreliable, maybe even misleading… Brevich suddenly feared that he might be late – but did not understand what for. He spent the whole evening and half the night sitting at his laptop fruitlessly searching for new clues, revisiting links from one prophet, one religion and one sacred text to another – only to become more confused. Then he finally fell asleep, but just for a little while: the tension would not leave him; his damaged mind hurtled around in a circle. The thoughts were becoming increasingly feverish and restless, jumping from one futile idea to another.

In the afternoon, Dara took him to a temple built recently with money from an influential police boss. Tourists didn't go there; its grounds with a large park were deserted and very quiet. They were met by an elderly monk who led them deep into the park and sat on a mat under a sprawling tree. He resembled a boa constrictor; there was something serpentine about his manner. Perhaps somewhere deep inside him beat the heart of a snake. For some reason, this made a positive impression on Brevich.

Dara took a long time to explain what their business was. Finally, the monk stopped her, indicating with a gesture that everything was clear. Then, gazing to one side, he said, "We're all scared of death but, if one ought to fear anything, it should rather be the rebirth that will follow it." Dara translated. Ivan nodded in agreement. This was easy to agree with: of course, the danger lay in the chance that out there, *afterward*, he might not get to meet Nok. The monk meditated a bit and added, "It is harder for those who remain behind" – and Brevich became confident they understood each other well.

Then the conversation started – the monk, with his eyes half closed, spoke for a while about the Buddhist way. "Calm is within us… Compassion and tolerance… At the core of everything is the law of karma…" Dara translated diligently. Soon Brevich's patience evaporated; he began to get agitated, fidgeting and breathing heavily. The turmoil of the last night returned; his mind continued to race round in circles. The circuitous phrases made him even more confused and distracted. Ivan began to look angry and finally raised his hand.

The monk immediately fell silent. "Tell him we don't have time for bullshit," Brevich said sullenly to Dara. "Ask him where she is waiting for me; how do I get there? I need a place, a time, a way."

Dara translated the entire tirade to the monk, noting his barely perceptible smile at the English word "bullshit." "Oh, and here's another thing…" Brevich suddenly started up, but the monk raised his palm in turn, interrupting him midsentence, and calmly said, "You are at the very beginning, but you want to jump right away to the end. That's why you think time and place are so important. But you see, the end is not the end – not by a long shot – and this, in fact, is the whole point."

Brevich fixed him with his gaze. Then he turned to Dara, "What? What did he say?"

Dara repeated everything. Ivan nodded silently and stared at the monk again.

"The moment of novelty follows another moment," the latter mumbled monotonously. "Drop by drop, the lake becomes full. Your karma changes, and every change is inextricably linked with the previous ones, with every reflection on the lake's surface. One candle is lit by another; a new flame comes into existence – but can you distinguish it by sight? No, it has the same essence; it's the same candle flame… I have answers to your questions, but you must accept what I say with all your heart. You must pass the words through your heart; otherwise, they will mean nothing to you."

Dara translated, thinking that Brevich would now become even more anxious, but he just briefly promised, "I'll accept."

The monk looked at Ivan sharply, then closed his eyes again and continued, "There is the energy of life and there is something that directs life.

There is an energy of the will – of your own will – it is hidden deep inside you, but it's still more powerful than anything else. Time changes your karma and your ability to govern your life. The energy of the will is the quintessence of karma: the pollen in the flower, the summary of all that you are. At the right moment, it and nothing else can carry you – from flame to flame, to a new existence, to a new shell... Do you understand what I am saying?"

Ivan thought and said, "I have the will." And he added, "I know how to govern my life."

The monk nodded, paused and spoke again, "The world of life – the world of the body – is not the main point. There is a cause, the most primordial one – it's the world of experiences, the reflection of the flame in innumerable mirrors. This is how the energy of your will manifests itself – and hurls you inside the flow from one world into another, where your flame takes shape, turns into life itself. If the flows draw close to each other, if their pulsations are similar, then the worlds in which the flame will relight can coincide..."

For another quarter of an hour, he talked about energies, about rebirth and karma, the sequence of incarnations and the continuity of manifestations. Brevich listened without interrupting, feeling that something was really penetrating his heart. In a hazy mixture, in a fever of thought, the germ of the fruit crystallized. The circle was converging toward a certain dot – there was no need to interfere, only to remain patient for a little while.

"You cannot leave the flow, and you cannot swim against it, but the flow can bring you to your goal. Your will is capable of helping, but remember: it's only a form of karma, nothing else," the monk said and fell silent.

Brevich also paused, listening to himself, and asked in a strange voice, "But there, near the goal, in the new flame, whatever it's called... There, in the new world, if it happens to be the same for us, will we be able to recognize each other?"

"I won't say 'yes,'" the monk shrugged. "The Buddha does not teach there's some unchanging 'I' that passes with its life experience from one life to another. But I won't say 'no' either – because the Buddha himself remembered his past lives. Why shouldn't you experience recognition – for instance, by sensing your mutual closeness?"

Dara translated this word for word and immediately regretted she hadn't exaggerated it a bit, but Brevich seemed quite satisfied with the answer. He sat quietly, without changing his posture, only squinting slightly – the sun had broken through the branches, playfully dappling his face. Now he had no doubt: the point of the resolution was getting closer. He and the monk were progressing toward it gradually, one move after another, like in a game of chess, together building a position on the board.

"You need to know," the monk spoke again. "There are three basic types of karma. The first, the foremost, is 'weighty' karma, as the Buddha called it. It is determined by the most consequential, the most significant actions. Those that changed your life, made you different. And I must be frank with you: sometimes damage to the karma is irreversible. Thus I have to ask you – have you ever had to kill?"

Brevich thought: it was just as well that Danilov was dead and "Valyok" Sakhnov had disappeared without a trace and could not be found. He had often fantasized how he would break their bones and pump them full of bullets. With enough money, it was quite possible this fantasy could have been turned into reality... The killing of the two perpetrators in jail didn't count, he decided. They weren't important, and besides, he hadn't carried out the act with his own hands.

"No," said Brevich firmly. "I've seen a lot, but I've never had to kill."

"Let it be so, but still..." the monk kept on. His serpentine eyes looking into Ivan's soul. "But still: you see, you've never previously taken the teachings of the Buddha seriously. You did not know the Path and have now decided to embark on the Path. What caused you to choose it? What gave you the impulse to turn your gaze toward it?"

"A few lines written down in a notebook," Brevich said.

"No," the monk shook his head. "I think your answer is too hasty. Those lines were just the final straw. Listen to yourself intently – and be honest."

Ivan thought a few minutes and quietly but clearly said, "The pain."

Dara translated and noted – both the word itself and the way Brevich pronounced it. The monk nodded in satisfaction as if he had been waiting for this very answer himself. "Good," he said, "now I believe you."

The chess game continued, the figures moving slowly like the shadows of the branches on the grass. Dara took out a bottle of water and offered it to Ivan, but he refused, waving it away. And, after a long weary pause, he asked, "What is the second type of karma?"

"The 'karma of habit,'" the monk replied. "A reflection of what is happening every day. The result of what you do repeatedly, without thinking, without noticing. It seems imperceptible, unimportant, but the vessel fills up – life is long. And thus it transpires that the influence of the routine is very great."

Brevich thought about his habits. He couldn't recall any persistent ones, except, perhaps, his liking for alcohol.

"Yes, I understand," he nodded. "Repetitive, unnoticeable… And what is the third?"

The monk paused, bowing his head. Then he raised his eyes and spoke softly, looking Brevich directly in the eyes, "Before you are born again, you must die. Your 'end-of-life karma' provides the impetus for your rebirth – this is the third type. Karma on the eve of death – it's shaped by what you are feeling, perceiving in your final moment. And in your case, this might be the most important of all."

Dara translated. Brevich listened and became thoughtful, retreated into himself. Having reflected, he frowned and was visibly alarmed. The point of resolution was near, but he couldn't step toward it. The tension in his brain intensified even more; some abscess was growing there.

He cleared his throat and spoke with an effort, trying to make his voice sound even, "Regarding me, it's clear, but my Nok, did she… What did she manage to perceive and think about before her death? What was her impulse, where did it take her? We do not and cannot know!"

"Your Nok," the monk said calmly, "is still thinking about it to this day."

"You mean?…" Brevich exclaimed, his forehead creased with suffering. Something started to ring in his head; he was finding it difficult to control himself. What the monk had said excited his hopes, misconceptions and doubts all the more. He completely ceased to sense what could be believed and what could not. His mind was frozen at the peak of a mountain, on the tip of a needle, barely keeping its balance.

The monk shrugged, "There's nothing to question here. She was killed; she died before her age of death – which is why her spirit has not found rest; it is still troubled. Rushing about, searching, waiting for a sign…"

"Her spirit?" Brevich interrupted him, squeezing his face with his hand and swaying backward and forward. Then he stopped, let out a loud curse and burst into laughter. Dara and the monk stared at him in alarm. His eyes were crazed; the feral grin on his face looked genuinely scary.

"Her spirit!" Ivan repeated and muttered a few Russian words. He grimaced, gritted his teeth – and suddenly his facial features smoothed out, the grin disappeared. He shook his head and asked Dara, "Please, could you repeat this."

She began to translate again, word for word. Brevich nodded, listening not so much to her but to the dissonance of his thoughts. They gyrated around some kind of stable center. "A restless spirit," Ivan said quietly and stared downward, fidgeting with the weave of the mat.

He knew: he had just experienced a revelation like the one he had had in Nok's room. The vitalizing freshness of simplicity replaced suffocating complexity. The truth of simplicity – he had been wandering in a maze and now he had found his way out. The abscess of his consciousness burst forth; his mind no longer balanced on a summit. His thoughts, which had been dancing on a needle, tumbled downward to the foothills, into one of the valleys. What the monk said was the final push that made everything clear.

Of course, the words spoken were naive, but in them, beyond them, as if behind a nondescript shell, the most important of contents was concealed. Everything fell into place; the epitome of the faith he had been trying to elicit from the city took on a specific form – a restless ghost seeking the same thing that he was. Other concepts, teachings, dogmas, theories quickly faded away, turned into dust…

Brevich raised his head and looked around as if reacquainting himself with his surroundings. Then he said in a firm, irrefutable voice, "First: How do we find her spirit? And second: How can we get into contact with it? I need details – of a very practical kind!"

The monk began to mumble – about the wanderings of ghosts and the fates that awaited them. There was nothing practical in his words, but Ivan was hearing something completely different. The game of chess continued, but the pieces on the board were now being marshaled by another player. Dara had entered the game – and was making moves for everyone.

She did not need any help: the ghosts of the dead, scurrying everywhere, occupied a large place in her picture of the world. Like any Thai woman, Dara knew a lot about them and could discuss the topic for hours. Now, under the guise of translation, she was making things up on the go – how Nok's spirit had remained close at hand to the unsuspecting Ivan. How it had followed him everywhere and, of course, had returned with him to Bangkok – for where else could it go to gain its freedom? From who else would it expect a sign signaling its liberation, if not from the man Nok was in love with? Even now it was circling somewhere nearby, finding temporary shelter for itself, as all spirits do, in someone it had chosen at random. And this "someone" would appear in due time, would make himself or herself known, ending up nearby. All that was needed was not to miss this chance…

Ivan listened carefully without asking questions. The image, the long-awaited solution to the puzzle, was forming in his head. And Dara fantasized swiftly, sensing that her own chance was waiting nearby and she must not let it slip through her fingers. And indeed, it really did soon arise.

The monk suddenly stopped talking, raised his head, as if looking for something in the crown of the tree, and, after a pause, said quietly, "But there is one problem."

Dara translated, and Brevich grimaced – this was not the time for new problems.

"You want to run ahead," the monk continued, "but we must go back to the beginning. I assume your Nok was a good girl?"

Ivan nodded grimly. "Then," the monk shrugged, "you're facing a difficult task. According to the law, your karma should be no worse than that of the person with whom you want to be reborn together. Your wife's karma was pure, but what is yours? Are you ready to make the effort to render it better, cleaner?"

Dara readied herself: it was clear the goddess Nang Kwak had given her a cue. In the game of chess the time had come to bring the queen into play. She translated the monk's words but changed the question slightly by adding, "Are you ready to give a lot?"

"I am ready," Brevich answered firmly. "What exactly do I need to do?"

He could barely restrain his impatience. Evidently, the problem that had arisen had a solution – which meant he would solve it.

"He says he wants to help with money," Dara translated to the monk. "He wants to give it to the poor – this will improve his karma, right?…"

Thus, the subject of money arose, causing the monk to become quite animated. He burst into a speech stating that, yes, helping the poor was the right way, but one cannot just buy karma in a single transaction. Giving to the poor must become a habit – hence forming a karma of habit. This must be done as a routine, almost imperceptible to yourself.

"Buddha lived one of his lives as King Vissantara," the monk said. "Having become enlightened, Vissantara chose generosity as his main tenet. He donated to peasants his luxury carriage, then his horses and servants. He gave his wealth and title to his brothers. He sent his children to work on someone else's farm and even gave away his magic white elephant…"

This all played into Dara's hands; she didn't even have to add anything. Brevich listened, nodded, memorized, looking intently at the monk's face. The latter's steady serpentine gaze was easy to believe.

After the story of Vissantara, the monk considered the subject of money to be over. He again began to speak about the path of a true Buddhist, about abstinence and rituals, ceremonies and prayers, but Dara "translated" something quite different. She firmly stuck to the single concept: the need for Ivan to donate. The need to rid himself of his possessions, which only hindered him. The need to make life easier for others – this was the best recipe, perhaps the only one available. This was the way to ascend the karmic ladder, to step from one level to another, to feel like the ancient king – although, of course, not everyone had a magical elephant to part with. Ivan didn't have one either – yet perhaps he still had enough to achieve his goal…

"From one level to another…" Brevich repeated after her. His brain was computing what he had heard and was finding no flaws in it. Everything sounded right, aligning with his own views on how fate might be working.

"A white elephant, ha?" he grinned. "One can buy an elephant too… Anyway. Tell him that I can, I am ready to help the poor, even whole villages – but what will happen next?"

Dara had a ready answer to this. She asked the monk something, listened to his long tirade and mistranslated the reply: "You have no guarantee. There is only a chance, and you can turn it to your advantage. Sooner or later, Nok's spirit will make itself known. It will be next to you, everything will converge, and then – if your karma is ready – you will find freedom together, simultaneously, with your thoughts directed toward each other. Alas, it's impossible to demand more, but this is still a lot – at least, much depends on you yourself in this case!"

"Probably…" Ivan muttered and felt that yes, he could not demand any more. Neither from the monk with his snakelike demeanor nor from others – anything extra would be too good to be true.

"It's important to remember what the Buddha said – 'by oneself, one is purified,'" said the monk, summing up and indicating that the meeting had come to an end.

"It's important to remember that generosity knows no limits," Dara "translated."

"Our spirit will still remain and seek out through the need of attachment," the monk quoted, getting up from the ground.

At that Dara muttered, "That's strange…" On the street outside the temple gate she touched Brevich by the sleeve.

"Do you know what he said at our parting?" she asked with a short laugh. "This is a Thai saying, and it means something like 'Hold on to your star; it will show you the way.' But my name translates as 'star' in English. Maybe it was not by chance that we met?"

Brevich smiled with her. Then she said, "Are you satisfied with my work? Do you think you may still need my help? Bear in mind: in this country, as soon as anyone finds out you have money, they will try to cheat you in every way."

Brevich frowned, thought for a moment and asked, "Would you like to work with me for a week or two, maybe three? I'll pay you well."

"What can I say?" Dara sighed. "I've already started; how could I now leave you halfway through? It wouldn't be right – and I need to care about my karma too…"

In the taxi, she asked Brevich, "Where to? The hotel?"

"Yes, to the hotel, to the bar," Ivan answered. He urgently needed a drink; the conversation in the temple had drained him of his strength. But he couldn't complain, of course – so much had been revealed to him at last! His head still rang a little, but the feverish agitation was almost gone.

In the bar, Ivan, despite his drinking habits and resistance to alcohol, quickly got drunk. Then he continued to drink in his penthouse, which he retired to together with Dara, taking a bottle of gin along with him. Finding herself with a drunk *farang* in a hotel room, Dara felt entirely in her element. It was so easy to anticipate his desires, to make him happy…

They spent the whole afternoon together. Dara ordered food; she almost spoon-fed Brevich and topped up his drinks, ensuring he did not sober up. Ivan relaxed completely; his mind, weary of fighting insanity, gave insanity the upper hand. It was granted the freedom to do whatever it wanted – however, Brevich himself did not want much; he just needed rest.

He mumbled something with a meaningless smile on his face, "The jagged edge of an eggshell in a nest… A diamond cutting glass-aluminum… In the crack of a gate, a ragged goldfinch…" It was so pleasant – to enjoy the absurdity to the full. Dara nodded to him, stroked his arm. She did not understand the phrases he was mumbling, but she sensed: no words could become an obstacle for her anymore.

Later in the evening, she dragged him to the bathroom and washed him with soapy water, whipping up the foam. Then she began to give him a massage in the bedroom – during it she casually undressed herself, but they didn't get any further than that; Ivan simply fell asleep. "Well, okay," Dara said out loud. She poured herself a gin, put on a lavish bathrobe and went to the window.

Bangkok beamed, played, sparkled with light. It emanated waves of seduction, the itch of desire, the energy of action. Dara flung open her robe, revealing herself to the city, and bit her lip – her own desire was becoming acute. A lot of money loomed up ahead, and this, coupled with the iridescent lights prostrated before her, excited her in earnest.

She ran her hand between her legs and turned toward Brevich. He lay on his back, completely naked, snoring softly.

"Shall we have a bit of fun..." Dara murmured, throwing off her robe and stepping toward Ivan. He did not look like he was going to wake up. She took his hand, stroked herself with it, then climbed onto the bed and crouched over his face, sensing the moisture draining out of her. Brevich was still snoring; carefully Dara lowered herself onto him and buried her slippery crotch onto his face. He breathed heavily, smacking his lips. "O-oh..." she moaned, approaching her climax. And then again, "Oh, oh, oh-oh..."

Her desire was unbearable; Dara almost lost control of herself. She crawled all over Ivan, screaming and moaning, pinching his nipples. When she was coming, he groaned too – succumbing to her emotions, she had pinched him too hard, digging in with her sharp nails. But Dara couldn't think of this; her convulsions shook her. Only after taking a short breath did she notice that one of Brevich's nipples was almost bleeding – and that his manhood was irrepressibly rearing skyward.

"Wow," she whispered; then, with skillful hands, she brought Ivan to orgasm. He still didn't wake up, just turned over onto his side and stopped snoring, now breathing silently, peacefully, like a big child. Dara covered him with a sheet and sat next to him for a while, looking at his powerful shoulders. Then she wrote him a note with a promise to call the next morning, got dressed and went back to her apartment.

CHAPTER 29

THE NEXT DAY, Dara invited Brevich to lunch. She arrived in a simple pants suit, not even a hint of frivolity. Right away, she announced she wasn't hungry, ordering just a coffee and some sponge cake. And she proceeded to break off small pieces from it, affectedly sticking her pinky out – in the same way she had seen English ladies do when she was living in London.

Brevich, for his part, ate with a hearty appetite, despite his hangover. He felt full of strength and looked purposeful, ready for action. The notion of Nok's restless spirit was fixed in his head firmly. He had been thinking about it all morning, becoming more and more convinced that the monk was right, that a solution had been found and the plan was almost clear.

Only the technical details remained, and it was precisely about these that Dara was speaking, with Ivan listening in silence. She described the needy and the poor, about those in difficulty whose wretched lives could be eased by Brevich's money. The farmers' families living in poverty whose land had been taken away. The girls who were sold to go-go bars. The homeless children of both sexes who swarmed the streets of Bangkok – those whom the mafia networks would inevitably force into street begging or petty thievery and the sweeter-looking ones into sleeping with rich perverts...

Hearing about the children, Brevich felt a lump rise in his throat. He remembered his and Nok's child, destined never to be born, his heir and successor. No grief or poverty were awaiting him; on the contrary, only the happiest of destinies, but this had not made any difference...

The muscles in Ivan's face froze; his fists clenched tight. Dara noticed something was up but, not knowing how to react, continued to speak. After a minute, Brevich managed to control himself, cleared his throat and stopped her with an impatient gesture. "I have decided," he said. "It will be children."

"Very good," Dara nodded. "I'll get in touch with someone today. But I have to have an idea about the amount – at least an approximate one."

"Let it be ten million," Ivan shrugged. "Well, give or take... It just needs to be divided into portions. So that it becomes like a habit."

"Ten million Thai baht?" Dara clarified. It was a lot of money: the price of a very nice house.

"US dollars," Brevich grunted and went back to his tom-yam soup, which was causing beads of sweat to form on his forehead. After eating two more spoonfuls, he continued, "Well, if everything goes right, you can double it – why not. If it really becomes a habit..."

"Oh, okay," Dara nodded. "I see."

She was almost speechless, lost for words. "I can start searching and negotiating right away," she barely managed to say.

"Well, yes," said Brevich. "Right now. Why wait."

Dara quickly wound up the conversation and left. In the taxi she was dizzy, so she asked the driver to crank up the air-conditioner, pinched herself and rubbed her cheeks. Then, in her small apartment, she immediately climbed into the shower – this always helped her to gather her spirits. So it turned out this time – wiping herself down with a towel, Dara felt able to reason sensibly again. At least two things were clear to her. First, despite the fantastic sum he'd mentioned, Brevich was not lying; he really did have this money. And second, her Khmer tattoo was not the main reason for the lucky breaks of her past, and now it was not being of any help. Because good fortune of this magnitude could only have been granted by the goddess Nang Kwak.

She sat with her legs up in a comfy chair and began to figure out her next steps. Soon a third thing became clear: she would not be able to deal with this alone; she needed a partner.

Of course, this greatly complicated everything. Dara knew it was always better not to involve anyone in your business – "partners" would most likely let you down or deceive you. You could only trust in yourself – but here this just wouldn't work. The quantity Brevich had talked about went far beyond her usual purview. She had no idea how people who deal with such sums behave, how to move in their circles, what to say. This was unfamiliar territory to her, and thus, Dara concluded, she would make fatal mistakes. Because – she knew this for certain – very quickly someone would appear who would force her into making mistakes to catch her out with them. Big money attracts mean predators; she would not be able to cope with them on her own.

Fortunately, she had the right man in mind. Dara thought a little longer, then picked up her phone and dialed a number. "Hello, horny daddy," she said briskly, "it's me. Something new has cropped up; we need to meet – urgently! What are you doing after five?…"

Then, putting the cell down, she sat back in her chair and finally allowed herself to relax. She had done everything right and most probably had managed to take another step toward a new happy life. Toward some tempting future… Dara imagined Brevich, his heavy figure and sullen face. He was a strong man, but still, he had no chance against her cunning. Because behind it lay the treacherousness of Siam in all its entirety… She thought back to her childhood, to the slums of Buriram. Then to her youth spent in Bangkok bars, among *farang* clients. She remembered her past and whispered out loud, "So proud to be Thai!"

The man Dara was counting on was called Jeff. Once a successful Boston lawyer, he'd been caught fabricating legal documents, lost his license, abandoned his family and relocated to Thailand. He'd met Dara soon after her return from London – just like Brevich, he had contacted her for help with translation. Then he'd needed her assistance again; they became friends, occasionally slept together and soon saw through their first joint deal sending Thai-made fakes to Europe. Dara was great at smoothing things out with customs; Jeff was impressed by her composure and ability to hold her nerve. Then they worked together some more and got used to each other. Jeff saw big potential in Dara, and she, in turn, appreciated him as her "entry ticket" into the Western world – where serious money sloshed around and wealthy men were to be found.

Mainly, Jeff worked with investors who flew to Asia for an easy, not always legitimate, profit. He was also not averse to petty fraud, thanks to which he had made some acquaintances among the Thai police. During his five years in Bangkok, he had not yet lost his American polish – he knew how to wear good suits and, if necessary, look like "a million dollars." Dara couldn't have found a better partner for any kind of a serious put-up job.

They met at Jeff's house, drank a little, had a laugh and a joke. Then he tried to drag her to bed, but Dara shooed him off. "Wait," she whispered, "I've come here on an important matter – you have no idea how important. Yesterday I met a Russian psycho…"

She told Jeff the whole story. He did not believe her at first, but, after some thorough questioning, he was convinced she wasn't making things up, trying to pull a fast one. That evening, they worked out a plan of action involving a scam that would see Brevich's money ending up in a Hong Kong bank. And they agreed to open a joint account for this purpose the very next day through a banker Jeff used to work with.

Dara had clear doubts when it came to the bank account in faraway Hong Kong, where she didn't know anybody. She demanded assurances that Jeff would not cheat her and pocket all the profits. He had to promise that the money could only be withdrawn from the account by the two of them, using an order with both of their signatures.

"Well, that's fine," said Dara. "Just remember, darling, if you blow me out, I'll find a way to get even. As jealous Thai wives say, 'I'll give your dick to the ducks.'"

"What are you saying, honey? Why would I do that?" Jeff grinned, walking up behind her and running his hand under her T-shirt. "You and I have a long, bright future!" At the same moment, he was thinking it wouldn't be difficult to copy Dara's signature onto a fax.

"Only, there's one thing I'm worried about," he added, turning her to face him. "Are you sure this Russian has fallen for your bull completely? What if he suddenly suspects something and wriggles off the hook, having screwed you up every possible way first?"

"This is strange," Dara thought. "Jeff is a serious man, of course, and we've done some real business together, but he still doesn't understand the most obvious things…"

She, however, did not betray her surprise. She just shrugged and explained patiently what any bar girl knew by heart. "First," she said, "*farangs* are stupid when it comes to money. Second, they are even more stupid when it comes to women. And third, he cannot get away, because…" And she declared with pleasure the favorite mantra of every night fairy from Sukhumvit to Patpong, from Pattaya to Phuket: "Because Thai pussy is number one!"

Two days later their scheme was ready. They had a meeting with Brevich, where Jeff showed his best side. He looked like a solid official, not some second-rate swindler. He introduced himself as the head of an international program, presented a business card for one of his charitable foundations and immediately offered to show the foundation's website, which he had just created that day. The site looked no less impressive than Jeff himself. It was full of striking photos – using them as a backdrop, Dara told several stories about the starving children of Isaan, about them being sold to strangers in the capital by their parents and the efforts of the foundation to help them survive…

It all sounded and looked authentic. Consumed with anticipation, Brevich wanted to and did believe everything. He could not wait to make a start – Nok's spirit seemed to be sending him silent signals: come quicker, quicker.

"What do you think," he asked, "how frequently should I actually send the money? So that it'd be best for my karma."

"Do it every morning before breakfast," Dara suggested. "What could be more natural than a morning habit?"

Ivan felt that he, as always, had no objections to anything she said. The rightness of the simplicity gave her words an extraordinary persuasiveness.

The next morning, he made the first transfer. Then, after breakfast, Dara took him out of town. On the way, they drove into the market and bought two dozen live fish, which were placed in plastic bags of water.

"This is a good Buddhist gesture – it's as if we are giving them a new life," said Dara. They stopped at a pond in a small grove, went down to the water and began to set the fish free. Ivan watched in fascination as they beat their tails, then came back and ate the bread thrown by Dara. He smeared his face with the water they sprayed up and was as happy as a child – and she, looking at him, was happy too; they were almost sincerely full of joy and carefree. Then it was lunchtime, and a message came from Jeff to Dara in the restaurant that the "donation" had hit the account.

She told Ivan, "Your money has been received. I am so proud of you – you are doing such a good thing!"

Brevich, suddenly and acutely, felt relieved. As if the money he had given were like a burden lifted from his shoulders, at least some part of it. He relaxed, lounging complacently on his chair with a glass of beer, then suddenly started and muttered, "You know, I want to send some more tonight. Do you think it might be too much?"

"No," she replied, "this is your first time. It's very logical you're impatient the first time. This is how all good habits begin."

Returning to the hotel, Ivan turned on his laptop and made another transfer. Then Dara gave him a massage, but nothing followed it; she did not even bother to undress. When she was getting ready to go home, a downpour started. "Why do you need to go? Stay in the second bedroom," Brevich suggested. Dara agreed. Later that night, when she was already under the covers, her phone made a barely audible ping. Jeff had sent another message, confirming receipt of the second transfer. Dara, lying in her comfortable bed, lazily toyed with her clitoris and thought that perhaps she had never had such a perfect day.

Chapter 30

THE NEXT MORNING, Brevich woke up in bad spirits. All night something seemed to be looming – behind the curtains or next to the writing desk or in the corner near the closet. A couple of times he jumped up and shone his smartphone's flashlight, trying to spot his enemy. But the room was empty – or the enemy was hiding, not giving himself away...

Already fully awake, but without opening his eyes, Ivan tried to recall the fish released to freedom yesterday and his carefree joy, but for some reason, only the monk, resembling a snake, arose in his mind. The monk – and the interweaving of the shadows on the grass, which trembled with a quick shiver, causing Ivan's head to spin and nausea to rise. Making an effort, Brevich got up, went into the living room and made a transfer. This – a meaningful, practical action – brought relief but only briefly. Something was wrong with his mind, with his inner world; he could no longer remain unaware of it. His brain seemed to be covered with a foggy shroud, under which there was a seething, feverish bustle, invisible from the outside. Ivan growled, cursed through his teeth, but then the door of the second bedroom opened, and Dara came out. This calmed him somewhat – and at breakfast he behaved almost normally, even trying to make jokes.

Later, during the day, he began to feel uneasy again. Only Dara's presence seemed to help – realizing this, Ivan, looking askance and wrinkling his brow painfully, suggested that she move in with him for a while. Dara agreed – it couldn't have suited her better. They went to collect her things together – Brevich, gloomy, frowning, sat in the kitchen and waited for her to pack. Then they went to dinner, but he ate almost nothing and sat in silence, smiling strangely at times and turning gloomy again. Dara made a lot of effort – both in the restaurant and then in the hotel room – to distract him from his oppressive thoughts, to maintain his equilibrium and put him to bed. Finally, he fell asleep; then she climbed onto the sofa in the living room and thought hard – the situation was clearly worsening.

She understood this was the reverse side of the coin, the consequence of Ivan's abnormality, without which her and Jeff's scam would never have worked. But something had to be done with this flip side: Brevich's unpredictability could ruin everything. She needed to keep her finger on the pulse, but how was she to control this madness – even with her ability to adapt to men? What's more, Ivan was refusing to have sex – and this was another worry. For Dara, control over a man was largely linked with managing his erection…

At night, as she lay in bed, her mind continued to be preoccupied, and she couldn't even get to sleep – for her, it was something unheard of. She was becoming increasingly anxious: Ivan's unhealthy mind might destroy their plans at any moment. What if he were to lash out and really "wriggle off the hook," as Jeff had said? Today he had gotten what he wanted – her moving in – but tomorrow something might be needed again, something new. How could she surprise him?… The situation was as shaky as a rickety boat, and Dara didn't know which lever to pull to stabilize it. At the same time, she felt: the solution lay somewhere nearby. The right word was nagging her subconscious, unable to rise to the surface. Dara was angry with herself; she was pursing her lips and, as usual, pinched her forearm – and with another pinch the solution finally emerged. The word came; it had actually been in plain view; it was inseparable – from Brevich, from his gloomy gaze and his wounded nipple of a few nights ago…

In the morning, Dara went out to acquire the accessories she needed. There were a lot: clamps, wax candles, a seven-row needle wheel with a comfortable grooved handle and several pieces of clothing. The saleswoman offered her a set of dildos as well with a playful wink. Dara thought for a moment and shook her head.

In the taxi on the way to the hotel, she contemplated the upcoming scenario. It aroused her – Dara could hardly wait for the evening to arrive. After dinner, she retired to her bedroom but soon came out dressed in a bathrobe. She approached Ivan and innocently suggested, "Massage?"

Brevich was wandering around the room with a glass of gin in his hand, not knowing where to put himself. "Massage? Yes, a massage…" he murmured in response. Obviously, his head was occupied with other matters. They stood at the window for a while; then he went to his room, undressed and lay on his bed, face down.

Dara threw off her robe; under it was a short, semitranslucent nurse's uniform. Then she pulled on a black mask covering half her face – for some reason this gave her more confidence. After massaging Ivan for a quarter of an hour, she said, "You are too tense. I know a way to relax you – roll over, and let's cover your eyes from the light…"

Brevich looked at her outfit in surprise but said nothing. She put a blindfold on him, then lit a candle, stroked his arm and said, "Trust me." Ivan silently nodded. "And don't be afraid," Dara added, tilting the candle and dripping melted wax onto his stomach.

He stiffened convulsively but almost immediately relaxed, making a strange sound. Dara said, "Welcome to my world," imitating someone she'd once heard, although she couldn't recall who. Brevich breathed deeply, clutching the sheet with his fingers. She repeated, "Welcome," took two clamps and fixed them onto his nipples, carefully watching his reaction. Ivan did not resist, but his face was changing. From grimace to grimace, hinting at – suffering, comprehending, then acceptance…

She began to drip wax closer to his groin and noted a powerful erection. Then he started to twist, smacking his lips and turning his head as if he were looking for something. Dara realized he wanted her flesh. She climbed onto the bed on top of him, sank down on his face, wriggling domineeringly, as if forcing him to give her pleasure, and then busied herself with his cock. For almost half an hour she would not permit him to climax; she used three more clips and ran the sharp-toothed wheel along his thighs… Then she finally allowed him to spurt forth.

Brevich twitched spasmodically for a long time, and afterward, when it was all over, he burst into tears. He began to mumble incomprehensibly, mixing English with Russian words. Dara understood almost nothing, merely catching that he was complaining to her about something unbearable, something that was stronger than him. And this really was so – Ivan, for almost the first time in his life, was unafraid to appear weak, to elicit somebody's pity. Dara stroked his head, knowing that another important step had been made – she had managed to gain control.

Then Brevich quieted down; for some time they lay silently side by side. Soon, he fell asleep. Dara covered him with a sheet and went to her room.

From that moment, their "therapy" sessions were repeated every evening. They were a real discovery for Ivan – and, in a sense, a salvation. The physical pain pushed aside all other torments, forcing the brain to shift its accents, its "operational centers." It, the pain, became the center itself – like the common denominator under the fraction bar. Like an invisible substance, it penetrated the space, creating bridges between the mind and the body, between the tangible and the ephemeral, otherworldly. It caused sparks to scatter from his eyes – the light of unseen stars. The light of new suns, summoning to themselves.

Before the sessions, he and Dara would usually sit in the rooftop bar. They said little – just sipped their drinks and looked out at the night city. As always, by the evening, Ivan was beginning to get disturbed, winding himself up, his mind obscured by a viscous fog. But this could now be tolerated; he had a reliable healer nearby. Brevich knew that soon they would go to the bedroom and he'd surrender to Dara's initiative, concentrating on physical sensations. Pain, like a drug, like a merciful opioid, would relieve anxiety, the unbearable frenetic agitation of his brain. Its impulses would temporarily restore the semblance of order in the unsteady system, returning it from the tip of the needle back down to the valley, dampening the surplus of energy. In the same way that Goldstone bosons maintain orderliness, preserve asymmetry, Ivan might have said if he had known such words…

The sexual pleasure he experienced also came as a surprise. His body reacted to the test of pain with amazing enthusiasm, each time rewarding him with the most powerful orgasm. It suggested something masochistic, but Brevich was not ashamed of himself. Everything seemed natural – a manifestation of yet another of the features of his brutal nature. Indeed, his whole life as a major businessman full of challenges and constant pressure had been like a training exercise for this change of roles. Satisfaction from the work-related struggle had, in some way, resembled pleasure from pain. His many years in business had crystallized an invariant, manifesting itself now under the clamps and the hot wax…

After the sessions, Ivan, usually a man of few words, would become voluble, talking about himself freely, without any embarrassment. Such was the degree of his trust in Dara after he had transferred his tenderest spots into her power. However, this did not continue for long – quite soon Brevich would be overcome by drowsiness. His speech would become incoherent and turn into a satisfied snuffling. Then Dara would silently slip out of the bed and walk back to her bedroom.

She would have her own nightly ritual there, the most pleasant of all possible. Climbing under the covers with her new smartphone, she'd repeatedly count her share of the money she and Jeff had "earned" up to that moment. Every morning she would learn from Brevich about the latest transaction, and by the end of the day, she would receive confirmation that the funds had been credited to the account. She would carefully record everything and draw up the current balance before going to sleep. This calculation flowed smoothly into her dreams – about how she would manage her wealth once the whole action plan had finally been completed.

She tried not to think about the specifics of "the completion." It was clear Brevich would have to disappear from their lives – when this thought could not be driven off, Dara convinced herself that "disappearing" might have different meanings. For example, he could just leave Thailand forever – although, of course, in the depths of her soul she knew that half measures would not be enough. At best, they'd be able to persuade Brevich to vanish of his own free will, in pursuit of the liberated spirit of his beloved Nok…

However, she said to herself angrily, let Jeff deal with that problem. He was a *farang* and didn't believe in the Buddha – so let him spoil his karma. And as far as Dara's own was concerned, ever since her go-go past, she had always had plenty of solid arguments in reserve to salve her conscience. First, she was helping her family – this was her duty, the most important karmic factor. Second, Brevich was a foreigner, not a Thai; deceiving a foreigner was not such a big sin, maybe not a sin at all. It was merely the restoration of justice – why did they, the Westerners, have all the money and get to drive good cars and travel the world? Why did they get to buy what they wanted while she, Dara, had to climb mountains just to make ends meet? After all, she was Thai, a daughter of Siam – that meant she was objectively better than any *farang* and deserved her share of happiness...

The arguments were impregnable, flawless. Besides, Dara convinced herself, when she had the money, she would take care of her karma in the best way possible, much more efficiently than now. For example, every day she would give out some money to the beggars near the temples. This would become her habit – she remembered well the monk's words about the strength of "habitual" karma. For example, Dara estimated, she might donate a hundred baht every day. After all, she would have millions – no, tens of millions... It looked like a great deal. This was how you should spend your money on karma, not like this crazy Brevich. But then, of course, what could you expect from him – he wasn't a Thai!

However, Dara had to admit: she had an involuntary respect for Ivan. She even felt a certain affinity with him – they were doing an important thing together! She also gave Brevich credit for the sincerity with which he had immersed himself in the local milieu, for the way he perceived Buddhism – not in the form of notional entities but in a practical sense in order to resolve his problems. This coincided with how she regarded religion herself – in a utilitarian and pragmatic manner, as something capable of providing support on difficult days.

Yes, Dara told herself, this Russian was perhaps the best of all the *farangs* she knew. He was even better than Jeff, who had previously been the hands-down winner. Jeff was smart and crafty, yes, but Brevich belonged to a completely different league. He was fabulously rich and was making Dara rich as well. And, even though he had fallen for their bait and had let himself be deceived, he was still stronger than everyone. Dara knew, in some higher sense, he would settle his score with everything – with fate, with his enemies, maybe even with Thailand and Jeff... She only hoped it wouldn't occur to him to get even with her. By whatever means possible, she would have to get out of his way, as she would a speeding train, when he eventually lost it for good.

CHAPTER 31

MEANWHILE, IN MOSCOW, the investigation into Nok's murder had taken a step forward. Having drawn a blank with regards to Danilov's death and Sakhnov's disappearance, the detectives continued to search for clues, and at one of their meetings it was decided to look more closely at Brevich's ex-wife, Inna Vitzon. The wily operative who had conducted her initial, fruitless questioning doggedly pestered the prosecutor's office and gained access to the records of Inna's telephone conversations. Soon, an interesting picture of her calls to one of Danilov's numbers emerged, which had suddenly stopped shortly before the abduction attempt. Thus, Inna was summoned by the police and interrogated very thoroughly.

It lasted almost six hours. Inna cried, fainted and lost control several times but still intuitively chose the right tactics. In tears, she admitted that yes, they had been lovers, and she had known that Sanyok was plotting something to take revenge on Brevich, but it hadn't occurred to her that it might be for real – he was such a milksop! She'd left him because of this; she was sick of his moaning – and the fact it had happened two weeks before the tragedy was a coincidence, nothing more...

She was released on condition she stayed in the city, but information about the new development reached Colonel Sibiryakov. He decided to share it with Brevich and called Bangkok deep into the night. Half asleep, it took Ivan a long time to work out who was speaking and what he wanted. Finally, he understood, listened, paused and said, "Thank you. I'll think about it tomorrow."

"Yes, think about it," Sibiryakov's voice rumbled down the receiver. "Your ex is clearly as guilty as sin, even though there's no hard data against her. For the cops, she's not much of a prospect at the moment, but if they get paid, they can give her a serious working over as an accomplice of some sort. I doubt they'll be able to cook up a charge, but she'll remember it for the rest of her life for sure. That will be a payback of some kind, you see?"

"I see," Brevich grunted and hung up. He let loose a string of curses, hurled his cell phone to the far corner, lay on his back, spread his arms and remained like that without sleeping for most of the night.

It was immediately clear to him that Inna had been a part of the plot; he was only surprised he hadn't realized it right away. It could not have been otherwise – now, looking from a distance, he saw how much poison, bile and pent-up grievance at life had filled her soul. It was all bound to come out some time, and when it did it had emerged in full measure... Brevich ground his teeth and clenched his fists. An impulse raged in him – to avenge himself on Inna, to ruin her life. To set the detectives on her – let them put her through the grill, mangle and crush her personality!

And then doubts began to arise – what if this were to harm his karma, which he had already worked so hard on? What if Inna were innocent – or, maybe, only a little bit guilty? What if revenge were to cancel out in one stroke all his help for the Thai children and his confidence that he was on the way, on the right path to a new life? The future was calling; it meant so much more than a futile face-off with a worthless past!

Then he thought about Inna herself, about the miserable years they had spent together. His memory presented a half-eroded image that contained little – mostly her petty snobbery and a tendency toward hysterics as a manifestation of her "delicate feminine nature." He recalled her tedious philosophy of life full of clichés parroted from the internet and her large, sluggish vagina resembling a dead mollusk... Looking at his past from here, from Bangkok, he saw clearly: she had been terribly unlucky. Unlucky with her place of birth, her upbringing and personality. With her environment, her genetics, her overall mind-set... She's already been punished by fate – maybe this was the whole point? Maybe it was only worth feeling sorry for her, no more?

With that, Ivan finally fell asleep, but in the morning he woke up in an agony of confusion. Inna's name had raked up his memory; demons, startled by the nighttime phone call, pushed his madness closer to the edge. He sat on the bed, clutching his face in his hands, and screamed in a beseeching voice, "Dara!" And again, "Dara, come here!"

Dara was in the living room; hearing the scream, she immediately ran to him. Ivan, not rising, drew her to himself, clasping her hips and pressing his head against her tummy. She froze, not knowing what to do. Brevich inhaled the smell of her body and said hoarsely, "Let's go and see the monk. I don't understand – how much longer do I have to wait?"

"Of course. We'll go," Dara said softly. "I'll arrange it, but let's have breakfast first…"

It was obvious: the situation had worsened again; it needed to be straightened somehow. Not really understanding how, Dara tried to win more time. She called the temple and made an appointment with the monk for two days later.

"He's gone up into the mountains," she explained to Ivan. "He's meditating alone; he needs it. Probably wants to get closer to Nirvana."

"Nirvana, fuck!" Brevich frowned. "Well, okay…" He made a circle around the room and lay down on his bed.

"If you don't need me, can I go out for a little while?" Dara asked. She wanted to discuss everything with Jeff.

"No, you can't," said Brevich. "Stay here; without you I feel terrible. If you need something, call the concierge; they'll buy it and bring it up."

"Well, as you say," Dara reassured him. She was increasingly alarmed at the way he was looking. "Maybe you'd like a massage? Or shall we play some games?"

"Not now," he grunted without glancing at her.

Dara cooed something soothing, climbed into a chair with her legs up and wrote to Jeff: "He's freaking out. Just a bit more and he'll lose it completely."

"Arrange things so that he transfers the remaining amount in one go," he answered.

"How the fuck am I supposed to do that, genius?" Dara snapped. Then, having calmed down a little, she added, "The day after tomorrow we're going to the temple. I'll try to think of something. In the meantime, we need to cheer him up."

"Show him our website this evening," Jeff responded. "And don't worry, I believe in you. Thai pussy is number one!"

After dinner, Dara took Brevich out to the hotel bar and showed him the updated "charity fund" website. Jeff had made some effort: the news section was full of notes of gratitude to an anonymous donor. On another page, an entry showed what the fund was planning to do with the money – who was supposed to receive it, and how it was going to help. There were also photographs – of appalling slums, garbage dumps and the unfortunate children, whose fate was about to change with Brevich's assistance.

For a while, Ivan looked at the pictures and read the messages. Then he suddenly turned to Dara, his eyes glowing. "I sense," he said, "I am ready. My 'weighty' karma is ready. I want to free myself – there is no point waiting. We must find her spirit!"

Dara realized that the conclusion, whatever it was, was inevitably approaching. "I agree with you," she nodded. "We'll put some pressure on the monk – he's the only one who can help. I think after the mountains, his head should be somewhat clearer... And by the way, since you're getting closer to liberation, why don't you give your karma a decisive push? A few days ago, I got a call from the charity – they're planning to build a shelter. Imagine: you'll be providing street children with a real home. This would be no worse than a magic white elephant!"

Ivan stared at her hard; she had to strain with all her might not to look away. "Well, I will," he said slowly. "I'll do it when her spirit is with me. Just before I'm liberated – I must be sure. I must feel it – and I will feel it; you'll see."

It was evident he couldn't be pressured any further. "Yes, of course," Dara said and took his hand. "You're right – don't worry; your intuition won't deceive you."

That very evening, she noticed that Brevich's reaction to the pain had changed. There was no erection; he simply endured it – undistracted from his thoughts. The pain no longer calmed him; its quanta could not restrain the chaotic buildup. His mind was thrashing about, denying order, and no boson particles could return it to tranquility.

Ivan spent almost all the time before the meeting with the monk on his bed, sipping gin. Any action seemed incongruous to him; it would only have weakened his focus. Dara was with him – she sat nearby, doing crosswords in a Thai magazine.

On the way to the temple, Brevich suddenly cheered up. "Now!" he said to Dara. "Now it will be decided, one way or another." She nodded in agreement, still not knowing what to do if the meeting came to nothing.

The conversation with the monk did not last long. Casting a brief glance at Brevich, he said right away, "Explain to him: to kill yourself is a trap, a dead end."

"He isn't asking about that," Dara tried to protest. "He just can't wait any longer for her spirit to show up. He has come to ask for advice…"

"Whatever he's come for," the monk interrupted her, "I can see what's going on in his head. Killing himself will mean no reunion. And what's more, if he takes someone else's life with him, his karma will be ruined forever."

Dara began to translate, the monk not taking his eyes off her. For some reason, she didn't dare misinterpret his words. "He stresses," she said, "that your liberation should come of its own accord. He insists that I make this clear: the Buddha does not accept suicide!"

Ivan waved her away, "I know, I know. Nothing like that will happen; we'll simply fly away like birds… Tell him we haven't come to discuss this. Tell him that the children have been saved, a lot of them, and that soon I'll build them a house. That I won't be taking revenge for the past – tell him that I am ready, *ready*! All that remains is to get to know – where, when, how? Where to find her, and how to give her a signal?"

"What-what?" Dara asked. Brevich's speech was slurred. The veins on his temples stood out; he was frowning and looking unhappy.

Ivan repeated himself, and she obediently translated. "You can only meditate and pray," the monk shrugged. He obviously had nothing more to say. Dara understood: the entire plot was hanging by a thread.

"Your thought determines… Your intention determines… The energy of the will…" the monk muttered and got up. Brevich turned away and stared into the distance. His nerves were stretched taut like a string.

Muffled peals of thunder could be heard; a thunderstorm was gathering. The monk looked anxiously at the sky, and then it suddenly dawned on Dara. "He means," she translated to Brevich, "that the energy of your will is accumulating like a thundercloud. It will strike like lightning – this will be the sign. It will flash – and you will see everything in its light."

Brevich's eyes bored into her. "Lightning?" he asked and repeated the word, chewing his lips, as if tasting it. Then he shouted, "Yes! Lightning – it makes sense!" He jumped to his feet and hastened Dara along, "Let's go home!"

The taxi crawled for ages through the city's traffic. Brevich was silent, thinking intensely about something. Dara did not dare interrupt him, but when they entered their room, she nevertheless said, "You probably need to collect your emotions, gather them together – to attract the lightning strike. There should be a match – between what you are experiencing now and something she has been feeling at some point in the past. Try to remember where the two of you had some important, highly charged moment together?"

She was acting on a whim, without any plan; she was just improvising, not knowing where it would lead. Someone seemed to be choosing the right words for her – perhaps the very same goddess of fortune.

Brevich pondered her question, thought for a few minutes and suddenly exclaimed, "Yes!" He walked around the room, gesticulating excitedly, then stopped, turned to Dara and said, "Get ready. Put on your most beautiful dress – we are going to have dinner in a plush place I know. On the roof of a skyscraper; you're gonna like it. Lightning is drawn to high places – mine will strike there!"

He laughed and ran around the room again. The look on his face was totally insane. He waved his arms, squinted his eyes and muttered utterly meaningless things. "I counted the hints on my fingers… they fly in a cart to the end of the world… your plate has been smashed into a multitude of pieces…"

Dara still had no idea how the situation would play out, but she saw that nothing depended on her anymore. There was no contradicting

Brevich; she could only obediently follow him. As if, indeed, the energy of his will and his desires had curved space, changing the reality around him – just as the Buddha taught.

The rumbling continued beyond the window; then the heavens opened up, and the downpour began. "Ha-ha," Brevich laughed angrily, running to the window, "the tricksters! They're prompting me, but I know it myself already!" And he asked, turning to Dara, "A massage?"

This session ended up being very intense. Brevich reacted acutely: his face twitched, he groaned through his teeth but did not resist, allowing Dara to do whatever she wanted. "Yes," she whispered, "I feel you are close to the limit; your receptors are more sensitive than ever. You're electrified – you're ready, yes, ready. Wow, what a hard-on you have!…"

After a furious orgasm, instead of becoming drowsy as usual, Ivan felt refreshed, full of power. He climbed into the shower and sang songs, screaming them out at the top of his voice. Dara didn't know what to think, what to expect; she only sensed that the outcome was very close. She grabbed her phone but shook her head and put it down. Then she picked it up again, started writing a message to Jeff, thought about it a little and deleted it. There was nothing he could do to help her.

In the restaurant, at Brevich's insistence, they were given the same table where he had once sat with Nok. The air had cleared after the storm; the heat had subsided. Ivan happily turned his face to the wind, rubbed his hands and kept looking around. Dara was on edge, not having the slightest idea how to behave.

Nevertheless, something needed to be done. Having ordered drinks, she took Brevich's hand in her own and muttered, "I can feel it: whirl-winds are emanating from you. I feel she is here; her spirit is almost within your touch. It's in our world and yet not in it; it's where it can and cannot be seen, heard and not heard…"

Ivan nodded, his fingers cold as ice. Minutes passed and nothing happened. Dara was in despair; she was running out of options. "Give me your palm, I'll have a look at it…" she began, but here Brevich squeezed her hand so hard it seemed her wrist might snap and exclaimed in a terrifying whisper, "There she is! Over there!"

Looking at his face, Dara understood that he wasn't joking. That, in some incomprehensible way, he really saw, heard and believed: the woman he needed was somewhere nearby. Dara followed his gaze. A girl stood by the rail, holding back her windswept hair with her hands. Her dress stuck to her body; it appeared she was ready to fly away on invisible wings. There was some kind of strangeness about her, some elusive flaw, a catch...

By an incredible coincidence, she was an almost exact copy of the image engraved on Ivan's memory – how Nok had stood on their last evening in Bangkok, here, in this same restaurant, next to the same rail. Only the bracelet on her thin arm was missing, but the bracelet wasn't important. The ghost, in search of a way out, might have neglected the bracelet, Brevich realized and again whispered, "It's her!" He whispered and then relaxed, suddenly becoming almost normal. Everything came together – fantasy and reality, the words of the monk and the gestures of fate. He had succeeded: the future was in his hands, and no one could stop him.

Dara didn't know what had come to her aid, but it was obvious: Brevich had no doubts. And once again, she mentally thanked the goddess Nang Kwak for her support. Meanwhile, the girl in the light dress had moved away from the rail and sat down at a table nearby, next to a European-looking man.

"Go and make their acquaintance," Brevich said quietly.

Dara nodded, got up and went to the ladies' room. On her way back, as she passed the girl, she asked her about something. They got into a conversation, and soon all four of them were sitting at the same table together. The couple introduced themselves. "I'm Tina," Tina smiled. "And I'm Theo," nodded Theo as he extended his hand.

CHAPTER 32

DARA DID NOT find it difficult to endear herself to the girl Brevich had identified. At first glance, it was clear she had Isaan roots and had most likely been born not far from Laos. This was half true but sufficient for Dara's purposes.

"Aren't you from Udon-Thani, sister?" she asked. This province was the main supplier of "employees" for Bangkok's go-go bars – Dara knew how the girls from there spoke and behaved. The conversation started naturally: two women from the same region meeting in a prestigious restaurant in the capital, both having apparently set themselves up well, both with *farang* men. This provided a lot of common ground for jokes, and Dara skillfully used it to amuse Tina. And then she exclaimed, "By the way, today is my birthday. Would you like to celebrate together? Ivan," she nodded at Brevich, "would also be happy if you'd join us, I'm sure!"

It seemed impolite to refuse. Tina and Theo looked at each other, shrugged and agreed.

"We also have a cause for celebration," Tina said proudly when everyone had introduced themselves. "Theo has just finished a great work. He is a scientist – he's studying what's going on in our brains."

"Another psycho," Dara thought. "How interesting!" she said aloud. "Maybe you can teach us how to read minds."

Theo frowned and waved his hand in the air. Dara immediately changed the subject, called the waiter, asked him for something and began to chat with Tina about Isaan in Thai.

Brevich, who had been sitting in silence up till now, grunted and stared at Theo. "Do you often come here?" he asked, trying to sound polite.

"No," Theo shook his head, "this is actually the first time, even though we live nearby."

"Okay," Ivan nodded, thinking: "It's all fitting together!" – and looked around with a benign smile. He was in a wonderful state of mind; inside him, for the first time in many days, peace and quiet reigned. The strangers, sitting opposite, personified his victory over the imperfection of the world, over its hostility, its cunning. All the chance coincidences of his recent past had congregated, converged into the desired vector. Into the pattern that satisfied his goals, consistent with his will.

The waiter brought snacks. Dara ceremoniously served Brevich, put a little bit on her own plate and, to maintain the conversation, asked Theo in a very courteous tone, "Well, how do you like Thailand?"

"It's ambiguous," Theo replied. Dara blinked in surprise. It was not the answer she was expecting.

"It has a vibrant palette, like an abstract painting. And what's contained in it can be interpreted in different ways," Theo tried to explain. "But, of course, I'm very grateful to Bangkok," he nodded at Tina with a smile.

Dara smiled back but flared up angrily inside. Like all her compatriots, she could not stand the slightest criticism of her country, the king and the Buddha.

"Many say Thailand is enchanting," she said thoughtfully. "Those who have been here always come back – its magic cannot be opposed."

"Magic… A little mystical mumbo-jumbo," Theo muttered with a grin. "I don't know; it's hard for me to judge. Although I have to confess, I can see: yes, it can draw people back again and again."

"Because we have real life here," said Dara, addressing Tina. "Don't you agree, sister? I lived in the West; it's cold and boring over there."

She disliked Theo, identifying him as an enemy – and it hadn't taken her long to get this feeling. The barely perceptible smile on his lips hinted at a superiority of some sort – and it was unclear to her what he felt superior to. Perhaps, to everything and everyone – and this annoyed Dara intensely, contradicting all her views on life. Theo was obviously not rich; he was dressed cheaply, but, at the same time, he considered himself entitled to look down from a height somehow... Or perhaps not? She couldn't figure it out, and this infuriated her even more.

"Thai smiles are often deceitful, yet true magic implies sincerity," said Theo, not addressing anyone specifically.

"*Ka*,"[24] Dara bowed her head in agreement. She understood suddenly: he was the type the bar fairies hated the most. Such men would never fall for a sob story or believe in love at first sight. They wouldn't lose their heads and later send money from abroad. And, after sex, they wouldn't even give a tip – or only a small one.

"However, Thais are very polite to each other," Theo continued. "And you have to respect that!"

"Ka-a," Dara purred and said to Tina, "You know, I spent a few years in England. They may have a lot of smart gadgets in their stores, but they still don't know how to live their lives – not even listening to those who do. They look at the world through their iPhone cameras and their large TV screens..." She turned back to Theo, "I also have a TV. I have an iPhone, too, and I love the camera. I take selfies and pictures of food wherever I go. But I know how to live – I see the path that the Buddha has laid out!"

"I don't have an iPhone," Tina smiled blithely. "I have a cheap Chinese phone, but I also know how to live – better than anyone, especially now."

"And me too. Especially now," Brevich muttered, half closing his eyes. Something indulgent and patronizing shone through his features; he looked like a man who really does know. Who knows everything that will be and understands there is nothing to argue about.

"Ha-ha-ha," Dara laughed. "Well done, sister. It's easy for us to live in peace because we carry the faith in us. And you," she turned again to Theo, "you deny any faith. For you, magic is tricks and mumbo-jumbo, but we can see it all around us everywhere!"

She was unable to control herself; Theo irritated her more and more. What he was saying seemed wrong, unacceptable. He was a foreigner; he

---

24   Yes (Thai).

must love Thailand, because, if you thought about it, her whole country was *number one*, and not just Thai pussy. A *farang* is obliged to spend his money here – Thailand has no other use for him. Then the *farang* is obliged to leave – his money will be put to use without his help. But while he is here, he should respect, appreciate and even marvel at his surroundings – despite no one in Siam respecting him for himself...

"Real magic is the B Object," Tina said, coming to Theo's aid. "And also the invisible arrow into the day after tomorrow."

"Real magic is mathematics," said Theo. "There is harmony and the greatest power in it, compared to which magic is mere child's play. But I agree – Asia is quite alluring."

"I have a magical tattoo," Dara squinted slyly. "It's a pity I cannot show it to you, ha-ha-ha..."

She suddenly felt calmer; the feeling of enmity had almost disappeared. "Mathematics... He really is a psycho," she thought. "He tries to be clever about everything. That means he'll screw up at a crucial moment."

"How do you like the food?" she asked everyone. "Personally, I'd prefer something a bit spicier."

They started talking about Thai food and then about Dara's birthday. Theo raised a toast; the atmosphere lifted. Dara began to talk about London, while Brevich surreptitiously glanced at Tina and thought – it was surprising Nok's spirit had chosen this young, strange girl who was so unlike her. Or maybe it wasn't surprising at all – Nok probably wanted renewal, rejuvenation. He himself, if he were in her place, would have preferred to move into not a world-weary middle-aged man just a little shy of fifty, but a young buck with burning eyes... Anyway, he didn't have the slightest doubt – it was Nok here, right next to him. Everything spoke of this: Tina's elusive aloofness, her slightly squinting gaze, even the bright-red streak in her hair. Yes, and her face – was is it really different? Thai faces, they may seem dissimilar and alike at the same time; you can never be sure...

After the appetizers, Dara led Tina to the ladies' room. Ivan refilled the glasses and proposed, "Let's drink?"

"Yes," Theo readily agreed.

"Actually, why don't we get drunk," suggested Ivan.

"Why not," Theo waved his hand. He felt pleasantly relaxed, like a man who has just completed a long and difficult feat – he deserved a rest. Maybe even an adventure, a slightly crazy one.

There was a freshness in the air, unusual for Bangkok; a light wind blew through the terrace. "It's good the thunderstorm broke this afternoon," said Theo. Brevich nodded with a grin, picked up his glass and took a long sip.

Then the women returned, briskly discussing something. "We have an idea," Dara announced. "Let's finish our food and get over to Jokey. It's a club next door," she explained to Brevich. "It's really cool and classy there."

"Let's dance!" Tina said in support and laughed. Theo noted he had never seen her like this.

They went to the club on foot. A narrow half road, half path looped through courtyards and buildings. Toxic scooters rushed along it, dogs scurried, food vendors pushed their carts. All four of them were having fun; the arguments were forgotten. Slipping and almost falling into a puddle, Theo turned to Dara and said in a slightly drunken voice, "I've just realized: in fact, I really love Thailand!"

"Liar!" she exclaimed with a laugh, slapping him on the shoulder. "A liar and a ladies' man!"

"Our home is over there," said Tina. "By the way, would you mind waiting for me? I'll literally be a minute. I just want to change my shoes."

They decided to wait in the air-conditioned hall. Brevich glanced around, then fixed his eyes on the doors of the elevator where Tina had just gone. He had no doubt: this was another sign Nok was giving him. She was revealing her location so that he wouldn't lose sight of her again… The evening might as well come to an end right now. All the details were clear; dancing in the club would add nothing. Nevertheless, Ivan hesitated; for some reason he did not want to part with these other two right away. Watching Nok in another person's body was somehow exciting, unusual, almost forbidden…

In the club, after a single glance at Brevich, they were offered the best table, with the most expensive champagne and scotch appearing on it. The girls went off to the dance floor, and Ivan and Theo lounged in their chairs, their glasses in hand.

"Give him a wave," Dara whispered to Tina, "so that he doesn't feel abandoned. Have you been with him long?"

"Two months," Tina replied honestly. "Although it seems like half a lifetime."

"Well, yes," Dara nodded. "That happens..."

Tina aroused more and more curiosity in her. Dara tried to understand why Brevich had so decisively isolated her from everybody else; why he, of his own free will, had been hooked by her, the simplest of lures – and could make no sense of it. She was also in the dark as to why Theo found her so attractive. For all his oddities, he still looked like a fairly presentable man – and in Bangkok, those were in great demand. Tina did not have any female tenacity, nor any special sexuality; in Dara's opinion, she was quite ordinary. Nevertheless, these two very eligible Europeans were fussing over her like she was a movie star!

They danced for a long time, and one way or another Dara tried to find a way to unravel Tina's mystery. She asked her about Theo, about the details of their lives. She inquired what her man liked to eat, whether he was stingy, if he had a big dick.

"I don't know," Tina answered, embarrassed, "I have nothing to compare it with."

"Oh, I see..." said Dara thoughtfully, and suddenly asked, "Do you love him?"

"Yes, probably," Tina shrugged. "And you? Do you love your *farang*?"

Dara hesitated and confessed, "Perhaps not. I am good to him, but I love myself and no one else." Then, succumbing to a sudden sympathetic impulse for a Thai sister, she added, "And you'd better do the same" – and she bit her tongue, remembering Brevich and his intentions that had so far remained unknown to her.

Meanwhile, Ivan and Theo were knocking back the scotch. Theo quickly got drunk and became talkative – he began to rant about Thailand and the West, about religions and myths, Christianity and the Buddha. Brevich nodded, almost without listening, thinking that, with or without gods, in rich countries or poor, this world was still ugly and maimed. Only sometimes, out of nowhere, a bright ray might appear, and everything would suddenly make sense – Nok had become just such a ray of light in his life. But then, if this ray were to die out, the repulsion against the world would become a hundredfold worse. And no one could help – neither a monk with the demeanor of a snake, nor the Buddha himself if he were to appear suddenly, nor a golden calf with a piggy bank full of diamonds. The diamonds just lit up the sky; among them – another sun. This was the only meaning that remained.

Two elderly American men walked past them, surrounded by several Thai girls. The latter affectionately chirped something, making eyes at their companions. "But these minxes," Brevich chuckled, "do they also follow the way of the Buddha?"

"I think," Theo replied, "they truly believe in him. The role of the gods is not to give us a way; the way is defined by only one thing – human nature, which cannot be changed by any 'supreme being.' The true significance of any god is only the abstract nature of its existence – a god is an idea so convincing that it captures human minds, pushes consciousness beyond the limits of the ordinary. We assign meaning to statues and figures, to sacred symbols and holy artifacts. Our minds and nothing else create the content associated with them – without the work of the mind, the gods as such would not exist at all. We invent deities and believe them to be omnipotent, but, in fact, we ourselves rule over the deities; the human mind is the highest thing there is."

"Yes," muttered Brevich with a grin, "my will is the most powerful thing there is. Today I had the ultimate proof of this."

He looked up at Theo, suddenly feeling a strange solidarity with him. The reason for this was the whiskey and – something else.

Theo continued, "By himself, the Buddha is essentially powerless. You can create any philosophy, however deep, a belief system around each individual god, but this will not be to his merit but yours. The belief system will reflect not the significance of the deity but only your own power of imagination. Standing before the Buddha, I know: he can only be what I dare to conceive, what I dare to have faith in. That is, depending on how big my balls are. On how big my dong is, as they say. Or not – ha-ha – not my dong, but my B Object!"

"What is the B Object?" Brevich asked suddenly in a completely sober voice. This was the second time he had heard the term, and for some reason, it piqued him.

"It's what remains after you have gone," said Theo. "It remains and, perhaps, lives forever. Maybe traveling to other stars."

"To another Sun?" Ivan narrowed his eyes. Theo's words alarmed him. They seemed to test the validity of what he had already understood and accepted. The coherent picture in his head, which did not need to be questioned.

"You could say that," Theo frowned, "but that's not the main point. It is better not to enter into this tangled maze."

"But then what is there – another life?" Brevich insisted.

Theo laughed drunkenly, "I don't like to fantasize on these topics. But now, because I'm not sober, I would reply: yes, you could say that too."

"My woman said the same thing," Ivan muttered.

Theo carried on without hearing him, "You could say that because no one knows for sure, including me. I can't reach there with my mathematics, and, overall, I have to confess, it's not easy for me to contemplate these matters. The thought of rebirth, of new lives, leads inevitably to the notion of the ultimate solitude."

"I've heard of that," Brevich grinned. "They say – it's frightening to get lost. Ha-ha... They said it to me but didn't have an idea who was capable of what... To get lost – fuck! They know nothing about me and my karma. I was a recruit of karma; I was taken into its service. I found my woman; she was with me, next to me. Now I am the champion of karma, and soon – soon I will become its knight! I will look into the distance from my horse. I will *see* into the distance from my horse. My winged horse will carry me forward..."

Something had changed in him; he suddenly began to look either drunk or not quite right in his mind. At the same time, his voice, facial expressions and gestures were filled with an animal power.

"A champion of karma – yes," said Theo. "That is exactly what the B Object is about..."

He felt uncomfortable, wanted to get away for a while or even leave completely. And Brevich continued in the same vein, "Your Object? Okay, say it exists. It exists and flies. It symbolizes flight, freedom… The ocean of tears tastes only of salt, but its dharma has the taste of freedom!"

"I get it," said Theo; then, making his apologies, he headed off to the bathroom. Ivan was lost in thought. He was not so much drunk as excited; clarity had returned to him. He had defeated this mathematician who had betrayed himself, showed his weakness, his fear of the upcoming – well, that served him right. A hopeless loner, that's what he is; no one ever will understand his ideas. Understanding is always based on faith, on the faith of society at large; that's where victory lies. Karma, ghosts, spirits – all this may sound pathetic, but the affirmations are all around. And the most important one was that he had again found Nok – and Brevich scanned the dance floor, looking out for Tina, as his indivisible property.

Returning to the table, Theo saw that Tina and Dara had come back to drink some champagne. With exaggerated courtesy, he set about looking after them, almost knocking the ice bucket over. "To you, our beautiful ladies!" he raised his glass of scotch, sensing he was swaying a bit. Tina gave him a worried look, but the music started again, and Dara whisked her away.

"To our beautiful ladies!" Theo repeated, raising his glass once more.

"Yes, to them," Brevich said quietly. He again became calm and complacent – it seemed nothing in the world could ruffle him.

"Speaking of the gods – you've probably heard this one: God is love," Theo turned toward him. "But love is much more than God! God is created by you yourself, but you can neither create nor destroy love. You can only betray it, become unworthy of it. This is your sole choice in regard to love: to betray it or not…" Theo leaned on the table, bent forward and confessed, "Here, with Tina, I realized: I know nothing about love. Including within the framework of my theory about B Objects!"

"That's true," Brevich said. "To betray, not to betray… My woman probably had the same thing in mind."

The music became louder; Ivan and Theo carried on talking but almost without hearing each other. Their words seemed disjointed, and Ivan's gaze was riveted on Tina and Dara dancing nearby. "I was a recruit of karma; I was taken into its service…" he repeated and looked – with an inexpressible tenderness that didn't correspond at all with his flabby face and rough, tough nature. "As if he was catching the tiniest bit of fluff in his fingers," Theo thought to himself and heard through the music: "At that very time... When I saw her the last time... When I lost her seemingly forever..." This sounded strange in relation to Dara – and, moreover, in Brevich's tone there was no sadness.

Suddenly, everything began to look surreal, phantasmagoric. Theo shook his head trying to return to his senses and felt: he didn't like something, and he couldn't understand what it was. A shiver passed through his body; for an instant, he was shaken by the impermanence, the unreliability of everything in the world – and especially of what you have and treasure the most. Does much really depend on him? What lay ahead – an insight, or maybe suffering? Some distant forefeeling rolled over – and retreated, teased...

Brevich noticed his companion's unease and stopped talking. He himself felt great; everything was perfect, exactly as he wanted it. His own forefeeling had come true and brought him to his goal. He no longer needed to contemplate, to look for something – let others do that. This Theo, for example, if he had such a karma. He, Brevich, was ready to pass the baton on to this man. Or to anyone else who wanted to take upon themselves the burden that was on his shoulders!

Ivan's drunken gaze blurred; reality split into different layers like tobacco smoke. Nok's slim figure appeared before his eyes, then the face of Nok, the face of Tina... He now saw: there was almost no difference between them. They had merged into one – and only one thought remained in his head: soon, very soon, he and Nok would be reunited; they would be liberated together. This anticipation was physically palpable; even his temples began to ache. And he suddenly felt an overwhelming impatience that was almost impossible to bear.

Brevich caught Dara's eye and with a gesture motioned her over to him. Soon both girls were sitting at the table; Tina held Theo by the hand and whispered something in his ear. Dara was struck by a realization: the connection between those two was extremely strong.

The same had become clearly visible to Ivan as well. He spun his glass in the palm of his hands, set it aside and declared hoarsely, without the slightest propriety, "Well, we've had our dance. It's time to say good-night; I have a difficult day tomorrow." And then barked at Dara, "Get your things!"

She quickly put her handbag over her shoulder. Ivan made a sign to the waiter and asked for the bill. Theo reached for his wallet, intending to pay half, but Brevich categorically dismissed the attempt. It was obvious there was no point arguing with him.

"Let it be my contribution toward mathematics – perhaps it's good for my karma," he said gloomily, and looked at Tina – right into her face, confusing her with his gaze.

In the taxi, he sat as dark as a storm cloud. "Is everything okay?" Dara asked.

"Not a damn thing is okay," Brevich growled. "The math guy is not going to let her go; he wants to take and hang on to what belongs to me. This problem needs to be solved – now. Today, tomorrow, immediately."

"Yes, of course," Dara nodded. "It's under control; we know where they live." And, turning to the driver, she said, "Stop here for a minute."

The taxi swerved toward the sidewalk. Dara got out and dialed Jeff. "Everything is settled," she said. "The client is all set, but there's a problem. We need to talk urgently – and not over the phone…"

Ivan looked at her through the car window and frowned, realizing he no longer wanted to see her. She lacked something essential – something that Nok possessed and, he guessed, Tina did too. But he didn't want to think much about it – now another thing was in focus. The finale that he had waited and suffered so long for.

His head was ringing from the drink; something flashed in his eyes – a reflection of the recent lightning? Brevich imagined: he and Nok were rushing toward each other through the rain and rumble, in the midst of the most violent thunderstorms. Through time and space, at insane speeds. Along trajectories that were about to intersect.

THE END OF QUARANTINE

CHAPTER 33

THE PLACE WHERE my phantom entity resides is immersed in half light. It is perhaps twilight, or maybe dawn – some time of day that doesn't change anymore. The sound of the copper string shakes me out of another short bout of drowsiness.

I am reclining in the same chair, in the same room, but its aspect has altered entirely. There is no exit out of it; instead of the door there is a solid wall. The wardrobe and the curtains have disappeared; beyond the window there's one and the same image: a winter park, a gloomy, low-hanging sky and snowflakes slowly sliding down. The main park alley narrows to the horizon. The touch panel no longer works; the landscape cannot be changed. And nothing can be changed: my quarantine is coming to an end.

I do not know what is happening outside my bedroom, the confines of which now make up the boundaries of my reality. I am not even sure I'm still in the same block, next door to Elsa. It's possible I've already been separated, isolated, abstracted. Maybe Elsa has a new roommate and they live their life in a different space disconnected from me. One way or another, these are merely my fantasies, nothing more. And, on the whole, I couldn't care less.

The screen now never goes out; it flickers a dim gray. In the middle of it there is a single word: SOON. The waiting drags on and on; I have lost track of time. I cannot say whether a day or three, five – or maybe a week or two have passed. This is as it should be; Nestor has warned about this. He, by the way, is the only remaining link between me and any kind of outside world. Sometimes the screen flashes, the word disappears, and in its place a familiar face with a high forehead emerges. His visits are not related to his duties; they occur during his rest hours – he just wants to talk. At least that's how he describes it.

"Bear in mind," he said the first time he came, "I shouldn't be doing this." And he added, somewhat caustically, "Although I haven't noticed that you particularly value my friendship. Maybe now you'll finally feel some remorse for that…"

Our conversations are short – I get tired quickly. My entity is aging; I notice it with every new sigh, every turn of my head, every glance at my hands. Everything is going according to plan, Nestor assures me, which is directly connected with the formation of the real me *there*. In my real new life, in my new infancy – with the beginnings of all the memories, all the knowledge that I have restored. They are activated naturally in their own good time, he said. When my new brain – the real brain – is ready to communicate with my B Object. When it is ripe for self-awareness. *Cogito me cogitare.*

Tired, I doze – in the viscous darkness without dreams. Then the string starts to resonate again – I start up in my chair, look at the screen and see the same message: "SOON." And I remember – how I woke up in an empty stairwell, how I got to know Elsa, argued with Nestor and worked vigorously on my theories. How I spent an amazing time in this place, the place of Quarantine. And how I finally decided to leave it.

Before the decision came, I remembered my death again – but the dream that led me to it took almost a week to emerge in full. It was formed out of shards, like a stained-glass window, negligently dropped onto the floor. I collected them together, step by step, filling in the blanks. The days stretched out as usual: walks with Elsa, who still nurtured her grievance, and short talks with Nestor – about nothing in particular, not touching on any serious matters. The Cloud of Objects, their grouping, the hidden rationale of the connection of destinies – it all seemed to be hanging in the air, waiting. Maybe I was getting used to the scale of the issues – and Nestor, sensing this, gave me time. Or he was being secretive for some reason – sometimes I suspected there was a cause for his silence, but I didn't want to betray my curiosity.

And then the stained glass formed into a whole – it was a long, deliberately detailed dream. The entire drunken night – the restaurant, the club, the chance acquaintance with the rich Russian and his girlfriend – was reproduced minute by minute, without cuts. I lived again, word by word, through our conversations, all their strange twists and turns. And when I awoke, I realized: somewhere near, here, beyond the nominal boundary, the most important memory of all lurked – and it wasn't difficult to reach it.

I got up, walked around the room, looked out the window. Behind it was an unfamiliar cityscape. I hastily moved away, not wanting to be distracted by it. Not allowing myself a disruption – it was clear that I had to choose: to remember everything up to the end right now or to stop, to put it off for later, out of hesitation or plain cowardice. I cursed through my teeth, sat down in my chair and closed my eyes. My memory was waiting for this very moment – pictures flashed past, one after another. There we were, saying goodbye to Ivan and Dara, walking home from the club. For some reason, neither of us was in good spirits, despite the alcohol and the fun in the club. Then Tina suddenly threw up her hands, "Why did I give her my number?" Once we were inside the apartment, she sat down on the bed and said, "Let's go away somewhere. Right away, tomorrow. Or maybe today?"

Her alarm was very sincere – I did not understand where the danger might be, but I didn't contradict her. We decided to rent a car the next morning and go to Hua Hin, to the sea. That night, we both barely slept – again, for no particular reason. Then the dawn rose – bringing with it the gloomy view from the window, low clouds, my hangover. Tina's anxiety had not dissipated; it even seemed to have become stronger; she was not herself. We began to pack; while Tina was busy in the bathroom, I decided to make coffee and discovered we'd run out of drinking water. So, I pulled on an old pair of sneakers and shouted to her, "I'll be back soon."

"Where are you going?" Tina asked, sticking her head out the door.

"To the 7-Eleven opposite," I said and added something witty.

Tina didn't smile; she looked at me intently and seriously. I winked at her and left the apartment. And I never saw her again.

I saw practically nothing else – just a few last disjointed frames. A hawker's stand right next to the door – the smoke from its brazier carried toward me. A rank of pink taxis by the sidewalk, a bus being loaded with tourists. A motorcycle emerging from the stream of cars and bearing two people in black helmets – suddenly the one sitting on the back, snatching a dark object from under his jacket. The sheen of steel, a long barrel – and myself, frozen to the spot...

I remembered all this from one second to the next, knowing: here it is, the end of my life. Again, as on the first day of Quarantine, an icy horror poured over me – but only for an instant, for a brief moment. The moment passed, and the horror receded. It was replaced by detachment, as if I had finally torn myself from the past, broken its umbilical cord. It had become independent of me, like a bundle of yellowed photos. I could place them in any order, view them from any angle. I could *perceive* as much as I pleased...

And little by little perception came, and with it the pain I sensed when sitting with Elsa next to the table lamp. The pain of loss, the scream of the nerve cells of closeness. Clenching my fists, squeezing back into my chair, I was living through it – once, twice, a third time – knowing I was incapable of sharing it with anyone. I tried to hide it deeper inside and realized I had already seen its shadow and reflection, heard its echo. That same night – in Brevich's eyes, in his hoarse voice, in his mirthless grin.

I didn't go to breakfast but stayed in the bedroom, pacing from corner to corner – for an hour, then another – muttering something in a low voice. I stood by the window for a long time, peering into the same urban landscape. It seemed the abstract city contained all the places I had ever lived but at the same time was dissimilar to any of them. Gray buildings, a river, bridges. Outlines, contours, silhouettes. Geometry, the interlacing of dotted lines, along which lives converge and diverge... The endless dashes of black ink – seemingly indicating your future in secret scrolls. In those that cannot be reached – on the metabrane, in the Cloud of Objects. Where your own conscion vortex is implanted into the structure of the world. It's controlled by overwhelming forces – they pull you by your strings, like a harlequin doll; they give you crumbs of happiness, brief moments of success, delight. And you rejoice like a child, and then you grieve when the dotted lines suddenly change course, each in its own direction – and run away from each other, rapidly, irreversibly. And all you are left with is a memory – you cannot switch it off; it is tyrannizing you from one life to the next. The memory – and your "I," your mind, your B Object, opened to the entire cosmos, helplessly subjected to the whims of fate…

At noon, Nestor appeared on the screen. I described to him – concisely and without emotion: the restaurant, Brevich, Tina and her anxiety, and then – the motorcycle, emerging from the traffic, two riders, their black helmets, the long barrel. At this point our conversation ended – Nestor realized I was not inclined to go on for long.

"It's a pity," he shrugged. "Actually, today I have a lot to tell you, but let's put it off till later…" – and with that the screen went blank. I sighed with relief but suddenly felt I was fed up with solitude. So, I got up, made another circle around the chair and resolutely pushed the door to the living room.

There was Elsa. "Finally!" she turned toward me. "A minute later and you'd have missed me. I was about to go out for a walk on my own – I'd given up all hope of seeing you today."

"I saw my death again," I said, sitting down at the table. "And I saw how I said goodbye to Tina for the last time. Our story was short; she did not linger in my life. Just like your boyfriends; you and I are alike in that respect…"

Then, on the seafront, for the second time that day, I recounted the morning's chain of memories – while feeling some new anxiety. It seemed to me now I hadn't grasped it all; I had missed something important and had lost its trace. Elsa listened without interrupting, holding my hand tightly, and when I finished, she said quietly, "I just wonder who these chance acquaintances were who sat down next to you?"

I shrugged it off, "Whoever they were, it wasn't about them. Brevich… Evidently, fate sent him to me, so that at the last I would understand some vital, crucial thing. There were some clues in his words; we talked about karma – and here, now, I'm thinking about it again but in a completely different way. On a different quality level; perhaps I might even succeed in putting it into formulas…"

The sun was shining; the sky was a clear blue. There were almost no waves; the triangles of the sails glided smoothly through the flawless ultramarine. In the middle of this idyll, it was strange to talk about death, especially about my own.

A couple walked past, engrossed in conversation. A girl with short hair was explaining something to her companion: "…when a hard, erect cock twitches inside me, I feel as if a string is ringing. And it's amazing!"

Her voice echoed all around, as if resonating from the railing, from the planks of the boardwalk. Elsa turned and looked at them. And I suddenly remembered the dialogue in the restaurant again.

"He called himself a karmic warrior," I murmured. "He said he was a recruit of karma and his woman was with him. Then they tried to lead him astray, but they could not – he had somehow found the answer. And he had become the champion of karma, and after that he was going to become a knight – which I don't remember…"

I suddenly shuddered – along with my words came the memory of the animal power emanating from Brevich; I recalled the way his face convulsed. I squeezed Elsa's hand; she looked at me briefly and nodded, "Yes, a karmic warrior – it sounds exciting. And in general – a warrior… I think his woman was happy with him.

"Well," she added, "and now, it turns out, you won't know what happened to your Tina afterward. You won't be able to dream her 'story' to its conclusion."

I swallowed the lump in my throat and turned away toward the sea. Then, forcing myself, I said, "Obviously, her life went on – I hope it was a long one. Or maybe it's continuing even now – tenses are irrelevant in this case. Time in the earthly reality and here, in this place of ours, flows in different ways. The connection between the worlds is only through B Objects, through the experiences encoded in them. A thin, invisible thread – stretching through indifferent space."

Then we just walked on in silence, and on turning back I suddenly remembered the morning landscape outside the window and my sad thoughts – about the contours and dotted lines, and the scrolls of fate in the Cloud on the metabrane, which cannot be read or touched. No, I didn't want to talk about it with Elsa – and yet I confessed suddenly, "I understood today – here, in Quarantine, it should become clear to everyone: the premonition of losing those you really care about is the main fear. It replaces the fear of death when you learn you are destined to live again. When you suddenly realize what it is to have, to lose and only wonder later whether you will find them again. You wonder and see, more and more clearly: the probability is very small."

The same couple came up to us again. Now the man was talking – almost inaudibly, bending down to the girl's ear. Only scraps came to us: "…slowly, like a river that turned into stone… But even the stone is flowing in its own way…"

This time I, not Elsa, turned around and watched them go. Then I continued, "The probability is tiny. Here you can be reborn at different periods, in different places, with unfamiliar faces and not recognize each other in any of your consequent lives. And one can only guess – whether you are in the same time, in the same point in space, whether you have a chance?"

Elsa suddenly stamped her foot and said angrily, "Does it occur to you that you are just stealing my thoughts? I have already told you – the very grouping of these Objects of yours is a direct path to misery. That's why it's not so wise to let someone into your heart… And regarding the fear of death, I was never too afraid of it anyway!"

We walked for a long time, longer than usual. Then I went straight to my room and waited for Nestor – although I was not eager to see him. He seemed to understand this – barely showing himself on the screen, he looked into my face and frowned, "You are still under the impression… Well, it's a personal matter, not for me to judge. Let's postpone our conversation to tomorrow…" And he stressed, "An important conversation; a lot will depend on it. Both for you, and, I have to admit, for me as well!"

I just nodded silently, squeezing back into my chair. Like that morning, I wanted him to leave me alone.

CHAPTER 34

THE PROMISED CONVERSATION took place the next day, at the five o'clock session. I came to my room a little early, but the screen was already lit. Nestor was sitting in one of his poses – as if clutching at the armrests of a chair – looking away, not noticing me.

"How are you?" he asked, turning when I coughed softly. "Did you manage to sort your emotions out? Have you pulled yourself together? Formally speaking, what is your status? Are you ready to talk about something important?"

I made an affirmative gesture. My emotions really had subsided, as if I had resigned myself to the inevitable, accepting the rules. The image of the motorcycle rider had faded, replaced by curiosity – Nestor sounded mysterious, probably for good reason.

"Well…" my counselor uttered and nervously rubbed his hands together. He seemed to be agitated and was concealing it with difficulty.

"Well," he repeated, "then let's get started. I admit I feel somewhat guilty – I have been predicting it, albeit without any purpose… Do you remember – about stories almost never having a happy ending? So, I do feel uneasy now, but, to make up for it, I'm going to tell you something – which will reveal a lot. And don't think this is about me being transferred away from you – no, the transfer is unclear now. Things have changed: yesterday a permission finally came through – regarding an idea I have been nursing for a long time. That's just a coincidence – irrespective of your dreams, I'd like to note."

"Is that so?" I tilted my head inquiringly.

"Yes, yes!" Nestor said with emphasis. "Permission has come through, and I am authorized. Authorized to make you a proposal: no more, no less. But initially, as an introduction, we have to open the remaining covers: I'm ready to tell you something I had to hide until just now. Something that was considered premature – you're about to find out what you accidentally stumbled upon in your first life. Remember, I hinted at the universality of the principle... An amazing development, leading far beyond – beyond all conventional views... Maybe I should also put a suit and tie on? After all, I'm going to reveal the whole picture to you!"

"The whole picture? Really?" I grinned, nevertheless intrigued. Nestor ignored my laugh. He looked down, took a deep breath, as if to calm himself, and continued, "To begin with, let's summarize, as always. Let us repeat in brief what we have already been through – a few days ago it seemed so significant... But everything is relative – so, let's establish the relativity. Let's compare – and please pay attention to my line of reasoning: correct me if I make a logical blunder."

He was regaining his usual confidence – like anyone approaching a subject he knows well. "So," he said, his chin jutting slightly, "let's consider first individual destinies, the interaction of B Objects with each other. The reality of this interaction has been confirmed beyond doubt – by different ways, including the rebirth statistics we spoke about. B Objects group together, attract each other, repel each other. They 'know' about each other's content – you and I projected this onto the interconnections of human lives and their mutual influence on each other. We talked about destiny and free will, about messiahs and missions, about karma from the point of view of mathematics and magic from the point of view of strict facts. We expressed a hope that your theory will perhaps permit us to look deeper into the interaction of the Objects, to describe the mechanism from within, to raise the veil on these interconnections from the inside out. How do the B Objects see each other? What aspects of the experiences encoded in them cause attraction or repulsion? What is more important here – the pursuit of one's passions or unsatisfied ambitions, or

maybe a thirst for love, or revenge? How do the initial conditions work
– place of birth, poverty, wealth? What is the impact of family? Or here's
another thing: Where does the crux of the matter lie – in the intention
or in the event itself, in what has been only planned or in that which has
already happened? How can we prioritize, apportion more weight? What's
better – to refer to the specifics or generalize, select categories, predicates,
subjects?…"

Nestor made a small pause as if giving me time to think, and continued, "Yes, it's extremely difficult to create a language for describing
individual fates, and moreover, I have to add, the links between destinies
are chronologically and spatially blurred. I mentioned the statistics from
maternity hospitals – they are, of course, illustrative, but other examples
are also known. For instance, some people here, in our world, who have
had brushes with the law, turned out to be connected by experiences from
their former lives, although back then they were completely independent
of each other. A similarity spread out in all metrics, so to speak, leading to
a less than obvious clustering – and there are many of these sorts of cases.
Every now and then new groups are revealed – for example, ruined finan-
ciers or, say, roving singletons of both sexes – with fleeting resemblances
in their past destinies, their previous lives. These 'fleeting resemblances'
can be separated by years, even decades, but still be related to the same
sort of events. Here these people can also exist in different places and
times, but the 'collinearity' of their lives is irrefutable… And so on and so
forth; you understood my point. And we can finish the summary there."

Nestor stopped, habitually pursed his lips and asked, squinting slightly,
"You're already excited by our conversation, aren't you? Remember how
thrilled we both were when we talked about the connections of fates for
the first time? Again, I'm never tired of being amazed, despite studying
them professionally for many years! And now, pay attention: I was not
being totally open with you before. Individual fates are far from being the
main issue. They are just the tip of the iceberg."

"It's not difficult to guess," I leaned slightly forward. "You have already
mentioned – evolution, dynamics… You probably have in mind the development of the system as a whole!"

"Hard to argue with your intuition," Nestor chuckled. "Considering your trained mind… And of course, you are right: my second point is the entire Cloud. Its dynamics, as you put it – obviously, the grouping of destinies is not static. It's not a frozen mosaic – it is a very volatile pattern. Everything flows, regroups – lives converge and diverge; their 'owners' are hurled here and there, scattered in time and space, then collide again, clasping on to one another. Moreover, all elements are interdependent – every B Object interacts with all others; a pronounced feedback is in evidence. So, we have a nonlinear dynamic system with a huge number of constituents – such as, for example, a planet's atmosphere, or a large eco-system, or the human brain that you are so familiar with. This system can also be described by its special language, formalizing not personal experiences and individual fates but the process of their collective evolution. And then, in the resulting parameter space, we can examine the dynamic portrait, the set of trajectories – from state to state, from one snapshot to another. We can look from above at our tragedies and triumphs, the divergences and convergences, the small local catastrophes. Overview the joint development of our lives – can you imagine it?"

I just nodded silently. For some reason, my mouth had gone dry.

"This, of course, is an outrageous challenge," Nestor continued. "The complexity of the task is inordinate, but, nonetheless, we have achieved something – after all, we have access to a lot of data. Turns and jumps from one perturbation to another in the present lives, in the past ones – we can classify, compare, extract something significant. Our findings may be only fragmentary, of course – we are floundering in a boundless ocean, navigating just by the wind – yet, there have been some impressive results. Several promising models have been built and are being researched. Phase portraits of the Cloud have been obtained – and I won't even try to sound mysterious. All the same, you'll say it yourself, if I don't do it first: yes, in terms of its evolution, the Cloud shows a typical 'chaotic' dynamic. Deterministically chaotic: the transformation of its states looks like a movement around an attractor – a strange chaotic attractor. Let's give it a name – for example, let's call it modestly the 'attractor of destinies'!

"It means the following," Nestor somewhat comically waved his hands. "It means: individual lives are not just interdependent – one depends on the other and on all of them together. This dependence has the most reliable basis. The cloud of B Objects is a self-organized system that does not develop randomly but in accordance with a global principle. This fact does not allow us to predict each individual fate. But it does confirm: none of the collisions and intersections of our lives are governed by chance. This is the true basis of causality. This is, if you like, the mathematical root of karma…"

"Things happen for a reason…" I mumbled and suddenly exclaimed, "Please, Nestor, this attractor – can I have a look at it? Can you draw it for me – even if only roughly, inexactly?"

Nestor frowned, "I would have liked to prolong the intrigue, but there's no point: you, of course, have already guessed. Yes, your 'face of thought' looks exactly like the attractor defining the evolution of the Cloud of B Objects – that is, of the entirety of our destinies. We, by the way, use a weightier name; we call it the fundamental ellipsoid!"

A stupid grin spread across my face. I gave out a short laugh and shook my head, not even trying to fully understand what I had heard. Nestor paused, enjoying my bewilderment, then assumed a dignified air and said, "Let's go over that again. The above is so important that we need to dwell on it in detail. So… According to 'Theo's theory,' our thoughts and memories are dynamic processes. The brain sequentially passes through a multitude of states thanks to the interplay between the quantum system of dipoles and the macroscopic network of neurons. This dynamic, por-trayed in the phase space, is a movement along 'chaotic' trajectories, around a typical 'chaotic' attractor. It is precisely this dynamic principle that allows the brain, on the one hand, to produce efficiently the proper thought, association or memory at the first, not even very distinct, hint, and, on the other, to hold on to it, concentrate on it and not be distracted, despite the constant bombardment by a multitude of various signals. Is that correct?"

I nodded. "Good," said Nestor, massaging the bridge of his nose. "Later. You got an approximate image of this attractor and called it the 'face of thought' – with absolutely legitimate pride. We also know that thinking in our world obeys the same principles, and the attractor of our thoughts looks exactly like yours – which adds universality to it and grounds for you to be proud. And finally, what I revealed to you today:

the face of thought also manifests itself in a completely different place. The same principle and the same image lie beneath the evolution of the Cloud – controlling our aspirations, hopes, fears. Now your pride may surge immensely: it seems everything related to the field of the conscions – and, therefore, to true consciousness – develops, changes over time in accordance with the same fundamental law. Both our individual thoughts and the totality of our life experiences, encoded in the Objects, exhibit the same, seemingly chaotic but in fact very deterministic behavior!"

I interrupted excitedly, "Experiences, thoughts... An analogy comes to mind right away: Maybe the Cloud, from the point of view of its dynamics, can also be considered as some kind of huge 'brain'? 'Super-brain' striving to reach some global 'super-thought'..."

"And this explains the meaning of all our lives, taken together," Nestor finished for me. "Well, this hypothesis is obvious in its own way. It has been expressed many times – an analogy between our thinking and the dynamics of the Cloud is very tempting! Of course, it remains only a speculation – on a par with other, no less appealing ones. How should we relate to them; should we believe them? I'd love to believe many of those, yes..." He made a dreamy face and immediately cut himself short, "However, let's postpone the speculating – save that pleasant activity for later. First, we need to finish with the facts – if, of course, you are still capable of listening and not floating in euphoria somewhere. Therefore... Therefore, let's go to the third point – let's even put down an exclamation mark, as you like it. A big fat exclamation mark – there is a reason. An even more important reason than the ones we've just discussed."

Nestor looked at me closely, then gazed down, moved something, thoughtfully rubbed his cheek and said, stressing almost every syllable, "Let us now consider the metaspace, the entire metabrane as a whole!"

For some reason, this immediately sobered me, even put me on alert, and he nodded, "Yes, as a whole – that frightened you, didn't it? You feel yourself on shaky ground – you are not a cosmologist; you're not so comfortable in the vast spaces of the universe? Okay, okay... So, overall, our science has not moved very far from yours, but in one aspect we have advanced significantly. We have learned how to detect the effects of gravity with great accuracy – including gravitational waves and their interference patterns. As a result, we can, quite realistically, model the evolution of the metabrane at different scales – from entire local universes to their galaxies, stars, even planets. I have already more than once mentioned the main conclusion that transpires from these efforts: geometry, the structure of the whole space is changing rapidly and at a high amplitude. We also mentioned the role of the field of the conscions in these changes: it seems that the metabrane moves its gambling chips – the local universes and the bodies within them – so that the Clouds of B Objects and the worlds, able to interact with them, intersect with one another. In other words, the field of the conscions directly affects the geometry of space, and vice versa: a change in geometry alters the field of the conscions, allowing its Objects and Clouds to develop, becoming more intricate and complex. Do you follow this logic?"

"Yes," I said shortly, sensing an anticipation of something new and huge ripen inside me.

"Then we can reformulate: in the case of the metabrane, we again have a nonlinear feedback system," Nestor said slowly. "It would be natural to expect its dynamics to manifest typical nonlinear properties – and we have discovered just such properties."

"An attractor..." I said quietly. "Your fundamental ellipsoid."

"Such modesty," Nestor sniggered. "You didn't say 'my face of thought'... Yes, even if our data is incomplete, we can say with certainty: the quirks of metaspace are not accidental. They – surprise, surprise! – obey the same laws that we have been repeatedly mentioning. Their phase portraits are nothing other than typical chaotic attractors, and – listen carefully: they, the attractors, are the same at different ranges. Yes, this is nothing else than fractal self-similarity – of universes, galaxies, star and planetary systems. In the dynamics of the metabrane we observe a symmetry of scales – this is of great significance in itself. Even more astonishing, however, something you are no longer even surprised about; for you this is routine, habitual. Yes, the dynamic portrait of the metabrane looks exactly like the ones we talked about earlier – like the face of thought and the attractor of destinies. Now you understand why we prefer the 'fundamental ellipsoid' term – it, at least partially, reflects its truly global role!"

"Incredible..." I mutter. "It's not just astonishing, it's... Incredible!"

"And most importantly, all this is reality," Nestor added. "A reality that asserted itself in scientific minds. These theories are already taught in universities, being studied by students. And as for the philosophers… Oh well. Let's summarize all of the above, from big to small…"

And he began to speak monotonously, like a bored master teaching a schoolboy, "The metabrane dynamically and structurally repeats itself in various different scales… Underneath its dynamic there's a stable order… Its name is deterministic chaos; its portrait is a strange attractor…

"We can say that metaspace sort of tends toward a certain perfection," the screen intoned. "In the process, it rearranges everything inside of itself – universes, galaxies, stars. It does this to maximize the cumulative 'rationality,' even 'intelligence,' if you like – that is, to increase the quantity and 'quality' of perturbations in the field of the conscions, forcing the vortices of this field, the B Objects, to be created and filled with content. The metabrane moves the Clouds of B Objects and the worlds that are or will soon be 'ready' to interact with the Objects toward each other. The amazing accuracy of this targeting is achieved by the symmetry of scales we just discussed: the geometry is 'adjusted' in accordance with the same laws at all levels, from universes to single celestial bodies!

"Exactly the same principle governs the dynamics of the conscion Clouds – that is, in a certain sense, all our lives taken together. At the deepest level, it lies at the heart of our thoughts and memories, the whole work of our brain. Both individual thoughts and the entire collective 'consciousness' of the Clouds seem to strive toward the same perfection as the structure of the global space. This striving determines, on the one hand, how we think, and on the other, everything that happens and will happen to us. Let's note here: what seemed to be a clichéd poetic metaphor – the whispering heavens, the music of higher spheres as sources of creative inspiration – is now a mathematical theory. The harmony of the cosmos has become inseparable from the harmony of thinking – in the most direct sense…"

I tried as hard as I could to grasp, visualize, imagine at least something; my head was spinning from his words, from the grandeur of what I was hearing. I had already felt like that a week earlier when I had first learned about the Cloud and the interlinking of fates, but now the picture was hundreds of times bigger. And Nestor continued solemnly, "So, the concept of dynamic chaos now gets greatly enriched with extra meaning. Its practical, so to speak, essence is as follows: the present really does determine the future, but no one can predict this future – nonlinearity, irregularity make it impossible to be calculated. And yet it, the future, is not accidental; it is determined. It may look like a triumph of disorder, yet it obeys a hidden but steadfast order. It's impossible to argue with this order; it decides each individual destiny. There's a strict causality evident, but it is not a debasing higher design, not a series of dead writings on scrolls of parchment; it is not static cast in stone. It does not bind us hand and foot – neither our thoughts, nor our fates, nor the universe itself. It gives us freedom – the highest freedom possible. It assumes development, not stagnation – it makes us able to rush from side to side, take contradictory steps, respond with the greatest shifts to the smallest changes, yet never – NEVER – losing sight of the ultimate goal. We can't get away from the attractor, from the fundamental ellipsoid, just as you, Theo, can't get away from your file!"

"Predestination, the whispering of the heavens…" I murmured after him. Echoing – either his voice or my own thoughts.

"Causality, continual feedback…" Nestor droned. "It is hard to even imagine the scale of the problems! Thinking, its mechanism; consciousness, its role and meaning; destinies, their interconnections; the universe, its formation. All this is tied into one – and awaits its unified theory. And while we don't have such a theory, we can play around with a fair few assumptions. For example, the question arises – what is space striving toward, what kind of ideal? And immediately, sublime ideas come to mind – is it maybe global consciousness of some kind that the metabrane fosters?

"Many serious people like this hypothesis. Many speculate as you do: that space is evolving, trying to focus on some 'thought,' like a gigantic metabrain with a gigantic metamind. And the parts of this mind – the Clouds of Objects carrying our life experiences – manifest the same dynamics themselves, trying to reach their own 'thoughts,' shuffling our lives and destinies in the process. And we in turn strain our Lilliputian minds, producing tiny views and judgments, nurturing the illusion of our own free will – and not even suspecting what gigantic forces we are trying to challenge. But still: without our microscopic brains, without their persistent, restless bustling, all these forces would have nothing to apply themselves to!

"There is also a suggestion that the metabrane is a giant self-learning computer," Nestor continued. "Or a powerful classifier aimed at solving some globally important task… Anyway, the hypotheses are countless. Current mathematics is such that some clever tricks may confirm indirectly the most incredible theories. Do you want to participate in the creation of an incredible theory?"

I was about to say, "Yes, yes, I do!" – but suddenly my strength left me. This hadn't happened to me for a long time – I had overextended myself trying to comprehend too much at once. I just whispered, "Sorry, I'm falling asleep now," interrupting Nestor in midsentence.

He grinned; I heard again, "It is only thanks to the dynamic chaos that we're not bored with living. And at the same time this 'chaos' is not chaos at all. Just like a death is not death…"

Did Nestor say this, or did I think it myself? There was already no difference. Stars floated before my eyes; my head rang. I buried my chin in my chest and fell asleep, without waiting for the end of the session.

CHAPTER 35

IN THE MORNING, waking up as if emerging from a deep pool, I rubbed my eyes and froze for a while, staring at the empty screen. I had slept a long time – a sound, healthy sleep with no dreams. This was what I needed – too much had been jammed into the last two days.

"The metabrane…" I whispered, trying to imagine some bizarre space structures – and forgot about them instantly. Abstruse concepts and mathematical abstractions faded into the background, moved to a distant corner. The day before yesterday's dream suddenly, authoritatively overwhelmed me – the restaurant, the drunken night and, most importantly, the separation from Tina.

The memory of her eclipsed everything. Reclining in my chair, I saw, as if for real, her innocent half smile during our most intimate moments, her way of shaking her wet hair under the hair dryer, her gaze – old beyond her years, inescapable, all falsehood powerless before it. The receptors of closeness again signaled a catastrophe; I was seized by the unimaginable – the helplessness of her pose, the scent of her heated body, the sense of my complete possession of her. And then, right after this: a terrible bitterness – a bitterness and resentment for both of us. A realization of the deepest injustice that cannot be reversed. We are in different worlds – is this not the evidence of the utmost malignancy of the creation, its soullessness, its imperfection? Its indifference – to us, connected by a great accomplishment and a shared secret…

I sat in a stupor, motionless, helpless. Then, somehow, I forced myself to get up, went to the bathroom and got into a hot shower, immersing my face in the jets of water. That helped; closing my eyes, I was driving out of my head all thoughts, all visions and then muttering to myself, "Ellipsoid, universal principle, music of the higher spheres..." I needed to switch, to change focus, to avoid surrendering to despair – so I whispered the words and then, sitting at the table, wrote and drafted – point by point. One logical step after the other – from the quantum model of the brain to the conscion vortex, the B Object; from the local halo, the Cloud of our destinies, to the geometry of the entire metaspace... I did manage to put something more or less coherent on paper – although I didn't feel I had penetrated deeply, to the quintessential depths. To the greatest meanings linked together – they seemed to be protected by an insurmountable barrier. Still, I tried hard – and ended up just praying: let it all be true! Not Nestor's fantasy, not one of his tricks. If it's all for real, then on my sheet of paper – the most alluring future waiting ahead. A future worthy of every effort to reach out to it – freeing oneself from the fetters, from stories with no happy endings. You could make a jump, grasp the crumbling ledge with your fingers, feeling the abyss under your feet and the chill in your soul. Pull yourself up with the last of your strength, dragging your body to the roof, and then stretch out on the warm asphalt and stare at the boundless sky, the new sky...

I came out to breakfast late; Elsa had already finished her coffee. I noted she was looking very homely, yet her outfit had been carefully thought out – a fluffy polo-necked sweater, soft ballet flats, close-fitting pants. "Do you want a sandwich or toast and jam?" she asked me. Then she got up, turned toward the refrigerator and, feigning indifference, asked, "Missing her?"

"I am infuriated by the injustice," I said through clenched teeth and fell silent, not wanting to explain anything. And immediately rushed into a verbose and inarticulate explanation.

Elsa didn't answer, busying herself with the grill; I couldn't see her face. Then the smell of toasted bread spread throughout the room. As soon as it was on the table, I grabbed the top piece, burned myself slightly, and this sobered me up. I began to eat in silence, alternately spreading apricot and strawberry jam.

"Listen," Elsa said suddenly, "I've been thinking about that motorcyclist of yours. I remember, in Southeast Asia hired killers often work this way. In a thriller I'm reading, there's a character like this. Perhaps you became an obstacle for someone, got in his way?"

I waved my hand in annoyance, "What sort of obstacle could I have been – a fence made up of integrals? A self-similar fractal trap? And I never crossed anyone – obviously, they just wanted to rob me. And they probably did, although they didn't get much."

Elsa did not argue but was clearly doubtful. Well, I didn't have any other conclusions or scenarios. I chewed my toast, sipped my lukewarm coffee and then added with a grin, "Nestor told me something yesterday. About how in the course of our lives the structure of the world is transmitted. But I have to admit: some Thai on a smelly motorbike doesn't look to me much like a messenger from the metabrane. And it's not the metabrane I hate but the man who shot me. I would gladly repay him in kind. Or even better, hang him up by the balls!"

"Yes," Elsa nodded, "I understand you. Although I'm not sure you'd pull the trigger."

I just grunted, then put the plates in the sink and began to wash them – again and again. Our very own tradition of senselessly washing dishes. Especially when you have nothing to say. I wanted to contradict Elsa, to convince her of something, but kept silent, realizing that any words of mine would sound unconvincing, lightweight. Because I myself wasn't totally convinced either – and, by the way, was Nestor yesterday all that convinced himself? Why was there all this confusion in my head – was he *convincing* enough yesterday?... I grimaced, rubbed my temple – and then it hit me. Now I knew what to do next.

For the evening session, I prepared carefully. I practiced several phrases in advance and even wrote one in my notebook. I was the first to make my greeting, barely waiting for Nestor to appear. He made a solemn nod, a perfunctory reply and suddenly, without pausing, said, "I have to make a confession: our last discussion contained an element of my own personal interest!"

"Hmm…" I drawled in perplexity, and Nestor continued, looking to one side, "It happens – we've noted it a few times: destinies become entangled and unable to go their disparate ways. I can even reformulate without fear of sentimentality: some people meet one day and then live their lives inseparably. Yes, inseparably – and now about my proposal, so to speak…"

He fell silent and picked up some thin-rimmed glasses from down below. He put them on but a moment later removed them and thoughtfully turned them over in his hands… "Remember, I also mentioned that your personality is being observed by a whole group of experts," he finally said. "That the time would come, and a conclusion would emerge – maybe quite an unusual one. Well, a conclusion has indeed been made – with my participation, I admit. They are ready to make you involved – in the real, serious work. Now, right away – that is, before you go through all the tedious journey of childhood, adolescence, maturity. Without waiting until you join our society naturally, so to speak, as a regular person. This is an exception to the rules, and for you – it's a very lucrative bonus. Just imagine: it's as if your first life is continuing – and what's more, the next one is not going to be canceled either… Although this continuation has some obvious restrictions, the main thing – your consciousness with all your memory that you restored so painstakingly – will remain intact, inseverable from you. And a roommate – you are guaranteed a roommate; that will be written into your contract. And I will be with you too – I have been approved as the link man. As the mediator between you and the specialists from *that* side – I mean, from this one, from our world. So, we have this development instead of my transfer – unexpected, isn't it?"

There was exultation in his voice, but he immediately restrained himself – "I understand, of course: this is first and foremost my chance. But for you, too, it's quite an opening, an opportunity – right away, only for your past achievements, so to speak, and the benefits are significant! And just think: together we make an excellent team. You keep the whole quantum field theory in your head, and I am a cosmologist, a very good cosmologist. And, of course, imagination, creativity – both of us have them in abundance. Moreover, we are already used to each other… Of course, you are blessed with good luck, and I am on a losing streak, but this does not mean much! You can judge my worth by the way I speak, the terms I use

– the choice of words is vital, right? It shows how intimate I am with the subject; it allows, maybe even forces, you to believe me. Or maybe not... Do you really believe me, Theo?"

He was noticeably nervous, and his agitation spread to me. I had no doubts: his proposal was no joke, no pretense, but I didn't know exactly how to react. Furthermore, I already had a plan, at least for this session.

"I believe – probably..." I squeezed out of myself. In my head everything was mixed up, the phrases I had prepared forgotten.

"Yes, probably," I continued with difficulty. "I am willing to consider this, but..."

Nestor became very tense at my "but." He looked at me point-blank, without blinking, almost biting his lip. For some reason, this made me angry, and I blurted out somewhat peevishly, "You know, I need something more substantial than your words, even if you select them perfectly. I need specifics; I want finally to feel some ground beneath my feet. The mathematics – I want to see it. Give me the articles – *scientific* articles. Why are you hiding them from me? It's strange. Please, don't think this is an ultimatum, but... Yes, in a sense, it is an ultimatum. Maybe in every sense!"

I made a point of stressing the "in every," expecting objections, grievances, but Nestor instantly relaxed, his features smoothed out and a sly smile appeared on his lips. He shook a finger at me, "You see, I can read you like an open book. This, by the way, proves we are on the same wavelength: I had foreseen this response of yours; it was as easy as pie! Look at the section of your closet where you found the notebooks. There is something there for you – I don't think you'll be disappointed."

I jumped up and opened the closet. The lower-right drawer was sticking out slightly; it contained a large pile of photocopies. I grabbed them, went back to my chair and sat down, not letting them out of my hands.

"Everything's in a familiar format," Nestor triumphed. "To appeal to your nostalgia – that was my idea as well. Slightly faint copy on poor-quality paper... What would you prefer – shall we talk some more, or do you want to read first?"

Stunned, I shook my head, glanced at the headline of the topmost article – "Quantum Correlation and Global Coherence" – and muttered,

"Later, later..." Then I hastily opened the next one. After a brief glimpse at the abstract, I looked up at Nestor and said imploringly, "I think I'd like to have a read if you don't mind..."

He grinned; the screen went out. I began to turn the pages; the work was devoted to the correspondence between M-theory and quantum fields – in my previous life this was known as the AdS/CFT duality. And so it was, but not quite: the equations made sense to me, although a completely unfamiliar part appeared in the main integrand function. The spectrum of oscillations of a hypothetical string expanded, but it did not look like supersymmetry...

"Good!" I declared out loud and took the next photocopy with the promising title, "On the Question of Effective Mass and the Dynamics of Gravitational Waves." The first thing I saw was the Einstein equations – but the space-time tensor in them was different. A bit different... No, not just a bit. Significantly, substantially dissimilar!

I grabbed a pencil, then put it down again – no, too early. I read through the article to the end, perused the conclusions – they looked strange. But here, one was clear – if we assume that the curvature changes evenly, without jumps. And what if we allow for a break, a singularity?... I went back to the beginning, rewrote the first equation, scratching at the paper, painfully trying to figure out what the mysterious symbols in the tensor diagonals meant...

Thus the next five hours passed, then, after a short sleep, all morning, followed by a day, two, four, six. A whole week, not allowing myself to be distracted, I floundered in an ocean of new concepts, unfamiliar transformations, axioms, theorems, on which the physics of this world was built. The feeling of powerlessness was giving way to delight, surprise, feverish impatience – and then again helplessness, irritation with myself, with the clumsiness of my mind... However, already by the second day, the first successes had emerged – I began to connect one thing with another, to build bridges between different, it would seem, sections and areas. Almost nothing was clear yet, but a premonition of the right direction had arisen – as if the arrow of an imaginary compass were pointing, shivering, precisely where my gaze was trying to penetrate. I clung to this premonition, and it did not let me down – gradually the blank spots shrunk, the gaps filled with content. My previous conversations with Nestor acquired new meanings; firm walls began to emerge under the chiseled vaults. And then the foundation appeared underneath – so, by the end of the week, I could see the contours of the entire building. Albeit without any details yet – only in outline, in a dotted line, in a sketch interrupted every now and then by voids, but it soared up in front of me, believable, almost real. And I did believe in it – late in the evening in my bedroom, wearily leaning back into the chair. I acknowledged my faith and closed my eyes, peering intently inside myself. Feeling how the fragility of this place, the place of Quarantine, was ceasing to be an impediment – now I had something solid I could rely on…

I stayed like this for a long time, an hour or two. I sat there, savoring my admiration for the harmony and grandeur of what I was beginning to comprehend. There were no more reasons for doubts; they had gone away. I didn't know yet how complete and consistent the new theories were – they most probably contained misconceptions, inaccuracies. But I was ready to work on any of them, bursting on ahead – there were so many tempting things ahead!

Then, sobering up, I opened my eyes. I looked around, taking everything in with a new gaze – sheets of paper, the stack of photocopied articles, the black rectangle of window. I had consciously made it darker recently, as if closing an imaginary curtain. Then I glanced at the equally black screen – yes, I was not communicating with Nestor much these days. Or with Elsa either – however, they reacted to this with understanding. I was lucky in this respect – both with my counselor and my roommate. A thought flickered through my head: What is she doing – maybe she is awake too?

I got up and went into the living room – suddenly realizing how exhausted I was from my feverish weeklong effort. Sensing that I needed to share with someone my shift in perception, my newly discovered faith. And indeed, my roommate wasn't asleep; she was sitting at the table, bending over her handiwork. There were florid paper figures and something resembling fine lace laid out next to her.

"I was waiting for you to come out," she said without raising her head. "Lately, you've been all radiant again – like when you remembered your

Tina. Glowing like a child who's been given a lollipop. But now, I'm sure, it has nothing to do with a woman… And I've been having trouble sleeping for several days now."

I was slightly hurt at her mention of Tina – especially since it was the first time Elsa had called her by her name. It also needled me because I was feeling a bit guilty. Over these last few days, Tina as well as my entire past had been relegated to the background. The novelty and power of the mathematics I had been exploring had overshadowed everything.

"Women have nothing to do with it," I muttered dryly. "I've been very busy – with the science of this new world. I have to admit, I am impressed by it – and, besides, some surprising things seem to have come together…"

And I began to talk, sharing with her everything – Nestor's proposal, the harmony of finely chiseled vaults, the enormity of the challenges and goals. I talked and felt: I sounded *convincing* – maybe more convincing than ever. A clear picture had taken shape in my head – all disparate thoughts were drawn toward it, like to an attractor in phase space. I talked, quite inspiringly, about the mission I had never doubted. It was binding, and it had given me a great chance; it was pushing me toward an understanding of lives, destinies, the first principles of underlying reasons, the true nature of aspirations. And from this, I could step further and further – toward the universe and its configuration, to the deepest connection of mind and space…

"You've managed to mix everything into one big pile," Elsa interrupted me suddenly. "I bet you're tempted to add your Thai girl to it too!"

Her tone was strange; it somehow knocked me off my train of thought. "Everything really is mixed up," I shrugged, once again jarred by the mention of Tina. And added, as if defending myself, "Universe and chaos – I can't argue with them for now. But I want to at least understand…"

Elsa sneered, "Not long ago, you claimed you'd want to bring to justice someone personally rather than blaming some abstract laws of the universe. But that was before you were given a lollipop. And, for instance, that man, Ivan, do you remember his words – 'recruit,' 'champion'?"

"'Karmic warrior,'" I muttered. "The recruit and the champion of karma…"

"Precisely," Elsa nodded. "And later – the knight. You see, he couldn't really understand, but he still decided to argue!"

"Oh, well," I grunted angrily. "If you prefer to put it like that…"

We were silent for a while, then I said, "It was easy for him, for Ivan, to argue; he didn't see the big picture. His opponent was something mercifully adapted for the crowd – lacquered, sweetened, very far from the truth."

Elsa sneered again, "Didn't you and your Nestor agree some time ago that the ordinary and adapted should not be discounted either? You yourself were ranting on to me about magic, karma – how they are playing in a new light if only to blow away the icing sugar. And you also love to talk about free will – listening to you, it's as if it doesn't exist at all. Everything controls you: people, their desires, then space, stars – and I wonder whether it isn't too easy to deny such a freedom to yourself? And to pin the blame for this denial on others or on some kind of mission…"

I just spread my hands.

"You also want," Elsa continued, "to tame something in there, throw a bridle on it, but, it seems to me, it's impossible to succeed this way. Purely in terms of dynamics, rhythm, tempo: one needs to jump decisively into a saddle, but you with your formulas are whirling around, capering in circles, dancing ritual dances in front of a deity placed on an altar. And what would a knight do?"

"Do you really think," I asked peevishly, "that a naive brute force is always the best option? That one can achieve something with it – at least sometimes, somehow, somewhere?"

"Maybe, in this case, one cannot," Elsa replied, straightening her hair, "But sometimes… Anyway, I'm not talking about the result, I mean the perception of the knight inside of yourself. You can surely achieve something with it for yourself, is that right?"

She moved her lace on the table; its pattern had changed. It had become irregular, senselessly chaotic. I wanted to point this out to her, but she suddenly mixed up all the pieces, almost dropping them on the floor, and said, "Maybe, of course, the whole thing is in the 'grouping' you spoke about – I admit, the word struck me. How was it in your theories – whatever the Objects need to accumulate within themselves, alone or in a group, we sense as decisions – our own, not someone else's? So, maybe you are repeatedly destined – not to depart far from your formulas. That's why your Tina turned out to be only a means for you – and for him, his woman was the meaning. He wanted to live through, and you – you only tried to examine it.

"By the way," she added, again attempting to put her pieces of lace into some pattern. "By the way: in this sense, you and I are alike. But still, if I were in her place… I would have wanted my man to fight for me, even with the entire universe, and not just use me to understand the universe, to unravel its puzzling secrets!"

She got up, went to the refrigerator, contemplated the contents for a couple of minutes, then poured herself a glass of milk. All the while, I looked at her silently, feeling how my thoughts crawled every which way, mumbling indistinctly. I shook my head and muttered crossly, "You always manage to turn everything on its head and bring it down to earth. With you, all science is transformed into a kitchen squabble!"

"Don't be angry," Elsa responded with a barely perceptible sneer; "I'm not attacking you. Neither you nor your finely chiseled vaults. You know my position: it's just that the universe is a bitch!"

"Good night," I said gloomily but, nevertheless, didn't move from my place.

"Good night," Elsa replied and sat down at the table drinking her milk. Then she carefully wiped her lips with a napkin and repeated, "Don't be angry. I'm saying all this, but, in actual fact, I'm thinking of something completely different. Namely, that we now have a chance."

I looked up at her. "Now it seems you're not going to leave the Quarantine any time soon," she explained. "Well, I'll stay here, too, and, putting all the grief aside, the fact remains: you and your Thai girl are in different worlds, but I am right next to you. Moreover, we don't have to fear getting attached to each other – in Quarantine nothing will tear us apart except ourselves. Nothing, including death – it does not exist in this place. Funny, isn't it? We can even expand our menu – I'll learn to cook something else besides fried eggs and toast!"

"Well… okay," I said, not sure whether she was being serious or joking.

"Yes, like that…" Elsa thought for a minute and added, "Now no one could say I'm not living a full life. Here fullness means only one thing: you are my roommate and I am yours, and we have been *made* for each other – as phantom entities, I mean. In my opinion, what could be more complete… We live in the same block – this means we are living in our common world. On one frequency, one wavelength – memories or no memories, but in general a roommate does not share a roommate with anyone. *I love Quarantine!*"

"Good," I said again and thought: jokes or no jokes, but for some reason, her words are more *convincing* than all of mine put together.

"Look how much we have already been through," Elsa shook her head. "The illusion of closeness, the illusion of betrayal, then the illusion of my jealousy – there's little now that can frighten us. The place of Quarantine is full of deception, but its unreality defeats any argument. As they say – the ocean of tears… For some reason, I remember it, even though I myself never cry. The ocean of tears tastes only of salt, but its dharma has the taste of freedom!"

Something pierced me through – a lightning, a discharge of current. Memory, like a merciless knight, had hurled a lance at me. It had broken through my armor, knocked me to the ground…

"What? What did you say?" I almost shouted, glaring at her. "I never told you those words – where did you hear them, from whom?"

Elsa froze, dumbfounded; her fingers convulsively squeezed her glass of milk.

"Try to remember!" I insisted. "This is important – you must remember!"

She very slowly, carefully raised the glass to her lips but did not drink and put it on the table. After a pause, she said quietly, "Just as I am able to bring things down to earth, so you have an amazing talent to spoil everything. To ruin everything – always, always!"

I didn't answer. Elsa got up and went to the door of her bedroom. On the threshold she turned, and I caught a glimpse of her face. I saw her pursed lips, her eyebrows drawn together. And her narrowed, unforgiving eyes.

CHAPTER 36

THAT NIGHT I hardly slept; my brain was working nonstop; ill-defined, half-smudged pictures flashed before me and unhurriedly floated away. Everything around seemed to be shaded with swirls of hoarfrost or threads of a cocoon that swaddled me like an infant. It was like looking at a familiar landscape sweeping along beyond the window of a train, trying to guess the stations and getting them wrong over and over again.

All this, however, did not matter – I myself, my dreams, my guesses, either right or wrong, played no role whatsoever. In wakefulness or oblivion, I had been caring only for what Elsa would tell me. Then the morning came, and I jumped up hastily – even though it was still too early. To kill time, I picked up one of the articles but immediately threw it away. Mathematics, quantum fields and outer spaces had become superfluous, unnecessary. Instead of my recent eagerness, I felt only irritation and incomprehensible anger.

Then, unable to bear it, I went into the living room, despite the odd hour. I opened the door and was surprised to see that Elsa was already there – she was walking from one corner to the other, straightening something, shifting things from place to place. I said hello; she nodded without uttering a word. I noticed an unfamiliar hard-edged crease mark on her face – an innate shadow of determination.

For a while we were silent. I fiddled with a pot of coffee, filled my cup and took the first sip. Then Elsa went to the kitchen cupboard and said without turning around, "It's good that sometimes I get up early. If you hadn't also happened to come out at this ungodly hour, you might still be under the impression everything gets tidied up on its own. It's convenient to think so, don't you find?"

"You said there were maids," I reminded her.

"Well, what can you expect from maids?" Elsa shrugged. "They just do their job; they don't make things cozy."

She poured herself a coffee, tore open a plastic packet and put some slices of bread in the basket on the table. Then she pushed it closer to me and said sarcastically, "Why aren't you eating anything; aren't you hungry? What else would you like for breakfast? We have kangaroo meatballs today. Tender as quail mousse. Just your thing!"

I didn't answer, only sipped my coffee, noting that my hand was trembling a little. It was clear: my roommate had remembered something important, and she wasn't happy about it.

Elsa sat down opposite me and meticulously inspected the table. "You know," she sighed, "for some reason, I don't like our tablecloth anymore. All that nonsense embroidered over it, all that baby babble... Really, it's time we had a makeover. We can hang something on the walls..." She glanced around and added in the same tone, "By the way, regarding those words that made you so concerned yesterday. I had a funny dream last night!"

I looked up at her. "Sorry," Elsa said, "'funny' is not quite the right word. Actually, completely the wrong word, although it all started amusingly enough: three years before my first death, I was with a lover in Bali. In ten days or so I got tired of him and went home early. I did not get a direct flight; the stopover was in Kuala Lumpur, Malaysia. For six hours, I was almost going crazy with boredom, and in the end that was exactly what happened..."

She finished her coffee, broke a soft, untoasted bun and covered her eyes with her hand. "*What* happened?" I could not hold myself back.

"Don't hassle me; I'm trying to visualize, to remember the details," Elsa said coldly. "So: there was not much time before my flight. I was walking toward the plane and suddenly stumbled upon some people staring at a television. One of those big TVs hung under the ceiling, and the entire screen was taken up with the distorted face of a man in the bright, roving beam of a searchlight. In one hand he had a megaphone, and in the other he was holding an Asian girl tight to himself – and she was also secured to him by a rope. There was some noise in the background – caused, as it soon became clear, by the helicopter on which the camera was located. I remember, I was dumbfounded by the unreality of the whole scene, and then he brought the megaphone to his mouth and screamed in bad English those words about the ocean, about dharma and – again and again – something like: 'I am giving us freedom!' 'You can all gain freedom,' he shouted, 'freedom from your losses.' And he continued: 'This is your Buddhist celebration of death, but we are not seeking death, we are looking for a new life. This is not a suicide,' he repeated, 'we are only liberating ourselves!'"

"Brevich…" I whispered and asked in a hoarse, tremulous voice, "And the girl? Tell me about the girl!"

"I didn't remember much," Elsa shrugged. "She was young, slim, and yes, there was a bright streak in her hair – in thick black hair down to her shoulders. And the most striking thing I remember was the terrible fear in her eyes. Unimaginable fear – of course, in her place, anyone would be scared, but she seemed to be afraid of something more, something I could not imagine. I don't even know how to explain."

"Well, and afterward?" I mumbled.

"Afterward…" Elsa shivered. "I remember, they were shouting something to him, probably the police, and the camera angle from the helicopter changed slightly, so that we could see wings attached to his back – big black wings. Then the subtitles came on – and I learned that everything was taking place in Bangkok, on the roof of an abandoned skyscraper. I even remember its name – Sathorn Unique. And… And then my flight was announced, so I went to the gate."

"You mean…" I could not believe my ears. "You left without finding out how it ended?"

"What was I supposed to do?" Elsa asked angrily. "Should I have missed my plane? This happened in a foreign country to people I didn't know. Despite the fact it was a real drama…"

I kept looking at her – as if not believing, as if even pleading for something.

"That's all," she said firmly. "All I can say is: both her fear and his insane look made an impression on me for a long while. But time passed, and everything was forgotten. And don't think," she added with irritation, "that I was hiding all this from you. It's just how my memory dealt with it – after all, yours also didn't come back quickly."

"No, it didn't," I agreed, looking into my cold coffee. "But, however, sooner or later..."

And suddenly I believed everything – Elsa's story, Brevich's insane cry and that Tina had been with him up there, on the roof of the skyscraper. All the parts of the puzzle finally came together. There was no one to ask for mercy, and no point in begging – to anyone or about anything...

I smashed my fist on the table with a mighty swing – the cups jumped, spilling their contents. I leaped up from my seat, ran to the window, then took a step back to the table – and again rushed away.

Elsa stared at me in fear. "The warrior? You were enchanted with the warrior thing?" I shouted at her. "Well here it is, the act of the knight with no brains. Only capable of destroying, never creating, achieving nothing, spoiling everything... I just don't understand how I could be so stupid, so naive and blind? Even Nestor saw something was wrong, but I kept waving it all away, mumbling nonsense about teasing shadows of meaning, an elusive twist ... A fucking elusive twist! Shadows of meaning – how do you like such shadows?"

Elsa got up, took a roll of paper towels, tore off a few and started to wipe the table. "I should have guessed!" I groaned, clutching the window sill with my fingers. "Everything was leading toward it: his intonation, glances, phrases and, most importantly – of course, he was not talking about Dara! I just didn't see what Tina had in common with the woman he was so obsessed with. But, undoubtedly, there was a connection... One can only guess – actually, I suspect he didn't need us personally. Something is prompting me: in his eyes we were just proxies who had stumbled in his way. And he decided to remove the obstacle!"

"He had made his decision, and he was unstoppable," Elsa said and smiled sadly. "Probably, this is what free will really is. Don't think I'm justifying it, of course…"

I did not answer her; I didn't even turn around. Just stood and looked out the window, in a gray haze over the hilly prairie. Then I said with difficulty, "It's easy to imagine what this freedom will turn into for him. The B Object will not allow him to slip away into oblivion, believing in success. He will remember and understand: his 'triumph' turned out to be empty; he achieved zero. It will be his payback – disappointment and shame. The payback for the 'knight,' the lot of the 'champion of karma.'"

"So, you're talking about your Objects again," Elsa narrowed her eyes. "Being too clever again, dancing ritual dances?"

I barely stopped myself from shouting at her. After a pause, I asked coldly, "Why don't you want to understand me? I am not trying to be clever; I don't give a damn about B Objects, all their groupings and the metabrane itself. I want to find, meet Brevich and shoot him with a long-barreled pistol. And this desire will remain with me forever!"

"And then what – disappointment?" Elsa asked, refusing to back down. "Or do you expect a different fate?"

"Whatever," I waved my hand, pressing my forehead against the glass. "I don't care. It's clear to me now: the only essence of freedom is that you accept, you agree to accept disappointment in what you do – in advance. You accept future shame for yourself – otherwise, it will torture you in the present. Only in this sense are you truly free."

"That may very well be," Elsa nodded pensively, and I felt I was no longer angry with her.

"Sit down, eat something," she added. "Do you want me to make fried eggs or toast?"

I refused, finally tore myself away from the window, paced around the room a few times and, in some sort of exhaustion, sat down on the chair next to her. Elsa drank her coffee, gazing ahead intently. The crease on her face had not gone. And she was all tense, like a spring.

"Well, we can report to our Nestors – our joint task has been accomplished," I said, forcing myself. "The intersection of our lives – admittedly, very indirect – has been found. So now what?"

"Now…" Elsa turned to me. Her gaze was cold and serious. "Now we can sum up. If you want me to do it, then okay, I will: that man, Ivan, undoubtedly did carry out his 'plan.' This means both he and your Tina went off into the same 'nonexistence' at almost the same time as you did. I, of course, understand little about this science of yours, but it seems to me that your destinies – with or without Objects – are so intertwined that it is difficult to divide them. And as for my fate – no, it is separated. No matter how hard I try, there is no way to connect it with yours. Because my lips become a blur when I speak. Because I don't have a real body. Because my scent is a fake."

"You want to say…" I began.

"There's nothing I want to say!" Elsa suddenly exploded. "This is how you want it yourself – *what* do you want yourself?"

She turned away in anger, remained silent for a few minutes and then continued quietly, "By the way, I remember you told me – time flows differently here and there. Thus, we don't really know – who ended up where and when. Ages also may happen to be different – older, younger – it's funny, isn't it?…

"Actually," she added after another pause, "time is a strange thing, but for some reason it can never be used as an excuse to back down…" And she shook her head, "I cannot believe I myself am saying this to you!"

Soon I went to my room and, before my session with Nestor, I sat alone, collecting my thoughts. I imagined Tina, picturing her as a captive, reliving her captivity – as if trying to empathize with at least a part of her confusion, her fear. Then my mind went astray. The fabric of the cocoon was torn apart; I now seemed to see Ivan Brevich, sitting opposite, in minute detail. I saw his sunken eyes, his flabby face and drooping cheeks, I heard his drunken mutter. And I recalled his gaze – the one with which he had been looking at his woman, somehow taking Tina for her… I saw an enemy in front of me – yes, now I had a sworn enemy. An extremely personalized one; he had a name. A name, a consciousness, a memory, a B Object…

And I was thinking, again and again, about my enemy, feeling the hate heavily turning inside me. It had no boundaries; it overshadowed 'Theo's theory,' the connections of destinies and the fundamental ellipsoid. The power of mathematics faded and failed next to it. Next to it and my desire for revenge.

Only the image of Brevich, growing in my inner eye, was not inferior to the scale of my hatred. He was huge, Brevich; his confidence that things would happen as he wanted seemed to build a rampart around him. His willingness to sacrifice everything released energy of the most sinister sort. I imagined its vortex, like a looming tornado; it might be I could even derive its formula. I could lock into the square brackets, place under the integral symbol the true nature of the self-proclaimed "knight." His resolve to subdue the principle on which all causality is based, to affirm power over it, to use it for his own purposes. He wanted exactly this, and he had made sacrifices for it...

"Ha-ha," I curled my lips caustically, "how naive!" And I meant the two of us: both Brevich and myself. His naivety was leading to a dead end; I saw it – but scribbling formulas also wasn't letting me reach much further. Formalization, perhaps, helped to extract the essence – but it greatly diluted the feel of life. All the formulas were flawed; they could not restore fairness or bring justice – in any world. They couldn't throw a weight off one's shoulders – or, for instance, return a woman, without whom life was not worth living. Yes, for instance... That's the instance of Brevich – and what is mine? Elsa argued that for me Tina was just a means. What are, really, the means and – the true goal, the meaning?...

Then Nestor appeared. "You can rejoice," I said coldly, instead of greeting him. "Your choice of dreams about Ivan Brevich has been justified one hundred percent."

"What are you talking about?" Nestor asked, perplexed.

"About the finale, the point of culmination!" I chuckled angrily. "About starting at the end and moving back toward the beginning, as you once suggested... Well, the news is: Elsa and I did find what was expected of us. Our memories intersected – with Brevich and Tina, no matter how surprising it is that all our lives are connected together. And, nevertheless, the connection is undoubtful!"

Then I briefly recounted to him Elsa's dream. Nestor pondered, bowing his head, and said, "Yes, it's hard not to be surprised. But on the other hand, this testifies in favor of our roommate-selection algorithms...

In any case…" He thrust out his chest and adopted an official tone. "In any case, now everything is simplified, is it not? I can put on my task list the tick everyone has deserved – you, me, your Elsa…" He paused, looked at me intently and asked, "This intersection you've found, it doesn't change anything as far the *main thing* is concerned, right? By the way, have you made your mind up in that regard? What have you decided?"

I ignored the question and said, "I have a request. Would you be able to make an inquiry – given my special status? Or even without my status: Can you try to find Tina – here, in Quarantine, or somewhere in your world – using my descriptions; I can systematize and clarify them for you? I will gather all the details together – there will be a multifaceted, detailed portrait."

"Like a police report…" Nestor quipped and snapped, "No. New bearers of B Objects cannot be identified using the features of the former ones – all the more so by private request. The inviolable secret of the past, you know, the right to a completely independent future. Maybe some of the newcomers do not want to be found in this way – no matter who is looking for them, even the close ones. *Former* close ones – are you sure that the women from your first life are so unreservedly striving to meet you again? Including your Tina."

"So that's how it is," I said thoughtfully. "Well… I understand the logic – and I don't have any more questions." The words "naive, naive" spun in my head again. And behind every naivety I sensed an impenetrable wall.

"If you don't have any questions of your own, maybe you can answer mine?" Nestor asked softly but persistently. "Have you decided anything – with regards to my recent proposal?"

"Oh, the proposal…" I muttered with deliberate indifference. "I need to think more, read the articles."

Nestor threw me a sharp look, pursed his lips and nodded, "Read, read." And then added, "Well, allow me to express to you my official – and personally sincere – condolences for Tina, who was evidently very precious to you. I regret that her first life was cut so short; you probably wanted it to have been different. Although now you understand: one never knows. Whether this would have been good or bad, I mean…"

"Thank you for your sympathy," I grunted and closed my eyes. Nestor was guilty of nothing, but continuing talking with him was unbearable.

CHAPTER 37

WHEN I LOOKED at the screen again, it was already empty. "The pro-posal…" spun in my head. "*Mierda!*" For some reason, my irritation with Nestor would not pass. I had to pull myself together – no, Nestor was not my enemy. I knew the enemy; there was no confusing him with anyone.

"What do you want yourself?" I repeated Elsa's words aloud. And fell silent, not letting the answer rise to the surface. My thoughts were in disarray; most of the day still lay ahead; it was going to stretch out far too long. I did not know how to spend it, what to do with myself. The main thing had already happened – so now what? Never in my life had I had that much free time. On the contrary, there had never been enough of it…

I took a few of the articles from the table, placed them in a neat pile, meticulously aligning the edges. I looked at the pile for a minute or two, then, surprising even myself, hurled the lot into the far corner of the room. They scattered like leaves in the wind. "*Mierda,*" I muttered quietly, and struck the table with my hand, hitting the touchpad. The black shutters slid over the window, the lights went out and the bedroom plunged into darkness. I began to jab randomly at the buttons, cursing under my breath. Then I jumped up, collected the photocopies from the floor and walked to the door, leaving the room in a purple half darkness, with gothic ciphers on the wallpaper.

Elsa was sitting on the couch with a book. I nodded to her, looked away and, without uttering a word, walked to the elevator. It was wrong; I should at least have said something – my roommate was certainly not my foe. But I didn't want to talk at all.

It was windy outside but warm. I wandered along the seafront for a while, speeding up suddenly, then slowing down again. I walked without noticing anyone, almost like in Bangkok, in my past life, after my argument with Tina. But no, this was not Bangkok with its wild mix of smells, colors and vices. I wasn't sweating; my clothes weren't sticking to my body. My body itself didn't really exist. And, most importantly, there was no Tina.

Then my surroundings gradually began to penetrate my consciousness. I looked around, peered at the oncoming pedestrians, tried to read their faces. I was probably looking too persistently – they turned away from me, some of the men frowning threateningly in response. I just grinned grimly to myself – maybe the fact of me being here, with them, was a caprice of the Cloud, a consequence of our Objects being in the same cluster? Maybe even later, during the new life, my fate will somehow depend on those who are now idly walking along the seafront? Maybe their whims and intentions will mix in with mine, will be getting in my way, or else pushing me somewhere? Or maybe not at all – I had no idea how and why the Quarantiners ended up here together. In any case, no matter what lay ahead, I did not care about them now. Their phantom entities didn't interest me in the slightest – and most probably none of them would want to know about the field of the conscions and its vortices. For them, like Elsa, just the result was important – and even then only to those who were capable of thinking about such matters as future lives. About the preservation of their memories, their unique personalities; about the journey of consciousness from one world to another...

I went down to the water and wandered among the rocks and scattered remains of seaweed. Then I sat down on a smooth boulder, warmed by the sun, and for a long time looked at the waves, trying to contemplate the cypher of their chaos, which is not chaos. I sat without moving, immersed in a trance, feeling something ripening within me – an urge, a desire? The cumulative vector of a multitude of destinies interlinked with mine? Or the fruit of my own free will, ha-ha?

I was brought out of my stupor by the sound – the chimes of a clock.

Then the loudspeakers, set up along the beach, came to life – announcing there was little time left until the evening counseling sessions. I didn't move – I just did not need another meeting with Nestor now. He might not be my enemy, but I still had nothing to discuss with him; it wouldn't make any sense.

The waves, however, were no longer fascinating me; their fragile magic had collapsed. After sitting for another half an hour, I got up and walked up the steps to the deserted promenade. Deserted, but not empty: a strange-looking car moved slowly along the seafront. Observing it, I realized it was an automated refuse vehicle collecting the bins standing by the rail and replacing them with empty ones. I caught up with it and glanced inside – there was no driver; only the lights under the windshield blinked.

I walked beside it for a few minutes and then, obeying an inexplicable impulse, glanced around stealthily, squeezed in and sat down on a plastic seat. It was cramped in the cabin; my knees squeezed against the front partition, but I put up with it – no one promised it was going to be comfortable. I did all this without any definite aim – not really knowing what I wanted to achieve.

At first, we barely crawled along, stopping occasionally; and then, probably having reached maximum load, the vehicle picked up speed. It wouldn't be easy to jump out of it now – and I didn't try, just sat and waited. Little by little the buildings became lower and shabbier, the entire area looking increasingly uninhabited. Afterward, squat blocks, looking like warehouses, stretched out – the road looped between them, moving away from the sea, and suddenly ended in front of a gate. The car had stopped. I knew I needed to seize the moment and get away, but for some reason, I hesitated – and then it was too late.

The gates swung open, and we drove into a large hangar with no lights. I just managed to catch a glimpse of some indistinct structures on both sides – high iron cabinets, narrow stairs between them – and that was it, the doors closed; complete darkness enveloped me. The vehicle started, accelerated and rushed off somewhere. I became frightened, then seriously terrified. My ears were ringing; I could barely stop myself from screaming; then suddenly a whistling signal rang out, the car braked sharply, and I let out a miserable wail, clinging to the seat with all my might. We turned to the right and stopped a minute later. A dim light switched on – it was coming from the ceiling and walls of a small room, more like a chamber in which my automated refuse collector barely fit. Directly in front of the windshield, there was a dark screen – the same as the one in my bedroom. Soon it came to life, and on it appeared an unfamiliar face with no hair or eyebrows and a smooth high forehead.

"Violation of the instructions," the man on the screen said casually. "Identification. What is your name? What is the name of your roommate? Do you remember the number of your housing unit?"

His lips barely moved; his eyes did not blink. I cleared my throat and answered his questions. It would have been silly to argue or get angry – I was obviously in the wrong. Having listened to me, the man nodded and disappeared from the screen, and in a quarter of an hour, my Nestor arrived in his place.

"I'm curious: you wanted to escape?" he asked and laughed his strange laugh. "The Count of Monte Cristo woke up inside you?"

I was sullenly silent. Nestor gave another giggle and continued, more seriously, "I must say that sneaking into the utility sector is a dangerous thing to do. For your Quarantine entity, it would have been fatal. It's good we have such a reliable control system here."

"Okay, I'll take note," I muttered with difficulty. For some reason, my tongue would not obey me.

Nestor bowed his head, carefully examining me, and asked, "Do you want to go back? Or maybe you *don't* want to go back? However, nothing else is on offer. The procedure is completely clear on that."

He covered his eyes, rubbed the bridge of his nose with his fingers and suddenly glared at me again: "Well, what have you decided? I'm talking about my proposal, of course."

"I'll give you an answer the day after tomorrow," I said dryly, feeling his persistence tiring me.

Nestor nodded and said in a bored, grumbling tone, "Well, you'll have to wait now. It'll take a while, but you only have yourself to blame."

The wait in the cramped room really did drag on – even my fake back-side seemed to go numb. A few times I tried to call out to somebody, but to no avail – there was no response; the screen remained dead. Only when

I got out of the car and tried to go around it, squeezing with difficulty between its frame and the walls, did a mechanical voice start, repeating over and over, "Return to the vehicle. Return to the vehicle..."

I got back in, and the voice went quiet. It was hot, stuffy; fake perspiration even seemed to break out on my back and forehead. I waited and waited and waited. It was unclear to me whether hours or even a day had passed; I had lost all track of time. My sense of place had also collapsed – it was like being suspended in a vacuum, locked in an iron box. Locked in a dungeon... I felt sorry for myself; my eyes were stinging. My fake body almost began to shed fake tears. My understanding – prefixed with a "mis" – of reality, of the entire boundless cosmos, had reached the point of absurdity. I felt, more acutely than ever, the alien nature of space, its vastness, power. I reflected on my measureless smallness and – suddenly I realized this absurdity was precisely what I needed. Within it and out of it something vital was crystallizing – the very thing that I had tried so hard to read in the chaos of the waves, that I struggled to formulate, that I had to decide – for myself, for everyone else, despite and thanks to everyone else. Now I knew what my mind needed to make a final small step – the lack of space, the almost complete immobility. The restraint of my freedom – to the extreme, to the limit toward which the place of Quarantine converged...

The same refuse vehicle drove me back to my block – in the dark, along a completely deserted seafront. I muttered to myself all the way, "You fool, fool!" – embarrassed at my weakness, at my listless stupidity. Yes, it's easy to lose your way in the blindness of "insight" – especially when you want it yourself. When you are almost happy to give up, surrender to the inevitable, to capitulate before it. And then revel in your small, parochial suffering – from one life to the next. It all seems so simple, and there's always a door visibly marked with an "Exit" sign, but getting out is not that easy. In your B Object – perhaps as a result of the regrouping, ha-ha – the incompleteness of your actions pulsates stubbornly, even if hopelessness seems to reign. That's how destiny works, how the Cloud connects your life with the lives of the others. That's how they – the Cloud and destiny – link all your past with all your future: throwing you rope ladders from impregnable rocks, building hanging bridges without handrails, luring and scaring with bright lights, with pyrotechnics of emotions and feelings, with flashes of local supernovae of your "ego"…

The car braked sharply at my front door. I went up in the elevator, passed through the empty living room and sat down, simply fell into my chair. Sluggishly, I thought to myself that I might be hungry but banished the thought and fell into a dream. I slept like an infant deeply and heavily until the morning.

The next day, Elsa greeted me with an ironic grin. "My counselor said you got lost yesterday," she said with exaggerated empathy. "They found you somewhere near the dump, he told me… Did you fall into a reverie and go the wrong way? Or were you trying to escape? From me? From your Nestor? From the whole shebang?"

I tried to laugh it off, but my jokes sounded inept. Fortunately, Elsa did not insist on an answer. She put some fresh toast on the table; we quickly ate breakfast and both got on with our own thing.

Nestor was similarly indifferent during our midday session – as if he wasn't interested in what I would say the next day. Our meeting lasted no time; then I went back to the living room and saw Elsa dressed for a walk – in a light raincoat and with an umbrella in her hands.

"Well," she said. "Let's go out and talk? It's drizzling on the seafront, but what are trifles like that to us…"

Soon we were wandering along the wet pavement of the promenade. Elsa held my arm firmly, looking at me sideways with very serious eyes; then she suddenly asked in practically the same words as Nestor, "So, what have you decided?"

"What do you mean?" I said somewhat disingenuously.

"Oh, that's how you want to do it…" Elsa sighed. "Okay, have it your way; I'll say it for you. Otherwise, perhaps you'll continue to have doubts and go running off to garbage dumps so that a whole team of Nestors will have to catch you and fetch you back to safety."

She fell silent – we passed by the street singer, sitting near the balustrade. He was covered with a huge raincoat; next to him, under a smaller cape, stood his guitar, leaning against the railing. I nodded to him, but he did not respond, completely lost in himself.

We walked on a few steps in silence, then Elsa said angrily, referring to the singer, "There's something strange, not quite right with him. I don't know about you, but I don't believe him anymore!"

I made a vague sound. "So," she continued. "Let's play a guessing game. Who is in the house and who is not? Whose turn is it to be 'it'? Who didn't hide, and whose fault was that?"

"I don't understand," I glanced at her.

"It's a pity I have to explain everything to you like a child," Elsa shook her head. "But that's all right. I'll say it more directly: you won't be able to create a theory of destinies without having lived out your own. You won't come up with an equation for karma without having sensed to the fullest how your karma is whirling you round, what this bitch of a universe really wants from you. Do you already know the answers? No, you don't. And your scribblings on paper aren't going to help you."

Her voice shook slightly; her fingers squeezed my arm, holding the umbrella, with a steely grip. I could feel her nails sticking into my forearm, even through the dense fabric of my jacket.

"I've been formulating this thought for a long time," Elsa confessed with a nervous laugh. "You see how many smart-aleck words it contains. But everything could be put much simpler: Your Asian believed you and in you – can you get away from this? That man, Ivan, deprived the two of you of each other – and you, what, forgave him? You have unfinished business – yes, you're lucky. I, for example, don't. I don't really have any-where to hurry off to!"

She gripped my arm even harder, then abruptly let go, turned away and muttered, as she had the morning before, "I can't believe I myself am saying this to you…"

Then we just carried on walking in the drizzling rain. The tension between us had disappeared as if we had just crossed over the summit of a peak, a rocky ridge with sharp jagged edges – and now we were slowly descending the slope. Something was spinning in my head – all the same familiar things, concerning enemies and revenge, and great accomplishments, for which you always need someone beside you. And also – what I had realized myself, what I had decided in the refuse vehicle. I could have said a lot to Elsa in reply – or at least I could have agreed with her – but for some reason, I felt that any words of mine would be inappropriate. They would simplify her effort, which was really difficult for her.

I just glanced at her sideways, remembering the crease on her face, her unforgiving eyes. I wanted something to happen right now – let the buildings collapse, the sea rise. I would have been so incredibly happy to do something for Elsa, to protect her, to defend, to save... But no, reality remained quiet and calm; it didn't want to help.

Elsa suddenly stopped, turned to me and exclaimed, "Well, why are you silent?" And, immediately, she drew me on farther, increasing her pace and speaking again.

"They probably won't like me pushing you away," she smiled wanly. "But what can I do; I have to be honest with you. I have to be a good girl – I still want to get to heaven sometime. Quarantine resembles 'heaven' to a point, but, let's agree, not quite."

We walked faster and faster; I was barely able to keep up with her. "I've been through so much with you... So many different stages," Elsa was saying. "You are the only man I have ever had this with. And there were moments when you were mine – even if only for a few hours, minutes. So, that's probably what it means to have 'a life fully lived'?

"So, now I know what 'fully lived' is," she murmured. "And the depths – now I know what there is in your depths. Nothing fucking good, that's what... You see, I just started to believe everything between you and me could be *for real* – well, as far as it's possible in this place, this *fake* place. And now I, on my own, have to do a terrible thing: push you away from myself, give you up to another one, who for some reason has more rights over you. And it's not even clear where this 'other one' is and whether you'll find her at all..."

On the left, from the direction of the sea, a gust of wind blew in, almost tearing the umbrella out of my hands. The spokes bent back, the black fabric flapped, light rain splattered into our faces. For a minute we fought with the umbrella, then the wind died down as quickly as it had risen, and we continued on. Elsa spoke more calmly, "Well, whatever. Here, in Quarantine, there can be no great losses anyway. Even virginity can't be lost here. And there is a logic in everything: as you explained to me – our bodies, our lives, are only needed to accumulate experiences in these Objects of yours. So that's what I will be doing – accumulating them, I mean – hopefully, there will be many. Even here – with one roommate, with another…"

She paused, then added, "Some of my future stories might turn out to be happy ones, right? I must admit: living through everything here with you, I felt I could indeed be happy at some time – seriously, really happy. And it is also clear to me now – you can only find true happiness after death. At least after one death!"

We reached the openwork gazebo with wet, empty benches and turned back. After taking a few steps, Elsa stopped, hugged herself and said, "Go home: I'll take a little walk on my own. No, no, I don't need an umbrella, I am good like this…" – and she quickly walked away. Soon she headed toward the stairs and began to descend to the sea. Without turning around, she waved her hand to me – as if to say, go, go…

I didn't see any more of her for the rest of the day. Having climbed up to the apartment, I looked around the living room, made some coffee for myself, took a sip and emptied the cup into the sink – it tasted terribly bitter. On the table was one of the articles – something about the quantization of gravity. I took it, went to my bedroom and sat down in my armchair – but instead of reading, I just looked at the wall opposite with its silent screen, thinking about everything at once.

The evening session with Nestor began exactly at five. He appeared with the same expression of indifference, as if to show that no one was rushing me, that he had all the patience in the world. After greeting me dryly, he asked, "How was your day? Lousy weather, isn't it?"

"Yes, yes…" I agreed absently. I wanted to tell him – as my counselor, as my *friend* – about my talk with Elsa and how she had walked away from me into the rain. About the street singer on the empty seafront and his guitar sheltering under a raincoat.

"Nestor…" I said and suddenly, surprising myself, asked, "Tell me, Nestor, how does knowledge of their new lives change people? You have plenty of experience; you see many of them at the crossroads. You witness how they become convinced that their former lives weren't really the end, that the first is followed by another and others afterward. They begin to firmly believe in that – without any further doubt or speculation."

Nestor narrowed his eyes, "So you want to philosophize? Well, it does calm the nerves. Although I wouldn't say you look too anxious anyway..."

He paused, chewing his lips as usual, and said, rather reluctantly, "My answer will surprise you. On the whole, it seems to me this knowledge makes a person better. I've thought about it; I have to admit – I've even written something on this matter."

"Makes them better – in what way?" I persisted.

"I repeat: *on the whole*," said Nestor with emphasis. "Because there are 'believers 'and there are 'thinkers' – and nothing can change the views and minds of the mass of believers; they're hopeless. And those who dare to produce a thought suddenly understand: you cannot run away from anything – ever. The B Object will not allow it, so it's better not to spend the time allotted to you by making things worse... And if there's more of this time than was commonly believed, it should only increase your focus, your sense of responsibility."

"Is it that simple?" I asked incredulously.

"What is there to complicate in this instance?" Nestor shrugged. "In your world, you tried to refine human nature by all possible means, and nothing worked – but give that human the knowledge that his existence continues, that everything is not in vain... Give him the confidence that this knowledge is not a trick, and he discovers amazing resources in himself. He begins to look at things differently – he may even sense some sort of connection with the universe, albeit only intuitively, without having the first idea about the field of the conscions. He even feels an interdependence – of destinies, lives, of everyone with everyone – despite never hearing about the Cloud and the clustering of Objects. As a result, he, all of a sudden, starts to believe that by giving and not consuming, he generates something real, an almost material outgoing flow that somehow affects the lives of others, adding significance and substance to them. His tiny attempts pushing others to make their own – and all this, by the way, is perceived without any mathematics. It sounds like a naive humanism, but this naivety suddenly gains an indulgence, an undeniable meaning..."

"Well, but still..." I interrupted. "A complication does suggest itself here – I mean nonlinearity, an explicit feedback. Fate first beckons you with a carrot, then teases you with a red rag, and you rush off – chasing after or intersecting, colliding. It lures you into a trap, where there is nothing but memory and pain – and immediately switches the means and the target, forcing you to move on… Nonlinear dynamics in its pure form, isn't that so?"

"What else is new?" Nestor snorted. "It's as clear as day: the feedback cycle – from hopelessness to an illusory goal, from seeming chance to one's own, so-called personal, unswerving aspiration… One can also speculate with regards to B Objects – to call on all those 'accidental' acquaintances to answer. Many of them, sooner or later, become unnecessary for your conscion vortex, not being able to enrich it anymore – and you free yourself, push them away. Yes, you push them away – or maybe not…"

Nestor paused, then waved his hand and added a little wearily, "And of course, speaking about meanings, all kinds of toys, treasure chests of riches, are left behind the brackets when going from one life to another. It also helps to add to the ranks – if you look from the side of the minority – or, if to glance from the other side, drop out of the ranks. Break out of the matrix, from unnamed but very firm agreements with society, from the stereotypes imposed by it. Human nature cannot be changed rapidly – yet, here, in our world, the power of public opinion is weaker. It's no longer so obvious what to consider as 'success' – that's a step forward, don't you agree? Some other things get transformed too – for instance, fears. It is fearful to accumulate disappointments and defeats; it's terrible to be a loser from one life to the next. Or to know that you are not doing what you do best – even if nobody believes in what you do best, even if you are laughed at by your own family. Well and…" Nestor moved forward, his voice somehow becoming thinner, his chin more angular. "And the fear of death: it becomes completely different from what it used to seem. Now it is nothing more than the sublimation of the two other things: the fear of idling and the fear of losing. And everything is intertwined: you aspire, they expect something from you, then they make fun of you, not really grasping what you have managed to achieve. And you accept it as the price of freedom from one of your fears – and immediately remember the second one and think with yearning: where is she, the one who cannot love you with all her heart, believing that only those who are near can be loved... I guess I answered your question? End of the session. The next answer is yours!"

I nodded at the blank screen, got up, walked over to the window. Looked at my reflection in the glass for a long time, thinking – and what is my own fear? Afterward, despite the late hour, I went into the living room, hoping to see Elsa. The room was empty, however; then I brought a clean notebook and pencil from the bedroom and sat down at the dining table. I began to write – and there were no equations, no formulas in my writing. I didn't think about my theories anymore – just as I didn't care what was going to happen to me next.

I was repeatedly crossing out what I had written, crumpling up the pages. I was wrinkling my forehead and starting again. And so it went on until late into the night.

CHAPTER 38

THE MORNING FOUND me half asleep and lethargic. I went to the bathroom, washed my face. Then I rotated my arms, even did a few stretches and squats. My phantom body responded as if it really had been refreshed; my head became clearer. I listened attentively to my inner self. There, inside, everything remained the same. My determination had not gone away.

I dressed carefully and went into the living room. There, I Immediately saw Elsa and could not restrain a surprised exclamation: her appearance had changed. Her dark-blonde hair had turned a bright red, and it altered everything – her smile, the expression of her face and her eyes.

"I just thought you might like it," she said, a little embarrassed. "I could have just had a streak like hers, but I decided to be original. And besides, a whole head of hair is more than a single streak…"

She walked around the room, then opened the refrigerator, took out a carton of milk and smiled, "It was not easy figuring out how to do the dyeing. I pestered my Nestor; at first, he refused to tell me, but then he relented and gave me precise instructions. He probably thought I was doing it for him. I, of course, didn't mention that's not exactly true. It wouldn't be wise to worsen our relations even more. Will you have eggs or just coffee? For some reason, I'm not hungry at all."

"Wait a minute!" I exclaimed. "Now I know how it should be…"

I ran to the bedroom, grabbed my notebook and crossed out the first line. "Now I know," I repeated to myself, writing another one in its place, hiding it from Elsa's view with my shoulder. And then I passed the notebook to her: "Here, I also tried to do something for you. Of course, my effort didn't come out as well as yours…"

Elsa quietly read aloud, "'One day I stole a red squirrel…'" and looked up at me, "Is this a poem? To me?"

I nodded, now tormented by awkwardness myself. Turning to the window, I mumbled, "Sorry, it has no rhyme."

Elsa read the rest in silence, came up to me, touched my hand and said, "I have never seen a more beautiful poem!"

I was nearly as thrilled to hear this as when Nestor told me about the universality of my "face of thought."

"Can I have it?" Elsa asked, and without waiting for an answer, she tore the page out of the notebook. Then we drank a cup of coffee and went to her bedroom to check the day's weather.

Beyond the window was a downpour of almost floodlike proportions. A sky the color of lead hung over the promenade and sea, dropping vertical jets of water. They stabbed the boardwalk, like steel-tipped arrows, splashing, gouging and turning into a muddy stream, raging alongside the balustrade. The horizon was hidden by a wall of water.

We silently looked out of the window, then Elsa asked in a very calm voice, "Are you leaving?"

"Yes," I replied, just as calmly, without emotion.

"When?" She turned to me.

"Maybe today," I said. "Immediately after the afternoon session, if I'm allowed. I don't know what the rules are on this matter."

"Yes," Elsa said quietly. "You never know with the rules on that. Like in our former life – basically, nothing has changed." Then she shivered and added, nodding at the rain, "It's good we don't need to search for a reason for skipping our walk today."

I kept silent. Elsa put the palm of her hand to the windowpane and examined her graceful fingers for several minutes. Then she removed her hand and said, "Forgive me for being a bit hysterical yesterday. I just felt I *needed* to tell you everything… Probably, this is what I really should have done for you; my red hair doesn't count."

I nodded, swallowing back a lump in my throat. Elsa grinned, "They told me – try to become his friend. Well, I tried as best I could – didn't I? They should appreciate that; in my opinion, I honestly earned my points. Who is to blame that at the same time, I wanted something else, wanted more? And I still do – no matter what."

The rain hit the window – likely the wind was rising. The jets were getting thinner and meaner.

"I wonder," Elsa muttered, "what my next roommate will be like? I'd prefer a tall, dark-haired man with strong hands... Do you think the fact that this is what I want will help me? You see, I can't just ask my Nestor for this directly!"

"It may well help," I responded as easily as I could. And joked, "I hope, 'having sensed' your desire, the field of the conscions will shuffle the pack as you wish."

"It's about time it did," Elsa quipped back. "Is it finally capable of making an effort? After all, I've never asked it for anything – I've only taken a few words on a tablecloth with me into my new lives. I can't be reproached for being selfish."

I put my hand around her waist, "I think you are the most unselfish roommate one could imagine. You made me breakfast every day."

"Yes," Elsa narrowed her eyes, "and you – you are self-centered, like all men. You used me – at least my fried eggs – to propel you to ever greater heights and horizons. Just like your Asian – without her, as far as I understand, not everything might have worked out."

"That's true," I agreed. "As a result, I have an accomplishment that can't be taken away, and she – she ended up with only a memory of us together. I admit it's not fair."

"That's why you feel guilty," Elsa sighed. "That's why you run off to garbage dumps and are now leaving Quarantine for good!

"No offence; I'm not being serious," she added. "I'm not angry with her at all. I think of your Tina warmly, even trying to imagine what she saw at the last moment before her death. What flashed before her eyes – probably the face of her unborn child? I've heard they look like aliens..."

The rain did not subside. After staying for a while by the window, we returned to the living room and sat on the sofa. Close, but a little apart,

404 | Vadim Babenko

not touching each other. Elsa picked up her book lying on the armrest but did not open it; she sat, turning away slightly, stubbornly pursing her lips. I glanced at her sideways – at the chiseled line of her cheekbones, her slightly upturned chin and her shock of bright-red hair.

"Actually, I'd like to become friends with her," Elsa continued in the same tone, as if there had been no pause. "We could go to the gym together, to the hairdresser, to the café. Maybe we would open some kind of business – a shop or a salon. Or we could just meet sometimes to chat, as girlfriends do – and we'd discuss men as well. She'd tell me what you are like in bed."

I laughed, even though I didn't feel joyful.

"You know," Elsa sighed, "I'll ask them not to give me a roommate right away. How can I live with a new roommate after you? I want to spend some time on my own – at least a couple of days. Or maybe even three days…" And she added angrily, "If you want to look at the clock, go ahead – you don't need to feel sorry for me."

I looked up. The hands were approaching twelve. A shiver ran down my spine; I leaned forward, resting my elbows on my knees.

Elsa moved closer, touched me with her thigh. "Right now," I said with difficulty, "I need to do three equally impossible things. To part with you; to announce to Nestor that I'm leaving – you could say, betraying him; and to actually leave, of my own accord, to no one knows where. I don't know how to do all this; I'm ashamed and scared at the same time."

"Get up," said Elsa. "Come with me." She took my hand and led me to the door of my bedroom. "Go and do this. Do this well."

And I stepped inside and closed the door behind me. In the second that it took me to walk to my chair, my mind became aware with the utmost clarity of many facts at once. For example, how I was going to miss my roommate – in any of my future lives. Or – that phantom closeness yearns in the same way as a living one. That it is just as painful, as unfair as it had been with Tina. Or – that I could not have done otherwise.

Looking at the blank screen, I also thought that our decisions inevitably cause pain to someone. And, at the same time, we ourselves experience it no less. This was the oldest of truths, but it revealed itself to me as if it were new.

As soon as he appeared and nodded curtly, my counselor asked without preamble, "Well, what is your answer?"

"Nestor," I said, looking him straight in the eye, "I want to leave Quarantine. I want to do it right now."

His face froze, but he did not look away. He kept silent for a while; then he bent his head and slowly said, "I confess, you have finally managed to surprise me. To surprise me for real: I understood you were having doubts, weighing up the pros and cons – and yet I was sure you would give me a different reply."

"Why?" I raised my eyebrows.

Nestor did not seem to notice my question. "I was sure – even when I saw you crouched in the cab of that refuse car," he said just as slowly. "Even knowing that once the process of escape has begun, it is difficult to stop it…

"I understood the past was pulling you back," he continued, rubbing his cheek with his hand. "I saw your introspection, the torment of your conscience, hanging like a heavy weight. But all the same: I firmly believed that, once the anger and confusion had passed, you would make a different choice. I assumed your conscience would give in at the last moment."

"But why, why did you think so?" I asked again and added, "Of course, I'm very sorry to disappoint you…"

"Disappoint?" Nestor grimaced. "Well, well… And what do you think I should have thought? Bearing in mind, for example, the curiosity of a scientist, the need for a talent to actualize itself… The scale of the task that awaited you… Of course, predetermination cannot be fooled, but sometimes you can get a respite, a break. This is no jaunt in a refuse vehicle; it is something completely real. You had a chance – such a rare, such a precise, unequivocal chance!"

He rubbed his face again and then said reluctantly, barely forcing out the words, "I hope you are aware of all the consequences of your decision, all its meanings, its side effects? You will have to go through childhood and adolescence, to grow up, to live and live – hoping that your destiny will somehow intersect with hers or his… I suppose you feel, albeit subconsciously, the boundless naivety of such a hope – having in mind the grouping of the B Objects and everything that happens in the Cloud

– a naivety comparable to your enemy Brevich's belief that things would always turn out the way he wanted. You are adjusting the probability of facts according to the yearning insistence of your faith, your desire – this is just the opposite of what a man of science should do. You…" And Nestor enunciated each word with the palm of his hand, "You are acting like some poorly educated – I'm not afraid of using this word – barbarian!"

"Well," I murmured, "I have heard that we often resemble our worst enemies. Otherwise, we'd be lacking common ground for hostility. As for my choice, I didn't have much of a choice. I simply felt I had to do the only right thing."

Nestor did not respond; he might not have even heard, did not want to hear me. He was reiterating his own point – monotonously, stubbornly: "And I also thought that, besides rational arguments, your fears would stop you. The ones we talked about: for example, the fear of never meeting your Tina – do you understand how scant the chance of such an event is? Or the fear of failure – who knows what will happen in your second life, who you will become, what you will be able to achieve? And then: Are you one hundred percent sure there will even be a second life? Where you are going? From what, from where? What this place really is, the place of Quarantine? Have you ever thought that this, perhaps, is basically all that's left for you? What if Quarantine is a computer simulation or, say, the last fantasy of your fading mind, which has been artificially prolonged – you may be in a coma from which you'll never wake up? And still, you've decided to take the risk…"

He paused and somewhat ridiculously, angrily, threw his hands in the air – as if signaling he had run out of arguments. As if showing he had nothing else to contradict my stupidity.

But now, it was me who had the arguments. "Yes," I said, shrugging. "All this, one way or another, has occurred to me from time to time. Yes, there were fears – and it was you who helped me overcome them. And I am very grateful to you, Nestor!"

My counselor focused his gaze on me. He stared at my face intently, then, gruffly, somewhat arrogantly, asked, "In what way? Let me know, if you'd be so kind, how I helped you?"

"Through your example," I spread my hands. "What else? Through echoes of your history, its shadows. Everything that made me understand that I, in some hardly formulated sense, am by no means a pioneer. There were others before me – for instance, someone was engaged in cosmology, wrote literary passages, yearning for a woman waiting in some unknown space-time, tried to break out of the social matrix, was laughed at by his own family… If it weren't for him, I would perhaps have been afraid quite differently."

Nestor was suddenly embarrassed, turned his head, began to hide his eyes. Then, little by little, he mastered himself. He groaned, cleared his throat and said wearily, "Let's assume we have outlined our positions – in general. I understand your motivation. Not that I accept or like it…"

For a while we sat in silence, both deep in thought, then he said, "Well… 'Right now' won't work; you'll have to wait. As with your rescue from the utility zone, the procedure is clearly defined; it cannot be speeded up. But we can initiate it immediately, why not."

"I'll probably need some special sanction?" I asked. "*Your* sanction – I remember, you said you are responsible for assessing my 'recovery,' so to speak, my suitability for a new life."

"Yes, it is needed," Nestor nodded, "but in this case, it is a mere formality. I have no reason to deny you the approval. If I did, I would probably be suspected of some personal motive…"

"And what about my enemy?" I persisted. "You know that I have an enemy."

Nestor frowned, "You mean revenge? Don't worry, this intention of yours is completely innocent. *All* your intentions and you yourself are completely innocent, Theo, whether or not you think otherwise. So…" He folded his hands in front of him and again rested his gaze on me. "So, it's goodbye; we can start the process. And that means… Goodbye!"

"You've just said goodbye to me twice," I muttered. "Although it's not customary to make long farewells here."

I didn't want to poke fun at him; I felt quite uneasy myself. It was clear: the procedure, having begun, could not be stopped. Until the very end.

"Yes, it is not customary…" Nestor agreed and again became pensive for a while. His shoulders sank; even his face sagged slightly. He no longer wanted or was able to hide his disappointment.

Then he suddenly shook himself, repeated once again, "Well, good-bye!" – and disappeared. The screen flickered; gray stripes and vague figures appeared on it. In a minute, they were replaced by the word "SOON." I looked around and saw the room beginning to change. Almost immediately my head started to spin…

And now there are – just the remnants of reality around me: the window with the view of the winter park, walls without doors, and also – a viscous web of time intervals of which I have long since lost count. Their duration is uncertain, the boundaries between them blurred; the passage of time is the strangest thing that is happening now, at the end of Quarantine. At first, it was slightly eerie, then it became easier. Either because I got used to it, or I've just gotten older.

I walk around the room, along the wall with the same unchanging pattern to the window with the frozen picture. Farther on – to the closet whose door does not open. Then – to the bathroom, where everything is dead: there is no water, no shower; the toilet lid is tightly closed. I limp slightly; my left hip joint hurts. Recently, I complained about this to Nestor. He was surprised, "Well, what did you expect?" "Nothing else," I'd agreed. "It's as it should be."

When my former counselor visits me, we talk amicably. Not getting angry, not trying to insist on our point of view. Our egos are lying low – at least mine is. Or maybe I just want to think so. Each time he says a lengthy farewell – as if in defiance of the customs of our past sessions. And each time I don't know if I'll ever see him again.

Occasionally we still tease each other, though. I told him once, jokingly of course, "You know, Nestor, I have always believed that cosmologists have a hidden handicap. An objective one, related to the scale of the quantities they deal with: just think about it – parsecs, millions of years, calculations in completely wild degrees by any normal standards. What is a human, if we are talking some sort of ten to the twentieth? The most appallingly terribly insignificant speck!"

Nestor, naturally, replied in a similar tone – my provocation was obvious. "I've often thought in a similar way," he said, "about those who work at a quantum level. They never dare to raise their heads to look around; their triumphs and catastrophes have nothing to do with what's happening in the real world. What is humanity to them – and at what scales do they search for their answers? The same degrees, only with a minus sign? Ten to the minus twentieth, if you round it up?"

"You've got a point," I agreed, and asked him right there, "Doesn't it seem strange that human beings – the size of our bodies, the lifetime of our bodies – are located exactly in the middle?"

"Well, whether it seems so or not, it means at least that human beings shouldn't complain about their own smallness," Nestor grinned. And he added, "Don't think, of course, that I have in mind you personally. Considering the extent of your pride…"

Or I told him once, "In your world, Nestor, God is replaced by the fundamental ellipsoid, but there is almost no difference. All the consequences are basically the same – and you don't know much more about it than we knew about God. And you rush about in life just like us, even though you were telling me fairy tales about stability – of perception, of understanding – as one of the goals of Quarantine. At least, judging by you."

Nestor was not offended; he saw that I was deliberately exaggerating, that I was a bit uncomfortable. "You are quite right," he nodded, "this discussion – about the divine in the laws of chaos – perhaps will never end. Because, you know – a convenient euphemism for the crowd will always be in demand. And we have preachers too – a whole caste of them… The essence, of course, has changed slightly – some of the veils have disappeared. Your religions represent God as some kind of animate figure – one that can think, compare, juxtapose, exhibit emotions, distinguish good from evil, formulate in clear terms certain rules and canons… We here know for sure: the highest power is none other than a specific universal order, which has neither a soul nor morality. In your world, God is feared and exalted, as a boss or lord, whom you can cajole or soften, whom you can beg for something, maybe even playacting shamelessly – well, we don't have any such dramas here. A so-called God can only be understood, calculated, brought into the framework of mathematical formulas. Yet at the same time, the universal order has more surprises and miracles up its sleeve than any invented deity does. And where there are miracles, there come preachers, only with a different bible. As well as all sorts of chicken-and-egg dilemmas…"

Thus we entertain ourselves, sort of joking around, but now and then we do venture into the jungle of overgrown seriousness. Especially me – the last time it happened was quite recent: two or three intervals back. I remembered Brevich's words and mulled them over – and I quoted them to Nestor during his next, as always unexpected, visit.

"Death is not so frightening; what's really scary is getting lost," I said. Nestor, of course, did not understand me. It was difficult to explain, but I tried, mumbling something about all of us resembling children wandering in a maze – regardless of what picture of the world we have in our minds. Us remaining like children, always being like children – with no discovery ever forcing us to grow up. Because we don't want to believe in the true cruelty of reality; it is too much for us. And if we acquire something – call it what you want, even if you are afraid of the word – if we find someone, we have only one desire, one dream: to preserve what we have found forever. We live, cherishing and nursing this dream, not wanting to know that it is impossible to achieve. We do not dare to part with it even in our next lives. Or maybe – *especially* in our next ones…"

"Here you are not being original," Nestor said to me, disgruntled. "You are breaking down an open door. Or a too-tightly boarded-up one… Basically, you are no philosopher!"

And I felt embarrassed. Later, justifying myself, I related the tediousness of my reasoning to my phantom old age, to the fading of my entity. And indeed, the fading is becoming more and more noticeable. It seems I have grown totally decrepit. My thoughts are slow; my fake body increasingly refuses to function…

Now I'm thinking about this, lying in my chair. Then I get up with difficulty, shuffle to the window, look blindly into the static outline of the world, and suddenly realize that it is no longer frozen. There, beyond the glass, everything is changing – slowly but distinctly, in the most persistent manner. It's difficult to explain what is happening: the horizon seems to be curving upward; space is collapsing into a multidimensional cocoon. I feel a momentary shock – sensing its unimaginable scale and, at the same time, the simultaneous displacement of all its points, their movements toward each other. I'm not able to see it; I can't even imagine it properly, but I do sense it – because the string is now ringing in my head.

Barely moving my legs, I go back, fall into my chair and notice the screen has changed too. The word SOON has vanished; in its place, even larger, the more expressive NOW has appeared. And I realize: I no longer have the strength to get up. I am chained to this chair to the end – until the end of my stay in Quarantine.

I am overwhelmed with a long-familiar feeling of boundless solitude – alone, face to face with the universe. The feeling of absurd incomparability – of its power and my infinitesimal weakness. Probably everyone goes through this from time to time. Maybe it proves that all of us – and the universe – are really connected by something. By some kind of invisible but incredibly strong thread.

The words of the old song play in my head: "*Ground control to Major Tom...*" I whisper them out loud, knowing that in my case there is no ground control whatsoever. There is neither a tower with an advanced radar nor a huge radio telescope dish – no one, not a single soul is observing my "takeoff." There is only the implacable, impersonal, deterministic but unpredictable, noncomputable but inevitable – who? Chaos? *Kaosa? Fowdo? Huru-hara?* Well, let's just call it that. What does it have up its sleeve for me? Is there really nothing more?

This thought once again frightens me for the millionth time. I frantically search for something to hold on to – like everyone, like we all do. We humans are clever at inventing fake hopes and clinging to them to save ourselves from despair... But it's easier for me; I have a theory. A theory, affirmed by mathematics. And I have my B Object.

"Now it is experiencing some changes," I whisper to myself. "Maybe going through another phase jump. And creating new perturbations in the global field of the conscions..."

I can't know for sure if this is the case – I just very much want it to be. So that all I've done hasn't been in vain. I almost pray: please, let things not be in vain! I have no gods; I pray to the metabrane.

Then my mind fades away. Before my eyes – something blurry, painfully dull. I blink once, twice, feverishly rub my eyelids, and, all of a sudden, I imagine clearly, almost see Tina – with the bright streak in her hair, with her childish grace – in all her fragility and helplessness, in all her strength, coming out of nowhere. And I try to yell – even if just a rattle escapes my feeble lips. I beg: give me a sign, call me, direct me. You are my wisdom and you are purity, clarity of thought, utmost innocence. I'm dependent on you again, as before. Do not abandon me – in space, all alone. We always believed that we were united by something more than life – more than one life…

And then all the sounds – and my hoarse whisper – are drowned out by the sound of the string. It grows, fills the room – and the world behind it. And on the screen, after more flickering lines, inscriptions appear, one replacing the other:

> The goal of your quarantine has been reached
> All its objectives achieved
> You know what is expected of you
> You know what you yourself want
> YOU ARE READY

The final statement makes me anxious. I want to object – no, no, I am still as confused and unsure about everything as ever. But there is no one to appeal to; the screen is empty. And then the command burns in the brightest light: "Repeat out loud!"

And I mumble, I repeat obediently, almost not hearing myself through the furious ringing of the string in my head.

> I can keep my first life a secret…
> I do not have to answer any questions…
> My choice of words and actions remain my own, although
> I am already incapable of renouncing anything…

The lines flash and go out, imprinted on my brain. I read them one by one, barely grasping their meaning. Barely… Almost not grasping… And suddenly the realization comes: everything is about to happen – yes, right now! I feel terrified, I close my eyes and scream, scream – into the walls, into the screen, into the curving horizon beyond the window…

And I think I can hear an answer. It is not a dead echo; it's a subtle but living sound. It has a source – in a distant and yet the only right place. On the edge of consciousness, at the very border. On one side of it, or maybe on the other.

Somewhere by the cradle.

Semmant

A Simple Soul

The Black Pelican

SEMMANT

An excerpt from the novel published in 2013

CHAPTER 1

I'M WRITING THIS in dark-blue ink, sitting by the wall where my shadow moves. It crawls like the hand on a numberless sundial, keeping track of time that only I can follow. My days are scheduled right down to the hour, to the very minute, and yet I'm not in a hurry. The shadow changes ever so slowly, gradually blurring and fading toward the fringes.

The treatments have just been completed, and Sara has left my room. That's not her real name; she borrowed it from some porn star. All our nurses have such names by choice, taken from forgotten DVDs left behind in patients' chambers. This is their favorite game; there's also Esther, Laura, Veronica. None of them has had sex with me yet.

Sara is usually cheerful and giggly. Just today I told her a joke about a parrot, and she laughed so hard she almost cried. She has olive skin, full lips, and a pink tongue. And she has breast implants that she's really proud of. They are large and hard – at least that's how they seem. Her body probably promises more than it can give.

Nevertheless, I like Sara, though not as much as Veronica. Veronica was born in Rio; her narrow hips remind me of samba; her gaze pierces deep inside. She has knees that emanate immodesty. And she has long, thin, strong fingers… I imagine them to be very skillful. I like to fix my eyes on her with a squint, but her look is omniscient – it is impossible to confuse Veronica. I think she is overly cold toward me.

She doesn't use perfume, and sometimes I can detect her natural scent. It is very faint, almost imperceptible, but it penetrates as deeply as her gaze. Then it seems all the objects in the room smell of her – and the sheets, and even my clothing. And I regret I'm no longer that young – I could spend hours in dreamy masturbation, scanning the air with my sensitive nostrils. But to do that now would be somewhat awkward.

Find out more about Semmant at www.semmant.com

A SIMPLE SOUL

An excerpt from the novel published in 2013

CHAPTER 1

ONE JULY MORNING during a hot, leap-year summer, Elizaveta Andreyevna Bestuzheva walked out of apartment building number one on Solyanka Street, the home of her latest lover. She lingered for a moment, squinting in the sun, then straightened her shoulders, raised her head proudly, and marched along the sidewalk. It was almost ten, but morning traffic was still going strong – Moscow was settling into a long day. Elizaveta Andreyevna walked fast, looking straight ahead and trying not to meet anyone's gaze. Still, at the corner of Solyansky Proyezd, an unrelenting stare invaded her space, but turned out to be a store window dressing in the form of a huge, green eye. Taken aback, she peered into it, but saw only that it was hopelessly dead.

She turned left, and the gloomy building disappeared from view. Brushing off the memories of last night and the need to make a decision, Elizaveta felt the relief of knowing she was alone. She was sick of her lover – maybe that was the reason their meetings were becoming increasingly lustful. In the mornings, she wanted to look away and make a quick retreat, not even kissing him good-bye. But he was persistent, his parting ritual enveloping her like a heavy fog. Afterward, she always ran down the stairs, distrusting the elevator, and scurried away from the dreary edifice as if it were a mousetrap that had miraculously fallen open.

Elizaveta glanced at her watch, shook her head, and picked up speed. The sidewalk was narrow, yet she stepped lightly, oblivious of the obstacles: oncoming passersby, bumps and potholes, puddles left by last night's rain. She wasn't bothered by the city's deplorable state, but a new sense of unease uncoiled deep inside her and slithered up her spine with a cold tickle. The giant eye still seemed to stare at her from under its heavy lid. She had a sense of another presence, a most delicate thread that connected her to someone else. Involuntarily, she jerked her shoulders, trying to shake off the feeling, and, after admonishing herself, returned to her contemplation.

Find out more about A Simple Soul at www.simplesoulbook.com

THE BLACK PELICAN

An excerpt from the novel published in 2013

CHAPTER 1

TO THIS DAY I remember the long road to the City of M. It dragged on and on, while the thoughts plaguing me mingled with the scenes along the way. It seemed as if everything around me was already at one with the place, even though I still had a few hours to go. I passed indistinct farms in empty fields, small villages and lonely estates surrounded by cultivated greenery and forest hills. Man-made ponds and natural lakes skirted the road and reeked of wetlands, which later, right before M., turned into peat bogs and marshes, with no sign of life for miles to come. The countryside was dotted with humble towns sprouting out of the earth, the highway briefly becoming their main street: squares and clusters of stores glimmered in the sun, banks and churches rose up closer to the center, a belfry whizzed by, silent as usual. Then the glint of the shops and gas stations at the outskirts said farewell without a word, and just like that, it was over. The town was gone, without having time to agitate or provoke interest. Again the road wound its way through the fields, its monotony wearing me down. I saw the peculiar people who swarm over the countryside – for a fleeting moment they appeared amusing, but then I stopped noticing them, understanding how unexceptional they are, measured against their surroundings. At times, locals waved to me from the curb or just followed me with their eyes, though more often than not, no one was distracted by my fleeting presence. Left behind, they merged with the streets as they withdrew to the side.

At last the fields disappeared, and real swamps engulfed the road – a damp, unhealthy moor. Clouds of insects smashed into the windshield; the air became heavy. Nature seemed to bear down on me, barely letting me breathe, but that didn't last long. Soon I drove up a hill. The swamps still sat a bit to the east, retreating to the invisible ocean in a smooth line overgrown with wild shrubs. Now the trees grew dense, casting the illegible calligraphy of their shadows over the road, until, several miles ahead, the road became wider, and a sign said I had crossed the city limits of M.

Find out more about The Black Pelican at www.blackpelicanbook.com

About the author

Vadim Babenko left his career in science and business to pursue his life-long goal of writing novels. Born in the Soviet Union, he earned master's and doctoral degrees from the Moscow Institute of Physics & Technology, Russia's equivalent to MIT. As a scientist at the Soviet Academy of Sciences he specialized in biophysics and artificial intelligence. After moving to the U.S. he co-founded a high-tech company. The business soon skyrocketed, and his next ambition, an IPO on the stock exchange, was realized. However, at the height of his success, Vadim dropped everything to set out on his journey as an author and has never looked back. He was a finalist in the National Bestseller Award (Russia) and the winner of the National Indie Excellence Award (USA).

Find out more at www.vadimbabenko.com